Other Books in The Vintage Library
of Contemporary World Literature

VASSILY AKSYONOV   The Island of Crimea

MANLIO ARGUETA   One Day of Life

THOMAS BERNHARD   Correction

JULIO CORTÁZAR   We Love Glenda So Much and A Change of Light

MARIA DERMOÛT   The Ten Thousand Things

JOSÉ DONOSO   A House in the Country

ARIEL DORFMAN   Widows

FUMIKO ENCHI   Masks

SHUSAKU ENDO   The Samurai

JIŘÍ GRUŠA   The Questionnaire

TADEUSZ KONWICKI   A Minor Apocalypse

CAMARA LAYE   The Guardian of the World

EARL LOVELACE   The Wine of Astonishment

TIMOTHY MO   Sour Sweet

ELSA MORANTE   History A Novel

MANUEL PUIG   Blood of Requited Love

DARCY RIBEIRO   Maíra

SALMAN RUSHDIE   Shame

WOLE SOYINKA   Aké: The Years of Childhood

MICHEL TOURNIER   The Four Wise Men

AT THE BOTTOM
OF THE RIVER

AT THE BOTTOM OF THE RIVER

JAMAICA KINCAID

AVENTURA

The Vintage Library of Contemporary World Literature

VINTAGE BOOKS   A DIVISION OF RANDOM HOUSE   NEW YORK

First Aventura Edition, March 1985
Copyright © 1978, 1979, 1981, 1982, 1983 by Jamaica Kincaid
Acknowledgment is made to *The New Yorker* for the
following stories, which first appeared in its pages: "Girl,"
"In the Night," "At Last," "Wingless," "Holidays," "The
Letter from Home," and "At the Bottom of the River,"
and to *The Paris Review* for "What I Have Been Doing
Lately."
The excerpt as the beginning of "Wingless" is from *The
Water Babies* by Charles Kingsley
Library of Congress Cataloging in Publication Data
Kincaid, Jamaica.
At the bottom of the river.
(Aventura: the Vintage library of contemporary
world literature)
Contents: Girl—In the night—At last—Wingless—
Holidays—The letter from home—What I have been doing
lately—Blackness—My mother—At the bottom of the river.
I. Title.
[PR9265.9.K4A7 1985]   813'.54   84-40701
ISBN 0-394-73683-4
Manufactured in the United States of America

For my mother, Annie, with love, and

for Mr. Shawn, with gratitude and love

Contents

᷈

GIRL · 3

IN THE NIGHT · 6

AT LAST · 13

WINGLESS · 20

HOLIDAYS · 29

THE LETTER FROM HOME · 37

WHAT I HAVE BEEN DOING LATELY · 40

BLACKNESS · 46

MY MOTHER · 53

AT THE BOTTOM OF THE RIVER · 62

AT THE BOTTOM
OF THE RIVER

GIRL

Wash the white clothes on Monday and put them on the stone heap; wash the color clothes on Tuesday and put them on the clothesline to dry; don't walk barehead in the hot sun; cook pumpkin fritters in very hot sweet oil; soak your little cloths right after you take them off; when buying cotton to make yourself a nice blouse, be sure that it doesn't have gum on it, because that way it won't hold up well after a wash; soak salt fish overnight before you cook it; is it true that you sing benna in Sunday school?; always eat your food in such a way that it won't turn someone else's stomach; on Sundays try to walk like a lady and not like the slut you are so bent on becoming; don't sing benna in Sunday school; you mustn't speak to wharf-rat boys, not even to give directions; don't eat fruits on the street—flies will follow you; *but I don't sing benna on Sundays at all and never in Sunday school*; this is how to sew on a button; this is how to make a buttonhole for the button you have just sewed on; this is how to hem a dress when you see the hem coming down and so to prevent yourself from looking like the slut I know you are so bent on becoming; this is how you iron your father's khaki shirt so that it doesn't have a crease; this is how you iron your father's khaki pants so that they don't have a crease; this is how you grow okra—far from the house, because okra tree harbors red ants; when you are growing dasheen, make sure it gets plenty of water or else it makes your throat itch when you are eating it; this is how you sweep a corner; this is how you sweep a whole house; this is how you sweep a yard; this is how you smile to someone you don't like too much; this is how you smile to someone you don't like at all; this is how you smile to someone you like completely; this is how you set a table for tea; this is how you set a table for dinner; this is how you set a table for dinner with an important guest; this is how you set a table for lunch; this is how you set a table for breakfast; this is how to behave in the presence of men who don't know you very well, and this way they won't recognize immediately the slut I have warned you against becoming; be sure to wash every day, even if it is with your own spit; don't squat

down to play marbles—you are not a boy, you know;
don't pick people's flowers—you might catch something; don't throw stones at blackbirds, because it
might not be a blackbird at all; this is how to make
a bread pudding; this is how to make doukona; this
is how to make pepper pot; this is how to make a
good medicine for a cold; this is how to make a good
medicine to throw away a child before it even becomes a child; this is how to catch a fish; this is how
to throw back a fish you don't like, and that way
something bad won't fall on you; this is how to
bully a man; this is how a man bullies you; this is
how to love a man, and if this doesn't work there are
other ways, and if they don't work don't feel too bad
about giving up; this is how to spit up in the air if
you feel like it, and this is how to move quick so that
it doesn't fall on you; this is how to make ends meet;
always squeeze bread to make sure it's fresh; *but
what if the baker won't let me feel the bread?*; you
mean to say that after all you are really going to be
the kind of woman who the baker won't let near
the bread?

IN THE NIGHT

*I*n the night, way into the middle of the night, when the night isn't divided like a sweet drink into little sips, when there is no just before midnight, midnight, or just after midnight, when the night is round in some places, flat in some places, and in some places like a deep hole, blue at the edge, black inside, the night-soil men come.

They come and go, walking on the damp ground in straw shoes. Their feet in the straw shoes make a scratchy sound. They say nothing.

The night-soil men can see a bird walking in trees. It isn't a bird. It is a woman who has removed her skin and is on her way to drink the blood of her secret enemies. It is a woman who has left her skin in a corner of a house made out of wood. It is a woman who is reasonable and admires honeybees in the hibiscus. It is a woman who, as a joke, brays like a donkey when he is thirsty.

There is the sound of a cricket, there is the sound of a church bell, there is the sound of this house creaking, that house creaking, and the other house creaking as they settle into the ground. There is the sound of a radio in the distance—a fisherman listening to merengue music. There is the sound of a man groaning in his sleep; there is the sound of a woman disgusted at the man groaning. There is the sound of the man stabbing the woman, the sound of her blood as it hits the floor, the sound of Mr. Straffee, the undertaker, taking her body away. There is the sound of her spirit back from the dead, looking at the man who used to groan; he is running a fever forever. There is the sound of a woman writing a letter; there is the sound of her pen nib on the white writing paper; there is the sound of the kerosene lamp dimming; there is the sound of her head aching.

The rain falls on the tin roofs, on the leaves in the trees, on the stones in the yard, on sand, on the ground. The night is wet in some places, warm in some places.

There is Mr. Gishard, standing under a cedar tree which is in full bloom, wearing that nice white suit, which is as fresh as the day he was buried in it. The white suit came from England in a brown package: "To: Mr. John Gishard," and so on and so on. Mr.

Gishard is standing under the tree, wearing his nice suit and holding a glass full of rum in his hand—the same glass full of rum that he had in his hand shortly before he died—and looking at the house in which he used to live. The people who now live in the house walk through the door backward when they see Mr. Gishard standing under the tree, wearing his nice white suit. Mr. Gishard misses his accordion; you can tell by the way he keeps tapping his foot.

In my dream I can hear a baby being born. I can see its face, a pointy little face—so nice. I can see its hands—so nice, again. Its eyes are closed. It's breathing, the little baby. It's breathing. It's bleating, the little baby. It's bleating. The baby and I are now walking to pasture. The baby is eating green grass with its soft and pink lips. My mother is shaking me by the shoulders. My mother says, "Little Miss, Little Miss." I say to my mother, "But it's still night." My mother says, "Yes, but you have wet your bed again." And my mother, who is still young, and still beautiful, and still has pink lips, removes my wet nightgown, removes my wet sheets from my bed. My mother can change everything. In my dream I am in the night.

"What are the lights in the mountains?"

"The lights in the mountains? Oh, it's a jablesse."

"A jablesse! But why? What's a jablesse?"

"It's a person who can turn into anything. But you can tell they aren't real because of their eyes. Their eyes shine like lamps, so bright that you can't look. That's how you can tell it's a jablesse. They like to go up in the mountains and gallivant. Take good care when you see a beautiful woman. A jablesse always tries to look like a beautiful woman."

No one has ever said to me, "My father, a night-soil man, is very nice and very kind. When he passes a dog, he gives a pat and not a kick. He likes all the parts of a fish but especially the head. He goes to church quite regularly and is always glad when the minister calls out, 'A Mighty Fortress Is Our God,' his favorite hymn. He would like to wear pink shirts and pink pants but knows that this color isn't very becoming to a man, so instead he wears navy blue and brown, colors he does not like at all. He met my mother on what masquerades as a bus around here, a long time ago, and he still likes to whistle. Once, while running to catch a bus, he fell and broke his ankle and had to spend a week in hospital. This made him miserable, but he cheered up quite a bit when he saw my mother and me, standing over his white cot, holding bunches of yellow roses and smiling down at him. Then he said, 'Oh, my. Oh, my.' What he likes to do most, my father the night-soil man, is to sit on a big stone under a mahogany tree and watch small children playing play-cricket while he eats the intestines of animals stuffed with blood and rice and drinks ginger beer. He has told me this many times: 'My dear, what I like to do most,' and so on. He is always reading botany books and knows a lot about rubber plantations and rubber trees; but this is an interest I can't explain, since the only rubber tree he has ever seen is a specially raised one in the botanic gardens. He sees to it that my school shoes fit comfortably. I love my father the night-soil man. My mother loves my father the night-soil man. Everybody loves him and waves to him whenever they see him. He is very handsome, you know, and I have seen women look at him twice. On special days he wears a brown felt hat, which he orders from England, and brown leather shoes, which he also orders from England. On ordinary days he goes barehead. When he calls me, I say, 'Yes, sir.' On my mother's birthday he always buys her some nice cloth for a new dress as a present. He makes us happy, my father the night-soil man, and has promised that one day he will take us to see something he has read about called the circus."

In the night, the flowers close up and thicken. The hibiscus flowers, the flamboyant flowers, the bachelor's buttons, the irises, the marigolds, the whitehead-bush flowers, the lilies, the flowers on the daggerbush, the flowers on the turtleberry bush, the flowers on the soursop tree, the flowers on the sugar-apple tree, the flowers on the mango tree, the flowers on the guava tree, the flowers on the cedar tree, the flowers on the stinking-toe tree, the flowers on the dumps tree, the flowers on the papaw tree, the flowers everywhere close up and thicken. The flowers are vexed.

Someone is making a basket, someone is making a girl a dress or a boy a shirt, someone is making her husband a soup with cassava so that he can take it to the cane field tomorrow, someone is making his wife a beautiful mahogany chest, someone is sprinkling a colorless powder outside a closed door so that someone else's child will be stillborn, someone is praying that a bad child who is living prosperously abroad will be good and send a package filled with new clothes, someone is sleeping.

❧

Now I am a girl, but one day I will marry a woman—a red-skin woman with black bramblebush hair and brown eyes, who wears skirts that are so big I can easily bury my head in them. I would like to marry this woman and live with her in a mud hut near the sea. In the mud hut will be two chairs and one table, a lamp that burns kerosene, a medicine chest, a pot, one bed, two pillows, two sheets, one looking glass, two cups, two saucers, two dinner plates, two forks, two drinking-water glasses, one china pot, two fishing strings, two straw hats to ward the hot sun off our heads, two trunks for things we have very little use for, one basket, one book of plain paper, one box filled with twelve crayons of different colors, one loaf of bread wrapped in a piece of brown paper, one coal pot, one picture of two women standing on a jetty, one picture of the same two women embracing, one picture of the same two women waving goodbye, one box of matches. Every day this red-skin woman and I will eat bread and milk for breakfast, hide in bushes and throw hardened cow dung at people we don't like, climb coconut trees, pick coconuts, eat and drink the food and water from the coconuts we have picked, throw stones in the sea, put on John Bull masks and frighten defenseless little children on their way home from school, go fishing and catch only our favorite fishes to roast and have for dinner, steal green figs to eat for dinner with the roast fish. Every day we would do this. Every night I would sing this woman a song; the words I don't know yet, but the tune is in my head. This woman I would like to marry knows many things, but to me she will only tell about things that would never dream of making me cry; and every night, over and over, she will tell me something that begins, "Before you were born." I will marry a woman like this, and every night, every night, I will be completely happy.

AT LAST

THE HOUSE

I lived in this house with you: the wood shingles, unpainted, weather-beaten, fraying; the piano, a piece of furniture now, collecting dust; the bed in which all the children were born; a bowl of flowers, alive, then dead; a bowl of fruit, but then all eaten. (What was that light?) My hairbrush is full of dead hair. Where are the letters that brought the bad news? Where are they? These glasses commemorate a coronation. What are you now? A young woman. But what are you really? A young woman. I know how hard that is. If only everything would talk. The floorboards made a nice pattern when the sun came in. (Was that the light again?) At night, after cleaning the soot from the lampshade, I lighted the lamp and, before preparing for bed, planned another day. So many things I forgot, though. I hid something under the bed, but then I forgot, and it spawned a feathery white moss, so beautiful; it stank, and that's how I remembered it was there. Now I am looking at you; your lips are soft and parted.

Are they?

I saw the cat open its jaws wide and I saw the roof of its mouth, which was pink with black shading, and its teeth looked white and sharp and dangerous. I had no shells from the sea, which was minutes away. This beautifully carved shelf: you can touch it now. Why did I not let you eat with your bare hands when you wanted to?

Why were all the doors closed so tight shut?

But they weren't closed.

I saw them closed.

What passed between us then? You asked me if it was always the way it is now. But I don't know. I wasn't always here. I wasn't here in the beginning. We held hands once and were beautiful. But what followed? Sleepless nights, oh, sleepless nights. A baby was born on Thursday and was almost eaten, eyes first, by red ants, on Friday. (But the light, where does it come from, the light?) I've walked the length of this room so many times, by now I have traveled a desert.

With me?

With you. Speak in a whisper. I like the way your lips purse when you whisper. You are a woman. Stand over there near the dead flowers. I can see your reflection in the glass bowl. You are soft and curved like an arch. Your limbs are large and un-knotted, your feet unsnared. (It's the light again, now in flashes.)

Was it like a carcass? Did you feed on it?

Yes.

Or was it like a skeleton? Did you live in it?

Yes, that too. We prayed. But what did we pray for? We prayed to be saved. We prayed to be blessed. We prayed for long and happy lives for our children. And always we prayed to see the morning light. Were we saved? I don't know. To this day I don't know. We filled the rooms; I filled the rooms. Eggs boiled violently in that pot. When the hurri-cane came, we hid in this corner until the wind passed; the rain that time, the rain that time. The foundation of this house shook and the earth washed away. My skin grew hot and damp; then I shivered with excitement.

What did you say to me? What did I not hear?

The mattress was stuffed with coconut fiber. It was our first mattress. It made our skin raw. It harbored bedbugs. I used to stand here, at this window, look-ing out at the shadows of people passing—and they were real people—and I would run my hand over the pattern of ridges in the cover belonging to the kettle. I used to stand over here too, in front of this mirror, and I would run my hands across the stitches in a new tablecloth. And again I would stand here, in front of the cold stove, and run my fingers through a small bag of green coffee beans. In this cage lived a hummingbird. He died after a few days, homesick for the jungle. I tried to take everything one day at a time, just as it was coming up.

And then?

I felt sick. Always I felt sick. I sat in this rocking chair with you on my lap. Let me calm her, I thought, let me calm her. But in my breast my milk soured.

So I was loved?

Yes. You wore your clothes wrapped tight around your body, keeping your warmth to yourself. What greed! But how could you know? A yellow liquid left a stain here.

Is that blood?

Yes, but who bled? That picture of an asphalt lake. He visited an asphalt lake once. He loved me then. I was beautiful. I built a fire. The coals glowed so. Bitter. Bitter. Bitter. There was music, there was dancing. Again and again we touched, and again and again we were beautiful. I could see that. I could see some things. I cried. I could not see everything. What illness was it that caused the worm to crawl out of his leg the day he died? Someone laughed here. I heard that, and just then I was made happy. Look. You were dry and warm and solid and small. I was soft and curved like an arch. I wore blue, bird blue, and at night I would shine in the dark.

The children?

They weren't here yet, the children. I could hear their hearts beating, but they weren't here yet. They were beautiful, but not the way you are. Sometimes I appeared as a man. Sometimes I appeared as a hoofed animal, stroking my own brown, shiny back. Then I left no corner unturned. Nothing frightened me. A blind bird dashed its head against this closed window. I heard that. I crossed the open sea alone at night on a steamer. What was my name—I mean the name my mother gave to me—and where did I come from? My skin is now coarse. What pity. What sorrow. I have made a list. I have measured everything. I have not lied.

But the light. What of the light?

Splintered. Died.

THE YARD

A mountain. A valley. The shade. The sun.

A streak of yellow rapidly conquering a streak of green. Blending and separating. Children are so quick: quick to laugh, quick to brand, quick to scorn, quick to lay claim to the open space.

The thud of small feet running, running. A girl's

shriek—snaps in two. Tumbling, tumbling, the sound of a noon bell. Dry? Wet? Warm? Cold? Nothing is measured here.

An old treasure rudely broken. See how the amber color fades from its rim. Now it is the home of something dark and moist. An ant walking on a sheet of tin laid bare to the sun—crumbles. But what is an ant? Secreting, secreting; always secreting. The skin of an orange—removed as if it had been a decorous and much-valued belt. A frog, beaded and creased, moldy and throbbing—no more than a single leap in a single day.

(But at last, at last, to whom will this view belong? Will the hen, stripped of its flesh, its feathers scattered perhaps to the four corners of the earth, its bones molten and sterilized, one day speak? And what will it say? I was a hen? I had twelve chicks? One of my chicks, named Beryl, took a fall?)

Many secrets are alive here. A sharp blow delivered quicker than an eye blink. A sparrow's eggs. A pirate's trunk. A fisherman's catch. A tree, bearing fruits. A bullying boy's marbles. All that used to be is alive here.

Someone has piled up stones, making a small enclosure for a child's garden, and planted a child's flowers, bluebells. Yes, but a child is too quick, and the bluebells fall to the cool earth, dying and living in perpetuity.

Unusually large berries, red, gold, and indigo, sliced open and embedded in soft mud. The duck's bill, hard and sharp and shiny; the duck itself, driven and ruthless. The heat, in waves, coiling and uncoiling until everything seeks shelter in the shade.

Sensing the danger, the spotted beetle pauses, then retraces its primitive crawl. Red fluid rock was deposited here, and now the soil is rich in minerals. On the vines, the ripening vegetables.

But what is a beetle? What is one fly? What is one day? What is anything after it is dead and gone? Another beetle will pause, sensing the danger. Another day, identical to this day . . . then the rain, beating the underbrush hard, causing the turtle to bury its head even more carefully. The stillness comes and the stillness goes. The sun. The moon.

Still the sounds of voices, muted and then clear, emptying and filling up, saying:

"What was the song they used to sing and made fists and pretended to be Romans?"

WINGLESS

The small children are reading from a book filled with simple words and sentences.

" 'Once upon a time there was a little chimney-sweep, whose name was Tom.' "

" 'He cried half his time, and laughed the other half.' "

" 'You would have been giddy, perhaps, at looking down: but Tom was not.' "

" 'You, of course, would have been very cold sitting there on a September night, without the least bit of clothes on your wet back; but Tom was a water-baby, and therefore felt cold no more than a fish.' "

The children have already learned to write their names in beautiful penmanship. They have already

learned how many farthings make a penny, how many
pennies make a shilling, how many shillings make a
pound, how many days in April, how many stone in
a ton. Now they singsong here and tumble there,
tearing skirts with swift movements. Must Dulcie
really cry after thirteen of her play chums have sat
on her? There, Dulcie, there. I myself have been
kissed by many rude boys with small, damp lips, on
their way to boys' drill. I myself have humped girls
under my mother's house. But I swim in a shaft of
light, upside down, and I can see myself clearly,
through and through, from every angle. Perhaps I
stand on the brink of a great discovery, and perhaps
after I have made my great discovery I will be sent
home in chains. Then again, perhaps my life is as
predictable as an insect's and I am in my pupa stage.
How low can I sink, then? That woman over there,
that large-bottomed woman, is important to me. It's
for her that I save up my sixpences instead of spend-
ing for sweets. Is this a love like no other? And what
pain have I caused her? And does she love me? My
needs are great, I can see. But there are the children
again (of which I am one), shrieking, whether in
pain or pleasure I cannot tell. The children, who are
beautiful in groupings of three, and who only last
night pleaded with their mothers to sing softly to
them, are today maiming each other. The children

at the end of the day have sour necks, frayed hair,
dirt under their fingernails, scuffed shoes, torn clothing. And why? First they must be children.

I shall grow up to be a tall, graceful, and altogether beautiful woman, and I shall impose on large
numbers of people my will and also, for my own
amusement, great pain. But now. I shall try to see
clearly. I shall try to tell differences. I shall try to
distinguish the subtle gradations of color in fine cloth,
of fingernail length, of manners. That woman over
there. Is she cruel? Does she love me? And if not,
can I make her? I am not yet tall, beautiful, graceful,
and able to impose my will. Now I swim in a shaft
of light and can see myself clearly. The schoolhouse
is yellow and stands among big green-leaved trees.
Inside are our desks and a woman who wears spec-
tacles, playing the piano. Is a girl who can sing
"Gaily the troubadour plucked his guitar" in a pleasing way worthy of being my best friend? There is the
same girl, unwashed and glistening, setting traps for
talking birds. Is she to be one of my temptations?
Oh, this must be a love like no other. But how can
my limbs that hate be the same limbs that love?
How can the same limbs that make me blind make
me see? I am defenseless and small. I shall try to
see clearly. I shall try to separate and divide things
as if they were sums, as if they were drygoods on

the grocer's shelves. Is this my mother? Is she here to embarrass me? What shall I say about her behind her back, when she isn't there, long after she has gone? In her smile lies her goodness. Will I always remember that? Am I horrid? And if so, will I always be that way? Not getting my own way causes me to fret so, I clench my fist. My charm is limited, and I haven't learned to smile yet. I have picked many flowers and then deliberately torn them to shreds, petal by petal. I am so unhappy, my face is so wet, and still I can stand up and walk and tell lies in the face of terrible punishments. I can see the great danger in what I am—a defenseless and pitiful child. Here is a list of what I must do. So is my life to be like an apprenticeship in dressmaking, a thorny path to carefully follow or avoid? Inside, standing around the spectacled woman playing the piano, the children are singing a song in harmony. The children's voices: pinks, blues, yellows, violets, all suspended. All is soft, all is embracing, all is comforting. And yet I myself, at my age, have suffered so. My tears, big, have run down my cheeks in uneven lines—my tears, big, and my hands too small to hold them. My tears have been the result of my disappointments. My disappointments stand up and grow ever taller. They will not be lost to me. There they are. Let me pin tags on them. Let me have them registered, like newly domesticated animals. Let me cherish my disappointments, fold them up, tuck them away, close to my breast, because they are so important to me.

But again I swim in a shaft of light, upside down, and I can see myself clearly, through and through, from every angle. Over there, I stand on the brink of a great discovery, and it is possible that like an ancient piece of history my presence will leave room for theories. But who will say? For days my body has been collecting water, but still I won't cry. What is that to me? I am not yet a woman with a terrible and unwanted burden. I am not yet a dog with a cruel and unloving master. I am not yet a tree growing on barren and bitter land. I am not yet the shape of darkness in a dungeon.

Where? What? Why? How then? Oh, that!

I am primitive and wingless.

☙

"Don't eat the strings on bananas—they will wrap around your heart and kill you."

"Oh. Is that true?"

"No."

"Is that something to tell children?"

"No. But it's so funny. You should see how you look trying to remove all the strings from the bananas with your monkey fingernails. Frightened?"

"Frightened. Very frightened."

❧

Today, keeping a safe distance, I followed the woman I love when she walked on a carpet of pond lilies. As she walked, she ate some black nuts, pond-lily black nuts. She walked for a long time, saying what must be wonderful things to herself. Then in the middle of the pond she stopped, because a man had stood up suddenly in front of her. I could see that he wore clothes made of tree bark and sticks in his ears. He said things to her and I couldn't make them out, but he said them to her so forcefully that drops of brown water sprang from his mouth. The woman I love put her hands over her ears, shielding herself from the things he said. Then he put wind in his cheeks and blew himself up until in the bright sun he looked like a boil, and the woman I love put her hands over her eyes, shielding herself from the way he looked. Then, instead of removing her cutlass from the folds of her big and beautiful skirt and cutting the man in two at the waist, she only smiled —a red, red smile—and like a fly he dropped dead.

❧

The sea, the shimmering pink-colored sand, the swimmers with hats, two people walking arm in arm, talking in each other's face, dots of water landing on noses, the sea spray on ankles, on over-developed calves, the blue, the green, the black, so deep, so smooth, a great and swift undercurrent, glassy, the white wavelets, a storm so blinding that the salt got in our eyes, the sea turning inside out, shaking everything up like a bottle with sediment, a boat with two people heaving a brown package overboard, the mystery, the sharp teeth of that yellow spotted eel, the wriggle, the smooth lines, open mouths, families of great noisy birds, families of great noisy people, families of biting flies, the sea, following me home, snapping at my heels, all the way to the door, the sea, the woman.

"I have frightened you? Again, you are frightened of me?"

"You have frightened me. I am very frightened of you."

"Oh, you should see your face. I wish you could see your face. How you make me laugh."

And what are my fears? What large cows! When I see them coming, shall I run and hide face down in the gutter? Are they really cows? Can I stand in a field of tall grass and see nothing for miles and miles? On the other hand, the sky, which is big and blue as always, has its limits. This afternoon the wind is loud as in a hurricane. There isn't enough light. There is a noise—I can't tell where it is coming from. A big box has stamped on it "Handle Carefully." I have been in a big white building with curving corridors. I have passed a dead person. There is the woman I love, who is so much bigger than me.

❧

That mosquito . . . now a stain on the wall. That lizard, running up and down, up and down . . . now so still. That ant, bloated and sluggish, a purseful of eggs in its jaws . . . now so still. That blue-and-green bird, head held aloft, singing . . . now so still. That land crab, moving slowly, softly, even beautifully, sideways . . . but now so still. That cricket, standing on a tree stem, so ugly, so revolting, I am made so unhappy . . . now so still. That mongoose, now asleep in its hole, now stealing the sleeping chickens, moving so quickly, its eyes like two grains of light . . . now so still. That fly, moving so contentedly from tea bun to tea bun . . . now so still. That butterfly, moving contentedly from beautiful plant to beautiful plant in the early-morning sun . . . now so still. That tadpole, swimming playfully in the shallow water . . . now so still.

I shall cast a shadow and I shall remain unaware.

My hands, brown on this side, pink on this side, now indiscriminately dangerous, now vagabond and prodigal, now cruel and careless, now without remorse or forgiveness, but now innocently slipping into a dress with braided sleeves, now holding an ice-cream cone, now reaching up with longing, now clasped in prayer, now feeling for reassurance, now pleading my desires, now pleasing, and now, even now, so still in bed, in sleep.

HOLIDAYS

I sit on the porch facing the mountains. I sit on a wicker couch looking out the window at a field of day lilies. I walk into a room where someone—an artist, maybe—has stored some empty canvases. I drink a glass of water. I put the empty glass, from which I have just drunk the water, on a table. I notice two flies, one sitting on top of the other, flying around the room. I scratch my scalp, I scratch my thighs. I lift my arms up and stretch them above my head. I sigh. I spin on my heels once. I walk around the dining-room table three times. I see a book lying on the dining-room table, and I pick it up. The book is called *An Illustrated Encyclopedia of Butterflies and Moths*. I leaf through the book, looking only at the pictures, which are bright and beautiful. From my looking through the book, the word "thorax" sticks in my mind. "Thorax," I say, "thorax, thorax," I don't know how many times. I bend over and touch my toes. I stay in that position until I count to one hundred. As I count, I pretend to be counting off balls on a ball frame. As I count the balls, I pretend that they are the colors red, green, blue, and yellow. I walk over to the fireplace. Standing in front of the fireplace, I try to write my name in the dead ashes with my big toe. I cannot write my name in the dead ashes with my big toe. My big toe, now dirty, I try to clean by rubbing it vigorously on a clean royal-blue rug. The royal-blue rug now has a dark spot, and my big toe has a strong burning sensation. Oh, sensation. I am filled with sensation. I feel—oh, how I feel. I feel, I feel, I feel. I have no words right now for how I feel. I take a walk down the road in my bare feet. I feel the stones on the road, hard and sharp against my soft, almost pink soles. Also, I feel the hot sun beating down on my bare neck. It is midday. Did I say that? Must I say that? Oh me, oh my. The road on which I walk barefoot leads to the store—the village store. Should I go to the village store or should I not go to the village store? I can if I want. If I go to the village store, I can buy a peach. The peach will be warm from sitting in a box in the sun. The peach will not taste sweet and the peach will not taste sour. I will know that I am eating a peach only by looking at it. I will not go to the store. I will sit on the porch facing the mountains.

I sit on the porch facing the mountains. The porch is airy and spacious. I am the only person sitting on the porch. I look at myself. I can see myself. That is, I can see my chest, my abdomen, my legs, and my arms. I cannot see my hair, my ears, my face, or my collarbone. I can feel them, though. My nose is moist with sweat. Locking my fingers, I put my hands on my head. I see a bee, a large bumblebee, flying around aimlessly. I remove my hands from resting on my head, because my arms are tired. But also I have just remembered a superstition: if you sit with your hands on your head, you will kill your mother. I have many superstitions. I believe all of them. Should I read a book? Should I make myself something to drink? But what? And hot or cold? Should I write a letter? I should write a letter. I will write a letter. "Dear So-and-So, I am . . . and then I got the brilliant idea . . . I was very amusing . . . I had enough, I said . . . I saw what I came to see, I thought . . . I am laughing all the way to the poorhouse. I grinned . . . I just don't know anymore. I remain, etc." I like my letter. Perhaps I shall keep my letter to myself. I fold up the letter I have just written and put it between the pages of the book I am trying to read. The book is lying in my lap. I look around me, trying to find something on which to focus my eyes. I see ten ants. I count them as they wrestle with a speck of food. I am not fascinated by that. I see my toes moving up and down as if they were tapping out a beat. Why are my toes tapping? I am fascinated by that. A song is going through my mind. It goes, "There was a man from British Guiana, Who used to play a piana. His foot slipped, His trousers ripped . . ." I see, I see. Yes. Now. Suddenly I am tired. I am yawning. Perhaps I will take a nap. Perhaps I will take a long nap. Perhaps I will take a nice long nap. Perhaps, while taking my nap, I will have a dream, a dream in which I am not sitting on the porch facing the mountains.

❧

"I have the most sensible small suitcase in New York.

"I have the most sensible small car in New York.

"I will put my sensible small suitcase in my sensible small car and drive on a sensible and scenic road to the country.

"In the country, I live in a sensible house.

"I am a sensible man.

"It is summer.

"Look at that sunset. Too orange.

"These pebbles. Not pebbly enough.

"A house with interesting angles.

"For dinner I will eat scallops. I love the taste of scallops.

"These are my chums—the two boys and the girl. My chums are the most beautiful chums. The two boys know lumberjacks in Canada, and the girl is fragile. After dinner, my chums and I will play cards, and while playing cards we will tell each other jokes —such funny jokes—but later, thinking back, we will be so pained, so unsettled."

❧

The deerflies, stinging and nesting in wet, matted hair; broken bottles at the bottom of the swimming hole; mosquitoes; a family of skunks eating the family garbage; a family of skunks spraying the family dog; washing the family dog with cans of tomato juice to remove the smell of the skunks; a not-too-fast-moving woodchuck crossing the road; running over the not-too-fast-moving woodchuck; the camera forgotten, exposed in the hot sun; the prism in the camera broken, because the camera has been forgotten, exposed in the hot sun; spraining a finger while trying to catch a cricket ball; spraining a finger while trying to catch a softball; stepping on dry brambles while walking on the newly cut hayfields; the hem of a skirt caught in a barbed-wire fence; the great sunstroke, the great pain, the not at all great day spent in bed.

❧

Inside, the house is still. Outside, the blind man takes a walk. It is midday, and the blind man casts

a short, fat shadow as he takes a walk. The blind
man is a young man, twenty-seven. The blind man
has been blind for only ten years. The blind man
was infatuated with the driver of his school bus, a
woman. No. The blind man was in love with the
driver of his school bus, a woman. The blind man
saw the driver of his school bus, a woman, kissing a
man. The blind man killed the driver of his school
bus, a woman, and then tried to kill himself. He did
not die, so now he is just a blind man. The blind man
is pale and sickly-looking. He doesn't return a greet-
ing. Everybody knows this, and they stay away from
him. Not even the dog pays any attention to his
comings and goings.

❦

"But things are so funny here."
"But where? But how?"
"We are going to the May fair, but it's July. They
are dancing a May dance around a Maypole, but
it's July. They are crowning a May queen, but it's
July. At Christmas, just before our big dinner, we
take a long swim in the warm seawater. After that,
we do not bathe, and in the heat the salt dries on
our bodies in little rings."
"Aren't things funny here?"
"Yes, things are funny here."

❦

The two boys are fishing in Michigan, catching fish with live frogs. The two boys do not need a comfortable bed and a nice pillow at night, or newly baked bread for breakfast, or roasted beef on Sundays, or hymns in a cathedral, or small-ankled children wearing white caps, or boxes of fruit from the tropics, or nice greetings and sad partings, or light bulbs, or the tremor of fast motor vehicles, or key chains, or a run-down phonograph, or rubbish baskets, or meek and self-sacrificing women, or inkwells, or shaving kits. The two boys have visited the Mark Twain museum in Missouri and taken photographs. The two boys have done many things and taken photographs. Here are the two boys milking two cows in Wyoming. Here are the two boys seated on the hood of their car just after changing the tire. Here are the two boys dressed up as gentlemen. Here are the two boys dressed up as gentlemen and looking for large-breasted women.

❧

That man, a handsome man; that woman, a beautiful woman; those children, such gay children; great laughter; wild and sour berries; wild and sweet berries; pink and blue-black berries; fields with purple flowers, blue flowers, yellow flowers; a long road; a long and curved road; a car with a collapsible top; big laughs; big laughing in the bushes;

no, not the bushes—the barn; no, not the barn—the house; no, not the house—the trees; no, not the trees, no; big laughing all the same; a crushed straw hat that now fits lopsided; milk from a farm; eggs from a farm; a farm; in the mountains, no clear reception on the radio; no radio; no clothes; no free-floating anxiety; no anxiety; no automatic-lighting stoves; a walk to the store; a walk; from afar, the sound of great laughing; the piano; from afar, someone playing the piano; late-morning sleepiness; many, many brown birds; a big blue-breasted bird; a smaller red-breasted bird; food roasted on sticks; ducks; wild ducks; a pond; so many wide smiles; no high heels; buying many funny postcards; sending many funny postcards; taking the rapids; and still, great laughter.

THE LETTER

FROM HOME

I milked the cows, I churned the butter, I
stored the cheese, I baked the bread, I brewed
the tea, I washed the clothes, I dressed the children;
the cat meowed, the dog barked, the horse neighed,
the mouse squeaked, the fly buzzed, the goldfish
living in a bowl stretched its jaws; the door banged
shut, the stairs creaked, the fridge hummed, the
curtains billowed up, the pot boiled, the gas hissed
through the stove, the tree branches heavy with snow
crashed against the roof; my heart beat loudly *thud!
thud!*, tiny beads of water gathered on my nose, my
hair went limp, my waist grew folds, I shed my skin;
lips have trembled, tears have flowed, cheeks have
puffed, stomachs have twisted with pain; I went to
the country, the car broke down, I walked back; the
boat sailed, the waves broke, the horizon tipped,

the jetty grew small, the air stung, some heads bobbed, some handkerchiefs fluttered; the drawers didn't close, the faucets dripped, the paint peeled, the walls cracked, the books tilted over, the rug no longer lay out flat; I ate my food, I chewed each mouthful thirty-two times, I swallowed carefully, my toe healed; there was a night, it was dark, there was a moon, it was full, there was a bed, it held sleep; there was movement, it was quick, there was a being, it stood still, there was a space, it was full, then there was nothing; a man came to the door and asked, "Are the children ready yet? Will they bear their mother's name? I suppose you have forgotten that my birthday falls on Monday after next? Will you come to visit me in hospital?"; I stood up, I sat down, I stood up again; the clock slowed down, the post came late, the afternoon turned cool; the cat licked his coat, tore the chair to shreds, slept in a drawer that didn't close; I entered a room, I felt my skin shiver, then dissolve, I lighted a candle, I saw something move, I recognized the shadow to be my own hand, I felt myself to be one thing; the wind was hard, the house swayed, the angiosperms prospered, the mammal-like reptiles vanished (Is the Heaven to be above? Is the Hell below? Does the Lamb still lie meek? Does the Lion roar? Will the streams all run clear? Will we kiss each other deeply later?) ; in the peninsula some ancient ships are still anchored, in the field the ox stands still, in the village the leopard stalks its prey; the buildings are to be tall, the structures are to be sound, the stairs are to be winding, in the rooms sometimes there is to be a glow; the hats remain on the hat stand, the coats hang dead from the pegs, the hyacinths look as if they will bloom—I know their fragrance will be overpowering; the earth spins on its axis, the axis is imaginary, the valleys correspond to the mountains, the mountains correspond to the sea, the sea corresponds to the dry land, the dry land corresponds to the snake whose limbs are now reduced; I saw a man, He was in a shroud, I sat in a rowboat, He whistled sweetly to me, I narrowed my eyes, He beckoned to me, Come now; I turned and rowed away, as if I didn't know what I was doing.

WHAT I

HAVE BEEN

DOING LATELY

What I have been doing lately: I was lying in bed and the doorbell rang. I ran downstairs. Quick. I opened the door. There was no one there. I stepped outside. Either it was drizzling or there was a lot of dust in the air and the dust was damp. I stuck out my tongue and the drizzle or the damp dust tasted like government school ink. I looked north. I looked south. I decided to start walking north. While walking north, I noticed that I was barefoot. While walking north, I looked up and saw the planet Venus. I said, "It must be almost morning." I saw a monkey in a tree. The tree had no leaves. I said, "Ah, a monkey. Just look at that. A monkey." I walked for I don't know how long before I came up to a big body of water. I wanted to get across it but I couldn't swim. I wanted to get across it but it would take me years to build a boat. I wanted to get across it but it would take me I didn't know how long to build a bridge. Years passed and then one day, feeling like it, I got into my boat and rowed across. When I got to the other side, it was noon and my shadow was small and fell beneath me. I set out on a path that stretched out straight ahead. I passed a house, and a dog was sitting on the verandah but it looked the other way when it saw me coming. I passed a boy tossing a ball in the air but the boy looked the other way when he saw me coming. I walked and I walked but I couldn't tell if I walked a long time because my feet didn't feel as if they would drop off. I turned around to see what I had left behind me but nothing was familiar. Instead of the straight path, I saw hills. Instead of the boy with his ball, I saw tall flowering trees. I looked up and the sky was without clouds and seemed near, as if it were the ceiling in my house and, if I stood on a chair, I could touch it with the tips of my fingers. I turned around and looked ahead of me again. A deep hole had opened up before me. I looked in. The hole was deep and dark and I couldn't see the bottom. I thought, What's down there?, so on purpose I fell in. I fell and I fell, over and over, as if I were an old suitcase. On the sides of the deep hole I could see things written, but perhaps it was in a foreign language because I couldn't read them. Still I fell, for I don't know how long. As I fell I began to see that I didn't like the way falling made me feel. Falling made me feel sick and I missed all the people I had loved. I said, I don't want to fall anymore, and I reversed myself. I was standing again on the edge of the deep hole. I looked at the deep hole and I said, You can close up now, and it did. I walked some more without knowing distance. I only knew that I passed through days and nights, I only knew that I passed through rain and shine, light and darkness. I was never thirsty and I felt no pain. Looking at the horizon, I made a joke for myself: I said, "The earth has thin lips," and I laughed.

Looking at the horizon again, I saw a lone figure coming toward me, but I wasn't frightened because I was sure it was my mother. As I got closer to the figure, I could see that it wasn't my mother, but still I wasn't frightened because I could see that it was a woman.

When this woman got closer to me, she looked at me hard and then she threw up her hands. She must have seen me somewhere before because she said,

"It's you. Just look at that. It's you. And just what have you been doing lately?"

I could have said, "I have been praying not to grow any taller."

I could have said, "I have been listening carefully to my mother's words, so as to make a good imitation of a dutiful daughter."

I could have said, "A pack of dogs, tired from chasing each other all over town, slept in the moonlight."

Instead, I said, What I have been doing lately: I was lying in bed on my back, my hands drawn up, my fingers interlaced lightly at the nape of my neck. Someone rang the doorbell. I went downstairs and opened the door but there was no one there. I stepped outside. Either it was drizzling or there was a lot of dust in the air and the dust was damp. I stuck out my tongue and the drizzle or the damp dust tasted like government school ink. I looked north and I looked south. I started walking north. While walking north, I wanted to move fast, so I removed the shoes from my feet. While walking north, I looked up and saw the planet Venus and I said, "If the sun went out, it would be eight minutes before I would know it." I saw a monkey sitting in a tree that had no leaves and I said, "A monkey. Just look at that. A monkey." I picked up a stone and

I threw it at the monkey. The monkey, seeing the stone, quickly moved out of its way. Three times I threw a stone at the monkey and three times it moved away. The fourth time I threw the stone, the monkey caught it and threw it back at me. The stone struck me on my forehead over my right eye, making a deep gash. The gash healed immediately but now the skin on my forehead felt false to me. I walked for I don't know how long before I came to a big body of water. I wanted to get across, so when the boat came I paid my fare. When I got to the other side, I saw a lot of people sitting on the beach and they were having a picnic. They were the most beautiful people I had ever seen. Everything about them was black and shiny. Their skin was black and shiny. Their shoes were black and shiny. Their hair was black and shiny. The clothes they wore were black and shiny. I could hear them laughing and chatting and I said, I would like to be with these people, so I started to walk toward them, but when I got up close to them I saw that they weren't at a picnic and they weren't beautiful and they weren't chatting and laughing. All around me was black mud and the people all looked as if they had been made up out of the black mud. I looked up and saw that the sky seemed far away and nothing I could stand on would make me able to touch it with my fingertips. I thought, If only I could get out of this, so I started to walk. I must have walked for a long time because my feet hurt and felt as if they would drop off. I thought, If only just around the bend I would see my house and inside my house I would find my bed, freshly made at that, and in the kitchen I would find my mother or anyone else that I loved making me a custard. I thought, If only it was a Sunday and I was sitting in a church and I had just heard someone sing a psalm. I felt very sad so I sat down. I felt so sad that I rested my head on my own knees and smoothed my own head. I felt so sad I couldn't imagine feeling any other way again. I said, I don't like this. I don't want to do this anymore. And I went back to lying in bed, just before the doorbell rang.

BLACKNESS

How soft is the blackness as it falls. It falls in silence and yet it is deafening, for no other sound except the blackness falling can be heard. The blackness falls like soot from a lamp with an untrimmed wick. The blackness is visible and yet it is invisible, for I see that I cannot see it. The blackness fills up a small room, a large field, an island, my own being. The blackness cannot bring me joy but often I am made glad in it. The blackness cannot be separated from me but often I can stand outside it. The blackness is not the air, though I breathe it. The blackness is not the earth, though I walk on it. The blackness is not water or food, though I drink and eat it. The blackness is not my blood, though it flows through my veins. The blackness enters my many-tiered spaces and soon the significant word and event recede and eventually vanish: in this way I am annihilated and my form becomes formless and I am absorbed into a vastness of free-flowing matter. In the blackness, then, I have been erased. I can no longer say my own name. I can no longer point to myself and say "I." In the blackness my voice is silent. First, then, I have been my individual self, carefully banishing randomness from my existence, then I am swallowed up in the blackness so that I am one with it . . .

There are the small flashes of joy that are present in my daily life: the upturned face to the open sky, the red ball tumbling from small hand to small hand, as small voices muffle laughter; the sliver of orange on the horizon, a remnant of the sun setting. There is the wide stillness, trembling and waiting to be violently shattered by impatient demands.

("May I now have my bread without the crust?"

"But I long ago stopped liking my bread without the crust!")

All manner of feelings are locked up within my human breast and all manner of events summon them out. How frightened I became once on looking down to see an oddly shaped, ash-colored object that I did not recognize at once to be a small part of my own foot. And how powerful I then found that moment, so that I was not at one with myself and I felt myself separate, like a brittle substance dashed and shattered, each separate part without knowledge of the other separate parts. I then clung fast to a common and familiar object (my lamp, as it stood unlit on the clean surface of my mantelpiece), until I felt myself steadied, no longer alone at sea in a small rowboat, the waves cruel and unruly. What is my nature, then? For in isolation I am all purpose and industry and determination and prudence, as if I were the single survivor of a species whose evolutionary history can be traced to the most ancient of ancients; in isolation I ruthlessly plow the deep silences, seeking my opportunities like a miner seeking veins of treasure. In what shallow glimmering space shall I find what glimmering glory? The stark, stony mountainous surface is turned to green, rolling meadow, and a spring of clear water, its origins a mystery, its purpose and beauty constant, draws all manner of troubled existence seeking solace. And again and again, the heart—buried deeply as ever in the human breast, its four chambers exposed to love and joy and pain and the small shafts that fall with desperation in between.

I sat at a narrow table, my head, heavy with sleep, resting on my hands. I dreamed of bands of men who walked aimlessly, their guns and cannons slackened at their sides, the chambers emptied of bullets and shells. They had fought in a field from time to time and from time to time they grew tired of it. They walked up the path that led to my house and as they walked they passed between the sun and the earth; as they passed between the sun and the earth they blotted out the daylight and night fell immediately and permanently. No longer could I see the blooming trefoils, their overpowering perfume a constant giddy delight to me; no longer could I see the domesticated animals feeding in the pasture; no longer could I see the beasts, hunter and prey, leading a guarded existence; no longer could I see the smith moving cautiously in a swirl of hot sparks or bent over anvil and bellows. The bands of men marched through my house in silence. On their way, their breath scorched some flowers I had placed on a dresser, with their bare hands they destroyed the marble columns that strengthened the foundations of my house. They left my house, in silence again, and they walked across a field, opposite to the way they had come, still passing between the sun and the earth. I stood at a window and watched their backs until they were just a small spot on the horizon.

I see my child arise slowly from her bed. I see her cross the room and stand in front of the mirror. She looks closely at her straight, unmarred body. Her skin is without color, and when passing through a small beam of light, she is made transparent. Her eyes are ruby, revolving orbs, and they burn like coals caught suddenly in a gust of wind. This is my child! When her jaws were too weak, I first chewed her food, then fed it to her in small mouthfuls. This is my child! I must carry a cool liquid in my flattened breasts to quench her parched throat. This is my child sitting in the shade, her head thrown back in rapture, prolonging some moment of joy I have created for her.

My child is pitiless to the hunchback boy; her mouth twists open in a cruel smile, her teeth becoming pointed and sparkling, the roof of her mouth bony and ridged, her young hands suddenly withered and gnarled as she reaches out to caress his hump. Squirming away from her forceful, heated gaze, he seeks shelter in a grove of trees, but her arms, which she can command to grow to incredible lengths, seek him out and tug at the long silk-like hairs that lie flattened on his back. She calls his name softly and the sound of her voice shatters his eardrum. Deaf, he can no longer heed warnings of danger and his sense of direction is destroyed. Still, my child has built for him a dwelling hut on the edge of a steep cliff so that she may watch him day after day flatten himself against a fate of which he knows and yet cannot truly know until the moment it consumes him.

My child haunts the dwelling places of the useless-winged cormorants, so enamored is she of great beauty and ancestral history. She traces each thing from its meager happenstance beginnings in cool and slimy marsh, to its great glory and dominance of air or land or sea, to its odd remains entombed in mysterious alluviums. She loves the thing untouched by lore, she loves the thing that is not cultivated, and yet she loves the thing built up, bit carefully placed upon bit, its very beauty eclipsing the deed it is meant to commemorate. She sits idly on a shore, staring hard at the sea beneath the sea and at the sea beneath even that. She hears the sounds within the sounds, common as that is to open spaces. She feels the specter, first cold, then briefly warm, then cold again as it passes from atmosphere to atmosphere. Having observed the many differing physical existences feed on each other, she is beyond despair or the spiritual vacuum.

Oh, look at my child as she stands boldly now, one foot in the dark, the other in the light. Moving from pool to pool, she absorbs each special sensation for and of itself. My child rushes from death to death, so familiar a state is it to her. Though I have summoned her into a fleeting existence, one that is perilous and subject to the violence of chance, she embraces time as it passes in numbing sameness, bearing in its wake a multitude of great sadnesses.

❦

I hear the silent voice; it stands opposite the blackness and yet it does not oppose the blackness, for conflict is not a part of its nature. I shrug off my mantle of hatred. In love I move toward the silent voice. I shrug off my mantle of despair. In love, again, I move ever toward the silent voice. I stand inside the silent voice. The silent voice enfolds me. The silent voice enfolds me so completely that even in memory the blackness is erased. I live in silence. The silence is without boundaries. The pastures are unfenced, the lions roam the continents, the continents are not separated. Across the flat lands cuts the river, its flow undammed. The mountains no longer rupture. Within the silent voice, no mysterious depths separate me; no vision is so distant that longing is stirred up in me. I hear the silent voice—how softly now it falls, and all of existence is caught up in it. Living in the silent voice, I am no longer "I." Living in the silent voice, I am at last at peace. Living in the silent voice, I am at last erased.

MY MOTHER

*I*mmediately on wishing my mother dead and seeing the pain it caused her, I was sorry and cried so many tears that all the earth around me was drenched. Standing before my mother, I begged her forgiveness, and I begged so earnestly that she took pity on me, kissing my face and placing my head on her bosom to rest. Placing her arms around me, she drew my head closer and closer to her bosom, until finally I suffocated. I lay on her bosom, breathless, for a time uncountable, until one day, for a reason she has kept to herself, she shook me out and stood me under a tree and I started to breathe again. I cast a sharp glance at her and said to myself, "So." Instantly I grew my own bosoms, small mounds at first, leaving a small, soft place between them, where, if ever necessary, I could rest my own head. Between my mother and me now were the tears I had cried, and I gathered up some stones and banked them in so that they formed a small pond. The water in the pond was thick and black and poisonous, so that only unnamable invertebrates could live in it. My mother and I now watched each other carefully, always making sure to shower the other with words and deeds of love and affection.

I was sitting on my mother's bed trying to get a good look at myself. It was a large bed and it stood in the middle of a large, completely dark room. The room was completely dark because all the windows had been boarded up and all the crevices stuffed with black cloth. My mother lit some candles and the room burst into a pink-like, yellow-like glow. Looming over us, much larger than ourselves, were our shadows. We sat mesmerized because our shadows had made a place between themselves, as if they were making room for someone else. Nothing filled up the space between them, and the shadow of my mother sighed. The shadow of my mother danced around the room to a tune that my own shadow sang, and then they stopped. All along, our shadows had grown thick and thin, long and short, had fallen at every angle, as if they were controlled by the light of day. Suddenly my mother got up and blew out the

candles and our shadows vanished. I continued to sit
on the bed, trying to get a good look at myself.

❧

My mother removed her clothes and covered
thoroughly her skin with a thick gold-colored oil,
which had recently been rendered in a hot pan from
the livers of reptiles with pouched throats. She grew
plates of metal-colored scales on her back, and light,
when it collided with this surface, would shatter and
collapse into tiny points. Her teeth now arranged
themselves into rows that reached all the way back
to her long white throat. She uncoiled her hair from
her head and then removed her hair altogether.
Taking her head into her large palms, she flattened
it so that her eyes, which were by now ablaze, sat
on top of her head and spun like two revolving
balls. Then, making two lines on the soles of each
foot, she divided her feet into crossroads. Silently,
she had instructed me to follow her example, and
now I too traveled along on my white underbelly,
my tongue darting and flickering in the hot air.
"Look," said my mother.

❧

My mother and I were standing on the seabed side
by side, my arms laced loosely around her waist, my
head resting securely on her shoulder, as if I needed
the support. To make sure she believed in my frail-

ness, I sighed occasionally—long soft sighs, the kind
of sigh she had long ago taught me could evoke
sympathy. In fact, how I really felt was invincible.
I was no longer a child but I was not yet a woman.
My skin had just blackened and cracked and fallen
away and my new impregnable carapace had taken
full hold. My nose had flattened; my hair curled in
and stood out straight from my head simultaneously;
my many rows of teeth in their retractable trays
were in place. My mother and I wordlessly made an
arrangement—I sent out my beautiful sighs, she received them; I leaned ever more heavily on her for
support, she offered her shoulder, which shortly grew
to the size of a thick plank. A long time passed, at
the end of which I had hoped to see my mother
permanently cemented to the seabed. My mother
reached out to pass a hand over my head, a pacifying
gesture, but I laughed and, with great agility,
stepped aside. I let out a horrible roar, then a self-
pitying whine. I had grown big, but my mother was
bigger, and that would always be so. We walked to
the Garden of Fruits and there ate to our hearts'
satisfaction. We departed through the southwesterly
gate, leaving as always, in our trail, small colonies of
worms.

❧

 With my mother, I crossed, unwillingly, the valley.
We saw a lamb grazing and when it heard our foot-

steps it paused and looked up at us. The lamb looked
cross and miserable. I said to my mother, "The lamb
is cross and miserable. So would I be, too, if I had
to live in a climate not suited to my nature." My
mother and I now entered the cave. It was the dark
and cold cave. I felt something growing under my
feet and I bent down to eat it. I stayed that way for
years, bent over eating whatever I found growing
under my feet. Eventually, I grew a special lens that
would allow me to see in the darkest of darkness;
eventually, I grew a special coat that kept me warm
in the coldest of coldness. One day I saw my mother
sitting on a rock. She said, "What a strange expression you have on your face. So cross, so miserable,
as if you were living in a climate not suited to your
nature." Laughing, she vanished. I dug a deep, deep
hole. I built a beautiful house, a floorless house, over
the deep, deep hole. I put in lattice windows, most
favored of windows by my mother, so perfect for
looking out at people passing by without her being observed. I painted the house itself yellow, the windows
green, colors I knew would please her. Standing just
outside the door, I asked her to inspect the house.
I said, "Take a look. Tell me if it's to your satisfaction." Laughing out of the corner of a mouth
I could not see, she stepped inside. I stood just outside the door, listening carefully, hoping to hear her
land with a thud at the bottom of the deep, deep

hole. Instead, she walked up and down in every direction, even pounding her heel on the air. Coming outside to greet me, she said, "It is an excellent house. I would be honored to live in it," and then vanished. I filled up the hole and burnt the house to the ground.

My mother has grown to an enormous height. I have grown to an enormous height also, but my mother's height is three times mine. Sometimes I cannot see from her breasts on up, so lost is she in the atmosphere. One day, seeing her sitting on the seashore, her hand reaching out in the deep to caress the belly of a striped fish as he swam through a place where two seas met, I glowed red with anger. For a while then I lived alone on the island where there were eight full moons and I adorned the face of each moon with expressions I had seen on my mother's face. All the expressions favored me. I soon grew tired of living in this way and returned to my mother's side. I remained, though glowing red with anger, and my mother and I built houses on opposite banks of the dead pond. The dead pond lay between us; in it, only small invertebrates with poisonous lances lived. My mother behaved toward them as if she had suddenly found herself in the same room with relatives we had long since risen above. I cherished their presence and gave them names. Still

I missed my mother's close company and cried constantly for her, but at the end of each day when I saw her return to her house, incredible and great deeds in her wake, each of them singing loudly her praises, I glowed and glowed again, red with anger. Eventually, I wore myself out and sank into a deep, deep sleep, the only dreamless sleep I have ever had.

❧

One day my mother packed my things in a grip and, taking me by the hand, walked me to the jetty, placed me on board a boat, in care of the captain. My mother, while caressing my chin and cheeks, said some words of comfort to me because we had never been apart before. She kissed me on the forehead and turned and walked away. I cried so much my chest heaved up and down, my whole body shook at the sight of her back turned toward me, as if I had never seen her back turned toward me before. I started to make plans to get off the boat, but when I saw that the boat was encased in a large green bottle, as if it were about to decorate a mantelpiece, I fell asleep, until I reached my destination, the new island. When the boat stopped, I got off and I saw a woman with feet exactly like mine, especially around the arch of the instep. Even though the face was completely different from what I was used to, I recognized this woman as my mother. We greeted each other at first with great caution and politeness, but as we walked along, our steps became one, and as we talked, our voices became one voice, and we were in· complete union in every other way. What peace came over me then, for I could not see where she left off and I began, or where I left off and she began.

My mother and I walk through the rooms of her house. Every crack in the floor holds a significant event: here, an apparently healthy young man suddenly dropped dead; here a young woman defied her father and, while riding her bicycle to the forbidden lovers' meeting place, fell down a precipice, remaining a cripple for the rest of a very long life. My mother and I find this a beautiful house. The rooms are large and empty, opening on to each other, waiting for people and things to fill them up. Our white muslin skirts billow up around our ankles, our hair hangs straight down our backs as our arms hang straight at our sides. I fit perfectly in the crook of my mother's arm, on the curve of her back, in the hollow of her stomach. We eat from the same bowl, drink from the same cup; when we sleep, our heads rest on the same pillow. As we walk through the rooms, we merge and separate, merge and separate; soon we shall enter the final stage of our evolution.

The fishermen are coming in from sea; their catch is bountiful, my mother has seen to that. As the

waves plop, plop against each other, the fishermen
are happy that the sea is calm. My mother points out
the fishermen to me, their contentment is a source
of my contentment. I am sitting in my mother's
enormous lap. Sometimes I sit on a mat she has made
for me from her hair. The lime trees are weighed
down with limes—I have already perfumed myself
with their blossoms. A hummingbird has nested on
my stomach, a sign of my fertileness. My mother and
I live in a bower made from flowers whose petals are
imperishable. There is the silvery blue of the sea,
crisscrossed with sharp darts of light, there is the
warm rain falling on the clumps of castor bush, there
is the small lamb bounding across the pasture, there
is the soft ground welcoming the soles of my pink
feet. It is in this way my mother and I have lived
for a long time now.

AT THE BOTTOM

OF THE RIVER

This, then, is the terrain. The steepest mountains, thickly covered, where huge, sharp
rocks might pose the greatest danger and where only
the bravest, surest, most deeply arched of human
feet will venture, where a large stream might flow,
and, flowing perilously, having only a deep ambition
to see itself mighty and powerful, bends and curves
and dips in many directions, making a welcome and
easy path for each idle rill and babbling brook, each
trickle of rain fallen on land that lies sloping; and
that stream, at last swelled to a great, fast, flowing
body of water, falls over a ledge with a roar, a loud-
ness that is more than the opposite of complete
silence, then rushes over dry, flat land in imperfect
curves—curves as if made by a small boy playfully
dragging a toy behind him—then hugs closely to the

paths made, ruthlessly conquering the flat plain, the steep ridge, the grassy bed; all day, all day, a stream might flow so, and then it winds its way to a gorge in the earth, a basin of measurable depth and breadth, and so collects itself in a pool: now comes the gloaming, for day will end, and the stream, its flow stilled and gathered up, so that trees growing firmly on its banks, their barks white, their trunks bent, their branches covered with leaves and reaching up, up, are reflected in the depths, awaits the eye, the hand, the foot that shall then give all this a meaning.

But what shall that be? For now here is a man who lives in a world bereft of its very nature. He lies on his bed as if alone in a small room, waiting and waiting and waiting. For what does he wait? He is not yet complete, so he cannot conceive of what it is he waits for. He cannot conceive of the fields of wheat, their kernels ripe and almost bursting, and how happy the sight will make someone. He cannot conceive of the union of opposites, or, for that matter, their very existence. He cannot conceive of flocks of birds in migratory flight, or that night will follow day and season follow season in a seemingly endless cycle, and the beauty and the pleasure and the purpose that might come from all this. He cannot conceive of the wind that ravages the coastline, casting asunder men and cargo, temporarily interrupting the smooth flow of commerce. He cannot conceive of the individual who, on looking up from some dreary, everyday task, is struck just then by the completeness of the above and the below and his own spirit resting in between; or how that same individual, suddenly rounding a corner, catches his own reflection, transparent and suspended in a pane of glass, and so smiles to himself with shy admiration. He cannot conceive of the woman and the child at play—an image so often regarded as a symbol of human contentment; or how calamity will attract the cold and disinterested gaze of children. He cannot conceive of a Sunday: the peal of church bells, the sound of seraphic voices in harmony, the closeness of congregation, the soothing words of praise and the much longed for presence of an unearthly glory. He cannot conceive of how emotions, varying in color and intensity, will rapidly heighten, reach an unbearable pitch, then finally explode in the silence of the evening air. He cannot conceive of the chance invention that changes again and again and forever the great turbulence that is human history. Not for him can thought crash over thought in random and violent succession, leaving his brain suffused in contradiction. He sits in nothing, this man: not in a full space, not in emptiness, not in darkness, not in light or glimmer of. He sits in nothing, in nothing, in nothing.

Look! A man steps out of bed, a good half hour after his wife, and washes himself. He sits down on a chair and at a table that he made with his own hands (the tips of his fingers are stained a thin chocolate brown from nicotine). His wife places before him a bowl of porridge, some cheese, some bread that has been buttered, two boiled eggs, a large cup of tea. He eats. The goats, the sheep, the cows are driven to pasture. A dog barks. His child now enters the room. Walking over, she bends to kiss his hand, which is resting on his knee, and he, waiting for her head to come up, kisses her on the forehead with lips he has purposely moistened. "Sir, it is wet," she says. And he laughs at her as she dries her forehead with the back of her hand. Now, clasping his wife to him, he bids her goodbye, opens the door, and stops. For what does he stop? What does he see? He sees before him himself, standing in sawdust, measuring a hole, just dug, in the ground, putting decorative grooves in a bannister, erecting columns, carving the head of a cherub over a door, lighting a cigarette, pursing his lips, holding newly planed wood at an angle and looking at it with one eye closed; standing with both hands in his pockets, the thumbs out, and rocking back and forth on his heels, he surveys a small accomplishment—a last nail driven in just so. Crossing and recrossing the threshold, he watches the sun, a violent red, set on the horizon, he hears the birds fly home, he sees the insects dancing in the last warmth of the day's light, he hears himself sing out loud:

Now the day is over,
Night is drawing nigh;
Shadows of the evening
Steal across the sky.

All this he sees (and hears). And who is this man, really? So solitary, his eyes sometimes aglow, his heart beating at an abnormal rate with a joy he cannot identify or explain. What is the virtue in him? And then again, what can it matter? For tomorrow the oak will be felled, the trestle will break, the cow's hooves will be made into glue.

But so he stands, forever, crossing and recrossing the threshold, his head lifted up, held aloft and stiff with vanity; then his eyes shift and he sees and he sees, and he is weighed down. First lifted up, then weighed down—always he is so. Shall he seek comfort now? And in what? He seeks out the living fossils. There is the shell of the pearly nautilus lying amidst colored chalk and powdered ink and India rubber in an old tin can, in memory of a day spent blissfully at the sea. The flatworm is now a parasite. Reflect. There is the earth, its surface apparently stilled, its atmosphere hospitable. And yet here stand pile upon pile of rocks of an enormous size,

riven and worn down from the pressure of the great
seas, now receded. And here the large veins of gold,
the bubbling sulfurous fountains, the mountains covered with hot lava; at the bottom of some caves lies
the black dust, and below that rich clay sediment, and
trapped between the layers are filaments of winged
beasts and remnants of invertebrates. "And where
shall I be?" asks this man. Then he says, "My body,
my soul." But quickly he averts his eyes and feels
himself now, hands pressed tightly against his chest.
He is standing on the threshold once again, and,
looking up, he sees his wife holding out toward him
his brown felt hat (he had forgotten it); his child
crossing the street, joining the throng of children on
their way to school, a mixture of broken sentences,
mispronounced words, laughter, budding malice, and
energy abundant. He looks at the house he has built
with his own hands, the books he has read standing
on shelves, the fruit-bearing trees that he nursed
from seedlings, the larder filled with food that he
has provided. He shifts the weight of his body from
one foot to the other, in uncertainty but also weighing, weighing . . . He imagines that in one hand he
holds emptiness and yearning and in the other desire
fulfilled. He thinks of tenderness and love and faith
and hope and, yes, goodness. He contemplates the
beauty in the common thing: the sun rising up out of
the huge, shimmering expanse of water that is the

sea; it rises up each day as if made anew, as if for the first time. "Sing again. Sing now," he says in his heart, for he feels the cool breeze at the back of his neck. But again and again he feels the futility in all that. For stretching out before him is a silence so dreadful, a vastness, its length and breadth and depth immeasurable. Nothing.

The branches were dead; a fly hung dead on the branches, its fragile body fluttering in the wind as if it were remnants of a beautiful gown; a beetle had fed on the body of the fly but now lay dead, too. Death on death on death. Dead lay everything. The ground stretching out from the river no longer a verdant pasture but parched and cracked with tiny fissures running up and down and into each other; and, seen from high above, the fissures presented beauty: not a pleasure to the eye but beauty all the same; still, dead, dead it was. Dead lay everything that had lived and dead also lay everything that would live. All had had or would have its season. And what should it matter that its season lasted five billion years or five minutes? There it is now, dead, vanished into darkness, banished from life. First living briefly, then dead in eternity. How vainly I struggle against this. Toil, toil, night and day. Here a house is built. Here a monument is erected to commemorate something called a good deed, or even in remembrance of a woman with exceptional qualities, and all that she loved and all that she did. Here are some children, and immeasurable is the love and special attention lavished on them. Vanished now is the house. Vanished now is the monument. Silent now are the children. I recall the house, I recall the monument, I summon up the children from the eternity of darkness, and sometimes, briefly, they appear, though always slightly shrouded, always as if they had emerged from mounds of ashes, chipped, tarnished, in fragments, or large parts missing: the ribbons, for instance, gone from the children's hair. These children whom I loved best—better than the monument, better than the house—once were so beautiful that they were thought unearthly. Dead is the past. Dead shall the future be. And what stands before my eyes, as soon as I turn my back, dead is that, too. Shall I shed tears? Sorrow is bound to death. Grief is bound to death. Each moment is not as fragile and fleeting as I once thought. Each moment is hard and lasting and so holds much that I must mourn for. And so what a bitter thing to say to me: that life is the intrusion, that to embrace a thing as beauty is the intrusion, that to believe a thing true and therefore undeniable, that is the intrusion; and, yes, false are all appearances. What a bitter thing to say to me, I who for time uncountable have always seen myself as newly born, filled with a truth and a beauty that could not be denied, living in a world of light that I called eternal, a world that can know no end. I now know regret. And that, too, is bound to death. And what do I regret? Surely not that I stand in the knowledge of the presence of death. For knowledge is a good thing; you have said that. What I regret is that in the face of death and all that it is and all that it shall be I stand powerless, that in the face of death my will, to which everything I have ever known bends, stands as if it were nothing more than a string caught in the early-morning wind.

Now! There lived a small creature, and it lived as both male and female inside a mound that it made on the ground, its body wholly covered with short fur, broadly striped, in the colors field-yellow and field-blue. It hunted a honeybee once, and when the bee, in bee anger and fright, stung the creature on the corner of the mouth, the pain was so unbearably delicious that never did this creature hunt a honeybee again. It walked over and over the wide space that surrounded the mound in which it lived. As it walked over and over the wide ground that surrounded the mound in which it lived, it watched its own feet sink into the grass and heard the ever so slight sound the grass made as it gave way to the pressure, and as it saw and heard, it felt a pleasure unbearably delicious, and, each time, the pleasure unbearably delicious was new to this creature. It lived so, banking up each unbearably delicious pleasure in deep, dark memory unspeakable, hoping to perhaps one day throw the memories into a dungeon, or burn them on an ancient pyre, or banish them to land barren, but now it kept them in this way. Then all its unbearably delicious pleasure it kept free, each thing taken, time in, time out, as if it were new, just born. It lived so in a length of time that may be measured to be no less than the blink of an eye, or no more than one hundred millenniums. This creature lived inside and outside its mound, remembering and forgetting, pain and pleasure so equally balanced, each assigned to what it judged a natural conclusion, yet one day it did vanish, leaving no sign of its existence, except for a small spot, which glowed faintly in the darkness that surrounded it. I divined this, and how natural to me that has become. I divined this, and it is not a specter but something that stood here. I show it to you. I yearn to build a monument to it, something of dust, since I now know—and so soon, so soon—what dust really is.

"Death is natural," you said to me, in such a flat, matter-of-fact way, and then you laughed—a laugh so piercing that I felt my eardrums shred, I felt myself mocked. Yet I can see that a tree is natural, that the sea is natural, that the twitter of a twittering bird is natural to a twittering bird. I can see with my own eyes the tree; it stands with limbs spread wide and laden with ripe fruit, its roots planted firmly in the rich soil, and that seems natural to me. I can see with my own eyes the sea, now with a neap tide, its surface smooth and calm; then in the next moment comes a breeze, soft, and small ripples turn into wavelets conquering wavelets, and that seems natural to me again. And the twittering bird twitters away, and that bears a special irritation, though not the irritation of the sting of the evening fly, and that special irritation is mostly ignored, and what could be more natural than that? But death bears no relation to the tree, the sea, the twittering bird. How much more like the earth spinning on its invisible axis death is, and so I might want to reach out with my hand and make the earth stand still, as if it were a bicycle standing on its handlebars upside down, the wheels spun in passing by a pair of idle hands, then stilled in passing by yet another pair of idle hands. Inevitable to life is death and not inevitable to death is life. Inevitable. How the word weighs on my tongue. I glean this: a worm winds its way between furrow and furrow in a garden, its miserable form shuddering, dreading the sharp open beak of any common bird winging its way overhead; the bird, then taking to the open air, spreads its wings in majestic flight, and how noble and triumphant is this bird in flight; but look now, there comes a boy on horseback, his body taut and eager, his hand holding bow and arrow, his aim pointed and definite, and in this way is the bird made dead. The worm, the bird, the boy. And what of the boy? His ends are number- less. I glean again the death in life.

Is life, then, a violent burst of light, like flint struck sharply in the dark? If so, I must continually strive to exist between the day and the day. I see myself as I was as a child. How much I was loved and how much I loved. No small turn of my head, no wrinkle on my brow, no parting of my lips is lost to me. How much I loved myself and how much I was loved by my mother. My mother made up elaborate tales of the origins of ordinary food, just so that I would eat it. My mother sat on some stone steps, her volumi- nous skirt draped in folds and falling down between her parted legs, and I, playing some distance away, glanced over my shoulder and saw her face—a face that was to me of such wondrous beauty: the lips like a moon in its first and last quarter, a nose with a bony bridge and wide nostrils that flared out and trembled visibly in excitement, ears the lobes of which were large and soft and silk-like; and what pleasure it gave me to press them between my thumb and forefinger. How I worshipped this beauty, and in my childish heart I would always say to it, "Yes, yes, yes." And, glancing over my shoulder, yet again I would silently send to her words of love and adoration, and I would receive from her, in turn and in silence, words of love and adoration. Once, I stood on a platform with three dozen girls, arranged in rows of twelve, all wearing identical white linen dresses with corded sashes of green tied around the waist, all with faces the color of stones found lying on the beach of volcanic islands, singing with the utmost earnestness, in as nearly perfect a harmony as could be managed, minds blank of interpretation:

> *In our deep vaulted cell*
> *The charm we'll prepare*
> *Too dreadful a practice*
> *For this open air.*

Time and time again, I am filled up with all that I thought life might be—glorious moment upon glorious moment of contentment and joy and love running into each other and forming an extraordinary chain: a hymn sung in rounds. Oh, the fields in which I have walked and gazed and gazed at the small cuplike flowers, in wanton hues of red and gold and blue, swaying in the day breeze, and from which I had no trouble tearing myself away, since their end was unknown to me.

❦

I walked to the mouth of the river, and it was then still in the old place near the lime-tree grove. The water was clear and still. I looked in, and at the bottom of the river I could see a house, and it was a house of only one room, with an A-shaped roof. The house was made of rough, heavy planks of unpainted wood, and the roof was of galvanized iron and was painted red. The house had four windows on each of its four sides, and one door. Though the door and the windows were all open, I could not see anything inside and I had no desire to see what was inside. All around the house was a wide stretch of green— green grass freshly mowed a uniform length. The green, green grass of uniform length extended from the house for a distance I could not measure or know just from looking at it. Beyond the green, green grass were lots of pebbles, and they were a white-gray, as if they had been in water for many years and then placed in the sun to dry. They, too, were of a uniform size, and as they lay together they seemed to form a direct contrast to the grass. Then, at the line where the grass ended and the pebbles began, there were flowers: yellow and blue irises, red poppies, daffodils, marigolds. They grew as if wild, intertwined, as if no hand had ever offered guidance or restraint. There were no other living things in the water—no birds, no vertebrates or inverte-brates, no fragile insects—and even though the water flowed in the natural way of a river, none of the things that I could see at the bottom moved. The grass, in little wisps, didn't bend slightly; the petals of the flowers didn't tremble. Everything was so true, though—that is, true to itself—and I had no doubt that the things I saw were themselves and not resemblances or representatives. The grass was the grass, and it was the grass without qualification. The green of the grass was green, and I knew it to be so and not partially green, or a kind of green, but green, and the green from which all other greens might come. And it was so with everything else that lay so still at the bottom of the river. It all lay there not like a picture but like a true thing and a different kind of true thing: one that I had never known before. Then I noticed something new: it was the way everything lit up. It was as if the sun shone not from where I stood but from a place way beyond and beneath the ground of the grass and the pebbles. How strange the light was, how it filled up everything, and yet nothing cast a shadow. I looked and looked at what was before me in wonderment and curiosity. What should this mean to me? And what should I do on knowing its meaning? A woman now appeared at the one door. She wore no clothes. Her hair was long and so very black, and it stood out in a straight line away from her head, as if she had commanded it to be that way. I could not see her face. I could see her feet, and I saw that her insteps were high, as if she had been used to climbing high mountains. Her skin was the color of brown clay, and she looked like a statue, liquid and gleaming, just before it is to be put in a kiln. She walked toward the place where the grass ended and the pebbles began. Perhaps it was a great distance, it took such a long time, and yet she never tired. When she got to the place where the green grass ended and the pebbles began, she stopped, then raised her right hand to her forehead, as if to guard her eyes against a far-off glare. She stood on tiptoe, her body swaying from side to side, and she looked at something that was far, far away from where she stood. I got down on my knees and I looked, too. It was a long time before I could see what it was that she saw.

I saw a world in which the sun and the moon shone at the same time. They appeared in a way I had never seen before: the sun was The Sun, a creation of Benevolence and Purpose and not a star among many stars, with a predictable cycle and a predictable end; the moon, too, was The Moon, and it was the creation of Beauty and Purpose and not a body subject to a theory of planetary evolution. The sun and the moon shone uniformly onto everything. Together, they made up the light, and the light fell on everything, and everything seemed transparent, as if the light went through each thing, so that nothing could be hidden. The light shone and shone and fell and fell, but there were no shadows. In this world, on this terrain, there was no day and there was no night. And there were no seasons, and so no storms or cold from which to take shelter. And in this world were many things blessed with unquestionable truth and purpose and beauty. There were steep mountains, there were valleys, there were seas, there were plains of grass, there were deserts, there were rivers, there were forests, there were vertebrates and invertebrates, there were mammals, there were reptiles, there were creatures of the dry land and the water, and there were birds. And they lived in this world not yet divided, not yet examined, not yet numbered, and not yet dead. I looked at this world as it revealed itself to me—how new, how new— and I longed to go there.

I stood above the land and the sea and looked back up at myself as I stood on the bank of the mouth of the river. I saw that my face was round in shape, that my irises took up almost all the space in my eyes, and that my eyes were brown, with yellow-colored and black-colored flecks; that my mouth was large and closed; that my nose, too, was large and my nostrils broken circles; my arms were long, my hands large, the veins pushing up against my skin; my legs were long, and, judging from the shape of them, I was used to running long distances. I saw that my hair grew out long from my head and in a disorderly way, as if I were a strange tree, with many branches. I saw my skin, and it was red. It was the red of flames when a fire is properly fed, the red of flames when a fire burns alone in a darkened place, and not the red of flames when a fire is burning in a cozy room. I saw myself clearly, as if I were looking through a pane of glass.

I stood above the land and the sea, and I felt that I was not myself as I had once known myself to be: I was not made up of flesh and blood and muscles and bones and tissue and cells and vital organs but was made up of my will, and over my will I had complete dominion. I entered the sea then. The sea was without color, and it was without anything that I had known before. It was still, having no currents. It was as warm as freshly spilled blood, and I moved through it as if I had always done so, as if it were a perfectly natural element to me. I moved through deep caverns, but they were without darkness and sudden shifts and turns. I stepped over great ridges and huge bulges of stones, I stooped down and touched the deepest bottom; I stretched myself out and covered end to end a vast crystal plane. Nothing lived here. No plant grew here, no huge sharp-toothed creature with an ancestral memory of hunter and prey searching furiously for food, no sudden shift of wind to disturb the water. How good this water was. How good that I should know no fear. I sat on the edge of a basin. I felt myself swing my feet back and forth in a carefree manner, as if I were a child who had just spent the whole day head bent over sums but now sat in a garden filled with flowers in bloom colored vermillion and gold, the sounds of birds chirping, goats bleating, home from the pasture, the smell of vanilla from the kitchen, which should surely mean pudding with dinner, eyes darting here and there but resting on nothing in particular, a mind conscious of nothing—not happiness, not contentment, and not the memory of night, which soon would come.

I stood up on the edge of the basin and felt myself move. But what self? For I had no feet, or hands, or head, or heart. It was as if those things—my feet, my hands, my head, my heart—having once been there, were now stripped away, as if I had been dipped again and again, over and over, in a large vat filled with some precious elements and were now reduced to something I yet had no name for. I had no name for the thing I had become, so new was it to me, except that I did not exist in pain or pleasure, east or west or north or south, or up or down, or past or present or future, or real or not real. I stood as if I were a prism, many-sided and transparent, refracting and reflecting light as it reached me, light that never could be destroyed. And how beautiful I became. Yet this beauty was not in the way of an ancient city seen after many centuries in ruins, or a woman who has just brushed her hair, or a man who

searches for a treasure, or a child who cries immediately on being born, or an apple just picked standing
alone on a gleaming white plate, or tiny beads of
water left over from a sudden downpour of rain,
perhaps—hanging delicately from the bare limbs of
trees—or the sound the hummingbird makes with
its wings as it propels itself through the earthly air.

〜

Yet what was that light in which I stood? How
singly then will the heart desire and pursue the small
glowing thing resting in the distance, surrounded by
darkness; how, then, if on conquering the distance
the heart embraces the small glowing thing until
heart and glowing thing are indistinguishable and in
this way the darkness is made less? For now a door
might suddenly be pushed open and the morning light
might rush in, revealing to me creation and a force
whose nature is implacable, unmindful of any of the
individual needs of existence, and without knowledge
of future or past. I might then come to believe in a
being whose impartiality I cannot now or ever fully
understand and accept. I ask, When shall I, too, be
extinguished, so that I cannot be recognized even
from my bones? I covet the rocks and the mountains
their silence. And so, emerging from my pit, the one
I sealed up securely, the one to which I have con-
signed all my deeds that I care not to reveal—
emerging from this pit, I step into a room and I see

that the lamp is lit. In the light of the lamp, I see some books, I see a chair, I see a table, I see a pen; I see a bowl of ripe fruit, a bottle of milk, a flute made of wood, the clothes that I will wear. And as I see these things in the light of the lamp, all perishable and transient, how bound up I know I am to all that is human endeavor, to all that is past and to all that shall be, to all that shall be lost and leave no trace. I claim these things then—mine— and now feel myself grow solid and complete, my name filling up my mouth.

Praise for the
Alpha Pack Series

"With *Primal Law*, J. D. Tyler has created a whole squad of yummy shifter heroes whom readers will fall head over heels for. Heroine Kira Locke is courageous and intelligent, with her own intriguing paranormal talents, while Jax Law is a sexy alpha-male werewolf who is both heroic and just dominant enough to give a girl wicked ideas. I can't wait for Tyler's next Alpha Pack adventure!"
—*New York Times* bestselling author Angela Knight

"What do you get when you combine top secret military teams and werewolves? Try Tyler's sizzling new supernatural series featuring the Alpha Pack—a specialized team of wolf shifters with Psy powers. In this launch book, readers are introduced to the various team members, with the primary focus on Jaxon Law. Tyler has set up an intriguing premise for her series, which promises plenty of action, treachery, and scorchingly hot sex."
—*Romantic Times*

"Sizzling and interesting, *Primal Law* pays homage to Lora Leigh's Breed series while forging its own paths. The characters are likable, and the work speeds along."
—Fresh Fiction

"*Primal Law* is riveting and carnal . . . full of testosterone-laden men, hot action, and unforgettable passion! In other words, a truly addicting series!"
—Reader to Reader Reviews

"In a genre where the paranormal is intense, J. D. Tyler may just be a force to be reckoned with. The book kept me riveted from start to finish." —Night Owl Reviews

The Alpha Pack Novels

Primal Law
Savage Awakening
Black Moon

Black
MOON

AN ALPHA PACK NOVEL

J. D. TYLER

A SIGNET ECLIPSE BOOK

SIGNET ECLIPSE
Published by New American Library, a division of
Penguin Group (USA) Inc., 375 Hudson Street,
New York, New York 10014, USA
Penguin Group (Canada), 90 Eglinton Avenue East, Suite 700, Toronto,
Ontario M4P 2Y3, Canada (a division of Pearson Penguin Canada Inc.)
Penguin Books Ltd., 80 Strand, London WC2R 0RL, England
Penguin Ireland, 25 St. Stephen's Green, Dublin 2,
Ireland (a division of Penguin Books Ltd.)
Penguin Group (Australia), 250 Camberwell Road, Camberwell, Victoria 3124,
Australia (a division of Pearson Australia Group Pty. Ltd.)
Penguin Books India Pvt. Ltd., 11 Community Centre, Panchsheel Park,
New Delhi - 110 017, India
Penguin Group (NZ), 67 Apollo Drive, Rosedale, Auckland 0632,
New Zealand (a division of Pearson New Zealand Ltd.)
Penguin Books (South Africa) (Pty.) Ltd., 24 Sturdee Avenue,
Rosebank, Johannesburg 2196, South Africa

Penguin Books Ltd., Registered Offices:
80 Strand, London WC2R 0RL, England

First published by Signet Eclipse, an imprint of New American Library,
a division of Penguin Group (USA) Inc.

First Printing, December 2012
10 9 8 7 6 5 4 3 2 1

PUBLISHER'S NOTE
This is a work of fiction. Names, characters, places, and incidents either are the
product of the author's imagination or are used fictitiously, and any resem-
blance to actual persons, living or dead, business establishments, events, or
locales is entirely coincidental.
    The publisher does not have any control over and does not assume any re-
sponsibility for author or third-party Web sites or their content.

ALWAYS LEARNING   PEARSON

To my lifelong best friend, Debra Stevens. You've been right there with me, celebrating all the rip-roaring wild times, and holding me up through the horribly bad. You understand me as no one else does, and you give me the strength and courage to go on when all I want to do is curl into the fetal position and give up.

You make me laugh until the tears stop, and you make me glad to be alive. My world is a much happier place with you in it.

I love you, girlfriend.

ACKNOWLEDGMENTS

Special thanks to:

My family, especially my children and my parents, for their unwavering support. I love you.

The Foxes—Tracy Garrett, Suzanne Ferrell, Addison Fox, Jane Graves, Julie Benson, Lorraine Heath, Sandy Blair, Alice Burton, and Kay Thomas. I don't know what I'd do without you, and I'm not about to find out! Bring on the wine!

My agent, Roberta Brown—my cheerleader, friend, and rock. I can't wait to see what fun surprises tomorrow brings for us.

My editor, Tracy Bernstein, for supporting and encouraging me when my personal life got really tough. You're a diamond who allows your authors to shine, and I'm grateful for you.

My personal assistant, Carla Gallway, for your enthusiasm and all the hard work you do. And to my Street Team, the Alpha Bitches (founded by Carla), for being my cheering section and spreading the word to those who love hot shifters as much as we do!

The art department for their gorgeous covers, and all the rest at New American Library who make my job so much fun and run so smoothly. You guys are the absolute best.

And to the readers, for welcoming my Alpha Pack shifters into your world and embracing them. May we have many more adventures together . . .

Darkness cannot drive out darkness; only light can do that.

—Dr. Martin Luther King, Jr.

Prologue

Kalen was thirteen when his grandmother told him that he'd been born under a black moon.

That didn't sound so great, and to be honest, Kalen didn't want to hear it. Wasn't he enough of a freak without adding another nugget of crap to the pile? His dad already had plenty of excuses to beat his ass, and like hell did Kalen need to give him one more. On top of that, it was Saturday—his dad's busiest day at the shop where he worked as an auto mechanic, which meant hours of glorious freedom. A whole day of no yelling, no fists. No new bruises. As soon as Kalen could get away and hurry to meet his friends, he'd make the most of it, too.

He squirmed as his grandma's old, gnarled hands gripped his. Who the heck cared about this moon thing? He resisted the suicidal urge to roll his eyes. Barely.

"A black moon is a rare occurrence in astrology, but you were born during the rarest of the four types—a month with no new moon or full moon at all."

Kalen suppressed a sigh and tried to appear interested. "Yeah, so?" He loved his grandma, and she loved him right back, but jeez. The guys had probably taken off on their bikes without him. "Do we have to talk about science stuff right now?"

Ida May's faded blue eyes bored into his. "Pay attention, my boy. You're old enough to understand what I have to tell you, and my stay in this world won't last forever," she said, the gentleness in her tone at odds with her intense expression.

All thoughts of his friends and a sunny Saturday of screwing around vanished as fear curled in his stomach. "Are you sick?" he asked in a small voice. "What—"

"Never mind that. Have you been practicing the arts?"

Flushing, he kicked the toe of his scuffed tennis shoe on the carpet. "Not much, since the last time Dad caught me." He swallowed hard, remembering the awful scene. How his mother had once again refused to intervene with his father. How he'd begged her to at least call Grandma. But she'd just stood there, grim-faced, as he curled on the floor of the living room, yelling in pain and fear while Dad kicked the shit out of him.

His grandmother's lips thinned. "You must keep developing your skills, no matter the danger. One day you're going to need every ounce of the incredible power you've inherited from my ancestors. Dark days are coming for you, my boy, and I won't be around to see you through them."

"Don't talk like that," he said hoarsely. "Please. I need *you*, Grandma, not some stupid magic."

She ignored his plea. "You're going to be the greatest

Sorcerer the world has ever known, your power beyond comprehension. And that means there are those who would seek to control that power, or take it from you altogether."

Kalen tried to calm his thundering pulse. The world's greatest Sorcerer? Dark days? He swallowed the smart-ass remark that threatened to burst from his mouth. Because Grandma was serious as hell, and she was never wrong when it came to the supernatural. *Shit*. "Okay. If that's true, what does it have to do with the black moon?"

"Everything." She paused. "The moon is protection, an omen of inner strength and good for our kind. A Sorcerer born during an absence of a new or full moon is at great risk for being swayed to the dark arts. For using his power for evil. Do you understand?"

"I—I guess," he said, though he didn't. Not really. The scope of what she was telling him was so vast and overwhelming, he couldn't grasp it. He picked at a ragged hole on the knee of his jeans. "So what am I supposed to do about it? Who's gonna help me if—if not you?" His throat almost swelled shut with grief at the mere idea of his beloved grandma not being around. She loved him, cared for him as best she could. She was the one soul in the world who did, and she could *not* leave him.

"That's why I asked you to come over, my boy—so I can give you something important."

Standing, she walked slowly and stiffly to an antique sideboard and slid open a drawer. She reached inside, withdrew a small wooden box, and returned to sit beside Kalen. Handing the box to him, she nodded for him to open it.

Curious, he raised the little hinged lid and peered inside. "Wow," he said, touching the cool metal object. It was a silver pentagram pendant about the size of a silver dollar, attached to a matching chain. Excited, he lifted the necklace and studied the swirling design etched into the pendant. "A Sorcerer's amulet?"

"Exactly."

"Awesome! This is mine?"

"Yes. It's been in my family for generations. The story goes that it was blessed by Druid priests to protect the wearer from all harm, no matter how great the source of evil." Again she hesitated, a shadow of sadness in her blue eyes. "It would've been your mother's, but she didn't inherit the gift. And then she married your father and he turned her mind against the arts and eventually against you. . . . Well, it doesn't matter now. It's yours. Perhaps I should've given it to you already, but I thought you were too young to understand the responsibility of owning it. Of taking good care of it."

And she'd given it to him today because she was running out of precious time.

The pendant shook in Kalen's grasp. "So I just wear it? That's all?"

"Wear it and never take it off, Kalen." Her bony fingers grasped his knee. "Not to shower, to sleep, to play ball or ride bikes. Not for *any* reason, *ever*. Is that clear?"

"Yes, ma'am," he croaked. Fumbling with the clasp, he lifted the necklace, reached behind his neck, and fastened it after a couple of tries. "There. Mission accomplished. I'm safe from all the creepazoids in the world." He tried a cheeky grin, hoping to lighten things up.

Grandma returned his smile, and though the shadows in her eyes remained, she seemed happy enough now. "That you are, little hellion. Run along and join your friends," she said with a throaty laugh. "You're practically vibrating with impatience."

Leaping to his feet, Kalen grabbed the box and gave his grandma a quick kiss as she rose. "Thanks! I promise not to take it off!"

The heavy visit at an end, he once again looked forward to his Saturday and all the promise it held. Jogging to the front door, he yanked it open. And suddenly stopped. Turning, he faced the woman he loved more than anyone on earth, hurried back to her, and impulsively threw his arms around her middle. Hugged her close and breathed in her sweet scent.

"I love you, Grandma."

"I love you so much, my boy. Always will." She kissed the top of his head. "Go on now, have fun. The day is wasting!"

Grinning at her, he turned and dashed out, down the porch steps, his heart light. He'd think about the bad stuff later. Everything would be cool. Right?

It might have been. If only he'd kept his promise.

And if only he'd known that the lingering warmth of her love, enveloping him like a cozy blanket as he pedaled away, would have to last him for the rest of his life.

One

Kalen Black stood apart from his team, awash in guilt. Impotent in his shame.

Right this second the Alpha Pack's beloved resident Fae prince, Sariel, might by dying. On top of that, Aric Savage's mate had nearly been killed a short while ago by the witch Beryl before Aric ripped out Beryl's throat, thereby putting an end to any information they might have gained from her.

The danger surrounding them all increased daily. Hourly. A traitor walked among Kalen's friends and colleagues, slowly drowning in the darkness clogging his lungs. Overtaking his soul.

And it's all my fucking fault . . . because the traitor is me.

As Aric tended to Rowan and the prince was rushed to the infirmary, Kalen hung his head. He tried to find comfort in the fact that Aric's mate was all right, but it didn't work. Then he wanted the earth to swallow him when Nick Westfall, the Pack's commander, ushered everyone into the conference room and demanded to know, "How the fuck did Beryl get out of Block T?"

"I let her out." His voice caught. "God, I'm so sorry—"

"Why? Did she seduce you, or was it Malik?"

Kalen died a thousand deaths during the questions that followed his confession and the truthful answers he supplied. In Kalen's wretched lifetime he'd suffered abuse and humiliation. Isolation. Starvation. More horrors than most people ever had to face.

But none of those were worse than *almost* achieving his dreams of a home, a job, a family of sorts, and most of all, acceptance among those who were as different as himself. Almost. Before Malik, king of the Unseelie and Sariel's evil sire, decided that Kalen Black—Sorcerer, Necromancer, and panther shifter—was exactly the sort of powerful ally he needed in his quest to rule the world.

And that he'd begin by taking over Kalen's mind. One wicked suggestion at a time.

Facing them all, Kalen whispered his admission. "Not her. Malik." He resisted the urge to squirm under Nick's hard gaze.

"He gained control of your mind long enough to make you let her out?"

"Yes, sir. I think Beryl spelled me back at the house where we caught her. My defenses are . . . crumbling. I can't keep him out for very long at a time."

The witch had placed a bloodied finger to the center of Kalen's forehead and whispered, *"Abyssus abyssum invocat."*

Hell calls hell.

"Jesus," Aric said, his tone dripping with horrified disgust.

The red wolf wasn't any more disgusted with him than Kalen was with himself. Though the spell wasn't Kalen's fault, and he hadn't known that Beryl would try to murder the Fae prince, it hardly mattered. He was to blame. He should've been stronger, even without the protection of his silver pentagram pendant. The one he'd given weeks ago to Dr. Mackenzie Grant, his onetime lover, and made her swear never to remove.

Nick cursed and rubbed his eyes. "Okay. We'll figure this out. At least now we have Malik's human name—Evan Kerrigan. Grant is tracking him down, gathering intel. With any luck we'll have his location and a complete profile soon."

The man Nick referred to was General Jarrod Grant, Mackenzie's father. Kalen wondered what the man would think of what Kalen had done to his precious daughter. He doubted the man knew—Kalen was still in one piece.

When Mackenzie walked into the room, her blue eyes briefly meeting Kalen's, they were filled with such pain it stole his breath. Kalen could feel nothing but self-loathing. As she looked quickly away, his gaze settled on the beautiful doctor, hungrily devouring the woman he could never have again, never allow into his mind or heart. The woman he had to protect at all costs from Malik.

From himself.

"I'm sorry to interrupt, but we knew you'd want word of Sariel. We believe he'll recover." Murmurs of relief sounded around the room. "But he was already weakened from some health issues stemming from being in our world, so healing will take time. He's stable, though, so I wanted to pass the good news along."

"Thank you, Mac," Nick said, bringing Kalen back to the present. The doc returned Nick's tired smile and left.

Without looking at me again.

Nick went on. "All right. I need to speak to Kalen. We'll adjourn for now and discuss this mess later."

Nick nodded at Kalen, indicating for him to follow. He trailed the commander, wondering if he could take the man in a fight. Nick was tall and muscular, strode with his broad shoulders back, head up, all easy grace and confidence. Yeah, this man could walk the walk, but he also had the power and skill to back it up. Kalen had seen him take on dozens of enraged Sluagh, huge batlike creatures that were Malik's drones. Just swat them down like they were flies and spit on their carcasses. The man didn't need the gift of sorcery; he could definitely dispose of Kalen with brute strength alone.

Not that Kalen *would* defend himself. No. Whatever the white wolf chose to dish out, he deserved.

In Nick's office, the man closed the door and walked to his desk, parking his ass on the edge of it. With a sigh, he ran a hand through his short black hair threaded with silver at the temples and crossed his arms. "Sit down."

Kalen complied without comment and waited.

"Tell me exactly what happened before you were compelled to set Beryl free. Don't leave anything out."

That was not a scene he'd wanted to revisit. Ever.

But the steely look in Nick's deep blue eyes said that Kalen wasn't getting out of telling the truth. He took a deep breath. "I was in my quarters about an hour ago and the bastard started prying into my head again."

They both knew the bastard he was referring to was Malik. "He told me that he'd never abandon me as everyone else in my life has done."

"Smart," he said, an edge of disgust to his tone. "He's isolating the vulnerable cub from the pack, playing the doting mentor."

"I'm *not* a cub." His youth was a sore spot. Always had been, ever since he'd been kicked out of the house at the age of fourteen. A lifetime ago, it seemed. He'd had to scrabble, suffer, for every morsel that eased the hunger in his belly. For every night not spent in a dirty alley under a cardboard box.

He didn't feel twenty-three—he must be a hundred.

"Trust me, you are, despite all that power the Unseelie asshole is attempting to harness in you. I don't say that as an insult," he said seriously. "What I mean is that in you, Malik has found a young, extremely powerful Sorcerer on the cusp of becoming all he is meant to be. As strong as you are, Kalen, you're nowhere near the level you'll be in a few years, then a few decades. With you, it's like when the very first coach ever saw Michael Jordan in action and said, 'My God, that kid is going to be the greatest player in the NBA one day.'"

In spite of himself, Kalen snorted a laugh. "What a comparison."

"But true. The Unseelie king knows you're a rising star and he wants you on his team. I can't let that happen. Do you understand?"

You're going to be the greatest Sorcerer the world has ever known, your power beyond comprehension. And that means there are those who would seek to control that power, or take it from you altogether.

A lump lodged in his throat at the memory of his grandmother's ghostly prediction, and he pushed it away. "Do you want me to leave after all? Or are you just going to take me out now and be done with it?"

"Just finish telling me how Malik manipulated you earlier."

It didn't escape his notice that Nick hadn't answered the question. "He promised me power, told me all I had to do to get it was surrender to him. He was . . . very seductive."

"In a sexual way?"

Kalen felt sick, and fought it down. "Yeah. The bastard touched me, and suddenly I wanted everything he was selling. God, Nick," he choked out. "What's wrong with me?"

Once a whore, always a whore, my pet. Malik's smug voice intruded into his head. *Don't forget you belong to me.*

Kalen shoved the Unseelie out with great effort.

The commander pushed from his desk and walked over to stand by Kalen's chair, gripping his shoulder. "There's not a damned thing wrong with you. Like the rest of us, you're trying to get a foothold on fighting the Unseelie, only for you it's worse because he's taken a personal interest in recruiting you. That means he'll stop at nothing to get what he wants. Creatures like him wield seduction like a weapon."

"I know. Just like I know him messing with me was nothing but a mindfuck, but that doesn't make it better."

"A mindfuck? How so?" Nick retreated to park his butt on the desk again.

"He sent Beryl to me in my room, or the illusion of

her since she was still locked up, and by then I was lost," he said miserably. "She seduced me, but when it was over, she just vanished. And here's the weird part—I was still dressed and I wasn't even fully hard. No evidence of sex at all. It was so real at the time, and yet it never happened! I'm losing my fucking mind."

Burying his hands in his hair, he held on as though he could keep his scrambled brains inside. "I called him Master, and I liked his approval. No, I wallowed in it and would've done anything right then to please him. So I guess you're right about the cub thing, huh?"

"Jesus Christ." Nick's gaze pierced him to the core. "Then what happened?"

Kalen lowered his hands to his lap, fists clenched. "He told me to let Beryl out of her cell. He said she had a task to perform before she left and that she was never meant to stay with us. I didn't know he meant for her to die, but I should have. Then I let her out, took her up to the ground level, where she attacked Sariel. Rowan and Aric went after her, and Aric killed her."

The commander fell silent for so long, fear balled in Kalen's gut. Finally he gathered his courage and asked once more.

"Are you going to kill me?"

"Would you submit if I said yes?"

Kalen nodded, the bottom falling out of his stomach. "Yes, I would."

"Why?" Nick cocked his head.

"Because you're a PreCog and that means you can sometimes see the future. On top of that, you're the commander and a good, fair man. So if the future is better without me in it, if my death will keep the Pack and other innocents safe . . ." He couldn't finish.

"On your knees, Sorcerer."

The commander's tone was cold, his blue eyes like the Arctic North. Legs shaking, Kalen slid from his seat and knelt on the stubby carpet. Placed his hands on his jeans-clad thighs and stared at his polished black fingernails digging in painfully. His heart thundered in his chest, threatening to break his sternum.

Then Nick walked around his desk and opened a top drawer. Reached in and lifted out the biggest fucking hand cannon Kalen had ever seen. The spit dried up in his mouth and he watched numbly as the Alpha wolf approached, went to stand behind him.

The hard muzzle of the gun pressed to the back of his head. So he'd die on his knees, execution-style. Quick and painless.

Oh, God. Take my soul before Malik can claim it, and look after Mackenzie, too. That's all I ask.

"I'm sorry, kid."

Kalen squeezed his eyes shut. Time crawled to a standstill.

The crack of a gunshot split the air.

Lightning before the storm.

"Dr. Grant?"

Mackenzie pushed an errant lock of curly dark hair behind her ear and looked up from the paperwork on her desk to see Noah standing there. The cute blond nurse was wearing a pleased expression as he hovered in the doorway to her office.

"What's up?"

"Blue's finally awake," he said, referring to Sariel. "Blue" was the name all of the staff at the compound had called the Fae prince, due to his long, gorgeous blue hair and matching wings. The Fae had eventually revealed his real name to Kira, Jaxon Law's mate. Kira had proved to be a godsend in the ensuing months, working with the creatures in Block R, or the Rehabilitation unit, where Sariel used to be housed.

"That's great news!" She smiled at Noah. "Does Dr. Mallory know?" Melina Mallory was her colleague and a damned fine doctor. Mac counted her as a friend, but the woman also ruled the roost in the infirmary as well as in their research on shifters and other paranormal beings.

"She's with him now. All his vitals are looking good—well, at least for what we know about faeries, anyhow. The prince has got some color back in his face, but he's still refusing to eat. I wouldn't be worried because it's not surprising that a patient wouldn't be hungry after being severely wounded, except Blue hasn't been eating well since he's been at the compound."

"We need to keep an eye on that," she said worriedly. "If his weight drops so much as another ounce, I want to know."

"You bet," Noah said. Some of his natural cheer returned. "But he's back with us and that's what counts."

"Yes, it is." Standing, she stretched. "Go and tell Blue I'll check on him in a short while. I've got a couple of things to do first."

"Yes, ma'am!"

With that, the nurse was gone. Mac couldn't help but be fond of the guy. Noah was a bundle of energy. He lived at the compound, loved his job, and rarely took any time off. He was in his element taking care of wounded Pack members, who were frequently injured in the course of battling rogue paranormals. He'd also started working with Kira and Sariel, rehabbing the innocent creatures like Chup-Chup, the resident gremlin, and even the prince himself, who had no one else to help them adjust in what was, to them, a strange world.

Noah was adorable, and fantastic at what he did.

After straightening her papers, she walked out of her office and down the corridor past the exam rooms, in the opposite direction of the patients' rooms. She headed toward the lobby of the infirmary, past the receptionist, and into the main hallway leading to the rest of the compound.

Only when she was alone did she reach up to touch the pendant hanging around her neck from its long chain. The weight of the disk was solid, comforting. She could feel the raised ridges that formed the pentagram within the circle, and the pendant seemed to warm in her hand. Almost as though it were seeking to reassure her that it would always do what Kalen had said—protect her from all evil.

Including Malik. The Unseelie slime had sent a Sluagh to attack her and Kalen in town a few weeks ago, and Mac had been scratched by the beast. This had somehow allowed Malik a portal into her mind, and the bastard had truly frightened her. Kalen had promptly given his beloved amulet to Mac, his sole possession of any sentimental value. The enchanted protection his grandmother had given to him was now Mac's.

Oh, but Kalen had shared so much more than that. Her footsteps faltered and she halted, remembering.

Breathy moans and tangled sheets. Messy black hair falling over his kohl-rimmed green eyes as he moved over her. Thrusting, possessing.

Making love.

And then it was over and he'd pulled into his isolated shell, claiming there could be nothing between them. He'd given her the pendant, made her promise never to remove it, and then put miles of emotional distance between them. They might as well be living on different planets, the chasm was so great.

Why?

A loud *crack* startled Mac, making her jump. The noise echoed down the corridor and, as it faded, she realized what the sound had been.

A gunshot.

Heart thundering, she took off in the direction of the noise. Kalen had used his Sorcerer's power to ward the compound against intruders, but perhaps a Sluagh or some other creature had gotten inside? Or maybe one of the creatures from Block R had become feral?

But no, the sound took her past Rehab, past the wings where the staff living quarters were located. Men from the Pack bolted from their rooms, came from every direction, rushed past her. She ran, at last realizing they were heading for Nick's office. She couldn't imagine what terrible thing could have happened.

Until she saw Nick standing like a statue over Kalen's prone body, a smoking gun in his hand.

Then Mac's eyes rolled up in her head and she saw nothing more.

I'm not shot. Holy fuck, I'm alive.

Kalen stared at the burned spot in the carpet right next to his leg for about five seconds before he slumped to the floor. His body simply refused to cooperate any longer, and he lay there in shock, hardly believing he was breathing.

"I had to know if you'd go through with it," Nick said quietly. "I'm sorry."

"Fucking hell," he croaked.

"Your last thought was for the safety of others, not yourself. You were willing to die for the greater good of everyone else, and that means Malik hasn't won. You're a good man at the core, and so there's hope."

"Nick, am I fighting this battle just to die anyway?" It was a question he'd asked before, and he received the same answer.

"I don't know."

"And you wouldn't tell me even if you could."

"That's right."

God, what a screwed-up mess. He wasn't sure how he would've responded, but the sound of footsteps, voices raised in concern, floated from the corridor. Kalen let out a deep sigh, humiliated that the guys, plus Rowan, were here to witness this and learn about Nick's little "test" of his worthiness.

"Shit, catch her!"

Her? Kalen sat up quickly, just in time to see Zander scoop Mackenzie into his arms and lift her against his chest. Kalen shot to his feet and, before he thought about what he was doing, grabbed the doctor from Zan with a snarl, holding her close. He glared at the man, warning him back.

Zan raised his hands, palms out. "Chill, man. Would you rather I had let her hit the floor?"

With an effort, he calmed himself. Zan was only trying to help. But inside, his panther raged at seeing Mac—*their woman*—in the arms of another male. He'd never felt anything like it in his life. It was confusing as hell.

"No. Sorry," he managed. "I'll just—"

"You can put me down."

Anxiously, he looked down into Mac's beautiful face. Large blue eyes fringed with dark lashes stared up at him, blinking away tears. His gut tightened, knowing he'd been the cause, in more ways than one.

"It wasn't what it looked like, exactly."

"Put me down. Please," she entreated softly.

Reluctantly, he did as she asked, but that didn't stop him from checking her from head to toe. "Are you okay? Are you hurt anywhere?"

"No." She glanced around at the guys who'd assembled there, cheeks pale as milk. Swallowing hard, she said, "I'm fine. Now tell me what the hell was going on in there."

"Nick gave me a test. I passed. The end."

She scowled at Nick. "What sort of test involves firing a gun at one of your men?"

Nick addressed the group, keeping the explanation to the point. "Kalen was willing to be executed rather than risk bringing harm to his team. That means there's still hope that he can be saved from Malik's control, so we'll see this through to the end. Anybody disagree?"

No one did. One by one each man plus their lone female swore his loyalty to the team. And that loyalty included Kalen. As he looked to each of them, he couldn't breathe. *Never* had anyone stood up for him. Stood by him. Not even his own parents, the people who should have sheltered him and loved him the most. The idea that these people who'd come into his life so recently would have his back, even in the wake of him letting them down, overwhelmed him.

He could hardly speak. "I swear I'll do my best not to fail all of you again."

Or he'd die trying. Suddenly the chaos inside him seemed to settle and his purpose became clear—he'd fight Malik with everything in him. And when the time came, he'd make the right choice.

Whatever that proved to be.

"Excuse me," Mackenzie said tightly. "But I think I'm going to be sick."

Spinning around, she dashed to a woman's restroom down the hall from Nick's office and disappeared inside. He would've gone after her, but Nick blocked his way.

"You should probably let her be right now."

It wasn't a suggestion. Quelling his pissed-off panther again, he nodded curtly and strode in the opposite direction, putting as much distance between himself and everyone else as fast as possible.

Just as he'd done all his life.

"Mac?"

"In here." Bent over the sink, Mac finished rinsing her mouth, then turned off the water. Glancing at Melina, she grabbed some paper towels from the dispenser, dried her face, and tossed them in the trash. "See? I'm fine."

"I don't think so." Melina's sharp scrutiny roamed over Mac's face, and she apparently didn't like what she saw. "To the infirmary with you. I'm going to give you a checkup."

"I don't need—"

"I didn't *ask*. I'm telling you. Doctors make the worst patients," she grumbled. "Let's go."

There was no arguing with her friend when she had a bug up her ass, so Mac relented. Though Melina was slight of frame and sort of resembled an elf with her short cap of dark hair, she was fully capable of making the toughest Pack member cringe in fear. She was a tough, militant bitch.

And that was when she was in a good mood.

Her friend hadn't always been that way, but that was before her mate, Terry, the Alpha Pack's former commander, had been killed in an ambush several months ago. Accepting Nick as the new leader in her mate's place had been hard on the woman, and she and Nick didn't always see eye to eye. But they'd found some peace between them, based on mutual respect.

Melina led Mac into an exam room and gestured to the table covered with the hated crinkly white paper. "Sit."

Dutifully, Mac did, and proceeded to subject herself to a complete physical. Melina checked her eyes, ears, nose, and throat. Checked her reflexes. All seemed clear, but the woman still wasn't satisfied.

"I don't like it one bit that you fainted," she said with a frown.

"For God's sake, I thought Nick had killed Kalen! Give me a break."

"How long have you been queasy? Don't think I haven't noticed."

She had? Mac blinked at her friend, hedging. "I don't know. A few days, maybe."

"How often have you been throwing up?"

Mac stared at her, silent. *Shit, shit.*

"O-kay," Melina drawled, brows raised. "Here's what's going to happen. Noah is coming in to take blood for a complete standard workup. Then you're going into the restroom to pee in a cup. Then you'll come back in here, sit down, and wait for me. Got it?"

She sighed. "Yes."

"Good girl."

Melina patted her knee and left. Soon after, Noah came in, swabbed the crook of her elbow, and took three vials of blood. When he was finished, he pressed a cotton ball over the injection site and topped it with a Band-Aid.

Giving her a smile, he pointed in the direction of the restroom. "Go do your thing."

She absolutely hated peeing in a cup. It was a dicey proposition at best, aiming just right. But she managed and in short order was sitting back in the exam room.

Where the clock on the wall ticked by with unbearable sluggishness.

Ten long minutes passed. Mac was starting to fidget when Melina walked in carrying a sheaf of paper. Her friend closed the door and slowly turned to her. The serious expression on Melina's face sent a bolt of terror all the way to her toes.

"What is it?" she gasped, gripping the edge of the table. "What's wrong?"

"Mac, honey. We have to talk."

Two

"What? Am I sick?" Mac asked, her heart thumping painfully.

"Nothing like that." Her friend blew out a breath and leaned her hip on the counter. "Mackenzie . . . you're pregnant."

The words blew through her like a hurricane. Left her gasping for breath. "What?"

"You heard me. Pregnant, knocked up—"

"Oh, God. But—but how?" Realizing how stupid that sounded, she flushed. "What I mean is, unmated shifters can't get their females pregnant! Right?"

Melina's voice was quiet, speculative. "A shifter, huh? Just who are we talking about here? I get that the father is none of my business, but I won't share anything you choose to tell me."

Mac paused, but just briefly. Even if their talk wasn't confidential, she completely trusted that her friend wouldn't say a word to anyone. "It's Kalen," she said hoarsely, searching Melina's face for the slightest sign of censure. She found nothing but concern.

Instead, the other woman laid the paperwork on the counter and reached out, taking Mac's hand. A surprising and welcome gesture. "That's who I suspected, considering how weird you two are acting around each other. Honey, Kalen's a Sorcerer first and foremost, and his black panther form is second. He's never been fully human and that makes him very different from the others. Besides, there's still so much we don't know about shifters and how their individual circumstances come into play. We can't take anything for granted."

Her friend's words struck a chord and she nodded. "Kalen said pretty much the same thing to me back when we were . . . together."

"How long ago was that?"

"About a month. Not long after Aric was taken captive, on the night Kalen and I were attacked by that Sluagh. I don't remember the exact date."

"I can get it from Nick. He documents all incidents involving the Pack."

"Oh, sure." And their boss would know her secret soon if he didn't already. Hard to keep much from a PreCog.

Melina fell silent for a few moments, consulting her notes, Mac's test results and personal information, as well as a paper calendar like the ones sitting on the counter in every exam room. "Going just by the dates of your last cycle, I'm guessing you're about four or five weeks along. We'll know more as you progress. And since we know next to nothing about pregnancies resulting from shifters and humans mating, I'm going to want reports from your ob-gyn, copies of your sonograms, stuff like that."

Mac's hand went over her tummy. "What if the doctor can tell this baby is special somehow? Where in the hell are we going to find a paranormal-friendly ob-gyn who knows how to keep her mouth shut?"

"Nick will find the answer to that, too. One step at a time, all right?"

Mac's head was spinning. Jesus, how her world had changed in the space of one morning. Kalen's too, though he didn't know it yet.

God, Kalen.

Who wanted nothing to do with Mac anymore.

Her eyes filled with scalding tears and she blinked rapidly, trying to stave them off. Her throat burned and she breathed through the grief that crushed her lungs. "I don't know if I can do this."

"Many women less prepared and much less capable than you have thought the same thing," her friend said crisply. "You're going to be just fine."

A tear slipped free anyway. "Kalen's going to flip. He's already given me the big brush-off."

"Tough shit," Melina said, anger creeping into her tone. "He helped make the kid, so he can deal."

Mac gave a watery laugh in spite of herself. "That simple, huh? Sure."

Her friend scowled. "You honestly think he won't take responsibility?"

"It's not that. There's something going on with him that has his head all twisted, and he won't let me in."

"Anything to do with the pendant he gave you?" Melina glanced questioningly at the silver disk and back to her friend's face.

"I think it has *everything* to do with it," she said, reaching to clasp the object. It was warm and comforting in her palm. "He gave this to me for protection."

"Against what?"

"More like *who*." Mac paused, clearing her throat. "Earlier, before I went in to tell them Sariel would probably survive, I might have eavesdropped outside the conference room door just a teensy bit."

"So? They never tell us shit about their ops unless we're patching them up or they have medical questions." The other woman pulled a face. "We get answers however we can. Go on."

"The one after Kalen is Sariel's Unseelie father, Malik."

"Is this the same being that encouraged Kalen to free Beryl?"

"They believe so. The bastard is trying to seduce Kalen to his side so he can use his power for whatever terrible reasons."

"If Malik is so strong, why doesn't he just go after Sariel himself? Use his son's power to his advantage, or kill him outright?"

"I don't know, but there must be a reason or he would've done it by now," Mac speculated. "If Sariel knows, he hasn't confided in me."

"Same here." The other woman shook her head. "But you've got more pressing worries. When are you going to tell Kalen about the baby?"

"You're assuming I am."

"Aren't you?"

Looking away, she felt crushed. "I'm not sure. The jerk couldn't get away from me fast enough after our one-night stand, so how do you think he'll react to the news that he's going to have a kid? He'll either hightail it out of Wyoming like the whole Pack is out for his blood, or worse—he'll feel *obligated* to be with me and take care of our child."

"You don't hold a very high opinion of your man."

"Kalen is *not* my man," she snapped. "He couldn't have been more clear about that."

"Well, now it's not that simple, if it ever was." Melina sighed and suddenly looked tired, showing an uncharacteristic crack in her usual armor. "Give him a chance to come around."

The anger bled from Mac's body, leaving her drained. Disheartened. "Maybe I will, eventually. But first I have to figure out how *I* feel about having his—our—child."

"Good point."

Melina shocked her again by closing the distance and pulling her into a warm, comforting embrace. That's all it took for Mac's tears to break free and flow. Her chest felt like it had cracked apart and was bleeding everywhere. The smaller, birdlike woman was, at this moment, the stronger of the two of them.

By far.

Kalen stumbled out of bed and stood blearily in the middle of the room, trying to get his bearings. From the slant of the sunlight filtering through the blinds, it was late afternoon. Seemed like it should be midnight.

After the fucking stressful morning he'd been through, he'd gone down hard the second his body was sprawled facedown on his bed. Not even Mr. Evil Unseelie had been able to break through his mental exhaustion, if in fact he'd tried.

The radio silence made him uneasy. It wouldn't last long. The bastard was likely crouching in wait, a spider ready to inject his venom at the worst possible moment. God, he despised being the tool of an enemy he didn't have a clue how to fight.

Walking to the bathroom, he felt a thousand years old. After taking care of business, washing his hands and splashing his face to wake up, he headed out in search of dinner. He wasn't very hungry, but it wouldn't help his cause to hole up in his room, isolating himself from the guys. He'd promised them he'd fight Malik, and he meant to do just that.

A couple of minutes later, he walked into the dining room and glanced around. Most of the Pack was there, settled around several tables where the food was served family-style. Mackenzie was present too, sitting with Melina, Jax, his mate, Kira, and Sariel. He hesitated, uncertain, his body flushing with heat at the sight of his beautiful doc.

Not yours, Malik intoned, darkly pleased.

"There you are, you crazy fuck," he muttered under his breath, tensing. "Don't you have some kittens to drown or something?"

No response. Just a lingering touch of cold fingers brushing down his cheek, his neck, then squeezing his shoulder in warning, digging in to grind painfully into muscle and bone before releasing him. Kalen sucked in a breath at the realization that the touch had been absolutely physical. Despite the wards Kalen had placed on the Alpha Pack compound, the Unseelie could actually hurt him from a distance, if he chose. Or harm one of his friends. *Goddamn him.*

But not Mackenzie. Ever. He'd made sure of that.

Shaken, he took a seat across from Hammer, the team's quiet giant, and tried to relax. The big, bald man simply uttered a polite, "Hey, whatzup?" and went on shoveling in his dinner like he'd never get another meal.

Kalen's muscles began to uncoil. Unlike some of the others, Hammer never forced conversation, pointed out Kalen's failings, taunted him, or poked into his biz, and for those things alone he liked the guy. Since the man didn't really seem to be waiting for an answer, Kalen didn't give one. Instead, his gaze fell on the dish of lasagna in the center of the table and he willed down sudden nausea.

He loved lasagna. Usually. But today the lumpy red sauce looked like blood, the wavy noodles and ricotta cheese like brains and gray matter. Just like what his head would've resembled if Nick hadn't moved the muzzle of the gun. Swallowing down bile, he scooped a square onto his plate and grabbed a bread stick from the basket beside the main dish.

The first bite of the gooey ensemble went down with difficulty, but he gagged on the second. Putting his fork down, he pushed his plate away and resigned himself to nibbling on the bread.

"You okay?"

He looked up to see Hammer studying him intensely, chewing his food. "Yeah, I'm good."

"That fuckin' creep screwin' around in your head again?"

"Not at the moment. I'm just wound a little tight."

"Understandable." Hammer didn't look like he much bought the simple explanation, but he nodded anyway. "Don't hesitate to ask for help, man. Do *not* try to deal with this on your own. We're a team. Remember that."

"And here I was just thinking how you never get into my business," he tried to joke.

"This doesn't count. What hurts one of us hurts all of us."

Like he'd needed the reminder. "I know," he said, his appetite now completely gone. He tossed the remains of the bread stick onto his plate. "Between the Pack and Malik, I'm not likely to forget, either."

"Hey, it ain't just you—we're *all* vulnerable to outside threats. That's why we work, train, and live as a unit. That's why we're in a remote building that's protected like a fuckin' fortress."

"And what if all that's not enough? What then?"

The other man eyed him in silence for a long moment. "It has to be."

But it wasn't. "I found out Malik can get to any of us, anytime he wants. Despite the wards I put on this place." Shame swamped him anew as he made his admission.

"What? How?" A twinge of alarm showed on Hammer's face before it disappeared.

"He touched me a few minutes ago." When the other man sat up straight and glanced around sharply, Kalen explained. "No, he's not here in body. But he projected some type of astral form of himself to me long enough to let me know he could get me whenever he wanted. Or anyone else, too."

"A warning," Hammer said in a low, pissed-off tone.

"Yeah."

"It's a bluff. Has to be."

"How so?"

"Think about it. If Malik could actually do significant physical harm to you or anyone here, he would've done it already."

"Maybe," Kalen conceded. The idea gave him a bit of hope.

"And if he could, wouldn't he just go straight for Sariel, perhaps snatch you as a bonus? I'm thinking it's smoke up our asses, man. If the motherfucker was all that strong, he wouldn't need you, and he sure wouldn't be so bent on murdering his own son."

"Makes sense." God, he hoped Hammer was right.

"Something else just occurred to me." The big man rested his elbows on the table and eyed Kalen. "Can he hear us talking? Can he hear *me*, right now?"

"Shit," he breathed, stunned by the question. Scouring his brain for past contact with the Unseelie, the creature's taunts, he shook his head. "I don't think so. He only seems to react to my thoughts or when I speak to him directly, or he'll project himself into my head and mess with me out of the blue. He likes to prey on my emotions, but I've never gleaned any hint of him listening in on my actual conversations with others. If he could do that, I'm sure he'd be driving me crazy with it."

"You mean, sort of like when you're in the room with somebody who's on the phone, you can only hear their end of the conversation?"

"Exactly. For whatever reason, it seems Malik can only tune in to *me*."

"Interesting. That's something helpful, anyway. But while that's good, you'll need to work on being careful about your thoughts, or blocking them altogether. Imagine a wall or some crap between your mind and his. Whatever helps."

"I'll try." He didn't hold out much hope of it working, but it was worth a shot. "Is Nick having any luck tracking down 'Evan Kerrigan'?" That the Unseelie was walking among the unsuspecting public, posing as a wealthy entrepreneur, was a source of real fear for the team. Involving innocent humans in their battles was always a frightening prospect, to be avoided at all costs.

"Not yet. He and his contacts have to tread carefully so they don't raise his suspicions."

"I have a feeling he won't hide forever," Kalen speculated grimly. "If we don't get him under surveillance before he comes out to play, it's gonna be bad shit."

Hammer snorted. "A handful of us against an Unseelie king and his army of giant, rabid bats? No fuckin' problem—we got it handled."

Those "giant, rabid bats" being the Sluagh—fallen Seelie who'd given themselves to evil and lived to serve Malik. God, they were all going to get massacred. Unless Kalen could pull off a miracle.

There are no miracles, my boy. Only the path that you and I will forge together. Once you learn to embrace your power, accept me as your master, we'll rule the universe.

"You mean the dark side of my power," Kalen hissed. "I won't use it to hurt innocents."

You will, pet. You have no choice.

"Fuck you."

"Kalen?" Hammer leaned forward, looking worried. "Is it *him*?"

Feeling sick again, Kalen pushed from his seat. "I have to go. Thanks for the talk."

Without giving the other man a chance to reply, he strode for the door. In the hallway, he leaned his back against the wall, sucking in a lungful of air and releasing it slowly. Searching for calm.

"Are you okay?"

Mackenzie had followed him out, and she stood in front of him with her hands tucked in the pockets of her lab coat, blue eyes apprehensive. Christ, he didn't deserve the concern on her sweet face.

As he fumbled for an answer, he noted that her eyelids were reddened. A bit puffy. Her expression was strained, her body tense, and he immediately went on alert. "I've had better days, Doc. Now, same question back at you. What's wrong?"

Some emotion that might've been remorse, or sorrow, flashed across her features and was gone. "Seriously? What's *right*? See, I can be evasive, too."

There was an edge to her tone that was new for the normally happy, bubbly woman. His heart sank. "It's me," he said softly, moving from the wall to get closer, touch her cheek. "I put that look on your face. Baby, I'm so sorry—" She stepped back to avoid contact, and the action skewered his gut like a blade.

"No. You don't get to do that," she snapped. "You don't get to *baby* me and act like you give a damn. I'm not your problem, remember?"

The dagger in his gut twisted. "I never said you weren't my problem or that I didn't care. I didn't mean to imply I felt that way." Just the opposite, in fact.

She crossed her arms over her chest in a protective stance. "Seemed like it to me. Anyway, does that really change anything?"

He looked away, heart aching. "Maybe not. But either way, staying far away from me is the best thing for you to do right now."

"Why? Because of this Unseelie character, Malik? He's the one who tried to get into my head a few weeks ago and now he's after you, right?"

He snapped his gaze back to hers. "Where did you hear his name?"

She glared at him. "I keep my ears open. I have to if I want to find out anything important around here."

"What, you eavesdropped on our meeting earlier?" In answer, she merely arched a brow, her militant expression daring him to make something of it. He'd never seen her temper spike so fast—in fact, he hadn't even been aware she had one. And he didn't like being the focus of it. "Fine. Then you know what I'm up against."

"What we're *all* up against, not just you!"

"You're the second person today to remind me of that."

"Then you should start listening before your stubborn ass gets us all killed."

He blew out a breath in frustration. "Working with a team isn't as easy as you make it sound. Not for me. I've been alone for almost half my life, and experience has taught me the hard way that the only person I can count on is myself. I can't change that sort of conditioning overnight."

Her eyes softened a fraction and some of the tenseness left her posture. "Life's been a bitch for you. I get that. But it hasn't exactly been a picnic for the other guys, either. Or me, for that matter."

"You?" He blinked at her. "Why? What do you mean?"

She gave a sad laugh and shook her head. "Did it ever occur to you to wonder why I gave up a lucrative private psychology practice to work out here, in the middle of nowhere, in a place that doesn't exist to the rest of the world?"

"Because your daddy—and our boss—the almighty General Jarrod Grant, hooked his baby up with a plum assignment?" The smartass comment did exactly what it was supposed to do.

It pissed her off.

"No, that isn't why, you jackass," she hissed, the fire back in those glittering blue eyes. "You know, if you'd wake the hell up and pay attention, you might learn a few things about the people who want to be your friends. I suggest you do that before it's too late."

"Yeah, everybody's got a shitload of great advice," he spat back. "And maybe I don't want or need any fucking friends."

"You know what? I'll talk to you when you're in the mood to act like an adult."

With a scathing look, she turned and walked briskly down the hall, putting distance between them as fast as she could. That's what he'd wanted. Right?

"Dammit. Mackenzie, wait!" he called, taking a step forward.

His path was blocked by a smirking, redheaded wolf shifter who had apparently seen too much of the exchange. "Way to go, Goth-boy. What'll you do for an encore? Twist the heads off her Barbie dolls?"

Of all the goddamned people to witness the scene with the doc, this guy was, hands down, the one he would've gone miles out of his way to avoid. He and Aric Savage hadn't gotten along since the night Kalen had met the Pack in the cemetery outside town. Kalen had been investigating a series of murders and was in the process of raising a corpse to get some information from it when he'd become aware of the shifters' presence. After a short but fierce battle, they'd gotten Kalen pinned and Jax had cheated by knocking him out.

After taking Kalen into the compound for questioning, the team had ascertained that Kalen was innocent. He learned that the Pack was looking into the same murders and that they were on the trail of Orson Chappell, the CEO of NewLife Technology. The man was using his scientists to conduct research on splicing human and shifter DNA, and he especially wanted shifters with Psy abilities like those in the Pack. Chappell and his men were murdering innocents in the process—thus the poor, mutilated bodies the local authorities had found.

But Chappell wasn't the Big Boss. To their shock, they'd discovered that Malik, masquerading as the wealthy Evan Kerrigan, was the real power behind the gruesome endeavor to create a breed of super-shifter soldier. He'd seduced the now-deceased Chappell and many others to do his bidding.

Just as he was now trying to seduce Kalen into joining him.

But that wasn't his most pressing problem right this second. He felt his lip curl as he glared at Aric. From day one, the Firestarter/Telekinetic had harassed and mocked him at every opportunity. How the asshole had managed to snag an intelligent, gorgeous mate like Rowan Chase—a former LAPD cop—was beyond Kalen's comprehension.

He tried to keep his voice even, but it betrayed his anger. "Fuck off, Aric. What goes on between me and Mackenzie is nobody's business, especially not yours."

"See, that's where you're wrong," the red wolf replied with a feral smile, clamping down firmly on Kalen's shoulder. "Mac is—"

"Get your hands off me."

Aric ignored his warning. "Mac is my friend. Everyone loves her, and none of us are going to stand by and watch you take a giant dump on her."

Kalen barely heard the words as Aric's face blurred. In an instant, memories assaulted him. Terrible ones, ghosts of other male hands in years gone by, many of them brutal. Taking what they wanted. And Kalen allowing the unwanted touches so he could put food in his empty, burning stomach.

Never again.

Mackenzie was the only one who had that right. Her hands were like heaven.

"Don't touch me," he said hoarsely. Inside, his panther stirred, rumbled in anger.

He's the enemy, pet, Malik cajoled. *Don't you see? He's done nothing but hurt you, laugh at you, just as all the others in the past have done. He would toss you back into the cold if he could. Do not give him your loyalty—he does not deserve it. Show him your power, boy! Do not accept this contempt from one so far beneath you! Show him what it means to fuck with a Sorcerer!*

Aric's lips were moving, but it was Malik's words that resounded in his head. They held the ring of truth, and anger boiled into a barely concealed rage. Under his skin, overwhelming emotions writhed like snakes, grew, and exploded.

With a snarl, he brought up a forearm and broke the other man's hold, then shoved him backward. Taken by surprise, the red wolf was unprepared when Kalen flung out a hand, palm up, and shouted a spell in Latin, releasing a blue sphere of pure energy.

The blast hit Aric in the chest and blew him off his feet, slamming him into the far wall hard enough to crack the plaster. His face registered shock as the energy hummed, spreading to his torso and limbs, causing his entire body to shake before it dispersed altogether. The man dropped to his knees, but just briefly. His head snapped up and his lips peeled back to bare his lengthening fangs.

"You wanna play dirty, kitty-cat? I can do that."

As Aric pushed to his feet, Kalen half-expected him to shift into his wolf form. He wasn't prepared for the other man to fling his hand out, answering Kalen's challenge with a plume of fire that rocketed toward his face. A shriek echoed in the hallway that he identified as Mac's frightened voice just as he brought up his hand and pushed his power at the fire, driving it back at his nemesis.

The wolf switched tactics, and the fire vanished. Before Kalen could react, he felt his body rise, feet leaving the floor. The fucker was using his gift of telekinesis to fight back, and quite effectively. Kalen's body spun around to face away from the wolf, making it almost impossible to throw a spell at him. Then he was body-slammed into the wall, his entire right side taking the hit. Pain shot through his head and arm, and he both heard and felt a sickening snap.

"Ahhg!" Agony swept him, and he was slammed again.

"Like that, kitty?" Aric sneered. "How does that feel?"

"What the fuck is going on here?" Nick's voice bellowed. "Savage, put him the fuck down!"

"You're the boss."

Kalen was unceremoniously dropped. He crumpled to the floor, trying to breathe through the terrible pain. And, as his head slowly cleared of Malik's coercion, shame. What had he done?

Hands rolled him carefully to his back and he found himself blinking at Nick's worried face. The commander's gaze went to Kalen's right arm.

"Can you lift it? Wiggle your fingers?"

He tried, and a bolt of white-hot fire shot through his arm as a cry escaped his lips. "No."

Nick glared at Aric, who was standing off to the side, jaw clenched. "You broke his arm. You'd better have a good goddamned reason for attacking one of your own brothers."

"First, he ain't my brother. The others, yeah. But not that freak," he said with undisguised contempt.

This time, the agony hit Kalen in a completely different place, and he struggled not to let it show as the man went on.

"Second, I do have a good reason. He attacked me first."

Nick's gaze returned to Kalen. "Is this true?"

Apparently the PreCog couldn't "see" everything. Kalen swallowed hard. "Yes."

A small crowd had gathered, some of the other guys muttering, one giving a low whistle. To his mortification, Mac stood with the others, looking at him in horror. Obviously she'd witnessed the whole thing.

"Why?" the commander bit off.

Such a simple question.

"Because he wouldn't take his hands off me." Such a sad answer.

Immediately, Nick understood and the anger began to drain from his face. "Flashback?"

"Yeah," he whispered. The awful memories threatened to overtake him again. "All I felt was his hands and he wouldn't let me go and I remembered . . ." He couldn't finish. But he didn't have to.

Finally catching on, Aric swore. To Nick, he said, "I thought he was just being a dick, especially after how he'd just talked to Mac. I didn't know."

Whatever Nick might've said was forgotten for the moment as Zander Cole, the Pack's Healer, knelt beside Nick, forcing him to make room. "Damn, that's a bad break. Lucky for you, I can fix it right up." He sent Kalen an encouraging smile, which Kalen couldn't quite return.

"If you say so."

"I do. The bad news is I've got to realign the bone first or you're going to be all crooked. Ready?"

"Do your worst."

Lifting Kalen's arm, Zan gave him an apologetic look. Working quickly, he pulled the injured limb with all his strength, popping the severed ends back into place. Kalen yelled, dark spots dancing in front of his eyes. Nausea pushed bile into his throat and he nearly passed out. How he kept from either throwing up or losing consciousness was sheer luck.

When Zan's fingers wrapped over the place where the bone had broken the skin, Kalen panted, sweat trickling down his temples into his hair. Then warmth enveloped the point of the break, and the horrible, stabbing burn gradually lessened. The heat felt good, and soon the pain was gone. Checking out his arm, he saw that his skin was covered in drying blood from the break, but the arm was as good as new.

"Thanks, Z-man," he said, giving the guy a wan smile.

"No problem. Here." Pushing to his feet, he offered Kalen a hand up.

He took it and stood awkwardly, not making eye contact with anyone as he waited for Nick to deliver his judgment. It came swiftly.

"I get what happened here," the commander said in a low, stern tone. "It's no secret that you two, in addition to your own problems, have had issues with each other from day one. But I'm not a fucking kindergarten teacher and this isn't a playground for you two to beat the shit out of each other while you work out those issues. Is that clear?"

Kalen winced. "Yes, sir."

"Yeah," Aric drawled, earning him a hard stare from Nick. He cleared his throat. "I mean, yes, sir."

"Find some common ground and do it on your own time. I've got a Pack to run. I don't have time for this bullshit and neither does anyone else. If this happens again, you're both suspended. Indefinitely."

"What!" Aric shouted. "It wasn't my fault! He—"

"And now you know why," Nick enunciated. He was fast losing his trademark patience. "You know how to read your teammate's signals better than that, Aric. I *know* you do. You should have stopped and read his body language, and if you had, you'd have known something was wrong. Then you would have let him go like he asked and diffused the situation with a bit of compassion. You're a better Pack mate and brother than this."

Aric glanced to Rowan, found her lips tight with disapproval. His high cheekbones colored and he hung his head in shame. "You're right, Nicky. I'm sorry."

"It's not me you owe the apology."

He didn't want to speak to Kalen at all. Anyone could see that. It hurt more than Kalen wanted to admit. But the man closed the distance and nodded.

"I'm sorry, Sorcerer. I fucked up."

"Kalen."

"What?" Aric's brow furrowed in confusion.

"You're always calling me Goth-boy, kitty, pretty boy, whatever. My name is *Kalen*," he said quietly.

"Right." Aric laughed without real humor. "Sure, *Kalen*, whatever."

Nick shook his head. "All right, everyone, show's over. Let's call it a day."

Kalen had never heard a better suggestion. As the group broke up, some of the guys clapped him on the back or gave him an encouraging word or two in a show of support. But none, he noted, actually stopped to *really* talk to him. To reach out.

Nobody ever had before. Why should now be any different?

Even Mac had left without speaking to him further. No reason she should've stayed after the way he'd spoken to her. Aric had been right and Kalen had been too angry to listen.

Now he was alone in the empty corridor, longing for companionship. He'd give almost anything for the joy of the easy friendships these guys shared. Not to mention a beautiful mate like Jax and Aric had found. It seemed those dreams were to remain forever out of his reach.

"Don't you have anything to say about that?" he asked Malik bitterly.

The bastard didn't respond, though. At that moment, he would've given anything for companionship, even the slimy Unseelie's, because then he wouldn't be so alone.

Which was, no doubt, exactly what Malik had planned.

And that was the most frightening thought of all.

Three

Kalen tossed in his bed, twisting in tangled sheets. The night was too hot, the room stifling. He'd lowered the thermostat in his quarters, but it hadn't helped. The cotton sheets clung to his overheated skin, sticky and miserable. For hours he'd fought for oblivion, but it remained elusive. He was restless.

So alone.

Can't sleep?

"You're quite the detective," he said sarcastically to the damned Unseelie. "What do you care? And don't the Fae sleep, either?"

A deep sigh sounded from somewhere outside, in the shadows. *I care more than you know, and I rarely require sleep. Come to me, boy. I want to show you something.*

A chill slithered across Kalen's skin, despite the uncomfortable heat. The Unseelie sounded almost ... friendly. Was this a new approach to try to worm his way into Kalen's confidence? "No, thanks. There's not anything you've got that I want to see."

You'll feel differently once you see it.

"Feeling sure about that, huh?"

What I'm certain of is that you're alone. That you're tired, so tired of walking through your existence with no one by your side who understands you.

"And you think you do?" Kalen asked tightly.

Yes. I know you better than you realize.

"What the hell does that mean?"

I'll show you. Come.

"Go to hell."

A darkly amused chuckle floated in the air. *That's not exactly an effective threat. While you're straining your mind for a more original insult, get out of bed and join me. You have nothing to lose. Deep inside, you know I'm right.*

The words filled him with despair. It didn't matter that he recognized the tactic the Unseelie was using—find the point of weakness in the prey and strike. Kalen's point of weakness also happened to be the truth.

He'd been alone and adrift since his grandmother died, not long after the day she'd given him the pendant. Ever since, he'd struggled to rise above the hatred, indifference, and ridicule thrown at him daily. It was hard to say which one hurt most.

With Kalen's grandmother no longer an obstacle, his father's abuse had worsened by leaps and bounds. Especially toward Kalen's mother. On that last, terrible night, Dave Black had started beating her for some small infraction, and the sight of her cowering under his blows, crying out, made something snap in Kalen's soul. He'd shifted into his panther form for the very first time and leaped onto his father, fully intending to rip out his throat. Only his mother's screams for him to stop spared the bastard his fate.

When Kalen had shifted back, his gratification at seeing dear old Dad's terror was brief. The bastard's fearful expression quickly morphed into outright, seething hatred. He ordered his son gone from the house immediately, and he was to take nothing with him.

Kalen's mother had remained silent, letting it happen. And his heart had broken.

That was his first experience with hatred. There'd been plenty of ridicule—Aric wasn't the first to call him a freak, to act like Kalen didn't deserve to breathe the same air as regular people. A recent run-in with a group of backwoods assholes at the Cross-eyed Grizzly came painfully to mind. And yeah, Mackenzie had witnessed that incident, too.

But now that he thought about it, the indifference might just be the worst. He thought of years of walking busy highways and lonely back roads. Everyone passing him by, no one caring where this drifter might be headed or what had brought him so low. Not one hand extended in welcome.

Until Nick Westfall had offered him a job with the Alpha Pack and a place to stay. Maybe—

Boy, don't get sentimental about the commander's gesture, Malik sneered. *You know as well as I that the man would've shown you the door weeks ago if you hadn't been of use to his team. Deny it!*

He couldn't, and misery swamped him anew. "I'm nothing but a tool to you, too. You're no different from Nick, if that's the argument you're going with."

I have something far greater to offer you, young Sorcerer. Something you long for badly that he can never give to you. Come and see, pet. Once you do, you'll be free to go if you wish.

"I don't believe you," he gritted. "You'll probably hold me prisoner or something."

No. I won't need to take such a drastic step.

Again, there was the ring of truth. Kalen was chilled, fear taking root deep in his soul. What could Malik possibly have that made him so confident Kalen would join him? What did Kalen want so badly that he'd give in to the darkness, as his grandmother had feared?

Acceptance, Malik said gently. *And a place to belong.*

Kalen's pulse beat hard in his throat. "You can't give me those things. You're evil, and you're lying."

I'm neither—merely misunderstood, like you. Let me prove it.

The temptation was too much. Kalen rose from the bed and dressed, hands shaking. He was glad Malik couldn't see them. After donning the jeans and T-shirt from earlier, he pulled on his boots and slipped from his quarters.

Moving as silently as possible, he made his way down the corridor to the compound's recreation room. Once there, he crossed to the door leading outside and soon found himself standing in the grassy area at the back of the building where the guys played football and other games to pass their free time.

Positive he'd escaped without being spotted, he strode for the edge of the forest. Once shielded from view by the cover of the trees and surrounding gloom, he took a deep breath and relaxed, calling his panther.

The beast responded with a glad roar at being free. It had been much too long. He hit the ground on all fours, lifted his nose to the air. The scents were much sharper in this form, the earth more pungent. Rich. He caught the scent of animals, too, small ones that would make tasty snacks, but he resisted the hunt. Tonight he had a different purpose.

His panther ran, exulting in stretching his limbs. In the simplicity of just being free. He'd often wondered if it might be better to live in this form forever, turning his back on humanity. It could be so easy.

Then again, perhaps not. The man inside craved acceptance, and unfortunately, Malik was right. He was curious to see what the male thought he had to offer. Even more puzzling, he sensed no imminent physical threat from the Unseelie. Why?

That question nagged him all during his run. He wasn't sure where he was going, but simply followed the pull that told him this was the right direction. The nearer he got to Malik, the stronger the force drawing him in.

He should've been alarmed once he passed beyond the boundaries of the wards he'd placed around the Pack compound, but he wasn't. For miles he ran, well into the Shoshone National Forest, far past where any hunter or camper would dare to venture.

At last he came to a clearing, and in that space stood a cabin nestled in the trees. Not a small, quaint one, either. The structure was made of logs, and a covered porch traversed the front and wrapped around both sides. The place was grand, like a hunting lodge a millionaire might own, which made sense. Malik was posing as the wealthy Evan Kerrigan.

Then again . . . the cabin was too far from civilization to be part of Malik's human cover. In fact, there was something different about this place. Something *other*. He became aware of a vibration along his nerve endings, sort of like a current, but one that caused him no discomfort. Immediately he identified the source—dark magic.

And it wasn't just coming from the cabin and surrounding area. No, this place *was* magic itself. A beautiful illusion created by a master of the dark arts, cloaked from all except those to whom Malik wished it known. He couldn't help but admire the skill involved in maintaining the facade.

But is it a facade if you can see and touch it, boy? I can disappear at will, so am I therefore not real?

Kalen shifted back to his human form, his clothes reappearing on his body. Quite a handy ability that none of the other guys possessed.

"I don't know. Why don't you vanish for good and we'll find out?" he muttered.

An amused laugh greeted Kalen's terse words, and a dark figure stepped onto the porch from inside. Backlit in the cabin's doorway, the man—or rather, the Unseelie disguised as a man—was very tall.

"Come inside, young Sorcerer," Malik said, gesturing him forward. "Let's have a nightcap to cure our insomnia."

The other male turned and went inside. Wary, Kalen followed him. Just because the Unseelie exuded a false sense of normalcy didn't mean Kalen was stupid. His years on the street had taught him that a friendly gesture always came with a catch.

And nothing about this creature was normal.

Mounting the porch steps, he trailed Malik into the cabin and took a surprised look around. Somehow he'd expected stark coldness and "evil" stamped on every surface. But the interior was the epitome of warm, rustic luxury. Dark leather furniture and plush throw rugs dotted the living space. A large stone fireplace graced most of the far wall, and an adjacent wall sported a walk-in wet bar.

"How civilized," he commented drily as Malik rounded the bar.

"Isn't it? And here you likely expected a dreary cave full of bats." The Unseelie reached for an expensive-looking bottle of Cognac and then removed two crystal highball glasses from the shelf. Smiling faintly, he poured them each a couple of inches of the liquor and then brought them both into the living area. He handed Kalen a glass. "Please, sit."

Kalen remained standing for a few beats longer, studying the creature who could pass for any human man. An exceptionally good-looking one. The form he'd taken as Evan Kerrigan was a few inches taller than Kalen's six or so feet, and he was well muscled without being ripped. Black hair dusted his shoulders and framed an angular face set with midnight blue eyes and a strong jaw. It was no wonder the creature had managed to seduce everyone who'd crossed his path.

He appeared to be anything but a monster.

There was an innate sexuality that radiated from the male's very pores. Although, despite the Unseelie's seductive approach, Kalen could honestly say he *knew* Malik's focus was not really directed at him in a sexual way—though he couldn't say *how* he knew—the bold scrutiny in the other's steady gaze unnerved him nonetheless.

"What are you so hot to show me?" Kalen asked, getting to the point.

"First I'd like to talk to you. Sit, please." Malik took a seat in a large wingback chair near the fireplace, stretching his long legs out in front of him and crossing them at the ankles. Casually sipping his Cognac, he presented the picture of cozy, urbane charm.

It couldn't last.

Slowly, Kalen lowered himself to the sofa across from the Unseelie and sniffed at the liquor. Reaching out with his magic, he could discern no spell placed on the drink. He took a sip and found it to be safe. But he knew better than to relax.

"This is good stuff," he said.

"Only the best for you."

"You sound as though you mean that."

"I do."

"Why?"

"Because I've waited for this moment for what seems like ages." Those piercing eyes bored into his.

Kalen shifted uneasily. "The way you said that . . . it's almost as if you know me."

"As well as I know myself," the Unseelie replied softly.

Something about that statement, Malik's tone, made every hair on his body stand on end. "That's not possible."

"It's as possible as the cabin you're sitting in quite comfortably, where no cabin should be."

"Is this how it's going to be? You talking in riddles the whole time? I don't know what the hell I thought coming here would accomplish." Self-preservation raised its head. He started to rise, eager to get out of there, but Malik held out a hand.

"Hear me out. Don't you want your questions answered?"

Yes, he did. Badly. He doubted prying them from the

fucker would be as easy as that, but he sat again, reluctantly. "All right. Let's start with why you want to hurt innocent people."

Malik affected a solemn expression, like a doctor about to tell someone he had a terminal illness. "Innocence is more of an illusion than anything my magic could possibly create. The sole innocent creatures are newborns, and all are eventually lost to temptation. There are no exceptions to this rule."

"You're wrong. My mother was innocent," he refuted tightly.

A flash of anger lit the Unseelie's eyes, then was quickly masked. "No. Your mother was weak. She did not protect you from the worm you called 'Father.'"

He sucked in a breath. "How do you know that?"

"She feared for herself more than she cared to protect her child, and that makes her among the most loathsome of her kind. I saw how she cowered while he beat you senseless, time after time. I saw how she ultimately handed your fate to David Black, allowed him to toss you into the street like a sack of refuse."

"And why the hell didn't you intervene, if you cared so much?" He glared at the Unseelie.

"I had to wait. It wasn't time."

"Wait for *what*?"

"For you to take your rightful place as my apprentice. To rule at my side."

"I was homeless, you fucker," he hissed. "I had to *turn tricks* to survive. You couldn't have contacted me a helluva lot sooner—like, say, when I was a scared teenager with not one person on earth to turn to?"

"I couldn't get near you, boy," Malik snapped, scowling. "The old woman made certain of that."

"Grandma?" The Unseelie waited for him to put it together. "The amulet. She said it would protect me from harm, no matter how great the evil. Hold up. Did she mean you, specifically? Did you know my grandmother?"

Kalen moved to the edge of his seat, gripping the highball glass so hard his knuckles whitened. He tried to push down the panic beginning to seize his lungs. What the fuck did all this mean?

"Yes, I knew Ida. She was a thorn in my ass for many centuries."

"Wait. What?" Kalen took a generous gulp of his Cognac, trying to get a hold on the conversation. "Centuries? You—you're lying."

"Hardly. Ida May Ventura was a four-hundred-twenty-three-year-old Seelie, and a very powerful one. Well, until her final days, anyway."

Eyes wide, Kalen stared at Malik, speechless. For several long moments he could do nothing but process what the Unseelie was really, truly telling him. Shock held him immobile.

"Are you saying . . . that I'm Fae?"

"Down to your last drop of blood. Sorcerers are not mere humans imbued with the gift of simple witchcraft."

"Oh, God." Mind spinning, he tried to assimilate this revelation.

"You're a rare breed. Very few Fae are powerful enough to become Sorcerers," Malik said, a slight smile playing about his lips. "Even I am not a Sorcerer."

"That's why you want me and why my power is valuable to you."

"I won't deny that as two Fae—a king and his sec-

ond in command—we'll be unstoppable together and
that I can accomplish my goals much more quickly
with you than not. But that's not the only reason I desire your presence."

"Why else, then?"

Malik shook his head. "You're not ready to hear it
yet. Soon."

Okay, that missing piece of the puzzle would have
to wait. Trying another tack, he asked, "How did you
know my grandmother? What's your connection to my
family?"

"The Fae are not a vast people numbering in the millions," he replied smoothly. "We had met."

"Yeah, but you said Grandma was Seelie. You're Unseelie. I seriously doubt she ran in your circles."

"True. However, we *had* crossed paths all the same,
arguing on opposite sides of issues before our royal
courts."

"All right. I'll buy that for now. So why did she live
her life posing as a human?" That she hadn't entrusted
him with her biggest secret cut deep. It hurt badly. He
realized his mistake when Malik immediately used that
emotion to his advantage.

Leaving his chair, the Unseelie moved next to Kalen
on the sofa, sitting beside him. Turning slightly to face
him, Malik set his glass of Cognac on the coffee table
and laid a palm on Kalen's thigh. The touch was surprisingly warm. Normally he would flinch, demanding
the offender remove his hand as he'd done with Aric.
But suddenly he was caught in the other male's gaze.
The warmth extended through his limbs, like sweet
honey, fostering a sense of peace. Of belonging. Companionship.

All the things he'd longed for these many cold years.

"I don't know why Ida made some of the choices she did, boy. I don't know why she lied to you."

Christ. It was true. His beloved grandmother had lied about something huge—the both of them being Fae.

"Maybe she wanted to protect me from something. . . ."

"Perhaps. But *did* she keep you safe?"

"No," he whispered, staring into the brown liquor in his hand.

"No," Malik repeated. "She didn't. All she managed was to keep you away from me, the one who could have taken you in after she passed on. Who could have fed and sheltered you. Cared for you. Instructed you properly in the arts—"

"The *dark* arts. She wanted to keep me from the dark arts, she said."

"Foolish boy. I know you feel compelled to defend your beloved grandmother." Again the squeeze. The sense of belonging. "There are no dark arts, merely dark uses. And we've already established that no one is innocent, no matter which side you're on."

"Maybe." Another thought occurred to him. "Why don't I have wings, like Sariel, if I'm Fae?"

Malik shrugged. "I don't know. Perhaps you took after your mother."

Kalen got the distinct feeling he wasn't telling the whole truth. "Hmm. You say my grandmother was Fae, but she looked like any old woman to me."

"Glamour. If she'd dropped it, I doubt she'd have appeared to be many years older than you are now."

"Then how could she die? Aren't Fae immortal?"

"Up to a point, we are. I'm guessing her life force was tied to the amulet. When she gave it to you, she accepted her death. She could also have been ill from using her glamour too long, living as a human who ages and gets sick. It's all speculation. Who knows?"

"I gave the amulet away. Will I die now?"

"No," Malik said firmly. "You won't. If your life force was in fact tied to the pendant, it isn't any longer. The link was severed the night you disobeyed your grandmother by taking it off."

He'd always had the sense that he'd made a dire mistake when he'd first taken off the pendant. Not the night he and Mackenzie made love in the hotel room, but years before. He'd been barely eighteen and had slept with a much older woman who'd admired the pendant. And like an idiot, he'd ignored his grandmother's warning. He'd set in motion something terrible and irrevocable that night.

"What?" He stared at Malik, stunned. "You were watching then, too?"

"I was." His lips turned up. "You were a young man trying to impress that older woman you fucked, letting her try the thing on. As soon as it left your hand, I made certain to sever its hold on you forever. It will protect the wearer now, as your grandmother said, but without draining the person's life force if removed or given away."

"So, a few weeks ago you forced me to give away the amulet to my . . . my friend Mackenzie. But you did so knowing I wouldn't be harmed by removing it."

Except by Malik himself, of course.

"As I told you, I knew one day you would belong to me." He paused. "I would have saved you from that harsh life years ago, when you first removed the pendant, but I didn't act quickly enough."

Kalen narrowed his eyes. "I thought you said you didn't rescue me because I wasn't ready."

"You weren't. But I would have anyway." He sighed. "There. Now you have a confession of one of my failings."

He wasn't so sure. Was Malik lying, or telling the truth about his part in everything? Or confusing him with half-lies, half-truths? God, if that was the case, Malik was succeeding.

That missing piece of the puzzle, the part of the story Malik wasn't yet telling him, nagged at him like a sore tooth. But he knew nothing would be gained on that score tonight even if he pushed. Instead, he brought the topic back to the original purpose of the visit.

"You wanted to show me something. To prove that you understand me and will stick beside me."

"Indeed." Malik paused, studying him intently.

He gave a humorless laugh. "Pardon me if I don't believe your bullshit."

"Why do you assume it's bullshit, as you say?"

"Really?" He gaped at the Unseelie, incredulous. "You kill people."

"So do you, and so does your whole team for that matter," Malik pointed out. "I suppose that makes you all evil to a man."

"Well, no, of course not! You're the bad guy!"

"Me? Why?"

"Are you serious? Man, you keep shifters and humans in cages so the scientists who're working for you—or for *Kerrigan*—can figure out how to splice their DNA and create super-shifter soldiers!"

"I don't keep my test subjects in cages. They're strictly volunteers."

"I can't believe you said that with a straight face." He shook his head, pushed angrily to his feet and paced a few feet away to put distance between them. "I saw with my own eyes two of our team members being held in cages. They'd been tortured and experimented on, one of them for months!"

Malik stood, looking troubled. "Ah. You're referring to Orson Chappell's and Dr. Gene Bowman's unfortunate decisions. They became a bit fanatical in their approach."

"You don't say," Kalen mocked. "And you didn't seduce or coerce them into performing the heinous shit they did in the name of science, I'm sure."

"I didn't, not that I expect you to believe me."

"I don't. You had to know what was going on."

"Whether you believe me or not doesn't change anything. And it certainly doesn't change my goal, which I must say is a worthy one."

"To create this perfect breed of super-shifters."

"Yes." The Unseelie's eyes lit with excitement. "What if we could perfect a soldier whose supernatural abilities far exceed any of the humans' weapons in existence? What if humans were no longer the top of the pyramid of intelligent life on earth? Can you imagine being a part of implementing the greatest fundamental change to civilization in the history of the universe? The soldiers would work for you and me, and the planet would belong to the Fae, shifters, vampires, and every other creature who's had to live in the shadows for centuries. Like you and I have been forced to live."

"That'll never happen. Powerful men in history

have tried shit along those lines and ended up with their heads on pikes."

"*Men* have tried. Never an Unseelie king."

Tired, he rubbed his eyes. "Show-and-tell time, Malik. Let's see what you've got or I'm leaving."

"I was getting to that before our little debate about what constitutes *evil*. And I happen to know that a bit of sacrifice is necessary for the greater good." He held up a hand before Kalen could voice further argument. "We'll put the super-shifter issue to rest for the evening. Follow me."

"Where to now?" he muttered.

But the other male didn't answer. Kalen followed the Unseelie through the house, turning over in his mind all the stuff Malik had told him. He still couldn't grasp, well, any of it.

Jesus fuck, he was Fae. Like Sariel, Malik's half Seelie–half Unseelie son and the Pack's good friend. Maybe he could trust the guy to answer some questions for him discreetly. Once Sariel recovered and got over the fact that Kalen had been seduced into letting the witch loose, who then almost killed Sariel on his daddy's orders. Yeah, the Fae prince would be happy to have a heart-to-heart with Kalen, become best buddies.

Right. That would happen.

Kalen was brought out of his thoughts when Malik reached a doorway off the kitchen. The doorway opened to a flight of stairs that led down. Right into a dark, creepy basement, it appeared.

Kalen balked. "You want me to go down there with you? I've seen this movie, and it didn't end so good for the stupid hero."

"I'm not going to harm you. You have my word."

"I'm sure that promise is worth framing and hanging on the wall."

Malik descended the steps, waving a hand as he passed. Several lights came on, and at least Kalen could see to the landing at the bottom. With a sigh, he went after the Unseelie. If he was making a mistake, this would likely be his last.

Kalen was completely unprepared for what he found.

In the center of the basement floor, hanging with his arms bound above his head, was a man he recognized. A big son of a bitch he'd met just once before—

That night, weeks ago, when the guy and his hick asshole buddies had attacked Kalen at the Cross-eyed Grizzly.

Billy Beer Gut.

Four

"What the fuck's going on here?" Kalen looked from the frightened man back to the Unseelie. "Why do you have this shithead tied up in your basement?"

The shithead in question darted his gaze from him to Malik, eyes bulging in fear. The sharp stench of urine reached his nose. It permeated the room, and a dark stain was visible at the crotch of the man's dirty jeans.

"I see you remember Billy," Malik said pleasantly, as though they were getting reacquainted over a nice dinner of wine and lobster. "He's been kind enough to join us for a brief reunion."

"Listen, I don't know what you're playing at, but Billy is good and scared now. Right, Billy?"

"Y-yeah! I got no beef with either of ya'll!"

"See? I'm sure that's what you wanted, and you've had your fun. Let him go and I'll wipe his mind. He won't remember this ever happened."

"What would be the point in that? He has to know what he's done wrong."

Before I kill him went unspoken, but Kalen was suddenly, dreadfully sure that's what Malik had planned. "He knows. Isn't that so, Billy?"

The man found his voice, nodding emphatically. "H-hell, yeah! R-right! I recognize the purty fella here, from that night at the Grizzly." He laughed nervously as though sharing a joke. "We don't git many dudes like him in our neck of the woods and we was just havin' us a little fun, that's all! I swear we wasn't gonna hurt him or nothin'!"

"As though you could." Malik scoffed in contempt. "Fat slug of a human."

"H-human?" He glanced around in confusion.

"Malik, please. Let him go."

"He must pay, my pet."

"For what? Him and his buddies ganging up on me? It's not the first time that's happened, and you can't go around killing everyone who tries to walk all over me. . . ."

He trailed off, seeing the catlike expression on Malik's handsome face. The triumph. And in that moment he realized two things.

First, the hapless Billy wasn't leaving this basement alive.

Second, Malik had killed on his behalf before. When? How many? Every single person in the entire time Malik had been following him, since he was a homeless teenager?

"Yes," the Unseelie answered his thoughts. "Every last one. And they were delicious."

"Christ." Kalen pushed a hand through his hair, feeling sick. Helpless. He couldn't think of that now. "You can't do this."

"I really can. More important, you won't stop me."

"You think not? I'm just as powerful as you, and I'm fully capable—"

"But you won't. My boy, this is why I brought you here—to show you that essentially there is no difference between you and me." He gripped Kalen's shoulder and brought their foreheads so close they almost touched. Kalen didn't pull away as Malik went on.

"You want this scum dead for what he did to you," Malik intoned gently. "He's a symbol of all those who've hurt you again and again throughout your life. You want him to pay, don't you?"

"No! Killing is wrong."

"You've been beaten and worse by men like this, when you were little more than a boy. Before you fully came into your powers. Am I correct?"

"Yeah," he said bitterly.

"Just once, you want to feel what it's like to show one of them what it means to be completely at *your* mercy."

"Yes." The word emerged in spite of his resolve to deny it.

The bound man started blubbering, tears and snot running down his fleshy cheeks.

"He's no innocent, Kalen," Malik soothed. "He has raped and murdered, left many battered and broken. Including his wife and three children. Like the slime you called 'father.' Look."

With a push, Malik shoved several of Billy's memories into Kalen's head. They rolled like old, grainy footage of a home movie, and the scenes were real. The bastard grabbing a waitress from the Grizzly, forcing her to blow him behind the bar, knowing she wouldn't tell or else he'd spin his own tale through the town, ruining her reputation. Other scenes were of Billy and his buddies burying a body outside town. Someone they'd killed for owing one of them less than a hundred bucks.

But the worst were the kids. He'd abused his children horribly, beating them with his belt and scalding them with cigarettes, hot water. Just last week, the little one had spilled something on the greasy carpet, and the bastard had forced the child to drink half of a bottle of carpet cleaner. In their backwoods craphole of a shack, the boy had almost died. The man promised his terrified wife they were all dead if she breathed a word to anyone.

Disbelief and horror at what Malik had planned here tonight became eagerness. Morphed into a terrible, seething rage that demanded justice for the ones Billy had hurt. Killed. Especially the children. And it was justice. No one else would do anything about this piece of filth.

"Do you see?" Malik asked.

"Yeah. He's a piece of shit." Power surged through his veins. The need for blood sang through him.

"What shall I do with him, boy?"

"Show him what hell really looks like," Kalen said coldly. "Then kill him."

Miles away, in the darkness of his quarters, Nick's pacing in his bedroom was brought up short by an awful vision.

He'd been restless tonight, just as he always was

when one of his own was suffering. And this man was in agony.

"Kalen," he whispered hoarsely. "No."

But he couldn't stop what was happening. There was no way he'd find Malik's hideout without Kalen's help, and the Sorcerer was already there.

Kalen's storm was on the horizon now, the thunder rolling. Lightning just beginning to flicker in the sky. The choices he made tonight, and the ones to come, he'd have to live with for the rest of his days.

However few those were.

The vision intensified.

Show him what hell really looks like. Then kill him.

"Oh, Jesus. No! Don't do it!"

But it was far too late. The Unseelie had finally managed to get his talons into Kalen, and the seduction had begun. The gradual slide into the pit of hell.

God help them all.

"No, no, please! I—I'll leave town! My wife and kids won't never have ta look at me again!"

Malik smiled, and his canines lengthened to protrude over his bottom lip. "They won't have to do that anyway."

With that, the Unseelie began to change. Kalen barely had time to register that Malik had dropped his glamour before his clothes disappeared and his form began to grow. His skin darkened to a grayish purple hue, and his straight black hair cascaded to his waist. His ears grew long, pointed at the tips, and his facial features sharpened to cruel angles.

His height quickly towered to at least seven feet. But the most frightening and impressive of all were his wings. Unlike Sariel's beautiful, feathered wings of electric blue, his father's were dark and leathery, almost black. They spanned nearly the entire basement in width, some fifteen feet.

The whole package that was Malik, undisguised, was cruelly magnificent. Something straight out of a nightmare.

And now he was Billy's nightmare. The man stared up at his tormentor, mouth open, no longer making a sound. He was learning now, at the very end of his existence, just how pathetic and insignificant he was in the grand scheme of the world. How powerless. A mindless bug headed for a zapper.

Kalen almost felt sorry for him. Except when he thought of what the asshole had done to his own kids.

"I'm not from hell, Billy," Malik said, his voice much lower and more gravelly than before. "I *am* hell. I have existed since before mankind walked upright, and for too long I have watched as many humans evolved to be not much more intelligent than the primates before them. You are one such substandard example of humanity. Are you following me, ape?"

The ape was beyond speech, his eyes fixed on the Unseelie in horror.

Malik reached out a hand, extended his index finger, and ran one razor-sharp claw down Billy's fleshy cheek. A thin line of blood trickled from the slice, over his jaw and down his neck. "And as a piece of undisputed filth, unworthy of being loose among even the weakest of humans, I cannot allow you to live. Even you with your limited cognitive ability can understand this by now, I'm sure."

Totally entranced, Billy nodded.

"Very well."

The Unseelie moved so fast, Kalen hardly saw what happened next. His arm shot out and he stabbed his claws deep into Billy's stomach. The man screamed, a high-pitched keen of sheer terror that bounced off the walls and became a gurgle as Malik thrust up, effectively gutting him.

Then Malik used his other hand to grab Billy's scraggly hair and yank his head back. The cords of the man's neck were exposed, and the Unseelie licked his lips in anticipation. And then he lowered his head and struck, tearing into the vulnerable throat of his captive, ripping it out. Drank and slurped, grunting in satisfaction.

Feeding on his prey.

The weak feed the strong, and the strong survive. That was Kalen's thought as he watched, transfixed by the sight of the powerful, muscled creature taking his fill. Why wasn't he horrified? Afraid? But he just wasn't. There was something darkly beautiful and primal about the scene before him. It called to his blood, to the dark power residing within him. Tightened his groin deliciously, stiffened his cock.

Abyssus abyssum invocat, Beryl had whispered to him a few days ago. *Hell calls hell.*

Now he knew why. The witch had been preparing Kalen for this night. For joining Malik, embracing his destiny. He never had to be helpless again, as he had been at fourteen. Never again had to endure the mockery of those like Aric. Never had to be alone. Because Malik understood.

The Unseelie raised his head, wiped the blood from his lips, and smiled.

"I told you that I do understand, my pet." Releasing his dead prey, he beckoned Kalen to him. "Come here."

Kalen obeyed, stepping so close he had to look up into that stunning, sharp face. "Yes?"

The other male lifted an arm and, with one claw from the opposite hand, sliced a cut in his wrist. Dark blood the color of merlot welled instantly. "Drink," he commanded.

Kalen hesitated, then took the wrist uncertainly, his heart pounding hard in his chest. A distant voice begged him not to do this, warned that this step would be irrevocable. Would bind him to the Unseelie until one or both of them died.

"Drink, and never be alone again," Malik said softly.

Kalen's tongue flicked out, tested the thick stream. The taste exploded on his tongue, sweet and rich as the finest red wine. A bolt of pleasure seared to his gut, his limbs, his cock, and he groaned, latching on more firmly.

God, it was so good. So fucking fine. He wanted more, would do anything to get it as often as his companion would allow him.

"Stop." The order barely filtered through to his consciousness.

Kalen blinked up at Malik and released his arm. Reluctantly. He licked his lips. "Please . . ."

Malik stroked his hair, studied him almost lovingly. "There will be plenty more. Do not worry. We are bonded now, and my blood will be your reward when I'm pleased."

"And when you're not pleased?"

"You do not want to know. Just make certain that doesn't happen."

He nodded, fear winding through his soul. What had he done? There was a lingering fog of lust that had banished all the caution he knew he should have. The guilt for having joined the enemy.

"I'm not the enemy, my boy. Does anyone blame a lion for killing and feeding upon a gazelle?"

"No, of course not. But—"

"I want to rid the earth of scum like Billy," he said, waving a claw at the corpse. "And I must eat, same as you or anyone. As a purebred Unseelie, I must have animal flesh and blood to survive, and if that means occasionally removing a violent, dangerous man such as this from the earth in the process, why is that wrong?"

He couldn't argue that point. Billy had been a mother-fucker. And now he was food. Probably the only thing he'd ever been useful for.

"What now?" he asked. "Will I live here with you?" The idea suddenly made him anxious. The Pack guys were his friends, too—well, except Aric. Most of them had made him welcome. Right?

"Not yet. You must go back to your compound. For now, it is where you can help me the most. You're going to practice the arts among them, beginning tomorrow."

"I won't hurt them," he said, body tensing. "Any of them."

Malik sighed. "Don't fight the darkness, pet. You can't win, now that you've accepted my bond. And why would you want to? Can't you feel the power flooding you, stroking your cock like a woman's lips? The ecstasy will only get better once you embrace our bond and let go of your previous inhibitions."

He swallowed a moan. "What do I do?"

"Good boy," he praised. "First, tell no one of our association. Practice on one of your teammates. Start small. Find a weakness and exploit it, discreetly. They mustn't suspect you're behind the incident. You'll be surprised by how wonderful it feels to wield such a weapon."

"And then?"

"Do as I say and you'll come to me again soon. I will tell you what to do next, after you've begun to enjoy exercising your superior gifts over the others."

"That's all?"

"For now. Eager already?"

He looked away, unable to answer. Too late, he was afraid of what he'd allowed to be set in motion. But the lure was so great, he didn't know how to break free. Wasn't sure he wanted to. But there was one certainty he had to make clear.

"I won't hurt Mackenzie. Ever," he said in a low, dangerous tone. "She's mine, and I'll kill you and me both before that happens."

The Unseelie smiled, showing off his fangs. "Have the woman. What do I care? She's merely a human and is nothing to my plans any longer, one way or the other."

"Fine."

With that settled, Malik shifted back into the form of an urbane, handsome man. He was once again fully clothed and one would never know he was anything but what he appeared to be. Unless they saw his half-eaten dinner hanging sightless in the middle of the room.

Together they went back upstairs, where they quietly shared one more glass of Cognac before Kalen took his leave in the wee hours of the morning.

Shifting into his panther, he ran back toward the compound. One thing Malik was correct about—the darkness sang in his veins. Demanded completion. Finding a nice grassy spot under the moonlight, he skidded to a stop and shifted back to a man. On his knees, he fisted his erect, aching cock and gave it a pump.

And another. Arching his back, he spread his knees and gave himself over to the night. To the heady pleasure that had needed release for the past couple of hours. His palm slid over smooth skin, electrifying his nerve endings. Up to the spongy head, weeping at the slit. Down to the base of his cock.

The other hand massaged his balls, playing with them. They tightened, drew upward. He had to come. Needed something more.

The second he imagined Mackenzie's mouth sliding along his shaft, sucking and licking, he was lost. With a shout he came, spurting ropy white streams onto the cool ground until he was spent and exhausted.

Finally, he'd be able to sleep. And he'd need plenty.

You're going to be the greatest Sorcerer the world has ever known, your power beyond comprehension.

Tomorrow he'd work on making his grandmother's prediction come true.

Mac knew there was something different about Kalen the second she spotted him leaning against the wall of the rec room. She just couldn't put her finger on what.

His animal form, a black panther, was typically secondary to his being a Sorcerer, but today he seemed even more catlike than usual. He rested his shoulder against the wall, arms crossed, watching some of the others. Aric and Zander were off to the side, playing a noisy game of foosball. Jax and Hammer were playing a war game on the Wii, and Sariel, Kira, Rowan, and Micah were watching a ghost-hunting reality television show they couldn't seem to get enough of.

And Kalen observed them all, the expression on his face almost . . . sly. Maybe even insolent. The sight chilled her, though it could be her imagination. She hoped it was. It could be that he was still smarting from the incident in the dining room last evening. He'd never seemed like the type to carry a grudge, but how well did she really know him, beyond a shared adventure and a hot night at the Wall-Banger Motel?

Yeah, she *so* wasn't going to think about that. Not when she had much bigger worries. Or little worries, like the one currently giving her awful morning sickness.

Lingering in the doorway, she figured she should just leave and find somewhere else to relax on her break. But that plan went out the window when Kalen's eyes met hers and he grinned, beckoning her to him with one finger.

Taken aback, she paused. Communication between them had been strained at best since he'd given her the brush-off. And now he seemed relaxed, the glitter in his jade green eyes almost playful. Composing her expression into what she hoped was cool indifference, she walked over to him.

"How's Sariel?" he asked, eyeing her.

Inside, she deflated some. A part of her had hoped he wanted to talk about mending their fences, stupid as that seemed. She took a breath, shoving down the disappointment. "His recovery is progressing slowly. He's still not eating very well, but other than that, he should be up and around in a few days."

"Do you think he would see me? I have some apologizing to do." He sounded sincere.

"I don't know, but I could ask him for you if you would like."

"I would, thank you."

"Just don't get your hopes up. He's been withdrawn since Beryl attacked him, and I doubt you're his favorite person at the moment."

He winced. "Ouch. I deserved that, I guess."

"You *guess*?" She frowned at Kalen and peered into his eyes. "Are you all right?"

"Sure, honey. Why do you ask?"

Gritting her teeth, she resisted the urge to shout not to call her pet names after what had transpired between them. After he'd walked away and broken her heart. Instead, she forced herself to think like a doctor and studied his eyes. They weren't right. "Your pupils are dilated."

"So?"

"Blown pupils are typically a sign of illness, concussion, or drug use. Have you hit your head? Are you sick?"

"Nah. Been smoking weed in my room." He winked. "Ya caught me."

She smacked his arm as he laughed. "That's not funny, Kalen. I want you to come with me to the infirmary and let me give you a checkup."

"I have a better idea—have lunch with me instead."

"What?" Her traitorous heart skipped a beat. "You've barely acknowledged my presence lately, and now you want to hang out in the cafeteria?"

"No. I want to take you to lunch. You know, in a real

restaurant in town, where we can sit and talk without two dozen of our well-meaning friends listening to every word."

Glancing around the room, she spotted several of those well-meaning friends quickly go back to pretending not to eavesdrop. "I don't know if that's a great idea."

"Please?" He affected a sexy pout.

Damn him for being so irresistible. "Checkup, *then* lunch. It's that or no deal."

"You drive a hard bargain, lady." He gave her a mock glare. "Fine. Poke at me or whatever. Then we'll go eat."

"I'm still not sure that's a good idea. The going out part."

"But you're going to do it anyway." Now he looked smug.

She wanted to smack him again. "Don't push your luck. Come on."

On the way to the infirmary, she did her best not to overtly ogle him. She had a weakness for guys that looked like rock stars, and even though he'd probably never touched an electric guitar in his life, the man totally did it for her.

On impulse, she asked, "Did you ever play in a rock band?"

He cut her a piercing look. "I've told you about my parents. They treated me like shit and threw me out on my ass. You think they forked over the cash for a guitar and lessons?"

She flushed in embarrassment. "No, but a lot of guys who are now well-known started with nothing. I just wondered, that's all."

They walked for a few moments before he responded. "Like a lot of kids, I had big dreams like that. Maybe if I'd pursued music and given it everything I had, I would've succeeded. Or maybe not. Some things aren't meant to be."

"And some things are, like you ending up here, being a part of the team."

He rolled his shoulders in what might've been a shrug. "Sure. Lucky me, huh?"

"Most of the Pack count themselves lucky to be here, yes," she said pointedly.

"You positive about that?"

"I know these men, so yes, I'm positive. Where is this coming from? You're in a weird mood today."

He flashed her a disarming smile. "Ignore me. Must be lack of sleep from last night."

"How often is that happening?"

"A night here and there. No big deal."

"I'll be the judge of that."

"Yes, ma'am."

"Where the hell is the sarcasm in your tone coming from? If I didn't know better, I'd swear you and Aric switched bodies."

"Do me a favor and don't compare me to him," he said curtly. "We're nothing alike."

"Then drop the crap and be yourself."

"I'm not sure I know what that means."

"I think you do, but if you insist on playing dumb, there isn't much I can do about it."

"Who says I'm playing? I don't even have a high school diploma."

"Is that another attempt to make me feel sorry for you?" So he didn't have to know it worked, she injected as much sternness into her voice as she could.

"Nope. Just sayin'."

Apparently she wasn't going to get any satisfactory answers. The jerk was enjoying baiting her way too much. So she decided to keep her end of the conversation strictly professional for the time being. If he wanted to have a meaningful talk at lunch, then he was going to have to work at it.

Suppressing a frustrated sigh, she led him past Noah at the reception desk. At seeing Kalen with her, the nurse gave her a look of concern, but she nodded to let him know all was well—and then hoped that was the case.

Ushering him into an exam room, she closed the door. "Up on the table, please."

Turning his backside to it, he hoisted himself up and parked his butt on the crinkly paper. Hands on his jeans-clad thighs, he arched a dark brow and grinned. "Have your way with me, Doc."

It was on the tip of her tongue to say, "Been there, got the reminder" but she refrained. Just barely. Instead she grabbed a blood pressure cuff and wrapped it around his biceps. Giving the bulb a series of pumps, she got the reading.

"Blood pressure is a bit high," she said. "Are you having any headaches, dizziness, anything of concern?"

"No, nothing."

Replacing the cuff on its wall hook, she removed a wooden stick from the jar on the counter. "Say *ah*."

"Ahhh."

Using her penlight, she peered into his throat. "No redness." She tossed the stick into the trash.

Next she checked how well he tracked her finger

with his eyes, then used a small rubber mallet to test his reflexes. "All normal on both counts, but I'd like to have Noah come draw some blood for a few tests—"

"No!" he barked, the word popping like a gunshot in the room. The sharp edge of panic flashed across his face before he made a visible effort to get it under control. "That's completely unnecessary. I'm healthy as a horse."

Startled by his outburst, she said evenly, "Then it shouldn't matter if we take a bit of blood to make sure."

"Not gonna happen. Did I ever mention I don't like needles?" Sliding off the table, he headed for the door. "You examined me, I'm great, and we're done. Ready for lunch?"

She was tempted to back out, for many reasons. But she was curious about what was going on with him. If she was honest, she was more than a little concerned, too. Could he be starting to feel sick from not mating with her? If so, he wasn't showing symptoms. As much as it worried her and went against her code as a doctor, it was probably best to let the other tests wait for now. Though she'd get that blood from him eventually. One way or another.

"All right. Let me get my purse."

"No argument from you about not poking on me anymore?"

"Would it do any good?"

"Probably not."

"Well, there you are."

She didn't miss the relief that briefly crossed his face as they left the exam room, and she wondered what he had to hide. Whatever it was, it must be the reason for his blown pupils. Was he doing drugs? Anything was possible, though she hated to think the worst. One thing she knew for sure—dilated pupils were a physical response indicating a possibly serious problem. No way around that.

After fetching her purse, she slung the strap over her shoulder and met him in the hallway. Together they walked back through the lobby.

"Noah, would you tell Melina I'll be gone for a couple of hours? Kalen's taking me out to lunch."

The blond made a face. "Must be nice."

"That's why I'm the boss of you."

Noah laughed. "Good point. At least it's quiet today—" He slapped a hand over his mouth. Every nurse and doctor knew better than to jinx a good shift with the Q word. "Sorry!"

"As long as karma bitch-slaps you and not me, it's fine." Giving him a little wave, she left, Kalen at her side. "Where to?"

"Not the Grizzly," he said thoughtfully.

"God, no! Our last time there didn't turn out so well."

"How about Italian? There's a great hole-in-the-wall place in Cody that has awesome spaghetti. I found it when I first hit town and had a few bucks in my pocket."

"Sounds good. I haven't had Italian in ages." Her stomach rumbled, reminding her she'd tossed breakfast after a nasty bout of morning sickness. She just prayed her body cooperated now that the nausea seemed to have settled for the day.

"Do you mind driving?"

"What, Nick still won't let you borrow another SUV?" she teased.

"After I let the last one I took get ripped up by a Sluagh? Fat chance. He won't even let me finish asking before he shouts no."

"Well, that's not fair. The damage wasn't really your fault." He made a disgruntled noise and she thought a second. "You can buy your own wheels now that you have a paying job with the team."

"I will eventually. Soon as I save more for a down payment. Maybe I'll get something cool like a Mustang Boss 302, fully loaded."

He sounded so excited, she couldn't help but smile. "Don't shoot big or anything."

"Of course not."

By the time they got into her car, Mac driving, some of the strange tension between them had lessened quite a bit. Glancing over at him, she noticed that vibe of malice, or whatever it was, that she had detected in the rec room seemed to have vanished. He looked like Kalen again, green eyes clear, face more relaxed.

But as he met her gaze and returned her smile, she saw his pupils were still much too large. Opting not to mention it again until later, she put her car in drive and started down the long road leading away from the compound.

There would be time enough to figure out what was going on with him.

And she wouldn't stop until she learned his secrets.

Five

"Wine?"

Mac shook her head. "I'd love a glass, but I'd better not while I still have half a day of work ahead of me."

"You're such a good girl, aren't you? Never do anything wild or spontaneous?"

She could think of *one* time. However, she opted not to go there in spite of his obvious baiting. "Not too often. I guess that's a hazard of being a general's daughter."

"I imagine he was tough."

"*Is* tough. You have no idea." She winced inwardly, thinking of how in the hell she was going to break the news of her pregnancy to her dad. Though she'd love to call him on the phone, blurt the news, and hang up, that wasn't going to cut it. Not for Jarrod Grant. He'd expect his daughter to face him like a woman, not hide like a kid.

That meant a flight out to visit him. Soon.

"Hey, where'd you go?" Kalen asked, breaking into her gloomy thoughts.

"Just thinking about Dad." That was no lie. "Being raised by him was no picnic, but he's a good father and a great man. I learned everything I know from him."

"You love him," he said, his tone wistful.

"More than anything."

Except this child. Your child.

"You're lucky to have even one parent who dotes on you. I have two, if they're still alive, and they're just about as worthless as two people can be. If they aren't already dead, I'd love to kill them both for the sheer pleasure of doing it."

She stared at him, taken aback. He'd never spoken against them outright before, and with such anger. "That's not a healthy emotion to live with," she said softly. "Have you seen a counselor?"

He returned her stare, started to deny it. "When the hell would I— Hold up. Yeah. On second thought, I guess you could say I am, in a manner of speaking. Someone who's helping me quite a bit, making sure I never feel like a victim again."

She paused. "Who are you seeing? Maybe I know the doctor."

"Didn't say it was a doctor, did I?"

There it was again. A terrible shadow on his face and in his eyes, a certain unkind vibe that sent a nasty shiver down her spine. Who could it be? Was he seeing another woman? Fucking away his pain at night when he couldn't sleep?

The awful nausea returned.

"You said you were raised by your dad. What happened to your mom?" he asked, changing the subject.

Thankfully he seemed oblivious to her upsetting thoughts.

"She died of leukemia when I was ten."

"I'm sorry." His eyes softened.

"Thanks. It was hard on us, especially him. My memories of her are distant now, but not so for him. She was the love of his life. My dad was never the same, and he never remarried. He threw himself into moving up in the ranks in the Navy, but he loved me and made sure I knew it."

The waitress came and took their orders, lingering longer and smiling more at Kalen than was strictly necessary. Mac tried not to bristle. After she moved off, Kalen went on, probing curiously into Mac's past.

"How the heck did your dad raise you alone and still have the time to become a general?"

"I stayed with my aunt—his older sister, Gena— whenever he was deployed. She was able to do all the mothering he couldn't, get me through the painful teen years when a girl needs a strong female in her life. He was gone less and less as the years went by, and now he's pretty much a fixture in Washington."

"Do you keep in touch with your aunt?"

"She passed away two years ago. Heart attack at age fifty-six." Studying her water glass, she swallowed against the sudden burn in her throat. "In many ways, she was my mother. She's the one I remember being there through all the skinned knees, awkward growing pains, boyfriend drama, and fights with best friends. She's the one who took me shopping for my prom dress, styled my hair, took pictures when my date showed up. . . . Losing her was the saddest day of my life."

One of Kalen's hands reached across the table and covered hers. "You've had your share of loss. I'd give anything to change that for you, but I'm a Sorcerer, not a god."

"I appreciate the sentiment, more than you know."

He paused. "So, did you always want to be a doctor?"

"Since I was a kid. I used to make dad and Aunt Gena sit for hours while I 'fixed' them with my plastic doctor kit. It would be years before I realized that you can't fix everyone, no matter how hard you try." Crap, she hadn't meant to say that last part. And sure enough, his curiosity was further piqued.

"Yesterday you asked me if I ever wondered why you left a perfectly good practice, came way out here in the middle of Bumfuck, and devoted yourself to studying paranormal creatures. And the answer is yes, I do wonder."

His hand was warm and comforting on hers, his expression open and encouraging. Unlike the tense, smirking stranger from earlier, *this* man cared. This was the man who held her heart.

She took a deep breath. "I suppose it doesn't make a difference telling you, since you could just Google my name and easily get the story."

"I'll do that if it's better for you not to talk about it."

"No, that's okay," she said, giving him a tremulous smile. "I was a psychologist, and a pretty good one, I thought. My practice was successful and I was content, if not totally happy and fulfilled."

"No boyfriend?" he probed.

"No one serious. I was open to finding someone special, but it was just so hard with me being married to my career. My practice was going so well, I got caught up in complacency. Forgot exactly who I was dealing with—people with problems. Serious ones. A couple of my patients were extremely disturbed, but I wasn't too worried. I was *good*, you know?" He didn't miss the self-deprecation in her tone.

"What happened?"

"I was attacked by a patient, in my office," she whispered. The memory still chilled her to the bone. "There was no warning. One moment we were having a nice conversation and he appeared fine, and the next he'd knocked me out of my chair, pinned me to the floor, and almost strangled me to death."

"My God," Kalen said hoarsely, eyes wide. "How did you manage to fight him off?"

"I didn't. I lost consciousness, and as I did, I believed I was dead. I thought of my dad and how grief-stricken he'd be to lose his only child, especially like that. Then I was gone. I woke up in the hospital and learned that my secretary had heard the commotion and run in to investigate. She and a couple of patients from the waiting room subdued the man and called for help."

"Jesus Christ." His face reflected the horror she had felt back then. "I can't imagine how terrible that must've been for you."

"It was. I never returned to private practice. Just the idea of being responsible for someone else's mental health, having all of that suppressed rage explode at me again . . . I couldn't deal with it, so I ran. Back to school to become a physician's assistant, and then my dad helped me get the plum assignment at the compound when it opened, just as you guessed."

He flushed. "I apologize. I didn't mean to imply you

didn't deserve your position or that you had it easy. I was just being a dick."

"Yeah, you were. But I accept." She gave him a small smile, letting him know he was off the hook. Almost. "So, why were you being mean?"

"It's complicated," he said, gaze dropping to the table.

Just then the waitress returned with their food and set down the plates, giving Kalen a thorough once-over as she did. "Anything else I can do for you?"

Mac's blood pressure rose, anger simmering.

But he barely glanced at the woman, then shook his head and answered politely. "No, thanks."

Taking her cue, the waitress left to see about other customers. The tension in Mac drained as quickly as it had come after seeing the girl devour him with her eyes. Maybe it was ridiculous to be jealous of a man who'd rejected her, but Mac couldn't help how she felt. The way her hormones were starting to kick in, a certain Sorcerer was damned lucky he hadn't responded to the bimbo.

"Mackenzie? Hey, where'd you go?"

"Hmm? Oh, sorry. Just thinking."

"About?"

"You. Gonna let me in on why you've been such a jerk to me lately?"

"Ouch." He winced. "I *am* sorry, for what it's worth."

"If the attitude is simply to keep me from stalking you or something, you can relax. I haven't been following you around begging you to change your mind, and I won't." Not that she didn't long to leave her pride in the dirt and do just that.

"I'm the one who should be begging for a second

chance," he said quietly. "Are you gonna make me do that? Should I get on my knees?"

She stopped twirling her spaghetti and her heart lurched. "What?"

"I got scared and I ran from you. I've fucked up in so many ways, you can't imagine." Setting down his fork, he rested both elbows on the table, clenching his hands.

"Why should I believe you?" she asked, barely managing to keep her voice steady. What she wanted to do was grab him, drag his body across the table, and kiss him until he passed out from lack of oxygen. Common sense told her to use a bit more restraint.

"You shouldn't. I'm a horrible prospect, honey."

"Because of your past? You *know* I would never hold that against you. That's not who I am." She touched his hand. "You did what you had to do in order to survive."

"It's not the past I'm worried about." His expression was agonized. "I've done something I'm so afraid I can't take back. I'm up against a force I don't know if I can fight, much less win."

"Tell me."

"I . . ." His inner struggle waged war on his face, and his eyes were bleak. "I went—" Suddenly he grabbed his head, grimacing in pain.

"Kalen, what's wrong?" she asked in a low voice, glancing around to make sure nobody else had noticed.

After a few quick, shallow breaths, he lowered his hands. His skin was pale and he looked shaken. "I can't tell you. He won't let me."

Fear washed through her like ice water. "Who? Malik?"

With apparent reluctance, he nodded. "Yes."

Beginning to connect the dots, she gripped the edge of the table. "This is the one who's giving you *meaningful* counsel, helping you feel *empowered*?" she asked in a low voice. At his miserable nod, the dread intensified. "What's this bullshit about him not *letting* you tell? What has he done to you?"

"I can't explain right now. I wish I could."

"Can't or won't?" Strained silence was her answer. "Is this the part where you ask me to trust you?"

"I can't ask anything of you, honey. But I'm hoping you do."

"Why should I?"

"Because without you—" With a sharp intake of breath, he stood abruptly, holding a hand under his nose. "Sorry. Be right back."

Mac stared after him as he retreated, presumably in the direction of the men's restroom. Slumping back in her seat, she let out a sigh and tried to calm her racing pulse. Malik was sinking his claws deeper into Kalen every day, and her Sorcerer was losing ground. This was bad. So very, very bad. Did Nick know how far the alliance had gotten between the two of them? He must have some idea. Would he follow through with his threat to execute Kalen? She couldn't bear thinking about that.

What had Kalen been about to say about why she should trust him, give him another chance? Two things she was almost certain of—Malik had stopped him. And if he had, the Unseelie must've had a good reason. That meant there was something specific the creep didn't want her to know.

Why not simply stop Kalen from being with her at

all? Now that he had Kalen, perhaps Malik didn't consider her to be a big enough threat to warrant denying his new apprentice a bit of pleasure.

"That's just sick," she muttered, tracing the beads of moisture on her water glass.

Recalling the night she'd spent with Kalen a few weeks ago, when the horrible Unseelie had come to her in a nightmare and attempted to sway her to his side, haunted her a lot these days. Because now she understood that it had been a ruse to get the Sorcerer to part with his amulet, to give it to Mac for her protection.

Leaving him vulnerable to Malik's twisted desires.

Why Kalen? He couldn't be the only powerful magic user in the universe. Why did he, in particular, matter so much to the Unseelie? Mac didn't believe Malik's choice was random.

She shouldn't care about Kalen's problems after the way he'd dropped her and walked away. But his problems were the whole team's, and now hers as well.

Okay, if she was honest with herself, concern for the rest of the Pack wasn't the only reason she cared. If she was a lesser person—or maybe a smarter person— she might walk away from *him*. Leave him to his fate.

But he was the father of their child. The more she got to know him, the more clearly she could see the kind of man he could be—*would* be—when he finally found his center. His inner peace. The wonderful lover and friend he could be as well.

She remembered how passionately he'd made love to her. There had been no deception in his touch, only pure need. That night, the man who'd held her close had been a man born to love. A man who'd had so little of it given to him in his life.

Glancing up, she spotted him returning, his gait slow and easy, like his half smile when he saw her watching. A wave of fierce protectiveness took her breath away and she knew one thing—

She was going to be the woman to give this man the love he deserved.

And she'd pray like hell the Sorcerer didn't crush her trust in his fist.

Kalen hurried to the men's room and ducked inside, trying to stem the flow of blood running from his nose. His head hurt so goddamned bad, it was like an ice pick being stabbed right through his temple and into his brain.

Leaning over the sink, he turned on the water. His stomach lurched as he watched the blood swirl down the drain. Ironic that he could kill a dozen Sluagh and not bat an eyelash over the slimy gore, but a nosebleed made him queasy. Not that the stabbing in his head helped.

"Son of a bitch," he rasped. Cupping the running water, he splashed his face, rinsing until the liquid became clear. Gradually the spike driving through his skull withdrew, leaving him shaken. Tired. Bracing his palms on the counter, he sucked in deep breaths.

You will not tell your woman, my boy. Not until our plan is well in motion. She is too soft to understand what must be done and why.

"You and your damned world domination," he hissed, anger at himself boiling his blood. He should've been stronger. Put up more resistance against Malik's evil. "What have I sold my soul for, you bastard? Just so you can rule the world, murdering anyone who resists you?"

He received no answer. But he did hear a shuffle to his right, and when he glanced around, he almost groaned to see a man standing uncertainly in the doorway, eyeing him as though he'd lost his mind. Fuck.

"Sorry," Kalen muttered, heading for the exit. "Not feeling so good, ya know?"

The guy gave him a wan smile. "Hey, it happens."

Brushing past him, Kalen pushed out into the restaurant again, cursing the man's rotten timing. He probably thought Kalen was on drugs, or worse.

What do you care for the opinion of some weak human? Today he might sneer, but he is a lesser being. After we've taken control of the earth, he'll get on his knees and vow his allegiance to us both, or he'll die.

"Shut up," he said under his breath.

Don't forget how much you'll savor bringing low all of those who've done you grievous wrong in the past. Remember how your heart gladdened to see Billy suffer for his terrible transgressions, and know that the pleasure will be tenfold when justice is delivered by your own hand.

The hypnotic voice lulled him, the lust for power snaking through his groin. An image was thrust into his head of the redneck tormenting his family. Then getting his just desserts. Yeah, he'd make sure assholes like that never hurt anyone else. God, it would feel so good to wrap his hands around that fat neck and—

"Kalen!"

Someone gave him a gentle shake, and he realized that fingers were lightly gripping his arm. Blinking, he found himself staring into Mac's worried face. "I'm sorry, what?"

"Where did you go this time? I called your name twice."

Suddenly he saw that he was standing in the middle of the restaurant like a statue, a few feet from their table. Jesus, he must look like a crazy person to everyone there. He noted a handful of curious stares. Raising his voice a little, he gave a short laugh and said for the benefit of those nearby, "Did you? Must've zoned out. I was trying to remember if I left my cell phone in the bathroom." He made a show of patting his pockets. "I can't find—oh, wait. Here it is. Stupid, huh?"

Her expression told him she knew what he was doing, but she didn't pursue it with others in earshot. Taking his hand, she led him back to their table. "Do you want dessert?"

"Not unless you do. Whatever you want, honey."

"Nah, I'm good."

He needed out of there. The atmosphere was abruptly claustrophobic and he had to vamoose, *now*. Not away from Mackenzie, but out of the building. Waving over their waitress, he mustered polite calm and requested the bill. They waited in silence, eyeing each other until it came and he paid, temporarily avoiding the elephant in the room.

Outside, Mackenzie took his hand as they walked to the car. "Okay, tell me what happened in there. Why did you rush to the restroom?"

"Nosebleed."

"Malik?" Kalen nodded, and her blue eyes went steely. "He did that to shut you up, to stop you from telling me you went to see him last night, didn't he? That bastard! We're going to find a way to beat him, sweetie. You just hang on. Do you hear me?"

"Yeah." Christ, he hoped she was right.

And that was when he realized that the Unseelie

wasn't in his head. That the awful dark thirst for blood and vengeance seemed to have lifted for the time being. "He's gone. I don't feel him anymore."

"For good?" At his look, her spark of enthusiasm vanished. "Of course not. That would be too easy."

"It's a ray of hope, anyway." However thin.

He was sure the reprieve now, and earlier in the car, had to do with the doc. He just had to figure out how, specifically. He mulled it over as his date pulled from the parking lot and onto the road, and for several minutes afterward. Until her sweet scent caught his attention as it had on the way to the restaurant.

Vanilla and roses. That was the tantalizing aroma making his senses tingle and his cock fill. In addition, the scent seemed deeper than before, richer somehow. His panther awakened, stretching, purring in joy at the familiar scent. The beast welcomed it and yearned to get close to the amazing presence of its mate once again.

Mate?

Quickly he envisioned a wall of solid steel around him, desperately trying to seal his thoughts from Malik.

No. She couldn't be his mate. Could she? Why had that word popped into his head? How could he know for sure? He'd seen what had happened to Jax and Aric when they'd met their mates—they'd gotten sicker until it was either claim their mates or die. But that hadn't happened to Kalen. He felt completely fine—well, other than Malik's horrible influence.

Admittedly, as a Sorcerer he was different. So his panther might be wrong about the mate thing.

Inside, it growled in displeasure at the direction of

his thoughts. Never had his other half been so vocal, so certain of what he wanted. His cat strained insistently, longing to shift, to rub his scent all over the woman, bite her, mark her for all to see. Kalen imagined doing just that, with his cock buried deep inside her warm, wet sheath. For the first time, instead of having to summon his panther, Kalen had to concentrate to hold him back.

The beast roared and he channeled his energy into soothing it. Imagining a pool of clear blue surrounded by a tropical oasis, he poured a stream of calming light over his cat until it subsided, curling up again with a huff of annoyance. Still not satisfied in its wants, but tame once more.

"You sure you're all right?" she asked.

He'd been off in his head again, and she'd been studying him the whole time. What did she see when she looked at him? A mess not worth keeping? He shifted uncomfortably. "I am now."

"Is that the first time that's happened?" She gestured to his face in general.

He nodded. "Yeah. Seems like he's got a trick or three up his sleeve to keep me in line."

"Are you going to talk to Nick about this and about last night?" Mackenzie asked softly.

"I'm going to try. And hope he doesn't shoot me for real."

"That's not funny."

"Wasn't meant to be."

"Do you want me to go with you to see him?"

Not having to face the boss alone was tempting. But the urge to protect her from the ugly reality of his situation was stronger—though it might be far too late. "I appreciate the moral support, but I'd better talk to him alone."

"Okay. Just know the offer stands."

"Thanks. That's more than I deserve from you."

"Oh, I don't know about that." A soft, secretive smile curved her lips.

A spark of light beamed through the gloom. "So you're not going to make me beg for another chance? You never did answer me, you know."

"No, I didn't," she agreed, sobering some. "To be honest, I'm not sure how to answer because I don't know where this sudden change of heart is coming from."

"It may seem like it's coming from nowhere to you, but it's not sudden for me," he admitted, gut churning. "I didn't want to walk away in the first place. I just . . . I know I'm about the worst thing that could ever happen to you, especially right now. But I can't stop wanting you."

The words came out raw, as if scraped with sandpaper. At least they were on the table, whatever she might decide. God, he was so afraid of the horror he could bring into her life. He was even more afraid of living his alone, with nothing but the temptation of evil for company.

"Wanting isn't the same as needing," she said softly. Her tone was contemplative rather than accusing. "Anyone can *want* something they don't *need*, or that isn't good for them."

He couldn't refute that, so he didn't try.

Mackenzie fell silent, brow furrowed in thought as she drove. Kalen wondered if she thought less of him because of his choice of wording, but what he knew about women and how their brains worked wouldn't fill the toes of his boots.

He'd been so lost in pondering the dilemma of the doc that it took him a few moments to realize she'd turned off the main highway and onto a dirt and gravel road that was little better than a path beaten out of the weeds.

"Um, where are we going?"

"You'll see."

"Finally decide to just take me out and shoot me yourself? Save Nick the trouble?"

"You're awfully preoccupied with being shot."

Because I deserve it. "Not really. Just curious about where you're taking me."

With a quick smile, she guided the car down the path, until at last it ended at a grassy clearing. Nearby was a creek and beyond that, a stand of trees where the forest resumed on the other side. The spot was beautiful, serene, and he told her so.

"This is gorgeous. It looks real peaceful."

She shrugged, but appeared pleased that he liked it. "That's why I come here sometimes, just to think. I've even brought a small picnic for one a couple of times, complete with a bottle of wine."

That seemed sort of lonely and sad, but he could hardly cast stones in the loner department, so he kept his opinion to himself. "What about your friends I met at the bar? You haven't brought them out here?"

"Amy and Shannon? No, they're good friends, but this place is mine."

"But you brought me," he pointed out, puzzled. "Why me and not them?"

"Because it's the sort of place you share with somebody special," she said, fixing him with those pretty blue eyes.

"Oh." His throat threatened to close up nice and tight. "Nobody's ever called me that, except maybe Grandma." Of course, that hadn't been the same at all.

Reaching out, she cupped his cheek. He couldn't help but lean in to her touch as she stroked, his cat stretching and purring in contentment.

"You are special," she said quietly, eyes growing moist. "You're amazing, talented, smart, and caring. And oh yeah, drop-dead gorgeous, too. You should be told those things every day of your life, and I'm sorry no one has until now."

Before he could respond, she leaned toward him, lips pressing against his. The touch was electric, shooting a bolt of sheer bliss through every cell in his body. Her lips were soft, gentle, searching. He opened at her insistence, met her questing tongue with his own, tasted her sweetness.

There had been no kisses in his life. No joy until Mackenzie. He couldn't walk away again. He wasn't that strong.

When at last they broke apart, she gave him a soft smile. "How about we go for a walk?"

"Sounds good," he managed.

Getting out, they met at the front of the car and automatically joined hands. He let her lead them across the clearing and simply appreciated the scenery—mostly the woman at his side. Just her presence was a balm to his troubled soul and he realized that though he'd forgotten to check his mental shields against Malik in the last few minutes, all was still calm in his head. He had no doubt she was the reason.

At the opposite end of the clearing, under the shade of the trees, was a creek. It wasn't wide, just a few feet across, and as they approached he saw it wasn't more than shin-deep. "Great spot. I can see why you like to come here."

"Isn't it beautiful? I like to sit on that grassy spot under the trees and just listen to the water, the birds, whatever else is moving. Day music, I call it. The sounds are much different than at night."

His protective streak reared its head. "You don't come out here at night, I hope?"

"No, silly." She patted his chest. "I'm not *that* stupid."

"Of course not. I just want you to be safe." Well, that was the mother of all ironies, considering she was with probably the most dangerous person around.

"I am. Don't worry, I never venture into the forest at night alone, unlike your Pack brothers when they have to let their wolves loose. Come on."

Tugging at his hand, she led him to her preferred spot, which was spongy and comfortable. Putting his back to a tree, he pulled her to sit between his spread legs, her back to his front. After giving him a look of surprise, and a bit of pleasure, he thought, she settled in and relaxed against him. He absolutely loved her warmth against him, her body pliant and trusting in his arms.

"I take it we're playing hooky this afternoon?" he murmured in her ear, wrapping his arms around her middle.

"Mmm. For a little while, if that's all right with you."

"More than. I'm a *play hooky* kind of guy."

"Why doesn't that surprise me?"

He heard the teasing in her voice and began to nibble on the shell of her ear. "It shouldn't. You knew I was a bad boy when you threw in with me."

"Is that what I've done?" she asked, shivering lightly as he nipped her neck.

"God, I hope so."

Flicking his tongue, he tasted her skin, the salty sweetness of her essence. His cat growled, loving that, ready to play. His cock hardened, lengthening to press along her butt and the small of her back. There was no way she didn't notice, but she remained relaxed, her body language letting him know that she was very much on board with his attentions.

Encouraged, he let his fingers inch under the hem of her blouse. For a few moments he savored the smoothness of her skin under the pads of his fingers. Her waist was trim, her belly flat. He explored her insy and she giggled some, wiggling in his arms. Chuckling, he let his hands roam to the flimsy fabric of her bra and hesitated. When she merely arched her back in invitation, he grazed the nipples, plucked them through the material until they were hard, tight peaks.

"Oh," she groaned, reaching around to cup the back of his head. She buried her fingers in his hair.

"Do you need me, baby?"

"Yes, please!"

That was all he needed to hear. Finding the front clasp of her bra, he deftly unhooked and parted the material. Her breasts spilled free and he sucked in a breath of appreciation as he let them fill his palms. Squeezing gently, he enjoyed her squirming against him and realized the mounds felt heavier, more full than they had been the one time they'd been together. But it could be his imagination.

"Spin around, baby."

He helped her maneuver so she sat straddling his lap, facing him. Before he could reach for her blouse, she stripped it off and tossed it aside, then slipped out of her bra. Her skin was creamy, flawless.

"You take my breath away," he said in a low voice. "You're so beautiful."

Bending, he tasted a dusky nipple, worried it carefully with his teeth. Moaning in pleasure, she buried her fingers in his hair and urged him on. He laved and suckled, first one nipple then the other, until she was writhing on his lap.

Reaching to the waist of her slacks, he hesitated and met her hungry gaze, asking silent permission. She nodded and he unbuttoned them, then helped her stand. Quickly, she shed her shoes, pants, and silky underwear. He stripped his shirt, boots, and jeans, then resumed his position on the grass, his erection pointed at the treetops.

He reached for her hand. "Come here and stand over me."

She took his hand and straddled him again, feet on either side of his thighs, and remained standing. Her look of eager excitement told him she knew what he was going to do and couldn't wait.

Neither could he. The first lick of her slit detonated his senses, sent an explosion of pure lust rocketing through his blood. There was nothing as fine as the taste of his woman on his tongue. Warm and wet. Inviting.

Prying her apart with his fingers, he laved her channel, getting as deep as possible. Tongue-fucked her as she pressed into his face, rubbing, needing more. He ate her, slow and easy, enjoying every second. As she made little sounds of ecstasy, he took himself in hand, spreading the seeping pre-cum around the head. After giving himself a few strokes, he couldn't wait any longer.

"On my lap, baby," he breathed. "Sit on my cock."

Kneeling, she positioned herself over him. Then, capturing his gaze with those gorgeous blue eyes, she lowered herself, sheathing him inch by inch. "Ah, shit! Good, honey. So damned good . . ."

Twining her arms around his neck, she gave him a feral look. "You like me fucking you like this, Sorcerer? Want me to milk your big cock so good your balls explode?"

Jesus! Who knew his baby had such a filthy mouth? Christ, he was a lucky bastard!

"Yes," he croaked. "Fuck me, honey. I'm all yours."

When she was seated, she began to rise and fall. As promised, she fucked him so fine, her pussy a hot, wet glove that stroked him from base to tip. Again and again. He let her control the pace, every aspect of their lovemaking. She quickened the tempo until she rode him hard, their bodies slapping in perfect rhythm, sticky with sweat, the pungent aroma of sex in the air.

His panther roared in pleasure, demanding that he sink his teeth into the vulnerable juncture of her neck. Especially when she tilted her head in what he believed was an unconscious gesture of submission.

Ours! Mate!

No. As much as he longed to bite and claim her, he couldn't do that without her agreeing to it. And it was much too soon for that, their relationship too new. Resisting his beast was the toughest thing he'd ever done, but somehow he won the battle.

Instead he lost himself in a red tide of desire and soon felt the familiar tightening of his balls, the quickening in his groin and the base of his spine that signaled impending orgasm. He came with a rush, slamming into her several times, pumping his seed on and on, filling her. Clasping him to her breast, she clutched at him as she found her peak as well and went over. Together they shuddered for long moments, until they clung to each other, replete.

He kissed her moist temple. "That was amazing, just like you. Thank you."

"Likewise."

Sitting back so he could see her face, he grinned at her smug expression. "Satisfied?"

"Very!"

"When did you get such a naughty vocabulary, lady?"

"The potential was always there, but it's just how you affect me, I suppose. You bring out my inner slut." She winked.

"Damn, now I *do* feel lucky!" Laughing, she eased off his lap. His softened dick slipped out of its cozy home and he winced at the mess. "I think a shower is in order for both of us."

"I think you're right. Was that an invitation?"

"Are you kidding? You can soap my back anytime you want."

"Well, what are we waiting for?"

As they dressed and gathered their clothes, Kalen smiled at this cool, playful side of Mackenzie's nature.

He loved it. He tried to recall a time when he'd felt lighter. Happier. Not in years had he felt this way, and he wished with all his heart that it could last.

A man could dream.

And he would, because dreams might be all he'd ever have.

Six

On the return drive, Mac went back and forth between cursing herself for a fool and basking in the sheer wonderment of making love with Kalen in her favorite spot.

Lord, that had been hot! No man had ever affected her the way he did, made her long to crawl under his skin and stay there. Made her need to hold him, feel his body moving against hers, possessing her.

The man was trouble, but he was *her* trouble. And she was falling for him harder every day.

There had to be a way to help him defeat Malik, and they'd just keep searching until they found it. Kalen couldn't go on much longer being torn between good and evil. Earlier, when he'd shown such hatred for his parents and when he drifted off a couple of times with that blank expression on his face, he'd frightened her. The Unseelie was doing his best to control the Sorcerer, but the longer she and Kalen were together, the more that seemed to help him come back to himself.

She fervently prayed Malik didn't catch on.

Kalen's hand came to rest on her thigh, bringing her back to the present. He just left it there, and she liked the way his palm on her leg felt warm and sort of possessive, as though he couldn't bear not to touch some part of her even for a little bit.

Stealing a quick glance at him, she admired his profile. She loved how his black hair feathered around his handsome face and fell to his shoulders. It was a noble profile, she thought, his nose straight, brow arched, with a jaw that wasn't square, but curved. His lips were full, and his air of vulnerability was at war with his strength—both figuratively and literally.

And studying his many physical attributes was making her panties wet. Again.

Something about this man made it impossible for her to resist. She felt a very real pull toward him that wasn't just physical but seemed connected to her soul as well. Which could find her paddling up shit creek very soon. However, she knew to her depths that this man was worth the fight.

How sad that only one other person in his life—his grandmother—had ever believed the same.

"Mackenzie?"

"Hmm?"

"I was just thinking that it's been a few weeks since we were together that first time. . . ."

She nodded. "Yes. And?"

"And, um, I haven't had any symptoms," he said slowly. "You know, like Jax or Aric."

"No mating fever, no aches or pains. I'd noticed." Still, she had to quell a jolt of disappointment at hearing him acknowledge that fact aloud.

"You're the doctor. What do you think that means?" Anxiety colored his voice. "Are we not mates? And if we're not, why is my panther trying to shred me from the inside out because I didn't claim you today?"

At that, she cut him a quick glance, unable to mask her surprise. "He is?"

"Shit, yeah." He grimaced. "The fucker's done nothing but snarl at me for the past fifteen minutes."

A glimmer of happiness unfurled in her chest. "I don't know why, exactly. But we do know you're not like other shifters. You're a Sorcerer first, a shifter second. You're magic personified. Your physiology isn't like the others', so it stands to reason there will be differences between you and them."

"So we *could* be mates?"

Gripping the steering wheel, she cleared her throat, trying not to sound overly eager. "It's possible. You say your panther feels a pull toward me."

"Not just him, all of me," he said.

"How would you feel about us being Bondmates, considering you wanted to break things off before?"

"Jesus." He blew out a breath. "Didn't I make my feelings clear by now? I want you in my life. I shouldn't because of the mess I'm in, because I'm afraid of dragging you down with me, but I can't help myself any longer. Can you give me another shot?"

Could she? There was no question, really. She wanted him. And she had more than her own life and happiness to think about. She laid a hand over his, which was resting on her thigh.

"I'd like that. Let's take it one step at a time, okay?"

"Yes!" Leaning over, he planted a big kiss on her mouth, almost causing her to run off the road. "Thank you, honey. I'll do my best to make sure you don't regret it."

Straightening the car, she laughed. "Just don't run us into a tree before we get to find out."

"Sorry." The wink told her he wasn't very repentant.

The day might've gotten off to a rocky start, but the second half of their outing was definitely a home run. Now if they could keep him safe from the Unseelie asshole, things would be fantastic.

Back at the compound, they walked in together hand in hand. Mac wasn't sure being open about their relationship was the best thing for Kalen. She didn't want him getting more grief from Nick and the Pack than he already had. Like it or not, Kalen was one of the rookies, while the guys had known Mac for years. They were protective of her, and Kalen was still a wild card to them. They were wary of which side Kalen would be on when the dust settled.

Mac was worried too, but she'd sided with her lover. Come what may.

Of course, fate decreed that the first guy they should run into was Aric. The obnoxious redhead was coming toward them down a corridor when he spied their linked hands and stopped in his tracks.

"What the fuck? No way." His lip curled, showing a hint of lengthening fang. "This cannot be happening. Mac, girl, I'd hoped you had more sense than to get down with the Great and Powerful Oz here."

Kalen started forward, snarling. "Shut your stupid mouth, you mother—"

Mac stepped between them, pushing Kalen back. "Stop! I can handle this." Her lover fumed, glaring at Aric, but made no move to circumvent her. She frowned at the wolf. "What Kalen and I do is our business. Furthermore, I don't think you have a lot of room to cast stones when it comes to being smart about a relationship."

His face flushed. "What happened with me and Rowan wasn't the same thing at all!"

"Maybe, but that doesn't change the fact that you were a dumb jerk when you almost killed yourself trying to spare her from mating with you and yet she loves you anyway," Mac pointed out reasonably. "Go figure."

Aric's eyes widened. "Damn, that's harsh."

"But true." She sighed. "Besides, hasn't there been enough animosity between you two? I don't believe either of you even have a clue why you're being such asswipes to each other."

The men eyed each other, both clearly reluctant to give any ground on the matter. But Kalen nodded first, resignation in his tone when he spoke.

"You apologized to me when we had our scuffle yesterday, but I never extended the same courtesy. For what it's worth, I'm sorry. I'm not used to being part of a team, but I'm usually a bigger person than to attack someone with so little provocation."

Aric ran a hand through his hair. For a few seconds he seemed to struggle with his reply; then finally his admission emerged with obvious reluctance. "Don't, man. I know where your buttons are and I enjoyed the hell out of pushing them—at first. As stubborn an asshole as I am, even I can see when it's time to cease and desist. Feuding is bad for the team. What do ya say we bury the hatchet for good and move on?"

After a tense moment, Kalen slowly offered his hand. Aric hesitated, then took it.

"I'm still gonna call you kitty and Goth-boy," Aric said with a smirk. "Out of affection, of course."

"No problem, Red."

As they shook, gradual smiles crept across both their faces. Mac resisted the urge to roll her eyes. Men were such dumb-asses sometimes; it was a wonder the entire planet wasn't dead by now.

"Good luck to you two. In spite of my giving you a hard time, I mean that," Aric said seriously. He looked to Kalen. "Your brothers are all in this fight with you. Remember that when things get rough."

"I will." Kalen looked away.

Mac could tell her Sorcerer was touched. So was she. Leaning toward the redhead, she gave him a peck on the cheek. "Thank you. I guess you're not such a dumb jerk *all* the time."

"Gee, thanks." Snorting, Aric bade them farewell and continued in the direction of his living quarters.

When the red wolf was out of earshot, Kalen said, "Do you think he was sincere this time, or was he just trying to keep the peace with you?"

"I believed him. You should too."

"Why?"

"Aric's not an easy guy to get to know, or like, but he wouldn't have made the offer if he didn't mean it. I've known him for years, so trust me on this."

"All right. Then I'll go along, unless he proves me wrong." Stepping close, he stole a leisurely kiss, then released her with regret. "I hate to interrupt our afternoon, but I've got a couple of people to see."

"Nick?"

"For one. And then Sariel, if you think he's up to a visit from me."

"I'll ask him. But as one of his doctors, I have to tell you that if your visit upsets him and sets back his recovery in any way, you'll answer to me *and* Melina. It won't be pretty."

He grinned. "I hate to tell you, baby, but you're just not that scary. Doc Mallory on the other hand . . ." He gave an exaggerated shudder. "She probably flosses her teeth with her victims' bones."

Mac snorted. "And on that note, I'll see you later. Thanks for lunch—and dessert."

She turned and started for the infirmary. But not before she'd glimpsed the total satisfaction in his green eyes at her suggestive parting comment.

Looked as though she'd snagged herself a Sorcerer. Now the question was how to keep him safe.

Kalen's steps slowed as he approached Nick's office. His gut clenched in dread at the thought of what might await him on the other side.

Did the boss believe Kalen was beyond redemption at this point? No, he told himself. If he did, Kalen would be dead already. The man wasn't the type to delay justice. It would come swiftly and painlessly.

With that bit of hope bolstering his spirits, he knocked. The commander issued a firm order for whoever was there to come in.

Kalen poked his head around the corner. "Got a minute?"

Nick looked up from some paperwork on his desk and sat back, stretching. "For you, I've got five. Close the door and have a seat, and put a shield over your thoughts."

Kalen followed the first order, wiping his palms

nervously on his jeans. Concentrating, he turned his magic inward and searched for the wall he'd erected earlier between himself and Malik. He found it to be wavering some but in place—though how long he'd be successful was anyone's guess. He met Nick's gaze. "I'm ready."

The man studied him for a long moment, expression hard as stone. "I know where you went last night. What I don't know is all of what happened while you were there, so why don't you start at the beginning?"

"How much *do* you know?"

"I know you watched him kill a man—and that you were seduced into enjoying it," he replied in a saddened voice. "Why, Kalen?"

Kalen swallowed hard. "He gets his hooks in me when my defenses are down. Then he showed me what Billy had done to his family and fed my rage. I went to him in the first place because I felt drawn to go to him last night. Compelled."

"Where is his hideout?"

"Where?" He frowned. "Deep in the forest, away from civilization. It's this really fabulous, rustic cabin that he told me is an illusion. I'm not sure I could find it again if I tried, unless he wanted me to."

"All right. Then what?"

"At first we just talked over a drink."

"Talked? That's it?" Nick's dark brow arched in clear skepticism.

"Yeah. He's quite the snake oil salesman, something I didn't realize before. Well, at least not firsthand."

"Most of your mad-dog, power-hungry world leaders are great at swaying the masses," the commander observed. "They start small, one soldier, one convert at a time, and before anyone truly catches on, they've decimated millions."

"Like Hitler." Kalen picked at his jeans. "Malik's a close comparison. Given enough time and resources, he could have every bit as huge an impact on history, with his super-shifter soldiers as the new Third Reich. In fact, he admitted that's his goal, to rule the world and make paranormals, the Fae in particular, the top of the food chain. He made some persuasive arguments for his cause and the way he wants to go about it."

"I'll just bet he did." Nick's face darkened.

"He had me half believing him, Nicky," he said quietly. "Now I know how masses of people can fall victim to that sort of tyranny."

Picking up a ballpoint pen, Nick tapped it on his desktop thoughtfully for a few moments. "Okay, so why *you*? Why does he want or need your help, in particular?'

"He . . . God, this is so wacked." Elbows on his knees, he clasped his hands together tightly. Nick waited patiently. "He claims that I'm Fae."

The commander's jaw dropped and his blue eyes widened. Obviously the boss hadn't seen that one coming. "What the fuck?"

"My reaction exactly." He gave a humorless laugh. "He told me that my grandmother was pure Seelie. In fact, he claims they knew each other ages ago, from when they were on opposite sides of issues between the Seelie and Unseelie courts."

"Do you believe him?"

"I'm not sure." He shrugged. "Grandma never told me about my heritage, and if she meant to, she died before she was able. I have magic, but I don't have wings like Sariel. And I know for a fact my blood runs red and not blue," he said, thinking of his father's fists and the many occasions they'd split his lip.

"What about your parents? Did he claim they were Fae also?"

Thinking back to the conversation, Kalen frowned. "He never really addressed my mom and dad in that respect, and I was so blown away by everything he was telling me that I didn't ask. He just said that I'm Fae down to my *last drop of blood*. His words. So I assumed my folks were Fae, too. Or at least my mom, since Grandma was *her* mother."

"Your father would have to be Fae as well, if you're a pureblood." Nick chewed on the cap of his pen.

"Which doesn't make sense at all if you knew my father. He's about as anti-magic as a person can get. He forbade my mother to even speak of such things, and I watched her slowly wither away trying to be what he expected." Kalen shuddered, remembering those awful years. "He kept an eagle eye on me, too. He was adamant that I'd be a 'normal' boy, not an aberration. Shortly after Grandma's death, when my powers began to grow, he kicked me out."

"He used that word, *aberration*?" Nick asked, puzzled.

"Yeah, and a lot worse."

"His attitude doesn't make sense if he's Fae."

"Tell me about it."

"It sounds almost as if he was afraid of your magic once it developed." He paused. "Do you know if your parents are still alive?"

"I've been gone for so many years, I have no clue." He looked away. "Even as badly as they treated me in the end, I'm ashamed to admit that I don't know and don't care much if they're still breathing or not."

"Hey, you were a minor when they kicked you out. You have nothing to be ashamed of where your feelings about them are concerned, kid. But we do need some answers about why Malik is so focused on you. I have a feeling your parents, if they're still around, have a couple they could be persuaded to share."

"Are you suggesting we pay them a visit?"

"I think that's a very good idea. And I think we should do it soon."

Kalen sensed their conversation was drawing to a close, and there was one other thing weighing heavily on his mind and heart. "What about Billy, the guy I watched Malik murder? You could take me out for my part in that—in fact, I'm surprised you haven't."

"I haven't because Malik was going to kill that man anyway, and I saw that there was no way either of us could've stopped him. You were under Malik's influence and you didn't touch Billy. But know this—if you kill out of pure bloodlust, and not in self-defense or defense of the team, I *will* terminate you. It'll kill me to do it, but I won't have a choice."

"I understand," he said softly. Christ, Nick didn't deserve to have the blood of one of his own men on his hands. If it came to that, Kalen prayed he had enough of his own mind left to take care of the deed himself.

Nick steered the topic to the present again. "Back to your parents. Give me your former address and I'll see if they're around. I might know something by this afternoon."

"Okay." Standing, he took his cue to leave. First he

took the pen and a scrap of paper from Nick's desk and wrote down his parents' names and address, if they were indeed still there. Then he reached out and shook the commander's hand. "Thanks for giving me a chance. I don't know how I'm gonna pull it off, but somehow I'll get rid of Malik for good."

"You won't be alone. We'll be there with you every step of the way."

That so closely echoed what Aric had said, Kalen's throat got tight. With a nod, he left Nick's office before he embarrassed himself by losing his composure.

Now for an overdue visit that he'd put off as long as he could.

Nick sat back in his chair and ran his hand down his face with a weary sigh. "Fuck!"

The kid was in so goddamned much trouble. All of them were. And he didn't have a fucking clue what to do next. Where was the line between doing his job and interfering with the future, the one thing he'd sworn off attempting? It blurred more with each passing day.

Suddenly a familiar buzz began in his head. A tingle began in his spine and the room went fuzzy as the on-coming vision gripped him. One he'd been plagued with before, but this time in more agonizing detail.

Nick was kneeling in the middle of a field, racked with pain as cold rain lashed down, stinging like needles. Lightning split the sky, took a jagged path to the soaked earth, scorching it in spite of the downpour.

All around him, his Pack battled the Sluagh. His brave men cutting a swath through Malik's batlike Unseelie minions, losing ground with every passing second. There were hundreds of the terrible beasts, swarming, screeching. Far too many for either fierce wolves or men with magical gifts to defeat.

They were all going to die.

High on a pinnacle stood the Sorcerer with his staff, holding it aloft. Screaming at the Unseelie enemy and at the heavens for help that would not come.

And then a bolt of lightning streaked from the boiling black clouds, making the night as day just before it hit the end of the Sorcerer's staff. A massive detonation shook the ground and the world fell away.

Fell and fell. Taking Nick and his men into the abyss.

Nick jolted back to himself, sucking in great gulps of air. His heart slammed against his sternum, wild with adrenaline. Fear.

"Oh my God."

That had been the end. The ceasing of life. But the question was, *whose*? Which side had Kalen chosen in that final act, that last devastating second? Eternal darkness or light?

One thing was for certain—unless Nick made a phone call right this minute, neither he nor the rest of the Pack would ever know that answer.

And he knew then that, for the first time in many years, he was going to break his vow never to interfere with destiny.

He picked up the phone. Hit speed dial. Within seconds, his friend answered. And he uttered the words he'd never thought he would say, not to this man.

"Jarrod, I need you here."

Instantly, the general barked, "When?"

"Yesterday."

"How many teams?"

He let out a sigh of relief, though he was careful not

to allow Jarrod to hear. God bless the man. "Several. Don't mobilize them yet, just have them ready."

"You're about to fuck up my life, aren't you, boy?"

He didn't object to his friend's use of the term "boy" even though he was much, much older than the general's human years. It was meant in affection, and was nearly his undoing. "Yes, sir. I'm afraid so."

Grant gave a quiet laugh. "Well, a cushy retirement was sounding awfully boring anyhow. Give me a couple of days to square things here. Then I'll be there. See you soon."

"Jarrod, . . . thank you."

"No need for that. Just don't tell my baby girl I'm coming. I want it to be a surprise."

Oh, it will be. For both of you. "Sure."

Nick hung up the phone and didn't move again for a very long while.

Kalen wasn't surprised to be met by both Mackenzie and Melina when he walked into the infirmary. The women stopped in front of him side by side, their stance more than a wee bit militant.

"I swear I'm not going to say or do anything to upset him," he said, holding up a hand before either of them could speak. "I just want to apologize."

"He's agreed to see you. But to be frank, I shouldn't even allow you near him," Melina said in a steely tone.

Kalen winced. "I won't hurt him. You have my word."

Won't you?

Shit! The shields had slipped without him realizing it, and he'd need to fully concentrate to shore them up again. Trouble was, his energy was shot from shielding all afternoon.

"You've got ten minutes. He's better but still not at full speed, and I won't have anything setting back his recovery. We'll be nearby."

"I'm sure you will."

Melina turned and stalked off, but Mac stepped forward and gave his hand an encouraging squeeze. "It'll be fine. He's in the third room on the left. Go."

"Thanks." Giving his lady a quick kiss, he headed for Sariel's room. Outside, he knocked.

"Come in."

He wasn't certain what to expect, but the sight of the Fae prince brought him up short just inside the doorway, guilt making another ugly appearance. The faery's cheeks were gaunt, the angles in his face more pronounced than usual. There were smudges under his golden eyes that indicated lack of sleep and illness. His long blue hair, normally a shiny sapphire shade, was dull and lifeless. As were the wings that drooped on either side of him, feathers hanging to the floor.

As he met Kalen's gaze, Kalen saw a weariness in those golden orbs that showed how extremely ancient a being he was, despite his youthful looks.

"Come and sit. I won't turn you into a toad," Sariel said in attempt at levity.

"I wouldn't blame you if you did." Moving to the prince's bedside, he took a seat in a vinyl chair. "I'm sure you hate the sight of me right now."

The prince cocked his head. "No, I can't say I do. What happened wasn't your fault."

"How can you say that? I let Beryl out and she nearly killed you!" He shook his head, trying to comprehend how the Fae could harbor no ill will toward him.

Sariel sighed, his tone resigned. "Kalen, the witch nearly killed me at my father's urging, not yours. My death has been his goal for the past few years, and these most recent months have nearly seen him succeed more than once. He won't cease until one of us is dead, and that blame cannot be laid at your feet."

Kalen felt anything but blameless in the whole deal. God, what must it be like to have your own father actively out to kill you? Kalen's dad had been a mean, abusive old motherfucker and he'd enjoyed hurting his son, but he'd never actually tried to murder him.

Yes, I want my spawn dead. I'll spread him on an altar in chains and use my own talons to slice off his wings. Then his balls and cock as he screams in agony, begging for mercy. And then I'll rip his heart from his chest and feast on it.

Kalen stared at the prince, shaken.

"Kalen? What's wrong?"

"Nothing." Gathering himself, he strengthened his shields. "Why does he want you dead?"

"I'm his only son, the product of his rape of my mother, the Seelie queen. My brothers are her legitimate offspring with the Seelie king who reluctantly raised me as his own. As Malik's progeny, I am the only being with the power to destroy him." He studied Kalen thoughtfully. "Or so I believed until recently."

Kalen ignored the prince's insinuation for the moment. "So why'd he wait until the last few years to go after you? You're something like eleven thousand years old, according to what I overheard."

"Yes, give or take." His smile was sad. "Though thousands of years are a mere blink in time to the Fae in general, some days it seems an eternity. Anyway, in most cases it takes millennia for us to reach our full potential. And when we reach our maturity, we get our wings as well."

Kalen's eyes widened. "Holy shit. That means . . ."

"Precisely." The prince sounded smug. "When you attain your full power, you'll get your wings, young Fae."

"Wha—how did you know?" he stammered.

"I've known you were Fae since the second you entered the compound."

"Then why the hell didn't you tell me?" he snapped in irritation. "Instead I had to hear it from Malik. And he claimed he didn't have a clue as to why I don't have wings."

Sariel made a face. "As humans say, my sire lies like a fucking rug. Don't believe *anything* that passes his foul lips, Sorcerer. I mean that."

"Okay. So how come you didn't mention my heritage to me?"

"To be honest, I wasn't certain that you *didn't* already know, and I didn't want to broach the subject until we were better acquainted."

"Fair enough. I guess *Hey, did you know you're gonna sprout wings in a few thousand years?* isn't exactly a great icebreaker," he muttered.

The prince smiled. "Oh, I doubt it will take that long."

He eyed the prince. "What makes you think so?"

"Your powers are quite remarkable, so I have a suspicion that your wings will emerge much sooner than mine did." The prince sobered, beginning to look tired. "That's also the reason my father has taken such an interest in controlling you."

"Yeah, but if I'm so damned superior, how *can* he

control me?" Kalen asked in frustration. "Because he's getting pretty fucking good at doing it and I don't have an inkling of how to stop him."

"He couldn't manipulate you unless you already possessed a thread of darkness that he can seize and mold into something terrible and useful for him. You know this."

"Jesus." He sighed. "You're right. But why don't *you* have some darkness he can pounce on? You're his son. Not that I'd wish that on you, because I don't. I'm just asking."

"I was fortunate that I was blessed with my mother's strong royal Seelie characteristics. That didn't save me from being cast out of my realm when he decided to target me, but at least he has no hold over my mind. For what it is worth, I'm truly sorry he does with you." The prince yawned, blinking slowly.

"Thanks." He could tell the guy meant it. They studied each other for several long moments, and as they did, Kalen couldn't help but feel a budding sense of kinship.

Was it simply because he'd finally found someone like himself? Here was a decent guy who'd been thrown out of his home, left to fend for himself in a cruel world, just like Kalen. They had a common enemy. They were both Fae. And as incredible as it seemed, he'd one day earn wings just like the prince. Maybe he'd live eleven thousand years, too.

He just hoped he wouldn't have to live even one of those years away from Mackenzie, especially not under Malik's rule.

"How do I defeat him, Your Highness?"

Sariel's head nodded as he attempted to stay awake.

"With your light and your love," he murmured cryptically. Then his lashes fluttered closed and his breathing became deep. Even.

Light and love? What the hell was that supposed to mean?

"Sounds like something a faery would say," he grouched as he stepped from the room.

Oh, wait—I'm a faery, too. Just not the light and love type.

That might explain why he was doomed.

He learned from Noah that Mackenzie was busy in her office on a personal phone call, so he strode toward the rec room. It wasn't until after he left that he remembered they hadn't been able to enjoy that shower together like they'd wanted. It would have to wait until tonight. In the meantime, they would have to finish their day drenched in each other's scent. Every creature in the building would know who the gorgeous doc belonged to.

And that suited him just fine.

Seven

Mac hurried toward Kalen's quarters, trying not to appear as though she was worried. But she had good reason to be.

Kalen hadn't showed at dinner. That in itself was cause for concern among the Pack—the men loved their food and rarely missed one of the cook's excellent meals unless one of them was sick.

She knocked firmly at Kalen's door. Waited and listened for signs of movement. No response. She rapped again, louder this time. Still nothing.

"Kalen!" Worry ramping up to dread, she started pounding. "Open this damned door right now or—"

It abruptly sprang open to reveal her Sorcerer standing there bare-chested, jeans slung low on his hips. His hair was rumpled in sexy disarray and he blinked as though he'd been napping. "Or you'll huff and puff and blow my house down?"

She scowled at him, determined not to let his mouthwatering, half-naked bod distract her. "I just happen to know a few wolves who would help me with that. Are you going to let me in or should I go fetch a couple?"

He gave her a lazy smile. "Feisty, aren't we? By all means, come in."

Stepping aside, he let her in and then closed the door behind them. Immediately he pounced, spinning her around and backing her against the wall in the small foyer. He looked just like a panther, she thought, jewel-green eyes glittering in the dimly lit apartment, expression hungry. Dangerous.

His mouth swooped down, capturing hers, his tongue thrusting inside. He kissed her like a starving man, causing every nerve in her body to tingle with delight. His lean hardness felt so good, and he smelled even better. Like the forest and pine, with a hint of musk. Raw and male.

He pulled back some, giving her a heavy-lidded look of pure need, and a prickle of alarm skittered along her spine. Not because of how much he obviously wanted her, but because the dark Sorcerer was back. The wicked one who would take no prisoners, show no mercy.

As if sensing her unease, he cupped her face and whispered, "I'll never hurt you. Never, I'd die first."

"I believe you." She laid a hand on his chest, feeling his heart beating so hard. Strong and steady. Like his gaze, full of fierce determination to ward off the shadows. For her. "Take me to bed. Please."

With a growl, he lifted her into his arms and strode for his bedroom. She'd never been inside his place, but it was the same layout as the ones belonging to the other Pack members, only more sparse in furnishings.

There were no decorations or personal touches at all. Given his background, that wasn't surprising, but it was sad. She'd change that if he'd allow it.

In his room, he set her gently on the covers as though she were the most precious gift on earth. Pulse jumping, she eyed him as he slid off his jeans and underwear, leaving him naked. The man was a delicious feast for the senses. Such a bad boy with those black painted fingernails and kohl-rimmed eyes.

She'd always had a thing for bad boys. Didn't a lot of good girls?

"I missed you at dinner."

"I fell asleep," he said as he knelt on the bed and crawled toward her.

"Aren't you hungry?"

"Oh, *yeah*." His lips curved up and he reached for the button on her pants. "Don't know why you even bothered to put these back on."

"Because I have a little problem with being naked in front of all the guys. Even if they don't have the same issue." The Pack didn't worry much about walking around in the buff, before or after shifting. Made for nice eye candy.

"There is that." In short order he had her pants and undies off, and her blouse and bra soon followed, joining the rest on the floor. The only item on her person was his silver pendant around her neck, hanging between her breasts. "You, my lady, look good enough to eat."

"Me first. Let me?" Reaching out, she wrapped her fingers around his erection.

Sucking in a breath, he rocked his hips toward her. "Whatever you want, baby."

Eagerly, she stroked his straining member, loving the silky hardness of his skin sliding through her palm. She enjoyed the rush of making a grown man tremble, reducing him to a quivering mass of want. Men believed they were so powerful, but when it came to a lover's touch, being fondled, licked, and sucked? They weren't so mighty.

Bending, she tasted the head of his cock, capturing the pearly droplet that escaped through the slit. He groaned, urging her on, and she took him in her mouth as she cupped his balls. She'd never get tired of this.

She sucked him slowly, taking him deep, to the base and up again to the tip. Bobbed and laved like he was a lollipop, while massaging his heavy balls. She even traced the treasure trail leading from his belly button to the trim, neat nest of black hair at the base. So manly.

"Honey, I'm not gonna last if you keep that up." Carefully he disengaged and gave her a smirk. "My turn now."

She let him push her onto her back on the bed, admired him as he crawled between her thighs and spread them. Bared her for his appreciation. Let him look all he wanted—although she wasn't into streaking in front of the whole Pack, she wasn't shy about her body. Never had been. No, as an adult, she'd always been a sensual woman, very attuned to her needs and not afraid to see them met when the opportunity came about.

And this man more than satisfied.

"You're beautiful," he murmured.

Lying down, he nuzzled her sex. Stole a taste. Immediately she melted, gave herself to his care. His tongue parted her folds, licked with slow thoroughness. She moaned, let her legs fall open wider.

"God, yes. Eat me," she begged.

He made a sound of pleasure and his tongue snaked deeper, stroking along her walls. She gasped, realizing he'd let his panther out just enough to allow his claws to dig into her hips and his cat's tongue to pleasure her in the kinkiest way she'd ever imagined. She almost came from that alone.

"So fucking sweet." His voice was gravelly. "Why did I ever think you were innocent? What a bad girl you are."

"Yes, and you love it."

"I do. And you're mine!"

"Yours! Please . . ." She clutched at his hair.

"Want my cock, baby?"

"Do you have to ask?"

Crawling over her, he smiled and met her eyes, and she got another surprise. His eyes were elliptical—those of his panther. They were captivating. Feral.

After positioning his cock at her entrance, he eased inside. Bracing his elbows on either side of her head, he pushed, burying himself to his balls. "Save me, Mackenzie," he whispered. "Drive out the darkness. Be my light."

Oh, God, she would try. For him.

As he thrust into her faster and faster, she began to spiral toward the edge of release. As she did, she noticed that his features sharpened even more. A half shift, she realized. She'd seen the men take their half forms on occasion, but never from this perspective. Sex like this was more than kinky; it was mind-blowing. And it triggered an internal red flag as well.

She couldn't heed the warning, even if she could've voiced what it meant. By the time she figured it out, it was much too late to stop what came next.

"Mine," he snarled, pounding her into the mattress.

"Yes! Fuck me!"

Just as that wonderful, familiar quickening began, Kalen buried his fingers in her hair, yanked her head back and slightly to the side. For one split second, she took him in, poised above her, fucking her senseless, his brutally handsome face all planes and angles, huge canines bared.

"Kalen, wait—"

Then he struck, sinking his fangs into her throat. The blinding pain was like nothing she'd ever felt—but it was instantly replaced by ecstasy that detonated her body. Her orgasm exploded and she screamed, clinging to his shoulders as they slammed together again and again. Rode wave after wave of euphoria so intense she almost passed out.

A golden thread stretched between them, strengthened. Somehow she sensed that this was the link that would bind them forever.

The bond he'd made without asking.

She was hardly aware of him drinking her blood, then finally removing his fangs and licking the wounds. Of him withdrawing and gathering her close.

Then the room and her lover faded away.

Kalen watched his woman—wow, his mate—sink into slumber and smoothed a curl from her face. A wave of happiness made him so weak it was a good thing he was lying down.

"You're precious to me," he told her sleeping form.

Love? Maybe not yet. But he was falling fast. She already owned a piece of his heart, and his soul would soon follow.

On the heels of that thought, he almost panicked. What if Malik had heard that? But there was nothing except silence in his head, and the new, miraculous tie binding him to his mate. He who'd never had anyone or anything to call his own now had a reason to fight. And to win.

Curving his body protectively against hers, he wrapped an arm around her, pulling her back as snugly to his front as possible. Then he settled the covers over them and drifted off.

Sometime later, he wasn't sure what woke him. Groggy, he reached for Mackenzie, only to find her spot empty. Sitting up, he let his eyes adjust and barely made out her form by the bed.

"What're you doing?"

"Getting dressed." Her words, like her movements, were sharp.

Fumbling for the lamp on the bedside table, he switched it on and blinked at her. "Why? Where are you going?"

"Back to my room." Her lips were pressed into a thin, angry line as she yanked on her pants.

Oh, crap. "But . . . I thought you'd stay here with me. What's wrong?"

"You just assumed, huh?" she snapped, pulling on her shirt. "Like you figured it was fine and dandy to bite me, to *mate* me without discussing it with me first?"

He shot from the bed, reaching for her hand. "Baby, listen to me—"

"Like you listened to me?" She jerked her arm from his grasp. "Don't touch me!"

This couldn't be happening. "My panther wanted to claim you so bad, he was tearing me apart! I couldn't hold him back," he said, voice rising with his fear. "And I thought you wanted it, too!"

"But you didn't ask!" she shouted, shoving him in the chest. "You took away my right to choose, and the tie between Bondmates can never be undone except if one of us *dies*."

That hit him hard, and he sat on the side of the bed. Crushing sadness nearly overwhelmed him. "I'm sorry. I'd undo it if I could, if that would make you happy."

That, of course, was another wrong thing to say.

"It's a little late to worry about how I feel, isn't it?"

"No. You always matter to me," he said quietly. "It's just . . . I thought you wanted me back. You didn't say no."

"I tried to ask you to wait," she hissed furiously.

"I'm sorry, but I didn't hear you. And how could I have stopped? Would you have refused to mate with me?"

"I don't know." She shook her head. "That's not the point."

"I disagree. I don't think it's fair to rip me a new one when you would've said yes anyway."

"Oh, I would have?" Her eyes flashed blue fire. "You arrogant ass. I'm done talking about this. I'm going back to my room, and I'd appreciate it if you left me alone for a while."

He swallowed the knot of pain in his throat. "How long?"

"Until I'm ready to talk. I'll let you know."

This time he didn't try to stop her. After she left the room, he hung his head and listened, catching the ominous click of the door shutting in the foyer.

The horrible burn started in his chest, spread to his throat, his eyes. Try as he might to stop it, he couldn't. He hadn't cried since the night so long ago when he'd finally gotten so hungry he'd given up his virginity in a dirty alley for a measly few bucks. He'd ended up torn and bleeding, left on the ground to rot with the rest of the garbage. And after he'd dried his face, he had sworn he would never shed another tear. Not for anyone, ever again.

But he'd never expected anything could possibly hurt worse than that horrible night. That he could ever again feel like something used and ugly to be discarded.

And he let the tears fall because he couldn't hold them back.

His cat yowled in distress, but there was no comfort to be found for either of them. He wasn't sure how long he sat there, naked and shivering in the dark, when he heard that voice. His voice, so low and reassuring.

Did I not tell you this would happen? Will you never listen? Care for these inferior creatures and they will hurt you time and again.

"You warned me," he admitted, heart aching.

I want you, my boy. I am here for you, so let your soul be at ease.

Someone out there cared about him. He so needed to believe that. He had to have something to hold on to, or he might as well check out.

I won't allow you to die. You are destined for greatness at my side.

He closed his eyes. "I can't stand this pain much longer. I can't take being alone, with no one of my own who gives a fuck about me. Make it stop. Please, I beg you."

You are the one with the power to end it, my boy. Don't you feel the power in your gut, flowing through your veins? Seize control. Focus your magic. Let all of that pain and anger be the fuel that guides it. Can you feel it?

The words throbbed in his skull, a soothing comfort in an ocean of chaos. Kalen found his center and honed in on the pulse of magic. Just there, residing in his core, ready to do his bidding. "Yes, I feel it."

Good. Now grab the thread of your anger and twine it carefully around the spool of light that is your magic.

Concentrating, he imagined his rage as a black ribbon, flowing freely through his body. Unfettered, without purpose. Then he took one end and began to twirl it through the sphere of light in his center, where the magic began. He twined the ribbon all around the magic, swirled it like peppermint candy—only with black instead of red.

"It's done."

Excellent, pet. You could destroy an entire city with the force that's inside you now. Do you see?

"Yes. It feels fantastic." No denying the truth.

You can do that anytime you wish. Use it well when you practice your skills against the posers who call themselves your friends. Do you remember what I told you to do?

"A small misfortune, a dark prank. Nothing too noticeable."

When will you begin?

"First thing in the morning. Breakfast."

Very good. Devise something especially unpleasant that you will enjoy watching.

"Oh, I will." He smiled at the prospect. "No one will hurt me again."

No, because you're going to get them. All of them, eventually.

His groin tightened at the prospect.

Now for your first real test. Lower the shields around the compound so that I may enter.

His resolve faltered. "What? Now?"

Yes. Lower them.

"I—I can't." His heart pounded in confusion.

You can. Don't you desire your blood reward?

"I do, but . . . you'll hurt them."

I will not. That is your task. To exact revenge on the ones who have wronged you.

He hesitated, in sudden turmoil.

Remember how rich my blood tastes, how delicious our bond? Just imagine it on your tongue, like chocolate and wine, as you will recall.

Waving a hand, he chanted a few words, and the wards fell. Immediately, a dark figure stepped from the shadows beyond the pool of light from the lamp.

"Come to me, boy."

Standing, he walked to Malik, uncaring that he was still naked. But it hardly mattered. The other male was in his true Unseelie form, in all his brutal, terrible glory. He was so tall, his head almost touched the ceiling, his leathery wings slightly spread, taking up the room. He was all muscle, raw strength, impressive as ever.

When Kalen was in front of him, the Unseelie cupped the back of his head and drew Kalen's face to the crook of his neck. "Take my blood in the way of our kind. I know you want to."

He did. His mouth was watering at the prospect. His fangs lengthened and he struck quickly, sinking them into the male's flesh. The dark nectar hit his tongue and he moaned, swallowing all he could. So good. The savage potency of it arousing him against his will.

The feelings weren't about Malik at all. But the lure of the darkness, the evil, that was another matter. The rush was a million times that of any street drug, and much more addictive. He could no more have stopped the ecstasy flooding his cock and balls than he could've stopped his heart from beating.

"You've had enough." The Unseelie pried him off, setting him back.

"No! Please, I need more." He hated the bastard for making him beg.

Malik grinned, looking a lot like the devil. "And so you will have it, the next time you please me. Report to me tomorrow, after you've completed your first task."

"Yes, Malik."

The Unseelie reached out and ran a claw down his cheek. Curiously, his expression softened. "You please me, boy."

Such a fatherly gesture, accompanied by words he'd longed to hear from his own dad. "Thank you." God, he was so messed up.

In a wink, the Unseelie was gone.

Falling back onto the bed, Kalen took his cock in hand. The flood of heady arousal had to be relieved or he'd lose his mind. If he hadn't already. The nectar flowed like heroin in his veins, seducing. Just, he suspected, as Malik had intended, but he didn't care.

Fisting his rod, he stroked firmly. Squeezed. His balls drew up and it took just a few more passes before his release blew, spurting come all over his belly. Even some on his chest. There was nothing like the ride the Unseelie's blood took him on. He could easily become addicted.

Like he could have to his mate had she not rejected him.

Obviously that had been a pipe dream. This, however, was real.

Before he dropped off to sleep, he chanted a few words, replacing the magical wards over the compound.

Though in some dark corner of his heart, he had been tempted to leave them down.

Breakfast was an interesting affair.

Sitting across from Ryon, Kalen studied the blond-haired man and contemplated the best method of getting to him. The man was a Channeler and Telepath. He could talk to spirits, and he hated his so-called gift. Now to find a way to turn that against him.

As a Sorcerer, one of Kalen's abilities was necromancy—he could raise the dead and talk to them. It came in handy at times, like in an investigation. Might be useful now.

Wasn't this going to be fun?

From the corner of his eye he caught Mackenzie's stare from the far side of the dining room, and for a few seconds his resolve faltered. Then the incredible pain of her walking out on him returned, strengthening it again.

Returning his attention to the silver wolf, he mulled

over his challenge. Kalen couldn't see ghosts like
Ryon could. In order to speak with them, Kalen had to
use his sorcery to call the spirit back into its former
body at the grave site. He was in short supply of
graves and bodies here, so that meant he'd have to
improvise. And the best way to do that was with an
illusion.

Ryon wouldn't know Kalen was behind what was
about to go down. If he suspected, it wasn't like he'd be
able to prove anything. Pretending to enjoy his eggs
and bacon, Kalen concentrated. Sent out a wave of
energy that drew from air and light and a touch of
shadow. The composition swirled to form a tall, menac-
ing figure draped in what appeared to be a dark cloak.
The white face was blank, and it stood beside the wolf,
reached out a skeletal hand and pointed a bony finger
at him.

The blond was engrossed in conversation with Zan
sitting beside him and at first didn't notice the eerie
presence. No one else in the room could see it, except
for Ryon and Kalen, who pretended he didn't.

Ryon laughed at something Zan said, and glanced to
his left. When he did, he choked on his food at the sight
of the cloaked creep. A thrill of satisfaction wormed
through Kalen's heart, even as it shamed him. Ryon
had always been pretty decent to him and—

Focus, Kalen. Make me proud.

Doubt subsiding, Kalen sent another burst of magic
at his creation, animating it briefly.

"You are no good to anyone with your worthless
gift," it hissed at Ryon. "Die."

Ryon immediately went white and nearly fell off his
seat. "What the fuck?"

Pushing a last surge at the figure, Kalen had it rush straight at Ryon and pass right through him before disappearing. The force of it knocked the wolf to the floor, where he landed on his ass.

"Jesus, man," Zan blurted, startled. He offered his friend a hand. "What the hell was that all about?"

"Didn't you see it?" He let Zan help him up and stood by his chair, clearly rattled. Wild-eyed, he spun in place, searching every inch of the dining room for the specter.

"I didn't see crap except you falling out of your chair looking like you'd seen a ghost. You did, didn't you?"

"Yeah. Shit." He tugged at his hair in distress. "But I've never had one attack me before. I felt the damned thing go right through me."

"No way," Jax said from nearby, frowning. "You all right?"

"Yeah. Or I will be, soon as I get the image out of my head of the Grim Reaper telling me I'm worthless and to die."

This caused no little alarm among his friends, who peppered him with questions. Kalen made sure to interject a couple as well, just to throw off any suspicion. When all was said and done, the group chalked it up as a random occurrence, not that Ryon was all that convinced. Appetite gone, the man excused himself and left.

Another twinge of guilt speared Kalen's chest. He'd upset a good man for nothing other than the sheer pleasure of watching another suffer. Worse, not everyone was fooled into thinking the incident was totally "random."

Mackenzie was glaring daggers at him. His chest

tightened as she stood and stalked to his table. "I want to talk to you. Alone."

Out of self-preservation, he went on the offense. "You didn't take a big enough chunk out of my hide last night? Want a knife so you can finish the job, baby?"

Leaning over, she whispered ominously in his ear, "I know what you just did. So unless you want everyone here to listen to our conversation, I suggest you come with me. *Baby.*"

Straightening, she marched out. *Fuck me.*

Ignoring the curious glances directed his way, he wiped his mouth, tossed his napkin onto his plate, and followed along. She led him down the corridor, not speaking again until she pulled him into the team's empty conference room. Perching one hip on the table, she crossed her arms over her chest and gave him a look of pure disgust.

"Want to tell me what the hell that was about back there?"

Damn, she looked sexy when she got all butch like that. It was a side of his doc that didn't come out often, and it turned him on. Probably not a smart idea to point that out right now.

Giving his full attention to her, he realized she wasn't just angry—she was disappointed. She couldn't hide the emotion in her blue eyes, or the exhaustion. He wondered if she'd slept any after she'd left last night.

He cared. Even though she'd rejected him, he cared far too much about her feelings. Her well-being. The thought of Mackenzie hurting, hurt him in turn.

"How did you guess it was me?" he asked hoarsely, slumping into a chair.

"I didn't have to guess. We're mates now, remember?" she spat. "I can't read your thoughts, but every emotion in you is coming through loud and clear to me. Including your rage and your guilt."

He tensed. "Since when?"

"This morning when you came to breakfast. I started to feel all of it, right after you walked in, and I know it's coming from you. If you focus, you can probably read mine, too."

"I don't need to feel them to get that you're upset," he muttered.

"Upset?" She stared at him, incredulous. "Kalen, what you did to Ryon may seem harmless, but the intent behind the act is very serious. Why would you do something like that?"

His gaze dropped to his boots.

"My God, that Unseelie creep has an even bigger hold on you than I thought. What does he have that lures you in?" Her anger dissipated, replaced by fear, and she gasped. "You haven't become . . . intimate with him, have you?"

His mouth fell open. "No!" He shook his head, stomach lurching at the mere thought—and that she would even *suspect* him of having sex with the Unseelie. His panther snarled in displeasure at the image of bedding anyone but his mate. "No way. Not like you mean. I'd never lie to you about that."

She blew out a breath and nodded. Some of her color returned. "Okay. Then how is it that he gets to you?"

"You know part of it. He plays to my insecurities

and sympathizes with all of the shit I've been through," he admitted with difficulty. "He tells me everything I've always longed to hear from my father. He tells me how proud he is of me, and when I please him . . . he gives me a blood reward."

She stilled. "His, or someone else's?"

"His. It's like a designer drug my system already craves, and now I don't know how I'll stop."

She lowered her head and fell silent. When a tear slid down her cheek, Kalen pushed to his feet, intending to gather her in his arms, but she put out a hand to stop him. "This is so messed up. I don't know how to deal with any of this, or with you."

Agony speared his heart. "If I'm just another problem you have to deal with, then maybe I'm not worth the fight. At least Malik thinks I am."

That was a low blow, and it produced instant results. Pushing from the edge of the table, she took a couple of quick steps forward and swung her hand. Her palm struck his cheek with a resounding crack that echoed throughout the room. He didn't move. Didn't breathe.

"Don't *ever* compare me to that murdering piece of scum, not ever again!" she shouted. "There isn't a single person in this building whose life he hasn't almost destroyed! Is that really what you want? To help that bastard kill your friends? Maybe even kill *you*?"

"No. It's not what I want at all." Any second, he was going to implode. How much more could he take?

"Then fight him! Otherwise, you're not the man I thought you were."

"But I can't—"

She wasn't listening anymore. Turning, she stalked

from the room, flinging open the door so hard it bounced against the wall and chipped the paint.

"I can't fight without you," he whispered to the empty air. His mate was the only good and pure thing keeping his head above water.

Without Mackenzie, he would sink into the depths of hell and never emerge.

Eight

Mac swept past the front desk, ignoring Noah's tentative question.

"Doc? You okay?"

She kept going. When she reached the sanctity of her office, she slammed the door shut and stood there, chest heaving. A wave of dizziness swamped her and the room began to spin. She wavered, put out a hand, realizing she was about to go down—

And a strong hand caught her arm, steadying her.

"Whoa! Easy there," Nick said soothingly. "Come on, sit down." He helped her into one of the two guest chairs in front of her desk and took a seat beside her, patting her hand.

"Thanks. I didn't see you there." She took a few deep breaths, rubbing the tears from her tired eyes.

"I just got here, thought I'd sit down and wait for you. Better now?"

"I think so."

"Do I have to ask what—" He halted in midsentence,

eyes widening. "Oh, Mac. Christ, don't tell me what I'm picking up is true."

"Depends on what you think it is," she hedged.

"Don't tell me you're pregnant with Kalen's baby," he said softly.

She swallowed hard. "Jeez, it's hard to keep a secret when you're living with a bunch of Psy-wolves."

Her attempt to joke fell flat. Nick's lips didn't so much as twitch. "Does Kalen know? I met with him yesterday and I didn't pick up on anything."

"If he knew, you would've been picking *him* up off the floor." She sniffled. "Things between us have been a roller-coaster ride, to say the least. No, the perfect time to drop the bombshell hasn't exactly presented itself."

"Not to mention how scared you are for your baby, and that's getting in the way of telling him the truth."

She nodded miserably, trying not to cry again. "I know in my heart he would never intentionally harm our child."

"*If* he were in full control of himself."

"Yes."

"Are you feeling okay physically? Other than the dizzy spell, I mean."

"I'm fine, really. That was probably because I've just started having some morning sickness and can't keep a lot down. I'm not as nauseated later in the afternoons, though, so I'm eating a little better then."

"That's good." The silence stretched between them as the commander absorbed the import of this development. Finally, he met her gaze and said, "What's going on with you and Kalen doesn't make what I've come to ask of you any easier. Quite the opposite."

"Whatever it is, you know I'll help any way I can," she told him with some unease.

"I know, and I appreciate it. Thing is, Kalen needs a lot of help—"

"Ya think?" Embarrassed by the sarcastic outburst in front of her boss, she grimaced. "Sorry. That wasn't very professional of me."

He gave her an understanding half smile. "I'd say you're entitled to some angst where our Sorcerer is concerned. I want you to know I'm just as worried about you as I am about Kalen."

"Nick, I'm fine," she tried to reassure him. But he wasn't buying.

"Mac, I know why you left Dallas. And even though Kalen isn't a patient of yours, the possible repercussions to you are just as devastating. He's more troubled and volatile than anyone you've ever dealt with, even the man who attacked you years ago."

Why did the man always have to be so reasonable? "True. But I honestly don't believe Kalen will hurt me." She had to believe that.

"I hope you're right." He leaned forward, his expression earnest. "We know Kalen is standing on the edge of a cliff, and it's not going to take much more to send him over. He needs all of us to be there, showing our support, ready to yank him back, if he's going to survive."

"I can't disagree with that." She paused. "Did you hear what happened at breakfast?"

"About Ryon getting knocked out of his seat by one of his ghosts? I heard. And?" He waited for her to explain.

"It wasn't one of Ryon's spirits," she said. "Kalen

created the thing as an illusion and scared the hell out of him for kicks."

"Damn, I was afraid of something like this happening." He gazed at her, troubled. "But I didn't pick up on it and neither did anyone else, as far as I know. How did you figure out what he'd done?"

"I felt his emotions. I read his intent through them."

His brows drew together. "And just how did you manage that when no one else could?"

"Because last night he claimed me as his Bondmate," she said with difficulty. Her face grew hot. "Without my permission."

"He did what? Jesus fucking Christ!" His laugh was completely devoid of humor as he shook his head. "I ought to shoot him now and put him out of everyone's misery."

She winced. "That might be a bit harsh. There were two of us getting hot and heavy, after all." At hearing her own words, she finally began to think that she might have been a little too hard on her lover. He had tried to explain, and she hadn't been willing to listen.

"I'm sorry, but in my old clan of born shifters, the penalty for claiming a Bondmate without consent is either banishment or death."

Never before had she heard him refer to his old life. She wondered where this clan was located and where they might be now. Whether anyone there missed him. But as curious as she might be, that was a line she didn't feel comfortable crossing with her boss, and they had a more immediate issue to discuss.

She brought the topic back to the purpose of his visit. "Well, you're not really going to shoot him or you wouldn't be here discussing our well-being with me. What do you think I should do?"

"He needs to talk with someone about his struggles, past and present," Nick said. "I know things aren't easy between the two of you right now, but he needs *you*."

"You think I should give him another chance."

"I think you should do what you know in your heart is right. I think his success in defeating Malik depends on his happiness with you."

"No pressure, huh?" Dammit! It was becoming very apparent he wasn't going to give up until she saw his point. Slumping in defeat, she nodded. "Okay. I'll try, but that's all I can promise."

"Noted." Visibly pleased, Nick stood. "Are you sure you're all right after that dizzy spell? Do you need me to call Melina in to take a look at you?"

"No, thanks. I'm all right now."

"Hmm." Which meant he'd probably do it anyway. "Well, take it easy and I'll see you later."

Giving Nick a halfhearted smile, she watched him walk out. And wasn't surprised when Melina hurried in less than a minute later.

"What the hell does he mean, you weren't going to tell me you've been dizzy?" she bitched.

Back to the exam room. *And just think—only eight more months to go, give or take.*

Yippee.

You won't be alone. We'll be there with you every step of the way.

But they couldn't follow through, no matter their good intentions, Kalen thought. The darkness inside him was taking root like a plant that had been dying of thirst for too long. He curled on his side and stared out the bedroom window at the deceptively bright day. At the lush forest beyond, beckoning his panther to go for a run. But even that small happiness had been taken away, unless he wanted to risk being drawn to Malik's lair again.

Idly, he gazed at his hand resting on the bed. Focusing on his panther, he allowed a tiny bit of a shift and one of his sharp claws grew from his index finger. A deadly weapon fit to skewer an enemy. Especially when he was one of them.

The claw would make a perfect razor blade.

Heart pounding, he placed the tip of the claw against the inside of his left wrist. Could he do it? Make a couple of deep gashes and simply wait until the pain was ended for good?

Nick's friendship, the Pack's support, even Mackenzie's love, were conditional. They would accept him as long as he didn't fuck up—which he did, frequently. He had nothing. No real home, a mate who didn't want him, and only an evil bastard who did. He would end up hurting everyone he'd never wanted to care about.

I will terminate you, Nick had said.

Why wait?

Then the memories of making love to Mackenzie stole into his thoughts unbidden. Of holding her close, skin to skin, just listening to her breathe. The bittersweet images gradually eased the turmoil in his mind. Calmed the desperation. Despite the heartbreak of the path he'd traveled to get to this point, he wasn't ready to give up.

Not yet. When and if he went down, his death had

to have meaning. Purpose. Until then, he'd hang on. Another hour. One more day. The claw retracted and he started to relax.

Come to me, boy. I have a task for you.

He started at the damned Unseelie's voice in his head, though he'd been half-expecting the asshole to intrude in the wake of his last thoughts.

"I can't do that," he snapped to mask his fear. "It's the middle of the fucking day. Everyone will want to know where I'm going."

Don't play me for a fool. You're a Sorcerer. Simply cloak your passing and nobody will know.

Not necessarily true. He could think of one who might, but he carefully guarded that name.

"It's an unnecessary risk."

And a test. Don't try my patience. Just get your ass here.

Kalen's brow rose. A crack in the Unseelie's normally cool, persuasive facade? Interesting. Whatever Malik was up to, it was a matter of some urgency, and his curiosity got the better of him. "I'll be there. Are you at the cabin?"

No. Follow our bond, and you'll find me.

"Or I could just follow the stench."

Agony knifed through his head as swift punishment, there and gone so fast he barely had time to draw breath. The connection between them vanished, but his orders were clear. God, how he wished he could tear out the bastard's throat. One day soon, he promised himself.

But he was the only one who could get close enough to learn Malik's immediate plans for his so-called super-shifters. To help the Pack stop him. If only he could hold on.

Considering his options, walking through the busy compound, even cloaked, didn't sound like a great idea. Nick or one of the others might still pick up on his life force moving in their vicinity. Using his magic to translocate was one way to go, but was a method he seldom used. It required a lot of concentration and zapped his energy much too fast. But right now, it was the best way.

Closing his eyes, he let the room fall away. Concentrated on his breathing, finding his center. Then he opened his mind to the black thread of the bond connecting him to the Unseelie. It stretched past the boundaries of the compound, beyond the forest, over the miles almost into the town of Cody. What was Malik doing there?

No time to dwell on it. Gathering his magic, he focused his power. Directed it into breaking every particle of his body down to nothing more than mist—a dangerous transition should he lose his grasp on the power. He let his body begin the journey, felt himself travel through space. Faster and faster, following the dark thread to the end, to Malik.

As he reached his destination, his form once again became corporeal. His boots touched solid ground and he took a deep breath, swaying a little. Blinking the spots from his vision. "Shit, that jacks me up every time."

"Perhaps you should practice more."

Malik stood a few feet away, wearing his guise of Evan Kerrigan. He looked like any classy businessman out for a midday stroll, his dark hair smoothed back, sunshades perched on his angular face.

"What do you want?" Kalen said with barely concealed venom.

"So testy." He smirked. "Watch your tone with me, boy."

"Whatever." Glancing around, he frowned. "Why are we standing in the middle of a park? Where are we, exactly?"

"We're in a small town not far from Cody. The name doesn't matter. It's a quaint little place, don't you think?" he observed, waving a hand at the peaceful, sculpted slice of town.

Across the expanse of lawn, a couple walked a yellow Lab. A man jogged past them on the paved, winding path, doing a double take at the undoubtedly odd sight of a businessman and a guy dressed in Goth attire loitering in the park.

"Yeah, it's nice. What does this place have to do with anything?"

"Are you so shortsighted? Look around us. It's the perfect canvas for the first swipe of our brush."

"Meaning what?" When Malik merely gave him a droll stare, dread crept through his stomach. "You're not planning to hurt any of these people, are you?"

The Unseelie scoffed at that. "How can someone who's lived your life still be such a bleeding heart? You wandered through many a town just like this one in your days of being starved and homeless. Did a single one of those people ever offer you a hand?"

He didn't answer that. Of course, nobody had.

Instead, he shook his head. "That doesn't mean people deserve to die for others' indifference. There would be nobody left on earth if—"

"Yes, yes," the Unseelie cut him off impatiently. "I've heard it all. Even so, none of these humans are without their failings. The jogger who passed us is cheating on his wife. The couple walking their dog over there closed the door in the face of a Boy Scout who was collecting cans for the local food pantry. That same Boy Scout struck another student at school just the day before, calling him names. No one is innocent, Kalen."

"But—"

"This beauty you see is a mere facade. That is why I brought you here, for a simple reminder. And a second exercise toward your tutelage, as well."

"What are you planning?" he asked, trying to hide his trepidation.

"My Sluagh are coming this way. They must travel by foot, as there are too many for me and you combined to transport them magically." His eyes were snakelike, glittering and cold. "They will level this pretty little oasis and devour everyone in it—while you and I stand here and laugh over their screams."

Kalen recoiled in horror. "There is no fucking way I'm going to allow you to slaughter these people, much less *help* you do it."

"You will." Reaching out, the Unseelie placed his palm on Kalen's forehead. "What's more, you will enjoy every bloody second."

"No, I—"

"*Abyssus abyssum invocat.*"

Hell calls hell.

Their bond opened and flooded every cell, the rush of inky blackness so strong, so painful, it nearly sent him to his knees. He fought against the rising tide of evil and knew instantly he couldn't fight this battle and win—not without the strength of his mate's love on his side. Not without her scent, her closeness, her belief in him. He had no footing.

He felt the change take place in his mind, felt the slide into depravity. He couldn't halt it completely. . . . But out of desperation, he snatched an image of Mackenzie's smile, the way she looked at him when she was happy. He seized that picture and tucked it close to his mind and heart, even as the corrupted part of his soul rejoiced in the prospect of inflicting his suffering on others.

"That's it, my boy," Malik's voice said in the maelstrom. "You've been hurt so much, haven't you? You want vengeance. Let it fill you."

Breathing hard, he struggled against giving in. It was almost easier *before* he'd claimed Mackenzie. At least then, without the strength of her bond to rival Malik's, there had been little sense of right and wrong to tear him apart. No light to battle the darkness . . .

Light and love. This is what Sariel had meant was his only savior. But the inner battle was killing him as surely as the real war would, when the time came.

"You will watch them suffer and die."

"Yes." No! He wouldn't do it.

"Excellent," he purred in praise, rubbing Kalen's shoulder in affection. Affection he knew the Sorcerer craved more than any alcohol or drug on the planet. "They'll be here shortly. You will remain by my side through it all. By the time your commander and his dogs learn of the attack, it will be much too late."

He stared at Malik, shaking his head to clear the fog. "No! I won't—"

"You heard me, boy." The Unseelie's face hardened. "You will not fail me."

The *or else* went unsaid, but it rang in Kalen's ears anyway as he glared back. There was just no way he could stand by while innocent people died. No matter how strong his tie was to Malik, no matter how badly his soul called out for blood. Ignoring Malik's shout of anger, Kalen vanished, teleporting back to the compound. In his own quarters, he paced the living room, fighting to strengthen his shields and push the evil back into a remote corner of his soul. He had to keep his wits about him. Combat this thing.

He'd tell Nick. Right now.

Pushing into the corridor, he hurried to the end and turned down the one leading to Nick's office. He rapped twice and heard Nick call out for him to come in. He stepped over the threshold, closing the door.

"You look pretty serious," the commander commented, pushing aside a stack of paperwork. "What's on your mind?"

Carefully erecting his shields, he met the other man's gaze. "I just saw Malik."

Nick bolted to his feet. "Here? How did—"

"No, he's not here," Kalen assured him. "He summoned me to a town not far from Cody to tell me his Sluagh are going to attack and kill everybody there."

Lowering himself into his chair again, Nick let out a vile curse. "When?"

"Any minute."

"Tonight?" At Kalen's nod, his expression darkened. "I've got reinforcements on the way, but they won't get here in time. We'll have to handle this on our own."

"What kind of reinforcements?"

"People I trust." He paused. "Now, where exactly is the attack taking place?"

"The—the east end of town." At that, pain lanced his temples and he gasped. Feeling dizzy, he sat in one of the guest chairs. "He ordered me not to tell you, but I couldn't just stand by and watch those poor people get murdered—oh, God."

Another blade seared his brain and the room spun. He barely registered Nick calling his name as he slumped to the floor, on his back. The commander's worried face appeared above his and he fought to make him understand.

"He . . ." A third spear of white-hot agony. Liquid ran from his nose. Blood. "Help them, Nick . . . *Ahhh!*"

The fourth time was too much. Writhing, he screamed as his brain was torn apart, molecule by molecule. In the distance, he heard Nick yelling.

And then there was nothing.

Mac was debating the wisdom of going to find Kalen, maybe breaking the ice, when a commotion exploded in the lobby of the infirmary.

"Get me some fuckin' help!"

Nick. Immediately she dropped the clipboard containing Sariel's chart and ran. In the hallway she almost collided with Melina, and the other woman took the lead. When they rounded the corner, her heart almost stopped.

Nick was moving toward them fast, Noah on his heels. But Mac's attention was focused on Kalen, limp in Nick's arms, head tilted back, eyes closed. Her mate's face was covered in blood. Christ, it had even run into his hair.

"First trauma room," Melina barked, gesturing them in. "What happened?"

"He collapsed in my office." Nick carefully laid his burden on the gurney and stepped back. "He was giving me some information about Malik, and this happened."

"You think the Unseelie is responsible?" Melina asked. Grabbing a penlight, she pried open a lid and shone it into one eye. Noah began taking their patient's blood pressure as Nick answered.

"Yeah. I know he is, but *how* is the question."

Mac spoke up, unable to hide the tremor in her voice. "My guess is he's using their bond to control Kalen. By trying to pass along information that would help you, he crossed the line."

"And now he's paying," Nick said grimly. "When I get my hands on that fucking demon, I'm going to kill him."

"You'll have to stand in line," Mac told him.

Noah piped up. "BP's normal, pulse is steady."

"Pupils are reacting normally as well," Melina put in, visibly relieved. "That's a good sign—though I'll feel better when he regains consciousness."

Suddenly Mac's throat burned with the effort it took not to cry. Her mate looked so vulnerable lying there, struck down by an unseen force. It must have taken a great well of inner strength to go against the leader of the Unseelie.

Fetching a sterile cloth, she cleaned Kalen's face. She noted he'd bled some from his ears and cleaned those as best as she could, too. His hair would have to wait until he could shower.

"He'll be all right," Melina soothed. She turned to Noah. "Let's move him to a room and keep him monitored until he wakes up."

Mac jumped to help the nurse and together they rolled his gurney into a private room. Noah assisted her in undressing him, stripping him down to his briefs. As they got him into a gown, she tried not to stare at her lover's perfect, lean body. But thinking of what he was going through sobered her quick enough.

As she stroked Kalen's hair, Noah slipped from the room. For several minutes she simply stood by him, painfully aware that she could've lost him. For the whim of an evil bastard, he could be dead right now. And she never would've been able to make up with her . . . mate.

"My mate," she whispered, tracing the line of his jaw. His lips.

She had a mate.

And if Kalen would give her another chance, she'd start being a real one to him.

Nine

Sprawled in one of the infirmary's uncomfortable vinyl chairs, Mac made a mental note to hit up Melina to order better ones. Not that her request would lead anywhere. The other doc was so tight with their budget she could make it squeal for mercy.

A small movement from the bed interrupted her musings and she sat up, scooting closer to Kalen's side. There was rapid twitching behind his eyelids and he moaned, started to thrash a little, maybe facing down an enemy in his nightmares.

"Kalen?" She touched his arm, watchful of any sudden moves. Patients who'd been through bad experiences could be violent upon waking—and she had extra reason to be cautious. "Hey, come back to me."

"M-Mac?" Licking his lips, he blinked slowly, trying to focus on her face.

She had to smile. "That's the first time you've ever called me by my nickname."

"Tired."

"I know, honey." She cupped his face, unable to get close enough. "You gave us quite a scare."

"What happened?"

"You don't remember? Nick says you collapsed in his office. You were telling him about the attack Malik planned on a small town outside Cody."

For a few seconds, he seemed to slowly process this, baffled, as though she wasn't speaking his language. Then a look of horror bloomed on his face as he tried to sit up. "God, the attack! How long have I been here? Has it happened already? Where's—"

"Slow down," she said, pushing him back gently, attempting to calm him. "You've been unconscious for about four hours. Nick sent a couple of the guys ahead to scout the area you told him about, but don't worry. They're going in quiet, looking to see where Malik and his Sluagh are before they bring in the rest of the team."

"I'm going with them," he said firmly.

"As one of your doctors, I strongly advise against any rigorous activity until tomorrow, at least. That includes battling the ugly Unseelie minions."

"Doc, I'm not asking. I'm telling you I'm getting out of this bed and leaving." With that, he sat up and began yanking at his IV.

"Stop!" She swatted his hand away. "You're going to hurt yourself. Let me get Melina and we'll discuss your options."

"No. I'm outta here. You can remove the IV or I'll rip it out. Your choice."

"Wait a second," she entreated. Waving a hand to encompass the room, she tried a different argument. "This is what Malik is capable of doing to you for telling his secrets. How bad will it be if you actually show up and fight against him?"

His jaw clenched. "I'm not going to sit here and hide like a coward while the rest of the team is facing him and his junkyard dogs, getting hurt or worse."

"But what if he takes you over again and you fight against your friends instead of with them? What then?"

Nick would have to kill him. They both knew it and that knowledge hung in the air between them.

"Then I'll get what I have coming," he said, his expression grim. Determined. "But I like to think I'm stronger than Malik. That I can beat him."

"Can he hear you now?" The possibility made her nervous as hell.

Kalen paused, then shook his head. "He's not tuned in to me at the moment. I'm guessing he's busy with his plans."

"You think he knows exactly what you told Nick?"

He frowned. "I'm not sure. I do know that my bond with Malik physically punishes me for going against him. Whether he's aware when it happens is something I suppose I'll find out."

And not in a pleasant way. "Please, stay here," she begged. "We can't lose you."

Falling silent for a long moment, he studied her, an odd look on his face. "You said *we*."

"We, the team." Her heart pounded furiously against her sternum. "That's all I meant."

"Suddenly you care? I don't know why." He looked away, green eyes bleak. "I claimed you without asking you first. I'm a piece of shit who's brought you and everyone else nothing but trouble."

"That is *not* true," she hissed. "Yes, I was pissed. But I realized that I was too hard on you. I should've listened when you tried to explain."

"Nah, you did the right thing." He didn't quite manage to hide the bitterness in his tone. "After I finish this thing with Malik, I'll probably hit the road again."

Her stomach lurched. "You're not serious."

"Come on, Mackenzie," he said with a sad smile. "It's not like I'll ever fit in here with these guys. No matter how many nice words they say about sticking together and being there for me, name one person who'll be devastated to see me walk away."

"Me," she whispered.

"You'll forget about me, in time."

"No, I assure you I won't." *God, you have no idea.* But if she told him the truth right now, he'd think she was just using the baby as leverage to trap him. What a damned mess. "Please, don't decide anything right now. Just . . . give it a while."

His voice was soft, his suffering all too apparent. "So you're willing to forgive me? Give me another chance? 'Cause that's the only way I'll stay."

Instead of answering, she showed him. Leaning over, she placed a soft kiss on his sensual lips. A kiss that quickly became heated, searching. And Lord, was her Sorcerer good at it. She longed to crawl inside him and never come out. No other man had ever made her feel this way, and it was no mystery as to why. He'd been made for her and she for him.

They broke apart and she caressed his cheek. "It's better when we're together, isn't it? I mean, you seem more yourself, more *here*, when we're with each other and in sync."

He nodded. "No doubt about it. I don't know whether to attribute that to our mating or the pendant," he mused, fingering the silver disk around her neck.

"Perhaps it's a bit of both."

"Could be." He held up the hand with the IV still attached. "You going to undo me?"

"Under one condition." Reaching behind her neck, she unfastened the clasp and removed the necklace.

"What are you doing?" Alarm spiked his voice and etched itself on his face. "Put it back on!"

"This is my condition. You wear this to go help the team, or remain here." Mac put her fingers over his lips to shush him. "No. I'm not going to sit by and watch you fall back into his snare if I can help it."

"That protection is yours," he argued. "I can't go off knowing you're exposed."

"Honey, *everyone* is vulnerable to that creep. But those of us who remain at the compound have an advantage—the wards you put over the building and the surrounding forest. They're still in place, right?"

"Yes," he admitted reluctantly. "No creature, not even Malik, can get through my wards unless I allow it. He might still be able to get into your head and harass you, but since I strengthened the spell, he won't be able to physically breach the property."

"Well, there you are. So take the pendant and go kick some ass!"

He wanted to. The yearning to join them as a true equal was almost heartbreaking to witness. When would he ever believe in his own worth? What would it take for a man who'd never been worth anything to anyone except his grandmother? *And now me.*

Slowly, he reached out. The second his hand closed

over the disk, he took a deep, shuddering breath. "Oh my God."

"What's wrong?" She studied him in concern.

"Nothing." At last, he smiled. "I'd worn this thing for years, and I'd already forgotten how powerful it is. It feels like the best vitamin shot ever invented."

"Really? It didn't affect me that way," she said thoughtfully. "I don't even notice it's gone, not in a magical sense."

"I'm glad, because if being without it affects you at all, I wouldn't take it, even for a few hours. And I'm giving it back the minute we return."

"I'm still worried about you going when you've barely recovered from the last round with that bastard."

"Don't be, sweetheart. I'll be back before you can blink, none the worse for wear. Now, what do ya say we get me unhooked?" He held out his hand.

Against her better judgment, Mac removed the IV needle and swabbed the site with alcohol. In truth, she couldn't have stopped him from leaving, but that didn't make her feel any better about the situation. When she was done, he pushed from the bed and stood unsteadily on his feet for a couple of moments. Then he straightened, waving a hand in front of himself and uttering a brief Latin phrase she couldn't quite catch.

His clothing appeared, his usual ensemble of black from head to toe, complete with his battered leather duster. The man looked completely badass, and good enough to eat. Later, with any luck.

Closing the short gap between them, he pulled her close against his hard, lean body. Nuzzled her hair, hands splayed on her back. Rubbing, comforting. "I'm going to be fine, and so are we. Together. If you want me."

"More than anything. Be careful, please."

"You bet."

Another kiss. This one long and drawn out, making her nipples pucker and the rest of her ache for his touch. For his cock to be buried inside, so deep she couldn't tell where one of them ended and the other began.

Her mate pulled back, gave her a wink.

And then he was gone.

Kalen appeared in the conference room, where the meeting to form a plan for intercepting the Sluagh was well under way. He retreated to a corner, making himself as unnoticeable as possible without actually cloaking his presence.

As he watched the proceedings, he couldn't believe how much better he felt already. It was as though the pendant had instantly washed all traces of Malik from his body. He suspected it was more like the blessed disk was protecting him from the effects rather than curing him, but he'd take what he could get for however long it lasted.

Nick paced at the head of the table, agitated. "No contact from Jax and Zander for the past twenty minutes. We give them five more. Then we head out."

"What about Malik's cover as Kerrigan?" Ryon asked. "Has anyone been able to pinpoint where 'Kerrigan' likes to hang out?"

"According to the employees at NewLife Technologies, Kerrigan continues to be a silent force behind their biological *research*," Nick said, letting the last word drip with sarcasm. "In other words, he's the man with the money, and they don't care who he is or where he is as long as the green keeps rolling in."

Aric spoke next. "What about other facilities where they're doing their nasty little experiments on humans and shifters? Any word on more locations?"

"None so far. With Dr. Bowman missing, and Chappell and Beryl dead, our leads on those have gone cold."

Rowan, Aric's mate, winced. She'd been the one to kill Orson Chappell, and Aric had taken out Beryl when the witch attacked both Rowan and Sariel. Maybe she felt a little guilty, though there was no need. "I suppose it's too much to hope for that we've already found and destroyed all the labs."

"I seriously doubt that," Nick said. "Wherever Dr. Bowman is, his heinous work continues. I don't think he's in it just for the money."

"He's not." Aric's eyes went cold. "Trust me, the motherfucker totally enjoys his *work*." He'd spent weeks under the crazy doctor's knife before Rowan and the team rescued him and Micah. They'd been fortunate to survive.

"If there are more labs, there might be more survivors like me," Micah put in quietly. All eyes swiveled to him and his gaze dropped to the floor—right about where his self-worth was located. One side of his face was like melted wax from the torture Bowman had inflicted on him, the other side unmarred, serving to remind him of the handsome man he'd never be again. He wasn't near healthy enough to go on their assignments yet, but the group had started including him in the meetings.

Mulling over Micah's speculation, part of Kalen hoped the other Pack members were dead, no longer suffering. The other part had witnessed a miracle when Micah was found and prayed for another one.

"If they're out there, we'll find them," Nick assured his newest member. Even though Micah had known the Pack since their days as Navy SEALs, he was new to Nick. Their commander was about to say something more when his cell phone blasted out George Thorogood's "Bad to the Bone," breaking the tension. Several of the guys snickered as their boss answered the call. "Whatcha got?"

After a brief exchange and a couple of questions, he ended the call and briefed them. "That was Jax. He said three Sluagh showed up and hid at the park while they were watching the east end of the town, obviously sent to keep an eye out for us since Kalen spilled the beans. Jax and Zan took them out."

"Just three?" Ryon asked. "Where are the rest?"

"Malik changed his plan, no doubt in hopes of avoiding us joining the fight, the cowardly bastard. The Unseelie is sending about a dozen Sluagh to the west end of town as we speak, where they're planning to attack the citizens. We need to move, now."

Chairs scraped on the carpet and a murmur of conversation ensued as the men began to file out, checking weapons and slapping each other on the back in support. Kalen was surprised when Micah stopped him.

"Be strong, man. If I can walk away from my hellhole, so can you." A half smile pulled at his ruined face. His brown eyes were glazed with whatever shit he was on to help him cope, and he was far too thin. But as fucked up as his life might be, here he was trying to reach out and reassure someone he didn't even know.

Kalen stood a bit taller and managed a smile. "Thanks, Micah. I'll remember that." Giving the man a nod, he headed after the group.

In the huge hangar that housed their land and air transportation, Nick led them to two of the sleek black SUVs for the trip. As the others loaded up, he turned to Kalen.

"I don't suppose it would do any good to order you to stay here?"

"Mackenzie already tried, so no. I'm in."

Nick's scrutiny fell on the pendant. "At least you had enough sense to accept protection."

"I didn't want to, but the doc wouldn't hear of me leaving without it."

"You need it more tonight. She'll be fine in the meantime, trust me."

"Easy for a PreCog to say."

"Isn't it? Come on, let's go kick some ugly Unseelie ass." With a half smile, he climbed into the SUV his best friend, Hammer, was driving.

His words so closely echoed Mackenzie's that Kalen wondered how much the man knew about what people said and did around the compound. It was freaky as hell. In the next instant, it struck him that Nick was joining in this time when he normally remained in command at the compound. From the looks some of the guys exchanged as they got into the vehicles, they thought it was unusual too, but no one questioned him. The more fighting on their side, the better.

Or maybe Nick foresaw something they didn't. Kalen got into the SUV Ryon was driving, and tried not to dwell on their boss's visions or his own part in the whole mess during the ride. On the outskirts of town, Ryon pulled over on an overgrown country road, parking behind Hammer. Kalen, Ryon, Aric, and Rowan piled out of one vehicle, Nick, Hammer, and A.J. out of the other.

Nine Pack soldiers against a dozen Sluagh. Not horrible odds, but it could've been better.

Rowan and A.J. carried plenty of hardware loaded with special bullets. Rowan was a newly turned wolf, A.J. a human, and as former cops they were both more comfortable with guns than fangs and claws. A.J. had also been a SWAT sniper years ago, and that skill had come in pretty damned handy once before—on the night Rowan had killed Chappell and they'd apprehended Beryl. The others would use a variety of man-made and supernatural weapons, whatever worked best in the situation.

"We'll cut through here," Nick said, raising his voice to be heard. "We'll meet Jax and Zan near the clearing about a mile away and intercept the Sluagh. Capture one alive if you can, but don't take unnecessary risks. Everybody be careful and get home in one piece."

Murmuring in agreement, the Pack started off through the trees. The area was pretty rural, no houses in sight. Just acres of forest, though Kalen didn't know if this was considered part of the vast Shoshone or not. Whatever. Traveling a mile through the undergrowth seemed ten times as long as walking down a stretch of lonely highway. He would know.

Kalen worried about all the noise they were making, no matter how cautiously they tread. But in the end, stealth didn't matter. The screams of terror reached their ears before they broke the cover of the trees. In the lead, Nick began to run and everyone else followed suit.

When they charged into the clearing, Kalen's blood ran cold. Across the meadow, a small house was nestled in the trees, a scene that might have been picturesque—except for the Sluagh ripping at the front door, tearing chunks out of the screen and wooden frame, trying to get inside. And the others at the windows, smashing glass panes.

"Go! Go!" Nick shouted. And in mid-stride, without shedding his clothes, he morphed into a big white wolf. His clothing simply vanished.

Kalen had been under the impression that he, as a Sorcerer, was the only one who could perform that particular trick. Born shifters like he and Nick must be different. But there was no time to dwell further on it. The Sluagh had broken into the house, and they were much too far away.

Kalen shifted too, letting his panther free to streak across the open expanse. As they neared, an adult male's voice yelled in anger and fear, trying to defend his family. The *pop-pop* sound of gunshots split the air, followed by the man's agonized scream . . . that ended in a horrid gurgle.

More screams. A woman and kids. Teenagers? God, what a clusterfuck!

As they reached the house, Kalen spotted two wolves already at the scene—one silver, one black—fighting Sluagh outside. Jax and Zan. Fangs and claws slashed as they attempted to get at either the heart or the throat of their opponents. They were two on two, so Kalen rushed into the house. The woman and children took priority.

Inside, the carnage in the living room was something Kalen never wanted to see again as long as he lived. Blood was everywhere, coating almost every surface. A man, presumably the father, lay sprawled on his back, eyes wide and unseeing, his head nearly severed from his neck. Still in his grip was a .357 Magnum, a weapon that would discourage almost any intruder.

Except minions from hell.

Half a dozen Sluagh were ransacking the living room and the tiny adjoining kitchen, mindless in their destruction. From down the hall behind a closed door somewhere, the woman and children were screeching, and from the noises, at least two more creatures were trying to get to them.

They had to get to the man's family. But first they had to dispatch these bastards. The Sluagh froze upon seeing their fun interrupted, then roared and charged to meet the threat. Kalen rushed one, quickly maneuvering behind him and slashing the back of its leg. He hit his target, slicing the thing's hamstring, and it went down squealing in pain.

Lightning fast, Kalen shifted back to human form and leaped on its chest. Shifting just his right hand to use his razor-sharp claws, he drove them straight into the Sluagh's heart. In seconds, the thing was dead.

Leaping to his feet, Kalen spun just in time to avoid the same fate as the unfortunate man whose family they were trying to save. He ducked and the Sluagh's big mouth full of long teeth snapped the air where his neck had been a second before. He took this one out almost like the first, stepping into its body and delivering the thrust to its corroded heart.

But this one didn't die easily. As Kalen stepped back

to let it fall, the creature made one last swipe with its claws, tearing right through his duster and the shirt beneath, into his side. Kalen swore as he stumbled back, clutching the tattered coat. Goddammit! He'd had that duster for years, and this asshole had messed it up.

Even wearing his pendant, he could get hurt. But he'd heal faster with it than without.

There would be plenty of pain to accompany the injury, he was sure. But for now, it hardly registered. A quick glance showed that the others had this part of the house under control. Kalen took off down the hallway just in time to see two Sluagh outside a closed door, one slamming his bulk into it again and again. As he burst through, pieces of wood went flying and the screaming inside ramped up to ear-shattering decibels.

"Hey, you fuckers!" Kalen yelled. The two attackers turned to face him, their wrinkled, batlike faces registering surprise.

Then they shrieked, flapping their leathery wings and beating their chests in an attempt to look scary. Mission accomplished. Fortunately these creatures ran on a severe shortage of brain cells. While they were busy attempting to see which one could appear the most frightening, Kalen uttered a word, held out a hand, and summoned his Sorcerer's staff.

After leaving his bed in the infirmary to come here, then doing battle, this was going to drain him. But it was the most expedient way to remove the threat from the wide-eyed woman and teens beyond the gaping doorway.

Softly, he began a chant directed at the enemy, the ones in front of him as well as any remaining Sluagh outside. Their macho posturing halted and they looked puzzled—and then their skin began to shrivel like raisins in the sun. Almost every creature on earth was made mostly of water. Take away that element and there wasn't much left. Malik's trained dogs were no different.

This method of Sorcery was one of the most disgusting he knew, but effective. The Sluagh began to whimper in fright and he almost felt sorry for them, but the image of the poor man in the living room erased that feeling in a hurry. The pair shriveled to husks, dead in moments, and then he simply waved his staff, reduced them to dust, and sent the particles floating away.

Kalen raised his gaze to the woman beyond the door—and she promptly fainted. A teenage boy and girl stared back at him.

"Fucking awesome," the boy said. The girl burrowed into her brother's side and remained silent.

Kalen started for the door, grimacing as the burning in his side made itself known. He staggered a bit, dizzy, but he wasn't finished here. Leaning against the doorframe, he nodded at the kids.

"What's your name, son?"

"Travis," he answered, his voice scared but strong. "This is Katie."

"Okay, Travis, I need your help. You and your sister get your mom up on the bed. Then all of you stay in here until we say you can come out."

"Where's my dad?" His chin quivered. Still so young, on the brink of manhood.

Oh, kid. I'm so sorry.

"Just stay here, all right?"

"Tell me where my dad is!" Travis was starting to panic, and that wouldn't do.

Holding out his staff, Kalen chanted a few soft words. The teens' eyes fluttered closed, and their bodies lifted along with their mother's. Gently, Kalen floated them all onto the bed and laid them down together. There they would sleep until the Pack could arrange to get them out of this place.

A hand clamped down on his shoulder and he turned his head to see Nick standing there, his expression grim. "Thanks for the help with those last few. There were more outside the house than we thought. Jax and Zan almost got their asses killed."

"They all right?"

"Yeah. Because of you."

Kalen flushed at the praise. It was nice, but strange to a guy like him. "What now?"

"We've got a dead civilian. Fuck!" the commander spat, losing some of his legendary cool for a moment. He heaved a deep breath. "I made a call to our buddy Sheriff Deveraux. The rest of the creatures hadn't yet reached the citizens in town, so we're okay there. He'll spin this attack to the public as an armed robbery or something. Random attack."

Kalen's lip curled at Deveraux's name. There was no love lost between him and Kalen. The asshole had tried to run him out of town more than once when Kalen had first arrived.

"A robber who bit a man's head almost clean off? Yeah, that'll fly."

"They aren't going to let that tidbit see the light of day." Nick gestured to the forlorn figures on the bed. "Did they see what happened to the dad?"

"I don't think so. The boy asked where he was, but I didn't tell him anything. Figured putting them to sleep until this is cleared away would be best."

"Good thinking. Can you do a mind wipe on them?"

Kalen considered it, and nodded. "That's about all I have left in me, but yes. I can. They'll wake up tomorrow with no memory of the Sluagh, us, or anything else that took place here. Then the good sheriff can spin whatever story he wants and they'll never know any different."

"All right. Do it so we can turn this over to Deveraux and get the hell out of here."

"You gonna warn him that there's more Sluagh where these came from?"

"Don't see any other way. He needs to know, and he'll call us if he or his men spot anything unusual."

Unusual. Now, there was an understatement. It was on the tip of his tongue to smart off that he could tell Nick used to be an FBI agent, but he refrained. Barely. Instead he walked on unsteady legs over to the bed and knelt. He wanted this over with quick.

Starting with the boy, he pressed his palm to the forehead and literally pulled the memories of the last half hour from his mind. The scenes were horrid, filled with the terror of monsters at the door, and he began to sweat as they flowed from the boy. When he'd retrieved them all, he set them free, letting them dissipate like so much noxious poison. Until the day the boy died, there would forever be a gaping hole in the day he lost his father. Same with the sister and their mother.

Finished, Kalen pushed to his feet, barely able to stand now. He was beyond thrilled to see the sheriff standing in the bedroom with Nick, both of them studying him in fascination.

"It's done," Kalen told them hoarsely. "They'll wake up tomorrow, and they won't remember a thing about tonight. Ever."

"Well, it looks like you're good for something other than hanging out in the cemetery robbing graves and disturbing corpses," Deveraux drawled, a hint of a snide tone coloring his words.

"Fuck you, douche bag."

"Jesse," Nick rumbled to the sheriff in warning. "Lay off."

"Oh, sure," the lawman said amiably. "Wouldn't want to hurt the princess's feelings, would I? Ya'll have a nice night, Nicky. And don't call me again for, say, twenty years or so."

"You wish. This is only the beginning, I'm afraid." Nick sighed. "But we'll keep all of it away from the public for as long as we can. Forever, if possible."

Nick shook hands with the prickly sheriff. Then he and Kalen turned to go. That was when Kalen's body decided it was finished being abused for the day. His knees buckled and Nick caught him, placing Kalen's arm around his shoulders.

"Easy, kid. I've gotcha."

"I'm fine."

"That would be more convincing if you could walk on your own and you weren't bleeding all over me."

"Shit. Sorry."

His side hurt like a bitch and his head was swimming. As they made their way through the house, Kalen took note of the others. His friends were all accounted for, battered, some bloody and limping, but alive. That was all he needed to know for now.

And these guys *were* his friends. No matter what lies Malik spewed.

He just prayed he could remember that in some distant corner of his mind when the darkness rose once again.

Ten

In her quarters, Mac stretched out on her bed with a grateful sigh. Nobody had clued her in about the fatigue that plagued pregnant women even in their first trimester. It was as if a giant vacuum cleaner had sucked out all her energy and left her unable to do anything but lie down for a long nap.

Despite her worry about the Pack's newest battle, and Kalen in particular, she was no match for the rigors of pregnancy. Her lids closed the instant her head hit the pillow and she drifted off into a deep sleep.

But her slumber was far from peaceful.

She'd been in this place before. A place of total desolation. Skeletal trees everywhere, no birds, no gurgling of fresh water. Fish carcasses littered the streambed, their rotting eyes staring up, accusing. She knew who had brought her here, but not what game he wanted to play.

"Show yourself, you son of a bitch!" she shouted.

Malik was here, watching and waiting. Trying to unnerve

her as he'd done before, the night she'd first slept with Kalen. The night they'd conceived their child.

What was his purpose in bringing her here again? Mac was neither a paranormal being, nor powerful. She was nothing but a simple doctor. She was of no interest or benefit whatsoever to the king of the Unseelie.

"That's where you're wrong, dearest."

She shuddered that he'd read her thoughts.

He stepped from behind a dead, gnarled tree as he'd done before, and she sucked in a shocked breath. Stood rooted to the spot, frozen in terror. She'd never seen an Unseelie in true form, and Malik was every nightmare rolled into one being.

He was tall, with black hair flowing past his waist. Huge, leathery black wings were stretched up over his back and outward, blocking the dull sky. His eyes were crimson, set in a sharp, brutal face that managed to be frightening and strangely beautiful at the same time. His presence was magnetic, and she couldn't help but be drawn to him in spite of herself. Many a sadistic ruler had possessed that particular gift, and the Unseelie was no exception.

She could see why Kalen or anyone else would be taken in by the male. He was the seductive dark to Sariel's brilliant light.

"What do you want?" she demanded, hoping she concealed her fear—for both herself and her baby. "I'm no threat to you."

"True." With a half smile, Malik stroked her cheek with one long, claw-tipped finger. "A puny human like you cannot hurt me."

"How astute of you," she said drily. "So why don't you leave my dreams in peace? Better yet, leave Kalen alone, too."

"I cannot do that, pretty doctor. Despite his unfortunate

failure in my latest test, he is too important to my plans for the future." The Unseelie's speculative gaze raked her from head to toe, making her skin crawl in trepidation. *"I used to believe the opposite about you."*

"What, I'm suddenly important?" She snorted to cover the fearful suspicion rising in her breast. *"I seriously doubt that. You've got your wires crossed and I'm not staying here to listen to any of your bullshit."*

But she couldn't escape him because there was nowhere to go. He stepped closer, a weird expression on his face. Almost one of . . . fondness? She took a startled step back, but her flight was halted when he grasped her wrist and stared deeply into her eyes.

"A mother should never underestimate her power in the world."

God, he knows about the baby! Gasping, Mac tried to twist her arm free, to no avail. *"Don't even think about trying to hurt our child,"* she snarled into his face. *"Or I swear I'll find a way to destroy you!"*

The Unseelie laughed. *"Such spirit! But why would you think for a moment I would harm a defenseless baby? Especially when I have a vested interest in his well-being."*

Cold slithered down her spine and she stilled. *"I fail to see how that could possibly be true."*

"It's quite simple, dear Mackenzie." Reaching out, he placed a palm over her still-flat belly, his expression the picture of rapt fascination. *"I had thought bringing Kalen to my side would be my greatest achievement, but now that triumph is twofold."*

Her heart pounded. *"How so?"*

"Because now I'll have not only Kalen, but my grandchild."

Mac stared at him dumbly for several seconds before the

*full import of his revelation washed over her, swept her away
in a tide of pure horror.*

*This time when she jerked from his grasp, he didn't stop
her. She ran, his ghostly laughter chasing her into the gloom.
On and on she fled the truth, tears streaming down her face,
blinding her vision.*

Her baby. Malik's grandchild.

And Kalen the Sorcerer . . . his son.

*She couldn't run anymore. Couldn't cope with the knowl-
edge. Fell to her knees and screamed . . .*

Mac shot upright in bed, heaving in gulps of air as
though she really had run for miles. Her pulse tripped
and her chest hurt like she was about to have a heart
attack.

"Just a dream," she whispered, looking frantically
around the room to make sure the Unseelie wasn't
really there. "No, a nightmare. That's all. Kalen is not
that creep's son! And our baby . . ."

No. It just wasn't possible. She wouldn't think of it.
Kalen didn't even know about their baby yet because
there hadn't been a perfect time to tell him. And she
sure wasn't about to upset him with what was either a
complete lie from a meddling Unseelie, or was simply
a figment of her overwrought imagination.

No matter how real it had seemed.

Gradually she became aware of a pounding noise
that she realized wasn't just her heart thrumming in
her ears. Someone was knocking, and they sounded
impatient. Pushing out of bed, she padded for the door,
attempting to shake off the groggy, disoriented feeling
left over from her nap.

"Mac?" Nick called from the other side. More knocking.

"Damn, hold your horses!" More than a little grumpy, she turned the locks and opened up. "What the hell's going on?"

"Why weren't you answering your phone?" he barked. "We need you in the infirmary."

Dread punched her gut. "I was taking a nap and never heard it ring. What's wrong?"

"We've got a handful of the team injured from the op. Minor stuff mostly, but Melina and Noah have their hands full."

"Hang on." Disappearing inside, she hurried and found her cell phone lying on the kitchen bar where she'd discarded it on returning to her quarters. Glaring on the display were five missed calls and several texts from both Nick and Melina. Crap. Sliding the phone into her pocket, she joined Nick and they walked at a fast clip.

"How's Kalen?"

"He took a swipe across the ribs from one of the Sluagh, and he's worn out from pushing his limit by using too much magic, but otherwise okay. He's clamoring to be released, like almost all the rest of the knuckleheads."

Thank God.

"Zander wasn't able to heal any of them?" she asked.

"Not this time. He's the worst of the bunch, out cold from a hard knock to the head. He seemed okay while we were getting ready to leave the site. Then he went down."

Damn. A head injury was much more of a problem than scrapes and bruises. "Has Melina done a CT scan on him?"

"I have no clue. I'm just the messenger."

Once they reached the infirmary, she left Nick to

hurry and find Zander. As much as she wanted to rush to Kalen's side, the Healer came first. She found Noah, who was bandaging a gash on Jax's biceps.

"Where's Zander?"

Noah glanced up. "Room seven. Dr. Mallory already ran the CT. I helped her get him prepped, but I haven't had time to ask her about the results."

"A CT scan?" Jax repeated with a frown. "Nobody told me it was that bad."

The RetroCog was worried about his best friend, and she didn't blame him. "One of us will keep you in the loop, okay?" He reluctantly agreed, as there was nothing else he could say. She turned to the blond nurse. "Thanks, Noah."

Flashing him a grateful smile, she jogged for Zan's room. As she arrived, Melina slipped from inside, closing the door softly behind her. "How's he doing?"

Melina waited, expression neutral. "He's got a pretty nasty concussion, and there's swelling putting pressure on his optic nerve. Both eardrums burst as well, and he bled some. When he wakes up we'll be able to better assess the damage, but I won't lie—I'm concerned about this. He's not healing as quickly as the other guys."

Mac nodded. "It takes a serious blow to injure a shifter to that extent. Has he regained consciousness?"

"For about a minute. The poor guy was totally confused and I don't think he knew I was there."

"Okay. I'll check on him and then see to the others. Who do you have left that needs to be seen?"

"Let's see . . ." She consulted some notes on her clipboard. "Aric, Hammer, and Kalen, all waiting in exam rooms. Thought you'd want that last one to yourself."

"You thought right." With a wink, she left her friend and walked into Zan's room.

He was asleep, collar-length dark hair feathered on the pillow. He really was quite handsome, and that wasn't just her penchant for dark-haired men talking. True to his nature as a Healer, he was kind and giving almost to a fault. There wasn't anything the black wolf wouldn't do for the ones he loved, and she admired that about him.

Moving his head, he moaned and opened his eyes. He blinked and stared at her in confusion, hardly able to focus. "Where . . . ?"

"You're in the infirmary," she told him, speaking slowly. "You tangled with a Sluagh and ended up here. Do you remember what happened?"

"I . . . yeah. One threw me against the side of the house. Hit my head. Still got him, though."

"Good for you." She smiled for his benefit.

"Doc?"

"Yes?"

"Can't hear you very good," he said hoarsely. "You're muffled."

Not good. Leaning closer, she tried to reassure him. "You took a bad hit, and there's some swelling inside. Your eardrums burst, too, so that's why you're in pain and having trouble hearing. We'll do more tests soon, but don't worry. Did you get all of that?"

"Sure." But his voice was barely a whisper, his lids drifting shut.

Briefly, she smoothed his hair from his face. "You're going to be all right, Z-man. Rest and float on the good drugs while you can, okay?"

But he was out again. Probably for the best at the

moment. On the way to her next patient, she fretted about Zan's condition. Another blow to the head as bad as that one, and he could be in real trouble.

As she turned to leave, a worried-looking Jax entered quietly. "I'll sit with him for a while, if you don't mind."

"Of course not." She touched his arm. "I'll be back later."

Aric was next, and true to form, he bitched the entire time she was cleaning and stitching his scrapes and slices. God bless Rowan for being around to tame the fiery wolf, because if he belonged to Mac, she'd end up smothering him in his sleep. She was more than glad to send him on his merry way.

Hammer was the complete opposite. The big, bald man was a huge teddy bear. A gentle giant among men to his friends, but a deadly fighter in the field. She'd known him for only a few months, since he'd joined the Pack with Nick, but she adored the guy. He took his doctoring without a cross word, unlike most of his buddies. When she was finished, he thanked her shyly and was gone.

That left a certain Sorcerer to see about. When she entered his exam room, she found him lying on his side facing the door, the table barely long enough or wide enough to accommodate him. His duster and shirt had been placed over a chair in the corner, and he wore only his dark jeans, which where stained even darker with blood.

He must've heard her come in, as his eyes fluttered open. "Hey, baby. Fancy meeting you here."

"Ha-ha, real funny. What am I going to do with you, stubborn Sorcerer?"

"Keep me?"

"I'll think about it." Her gaze found the ragged wounds on his side. "Those are some nasty souvenirs you've got there. Why don't I clean and dress those, then take you to my quarters to recover?"

He perked up considerably. "Best idea I've heard all day." He tried to sit up, but she moved over to him quickly.

"No. Stay like you are. It will be easier to get to the wounds this way."

Settling on his good side, he gave himself over to her care. After fetching the alcohol and some wipes, Mac began to clean the scored flesh. The tears were too uneven to stitch, but thankfully, they'd already started to heal. Next she retrieved some gauze, bandages, and tape, and helped him to sit up.

"Help me hold this," she said, placing several large gauze pads over the abused skin. He did, and she took the roll of bandages and began to wrap his torso. As she worked, she eyed the pendant dangling attractively on his smooth chest. "Thought that thing was supposed to protect you from evil."

"Yeah, but not so much from stupidity."

Mac couldn't help but laugh, and he joined her. Kalen didn't joke around much, and she loved how his eyes lit up on those rare occasions.

"I take it I'm going to live?"

"You are," she assured him. "Let me see who's going to monitor Zan tonight and then we'll get out of here, with any luck."

"Wait—what's wrong with Zan?" he asked in concern.

Quickly, she gave him the rundown on the Healer's

condition, something she couldn't have done in the human world. But HIPAA didn't amount to shit when the compound and everyone in it didn't technically exist.

"Damn," he said, sobering. "I hope he's going to be okay."

"He should be, but another head trauma like that one could cause serious complications." She patted Kalen's bare shoulder. "Hold on, I'll be right back."

She went in search of Melina, who assured her that she and Noah would split the night into two shifts and check on Zan. Mac could "nurse" her man tonight and take duty tomorrow night if the Healer hadn't been released by then. Grateful, Mac returned to Kalen.

"I'm clear. Ready?"

"Just a sec." Reaching behind his neck, he unclasped the pendant and walked to Mac, fastening it around hers once more. "There. Now I'm ready."

Having possession of the blessed disk again brought back the horrid dream she'd had about Malik a short time ago—and Malik's equally horrible revelation. Guilt speared her anew at keeping it from Kalen, but he didn't need that stress on top of everything else he was facing. Later, she'd tell him of the nightmare.

On the way back to her apartment, they met up with Ryon. The blond waved at Kalen and they stopped.

"Hey, you all right?" the wolf asked Kalen.

"Yeah, I'll live." The Sorcerer looked uncomfortable. "Listen, I've been meaning to talk to you, but there hasn't been a good time."

"What about?" He eyed Kalen curiously.

"I have a confession to make. It's about what happened in the dining room."

Ryon frowned. "The dining room? Oh. You mean when that spirit attacked me. What about it?"

"I caused it," Kalen confessed, looking ashamed. "It was me."

"What?" Ryon glanced between Mac and Kalen. "How?"

"With my magic. I'm so sorry."

His jaw dropped. "Are you shitting me? Why would you do something like that?"

"I gave in to Malik's influence. He wanted me to practice honing my darkness. I'm so sorry."

"Christ, that's jacked up." Ryon ran a hand down his face.

"I know. Please, forgive me. I'm trying so hard to beat this thing, but it's not easy. For what it's worth, I'm trying and I really am sick about what I did to you."

Ryon fell silent for a minute, visibly struggling with accepting the apology. But then he sighed, relaxing some. "Accepted. I appreciate you telling me. But if it happens again, to me or anyone else, and I find out it was you, I'll kick your ass."

"Fair enough."

After shaking Kalen's hand, Ryon went on his way, strolling as though he didn't have a care. Mac stared after him for a moment, thinking he was a good guy. He deserved a fabulous woman. But then, all of the guys did.

She turned back to Kalen. "I know that wasn't easy. I'm proud of you."

"It wasn't, but it needed to be done."

They continued in companionable silence to her quarters, Kalen sans his shredded T-shirt, his leather duster slung over one arm. When she let them in to her comfy apartment, he laid the coat over a chair.

"Is there a story behind that thing?" she asked curiously. "You never go anywhere without it."

"Everything has a story," he replied with a small grin. "I won it in a poker game on my twenty-first birthday. Took it right off a rich dude's back after I laid down a royal flush. Only time in my life I ever wished I'd bet more."

"What would he have gotten if you had lost?"

"Me in his bed for the night." His smile turned sad. "I didn't have anything else to wager."

She wanted to cry for the lost young man he'd been. "But you're a Sorcerer. Why didn't you just use your magic to win? To get whatever you wanted or needed out of life?"

"Because I'm many things, plenty of them not good, but I'm not a cheater, baby. My grandma raised me better. Besides, if I had given in to that temptation every time I was in a tough spot, I'd be just as selfish and evil as Malik by now."

"I'm sorry," she said contritely.

"Don't be. It's a perfectly understandable question anyone would ask." Closing the distance between them, he pulled her flush against his hard body. "What matters is that I survived. I'm here now, and this ass belongs to you."

A delicious little thrill zinged through her, arousing her past the point of no return. She had zero willpower where her mate was concerned. "Is that so? You won't mind if I take advantage of an injured man?"

He took her lips in a passionate kiss that left her

breathless. "If you don't take advantage of me and fast, the disappointment might set back my recovery."

"Well, we can't have that!"

Taking her mate's hand, she led him into her bedroom. Right where she wanted him. They stood looking at each other for several heartbeats. The desire building, the flames banking. His gaze was hot, full of need, making her feel like the most beautiful and desired woman in the world.

"I'm so sorry about how our last time together ended. I stormed out without trying to understand your side, letting you explain—"

"Shh. It's over, sweetheart. My *mate*. Let's move on, together."

"I can't think of anything I'd love more." She paused, took a breath. "I want you to claim me again. This time because we both want it."

"Oh, God, Mackenzie," he whispered. "Yes."

His hands shook a little as he reached out, began to unfasten her blouse. He unwrapped her as though she were a precious treasure, let the material drop to the floor, and removed her bra next. For several seconds he simply stared at her, such raw emotion etched on his face.

"Never have I had anyone of my own. Nobody who was just mine and mine alone to cherish . . . and to love."

"Kalen," she began, eyes stinging with tears of joy.

"Let me love you. And not just with my body—I mean let me *love* you. Please. I need you."

"You have me," she said, her voice breaking.

Scooping her up, he placed her on the bed and shed

his jeans and underwear. The emotion between them was so intense, she could tell this time would be much different than the last. Before, the sex was hot, raw, carnal. She'd almost combusted.

This time her mate was going to make love to her, lavish on her all the love he'd been longing to give his entire life. And she would love him back, as he deserved.

Crawling over her body, he lowered himself onto her, careful not to squash her, and kissed her so gently, the tears finally spilled over. He licked them from the corners of her eyes, shushing her softly, whispering sweet words she didn't quite catch but grasped the meaning of anyway.

Then he moved lower, paying homage to every inch of her skin. He nibbled the sensitive spot behind her ear, her neck, and her collarbone. Next, he suckled her nipples, tightening them to rigid peaks. Played with them until she moaned, needing much more attention in other places, too.

He was happy to oblige, trailing his tongue down her abdomen, tickling her belly button and making her laugh. Laughter during sex, who'd have thought? But what was happening between them tonight transcended sex—this was a sharing of bodies, connecting souls. Why shouldn't it be an occasion of joy?

Then he crouched between her legs, spread her thighs wider, baring her sex to him. She'd never been ashamed of her body, but this openness, the ease she felt with him, was unlike any relationship before him. This man was hers.

Cupping his hands under her bottom, he raised her some and began to feast on her pussy. Every cell in her body came alive, singing at his attentions. This was her mate, pleasuring his woman as no one else had the right to do, ever again. His possession nearly tipped her too far over the edge. As though he sensed how near she was to release, he grinned and lowered her to the bed.

"Not so fast, baby. Gonna make you come on my cock."

"Yes, please!"

Moving over her again, he placed the head of his hard cock at her entrance and began to ease inside. He impaled her slowly, and it felt so damned good. He was the perfect fit, stretching and filling her so she was nearly incoherent with pleasure. Then he began to slide in and out, stroking her inner walls, and she clung to him. Let him sweep her away in glorious waves of delight that drove her higher.

"I love you, Mackenzie," he said softly, holding her close. Thrusting his cock slow and deep. "God, how I love you."

"I love you, too. Have since the minute I saw you."

"Baby . . ."

His thrusts increased in speed bit by bit. His breathing came harsher as he picked up the tempo. Then he gathered her in his arms, and not breaking their connection, pulled them into a sitting position with Mac on his lap.

"Ride me just like this, sweetheart," he breathed. "Fuck me like this."

"Yes!"

She took the lead, clinging to his shoulders as she bounced on his lap. Fucked him with enthusiasm, spiraling them toward the inevitable climax.

"Gonna claim you, my mate. Never let you go."

"Please, Kalen!"

Needing no further encouragement, he struck. The instant his fangs sank into the curve of her neck and shoulder, the force of her release detonated her world. Mac was vaguely aware of screaming out her wild ecstasy as he reaffirmed their bond, pumped his come into her on and on.

When at last their shudders stopped, he still held her tightly, rubbing his palms on her back. Eventually he withdrew his fangs and licked the wounds, though she sensed that the beast in him had been reluctant to give up his hold.

"I meant what I said," he told her. "It wasn't just the heat of sex, either. I love you, Doc."

"And I love you, Sorcerer."

He smiled. "You make me happier than I have a right to be. But for once, I'm going to enjoy having what I want and worry about the rest tomorrow."

"There's the spirit." She kissed his luscious lips. "I suppose we should move."

"Ugh. Do we hafta?"

"Shower?"

He perked up. "Does that include shower sex?"

"If you're lucky," she teased.

"Sounds like a plan to me."

Carefully he eased her off his lap. Together they padded into the bathroom, started the spray, and let it get nice and hot. Then they proceeded to steam up the glass in more ways than one.

Afterward, Mac thought again about how she needed to tell Kalen about the baby. Crap, if they started sharing living quarters, he was going to be worried about her getting sick in the mornings.

And she'd have to tell him about the nightmare and Malik's claims.

She'd tell him about both soon. But she wanted this one night just for the two them, before reality intruded.

Surely that wasn't too much to ask.

With a sigh of contentment, she snuggled into his arms and slept better than she had in months.

Later, she would be very glad she hadn't known of the tragedy and heartbreak to come.

Eleven

The morning following claiming his mate for the second time—with much happier results—Kalen was flying high. So high his lover would've given him a drug test if she hadn't known for a fact it was natural.

So he should have known the buzz wouldn't last.

After Mackenzie had dressed and headed to the infirmary, Kalen went back to his quarters for a change of clothes. He was contemplating asking his mate if they could move in together when his cell phone rang.

Nick's name popped up on the display and he grimaced. A call from the boss wasn't typically cause for celebration, and this one was no different.

"I've got a location on your parents," he said without preamble.

"Well, *there's* some fantastic news," Kalen replied with all the sarcasm he could muster. This conversation required coffee. Maybe he'd add a dash of whiskey to it, too. "I can hardly wait for the heartfelt reunion. Should I bring tissues?"

"Funny. Don't you want to know where they are?"

"Not particularly. But I guess you'll tell me anyways." Yep, coffee. Better leave out the booze, though. He reached for a mug and stuck it under his single-cup brewer, then hit the switch.

"Your childhood address is still listed in their names."

Kalen froze, watching the fragrant brew steam into the mug. "You're kidding."

"No. The weird thing is that my contact says nobody can recall seeing the Blacks for years. Nobody going in or out of the house, no visitors, nothing. But the house is well kept, flowers planted, grass mowed, newspapers and mail picked up regularly. Records show the bills have been paid on time, et cetera. For nine years. All seems good on the surface."

"Except not a soul has seen them in almost a decade." A cold finger trailed down Kalen's spine. He didn't need Nick to tell him that something wasn't right. "When do we leave?"

"You don't have to go," the commander said, his voice softening. "You know we'll tell you what we find."

"I trust you. It's just . . . As much as I'd love never to set foot in my hometown again, I've come to realize I've got to go back and get some closure." He hesitated. "For me, and for Mackenzie."

"You and Mac, huh?" Nick's smile came through in his voice.

"I doubt it's much of a secret."

"You're right, it's not. You've claimed her—the right way this time?"

"Yeah," he said, glad the man couldn't see his red face over the phone. Or shit, maybe he could. "She's the greatest thing that's ever happened to me. I love her, Nick, and for some damned reason she loves me."

"I'm really happy for you, kid. And I agree closure is what you need. Can you be ready to leave in an hour?"

"I'm ready now."

"Eat some breakfast first, then be at the hangar in an hour. Aric is going to fly us there in the jet, and Ryon is going as extra backup. Those two are the least injured from yesterday."

"All right, see you then. And, Nick? Thanks."

"Don't mention it."

Kalen sipped his coffee for a few minutes, then tossed the dregs down the drain. The idea of facing his parents again after so long made his gut churn, and he wasn't sure about putting anything in his stomach. But there was no telling when he'd be able to eat next, so he'd better do as he was told.

Only about half of the guys, including Aric and Ryon, were in the dining room, stuffing themselves on pancakes and bacon. The rest must have been sleeping off the beating they'd taken from the Sluagh. Kalen stabbed a couple of pancakes with his fork, grabbed three pieces of bacon, and dug in. He was hungrier than he'd thought and made quick work of it. After telling Aric and Ryon he'd see them at the plane and saying goodbye to the others, he hurried to the infirmary.

A tired-looking Noah pointed him in the right direction, and Kalen found his doc coming from Zan's room. "How is he?"

"Improving," Mackenzie said with relief. "His vision is clear now and his hearing is almost back to normal."

"That's great news." He gave her a quick kiss—not nearly the hot, passionate one he'd rather lay on her. But it would have to do. "Will he be out of here soon?"

"By tomorrow, I'd say. So what are you up to?"

He released a pent-up sigh. "Going to see my parents. Nick wants to check out any connection they may have to Malik, considering his claims, and a couple of the guys are going along as backup."

"You mean his claims that he knew your family and that you're Fae." She gazed at him in worry.

"Exactly. I'm not sure my folks are going to be real cooperative, or if they'll even speak to us."

"Good luck, honey," she said, pulling him into a hug and squeezing him tightly. "I know how important it is to you to get answers."

"I just hope I can handle them once I have them."

"I wish I could go with you." Her pretty blue eyes were cloudy with concern. "But I have to take this shift with Zan. Noah is exhausted and needs to get some sleep."

"Don't worry about me, baby. I'll have Nick, Aric, and Ryon with me. I'll be fine. I promise."

She bit her lip. "Okay, but call me and let me know how it went. I won't be able to concentrate on much until you do."

"I will. See you this afternoon."

One hug and several long kisses later, he was on his way to the hangar. Christ only knew what they'd find in his hometown.

Kalen could feel the tension in his neck and shoulders as Aric guided the plane to a stop on the private runway they'd appropriated for their trip. He'd sworn he'd never return and here he was. Back in home-sweet-prison.

Except for Grandma. She'd been the sole positive influence in his life, and without her, he'd quickly become lost. Until Mackenzie.

There was no doubt that his mate drove the darkness back. In spite of Malik's terrible hold over him, his mate's was much stronger. She was what Sariel had meant by opening himself to light and love—all along, it had been Mackenzie.

Still, he worried about something happening to shatter their fragile new bond. That it could be crushed like a flower in a hurricane, simply swept away on a tide of cruel fate. He wasn't being paranoid. It had happened before, the loss of his happiness, his soul. If it happened again, he could become a slave to his own darkness, never to see the light again.

"Welcome to Mayberry," Aric quipped, bringing the jet to a stop. "Jesus, what do people do for fun around here? Knit afghans?"

"Yep. When the old folks are feeling *really* rebellious, they throw money in the pot for the Bingo winners. And I'm not exaggerating." His three companions snickered, and he smiled at the memory of Grandma boasting of her big score.

"Hammer would be right at home," Ryon observed as they disembarked. "He could start a knitting circle since everyone knows he's really a little old lady in disguise."

Nick laughed. "Don't let him hear you say that. He swears by the pastime, says it helps him relax."

Ryon arched a dusky brow. "Dude, I can think of

better ways to relax that don't involve yarn. Seriously, somebody needs to take that boy under his wing."

"That *boy*," Nick drawled, "lived so deep undercover for so many years he almost lost himself. He's dined with drug lords, walked the edge with homeland terrorists, and has taken out more dangerous criminals than the four of us combined. If he wants to live a quiet life while off duty, then leave him be."

Interesting. Kalen had often wondered about the big man, and the glimpse into his past made him even more curious. But now wasn't the time to dig. They'd come here for a reason, and the knowledge brought him back to reality.

A dark SUV was waiting for them on the tarmac, keys under the driver's floor mat. Ryon took the wheel and Nick called shotgun, leaving Kalen in the back. With Aric. Who eyed him before settling in, unbelievably, without a single snarky comment. In fact, when he did open his mouth, what came out was pretty damned decent.

"This thing with your folks, man, it ain't shit. You're gonna wrap up that part of your life, put it behind you. We've got your back. Remember that."

Their truce was uneasy, but it seemed to be holding. Kalen doubted they'd ever be BFFs, and the man took some getting used to, but he was all right. "Thanks. I appreciate it," he said, and meant it.

The ride was uneventful, and he checked out the town as they drove past the square. Not a lot had changed, except a few new businesses he didn't recognize. The trees were taller and fuller, and the city had done some work beautifying the place with flowers and such. Other than those minor details, it was like walking into a time warp.

A few minutes later, when Ryon pulled up in front of his old house and parked next to the curb, Kalen was sweating. He took a few deep breaths, willing himself to calm down. His father was like a pit bull—if he sensed the least bit of insecurity in his prodigal son, he'd go for the jugular and they'd end up having that fistfight that had been years in the making.

Kalen wasn't fourteen anymore. He wouldn't take the abuse lying down.

But he needed answers more than he needed to deck his father. They got out of the vehicle, four doors slamming. They started up the sidewalk, but Ryon halted in his tracks.

"Wait." The blond pushed a fall of hair from his eyes and looked around at the quaint, yellow frame house with the white gingerbread trim. The neighborhood was peaceful, leaves on the old trees swaying gently. Somewhere, a dog barked. A street or two over, children could he heard playing. A typical day.

"What?" Kalen asked, voice low.

"There are two spirits here," Ryon told them grimly. "They're warning us to leave."

"They say why?" This from Nick.

"Something about bad juju. Black magic."

Great. Just what they needed. "Somehow I should've expected this," Kalen told them. "Hang on, let me see if I can get a handle on anything supernatural."

Opening his magic, he let it flow outward, toward the house, seeking a like power. The backlash was instantaneous and knocked him backward violently. "Fuck!"

Aric caught him, saving him from smacking the pavement. "Whoa! Found it, huh?"

"Son of a bitch!" Straightening, he glanced at the redhead. "Nice catch."

"You're welcome. So, what's the deal?"

"Just like Ryon's spirits said—black magic. There's a thick net over the house, acting as a veil or protection ward of some kind."

"Can you get rid of it?" Nick asked.

"I think so." If not, they'd need a shovel to scrape him off the ground. But he refrained from mentioning that.

"Great. Just get us inside before somebody calls the cops," Aric muttered.

There was that. Blocking out thoughts of curious neighbors, Kalen closed his eyes and opened his magic. Let it flow, cautiously this time, toward the spiderweb of wards over the house. He probed the structure here and there, found points of weakness to exploit. He worked on those while expanding his gift, searching for the right type of spell.

It was a simple veil, constructed to deceive all who viewed the house so that they would see it as it had been long ago. And the signature belonged to a creature he was beginning to know well.

"Malik," he managed. "This is his work."

He heard a couple of curses at this news, but kept his focus on the ward. On breaking it down inch by inch until finally it collapsed and dissipated like dust. What remained, the true image of the home where he'd suffered as a boy, reflected what he'd expected to find.

The house was in a state of sad neglect, sitting in a weed-choked lot, the porch falling in. The windows resembled soulless eyes, broken and weeping. The once-cheery yellow paint was faded and peeling, making the house appear diseased. That wouldn't be too far from accurate.

Ryon started up the cracked, uneven sidewalk. "Christ, what a mess. Why would Malik bother to mask the actual condition of the house?"

"I can think of one good reason," Kalen said. "He didn't want anyone going inside."

"Be alert going in." Nick eyed the house warily. "We don't need any more of you laid up or worse."

They stepped onto the porch carefully, and the rotted boards groaned under their combined weight. It seemed to hold, though.

"Ladies first," Aric quipped, smirking at Kalen. At Kalen's glare, he immediately attempted to look contrite. "Sorry. Old habits."

Kalen laughed, surprising the redhead. The others smiled, too. If he was going to be a real part of this team, he'd have to learn to laugh at himself a little. Okay, a lot.

He tried the door and the knob turned easily. Every cell ready to spring into action, he swung the door open. All that met him was the scent of dust, cobwebs . . . and something he'd smelled dozens of times before, in cemeteries all over.

Decay.

The wolves must've picked up on the scent, too, because Nick laid a hand on his shoulder. "You can wait outside if you want. Nobody will think less of you."

He knew what they were likely to find. But Kalen hadn't come this far to face his demons only to back down at the last second. "No, I'm fine. Let's do this."

At the commander's nod, they moved inside and began to search the house, sticking close. The interior must've been covered in an inch-thick layer of dust. Cobwebs littered the corners. Ryon moved into the kitchen and in a moment he called out.

"Hey, come look at this."

Kalen followed them inside and stared at the mess. The stench of old, burnt food assaulted their sensitive shifter noses. Two pots sat on the old stove, charred black with something that must've been cooking at one time. Ryon opened the oven and started coughing, slamming it closed again.

"There's a pan of something in there that I think used to be meat of some kind."

"Gross," Aric said, wrinkling his nose.

Nick waved a hand at the room. "So, dinner was cooking. And then what?"

"Nothing good," Kalen said. "Let's check their bedroom. Mom would often come home after work and change clothes after she started dinner. She always said it was nice to unwind after a long day."

He really, really hoped they didn't find anything. He'd rather his parents just be gone without a trace than to discover what he was afraid they would. But his prayers were not answered.

The reality was so much worse than he'd imagined.

Nick, in the lead, stepped through his parents' bedroom doorway first and immediately spun around, holding out both hands. "You don't need to go in there."

"Fuck if I don't! Move, Nick."

Peering around their boss, Ryon gaped and Aric shook his head. "Nah," Aric said. "You really don't want to go in."

"I'm a grown man," he said evenly. "It's not as if I didn't know something was terribly wrong the minute I discovered that the wards belonged to Malik. Let me in so I can put an end to this part of my life."

After several beats of agonized silence, they parted to allow him entrance. What he saw assured him there were some things that were never truly over—for the living, that is. Sometimes there was nothing but horror that would remain with a person for the rest of his life.

The dried-out, mummified husks of his parents lay in the room, as abandoned and forlorn as their once-unhappy home. His father lay on the floor to one side of the bed, his clothing long turned to rags. But that wasn't the most chilling detail.

He'd been decapitated. His head was sitting on the dresser at the foot of the bed, overlooking the corpse of his mother.

She had been bound to the bed, wrists over her head, and from what he could tell, had been naked when she died. Her face was turned toward the severed head on the dresser, her mouth frozen in a silent scream.

"Their spirits are still here," Ryon whispered. "They're telling me Malik did this. He bound Mrs. Black to the bed, then killed Mr. Black while he made her watch. And then he left her here to die slowly, alone with the horror of her husband's murder and her own impending death." Ryon's wide, empty gaze found Kalen. "Mr. Black has a message. He says he hates you. You're a bastard, and he hopes you rot in hell."

Ryon's eyes rolled back in his head and he hit the floor.

Kalen's stomach lurched. "God. I'm gonna be sick."

He bolted for the tiny bathroom and barely made it

to his knees in front of the grungy toilet before he lost his breakfast. He heaved his guts until there was nothing left and he was sure his stomach lining must've turned inside out. A hand clasped his shoulder and he jumped.

"You all right, kid?" Nick gave a humorless laugh. "Dumb question. Come on, let's get out of here. I'll put a call in to Grant and have him send a team to make this mess go away."

"Grant? We don't need him, boss," Aric scoffed. He helped a shaken Ryon get up, then came to stand behind Nick at the threshold of the bathroom. "We can take care of this ourselves."

Nick thought about that for a moment, then asked Kalen, "Do you want anything from this place? What about the house?"

"My grandma's photo albums," Kalen answered hoarsely. "My mother got them when she died, and I'd like to have those. Then burn the fucking house down."

Aric nodded. "I can do that. With pleasure."

"Without damaging any other homes nearby?"

"You bet."

Nick gave Kalen a hand up and the guys rallied around him as they left the bedroom, blocking his view of the awful scene. Though it was too late for that, he appreciated the gesture.

The search for the albums was mercifully brief. His mother had kept them on a bookshelf in the living room, and his friends gathered an armload of several dusty books, taking them out to the SUV. Kalen trailed behind, turned and took one last long look at the place that held so many sad memories. So much horror.

Remembering his mother, a lump burned in his

throat. Whatever her failings, she'd loved Kalen once. But her many mistakes, like marrying his father, had sealed her fate. She might have loved her son, but she hadn't fought for him. She'd been too beaten down, without hope.

And whatever secrets she kept had died with her.

Or had they?

Malik was unusually quiet at a time when Kalen would have thought he'd be gloating, taunting him with riddles and more secrets. Not to mention punishing Kalen for his betrayal, for going straight to Nick and the Pack about the planned attack on the citizens. The mating bond must truly be stronger, and he was grateful for the reprieve.

"Cloak us, magic man, 'cause this baby's gonna burn."

Aric threw out his hand and a column of fire shot to the dilapidated porch. The house went up like dry kindling, and Kalen barely managed to get another ward in place before the entire neighborhood witnessed a spectacle they wouldn't soon forget.

They watched as the hungry flames consumed the structure. Reduced it to ash. In minutes it was over, only a heap of smoldering rubble left to mark where his life had begun.

Aric steered Kalen toward the SUV. "Ryon, get us the fuck out of here."

"I'll drive," Nick said. "Ryon's still a little out of sorts."

As they climbed into the vehicle, Aric muttered, "Jeez, this town may look like Mayberry, but it's really Freakville, USA. Givin' me the goddamned creeps. Whole town's probably full of goblins or some shit."

Kalen's lips curved upward in spite of the serious-
ness of their grisly find. Aric was just so . . . Aric. One
of a kind. They'd had their differences, but he was turning out to be a stand-up guy.

In less than half an hour, they'd returned the borrowed SUV to the spot where they'd found it and were
jetting toward the compound in Wyoming.

Toward home, and better yet, the woman he loved.

Mac's cell phone buzzed on her hip and she grabbed it
and read the text from Kalen.

Landing in five. XOXO.

XOXO back at u. How'd it go?

Bad. Tell u soon.

In my office. Come when u can.

"Crap." *Bad* could mean anything. She wished they
could talk in each other's heads like the wolf Bondmates, but while she and Kalen were more sensitive to
each other's emotions and the general direction of each
other's thoughts, actual telepathic communication didn't
seem to be in the cards for them. Anxiously, she paced
her office until finally a knock sounded.

She hurried over and flung the door open, and her
Sorcerer practically fell into her arms. "Oh, honey! Are
you okay?" She tried to pull back to check him over,
but he clung even tighter. Tucking her head under his
chin, he kissed her hair, his lean body shuddering.

"They were dead," he choked.

Oh, no. "Your parents?"

"Dead, like for *years*. Maybe since I left home. Christ,
they were *mummified*."

"Sweetie, I'm so sorry," she whispered, aching for him.
"It must've been such a shock, finding them like that."

"My mom was bound to their b-bed, and my father's head was on the dresser. The killer made her watch and then left her there with him like that. Just left her to die."

She held him for a long time, tried to comfort him while he shook. She felt so helpless, uncertain what to say. "Who do you think did this?"

"Malik's signature was all over the wards he left on the house," he said with difficulty. "Ryon said he killed them."

"What about the scene? Did you guys leave it alone?"

"No. Nick wanted to call your dad and have him bring in a clean-up crew, but Aric offered to torch it instead. It's gone, all except for Grandma's photo albums. I brought those back."

"That's good. I'm glad you were able to save something that belonged to her," she said gently.

He fell silent for a moment. At last she managed to extricate herself from his death grip and urged him into a chair. Taking a seat next to him, she held his hand. His eyes were red and he looked so lost, her heart went out to him.

"I feel like it's my fault that they're dead," he said quietly. He looked at her, his expression wretched.

She put on her therapist hat. "That's an understandable reaction. But let me ask you, were you there when they were killed?"

"No."

"And why weren't you?"

"Because my father had thrown me out."

"And you were only a fourteen-year-old boy. Therefore, there's nothing you could've done to save them. You might even have been killed along with them."

"Maybe, but I don't think so."

"Really? Why not?"

"They were the target of Malik's revenge, not me. If he had wanted me dead, I would be by now. I'm too useful to him to die. He's said as much."

She managed to hide her shiver of fear. They both knew that if the killer was Malik—and that seemed highly likely—the Unseelie could change his mind at any time. He could decide that Kalen was a liability he couldn't afford, especially if he failed to win him to his side. Through their bond, she felt Kalen's worry. He was strung out, on the edge.

"Why don't we go rest in my quarters before dinner? Zan was released earlier, so I'm free." She tugged him up and linked her arm through his as they walked toward her apartment.

"I don't deserve you," he murmured.

She burrowed close to his side. "Don't."

"It's true. All of the bad shit that's happening is about me."

"No. It's about Malik's quest for world domination. You had nothing to do with the birth of his plans."

"But from the time I was a child, those plans had something to do with me. He killed my parents, just like he's murdered everyone who's ever hurt me. And he hasn't done those things out of love—I'm important to him. Or rather, my power is." He gave a bitter laugh.

"But you're more important to me and to the Pack. Don't forget that."

"I'll do my best, baby." Squeezing her hand, he gave her a grateful smile.

The two of them continued to her apartment holding

hands and she enjoyed their closeness, the warmth of his bigger palm enfolding hers. Inside, she slipped off his duster and tossed it on the sofa, then pulled him into her bedroom. He gave her a questioning look, hope and desire flaring in his eyes.

"Make love to me, please," she murmured, skimming a palm over his chest.

He sucked in a breath. "Thought you'd never ask."

She took care of him, undressing him as he watched her, his expression as vulnerable as a boy's. But his body was all man, as evidenced by the desire rising to kiss his stomach. He was breathtaking, made of sleek, lean muscle. Dark and dangerous. All hers.

"I love you, Kalen."

"I don't understand why, but I'm glad. You make me so happy," he breathed. "Let me love you back."

He undressed her with just as much care as she'd shown him, then pushed her gently onto her back. This time there was wasn't a lot of foreplay. A few heated kisses on her lips, and he parted her thighs, moved between them. Found her moist center with the head of his cock and slid inside. Made sweet, leisurely love to her with sure strokes, bringing them to a breathless peak. Then sending them over.

Clinging together, they rode their climax until they lay spent. And afterward remained entwined, soaking up the golden glow of their bond.

He sighed, sated and spent. When he spoke, his voice was filled with wonder. "God, that was wonderful. What does a beautiful, intelligent woman like you see in a freak like me, baby?"

Rising up on her elbow, she frowned at him. "You are not a freak. You're the man I love and I wouldn't change anything about you, except for taking away your hurts."

He squeezed her tight. "I just wish I'd been born a normal kid from a regular, white-bread family. Then I could be an everyday guy for you."

"Well, if you had been born any different we wouldn't even have met," she said. "Besides, I love you exactly how you are. By saying you wish you were different, you're questioning my choices and my intelligence. Is that what you mean to do?"

Sucking in a breath, he hugged her tight as she cuddled into his side again, and dropped a kiss to the top of her head. "No, it's not. You're right and I'm sorry. You're the one good thing to come out of all of this, you know that?"

"*We* are the one good thing." She nuzzled his bare chest.

"Yeah. You make the darkness go away," he whispered. "You're my light."

Her throat tightened with emotion. "Then hang on a bit longer and we'll beat it together."

Mac awoke to a persistent knocking coming from somewhere beyond the bedroom. Disoriented, she glanced at the digital clock on the nightstand and realized it was seven in the morning. She and Kalen had missed dinner and slept all night.

The knocking came again, and she frowned, wondering who in the hell would be pounding on her door at this hour. Her cell phone lay silent beside the clock. If someone needed her, why hadn't they just called?

With a sigh, she rose and donned a terry cloth robe, ignoring the ominous rumble in her tummy that signaled an impending onslaught of morning sickness, and hoped the visitor didn't wake Kalen. Her poor mate was exhausted from all the crap he'd been dealing with and deserved to sleep. But later she had something to share with him that she hoped would make him happy. The idea of telling him gave her a little thrill.

She was thinking about whether to share the news over omelets or take him for a walk instead when she opened the door without looking through the peephole—

And found herself face-to-face with General Jarrod Grant of the US Navy.

"Dad!" she squeaked.

"Baby girl!" he boomed, giving her a big smile. "Surprise!"

Instantly she was wrapped in a huge bear hug, the stuffing squeezed out of her. "Oh my God! Isn't it, though?" Oh, shit. She was almost always overjoyed to see her dad. Except when her new Bondmate was lying in her bed, sexually sated and snoozing.

"Let me look at you," he said, setting her back from him a bit. "You're lovely, as always. Almost glowing."

Imagine that. "You look rather handsome yourself."

It was the truth. Her father was still a very good-looking man, even pushing sixty. Everywhere he went, he turned heads with his toned, military-hard physique. His dark hair was more salt than pepper these days and there were laugh lines in the corners of blue eyes that looked just like Mac's, but it all added to his ruggedly masculine appeal.

"Thanks, pumpkin." He glanced to the kitchen with a hopeful look. "Got any coffee?"

"You bet. Coming right up." *Please don't let the smell of it make me sick.* She kissed his cheek, then moved into the kitchen to put on a pot. They were all going to need it. Idly, she gestured toward his crisp dress uniform. "Here on official business?"

His happiness dimmed some as he took a seat at the small table. "You could say that. Got a call from Nicky a couple of days ago that I couldn't ignore. So here I am."

"That's rather vague," she said drily, fetching three mugs. She resisted the urge to bite her lip, figuring the extra mug wouldn't go unnoticed.

It didn't. "You got company?" he asked, tone carefully neutral.

"Um, you could say that." Ugh. How awkward. "But it's fine, really. In fact, there's something I need to—"

"Hey, baby. Do I smell coffee?"

Yawning sleepily, her Sorcerer walked right past her father seated at the table without noticing him. Her dad's eyes widened and his brow shot up. Thankfully, Kalen had put on his jeans before venturing out of the bedroom, but given his disheveled state, the top button undone at his waist, and no shirt, it was pretty darned clear that this man was her lover.

Her *enthusiastic* lover, who wrapped his arms around her and gave her a soul-melting kiss while her father smirked at her behind Kalen's back.

She managed to pull away with an embarrassed laugh. She was a grown woman and this was her life, but still. "Uh, Kalen, sweetie. There's someone I want you to meet."

"Huh?" Confusion furrowed his brow until she

turned him to face her dad. "Oh! Damn, sorry! I didn't realize we had company. I'm Kalen Black," he said politely, voice uncertain, as he stuck out his hand.

Her father rose to his full six-foot-four height, smirk gone. In her dad's place was the man who could—and had—made grown men pee their pants. "General Jarrod Grant." He took the offered hand, giving Kalen the unmistakable once-over that let the other man know he was being measured. And that the jury was out.

"Nice to meet you, sir." To his credit, Kalen didn't flinch. He stood straight and tall, meeting her father's gaze with a level one of his own, silently communicating that while he was respectful, he was no pushover.

"You too, Kalen." Her dad paused, narrowing his eyes as he released Kalen's hand. He glanced between his daughter and the man in her apartment. "You're the Sorcerer Nick was telling me about. You're the reason the Pack is having so much trouble with that Unseelie bastard."

"You've got the right Sorcerer but the wrong impression," Kalen said stiffly. "Malik doesn't *need* a reason to make everyone's lives miserable, but he's got a couple all the same, and his plans happen to include me."

"And what do *your* plans include? Balancing on the fence until you figure out which side you're going to land on?"

The temperature in the room seemed to drop about twenty degrees and Mac's stomach twisted. "Daddy, please—"

Kalen interrupted her plea. "That's a fair question. No, sir, I'm not sitting on any fence. I'm fighting as hard as I can against the asshole who wants me in his camp. And I'm determined to win, but if I don't . . ."

He swallowed hard, but held her father's steely gaze. "I'm prepared to do what I have to in order to protect your daughter and my team."

Her dad nodded, new respect easing the harshness of his face. "If it looks like you're going to fail, I'll help you do it. Believe that."

God. They were discussing Kalen, her mate and the man she loved, losing his life, right in front of her! Mac's stomach lurched again, and she knew she was going to be sick. She clapped a hand over her mouth.

"Excuse me."

She ran for the bathroom, hit her knees, and heaved. As she did, her father's incredulous voice floated in the air. Made her pulse pound with panic and regret.

"Sooo . . . when the hell were the two of you going to tell me that my baby girl is pregnant?"

Twelve

Pregnant?

What the fuck?

Kalen made like a statue, stared dumbly at the undoubtedly badass General Jarrod Grant and searched for an appropriate reaction. Unfortunately, his brain short-circuited and he gaped at the general with his mouth hanging open and his heart doing a weird stuttering thing in his chest. Maybe he was going to have a heart attack.

"What? Don't tell me you didn't know," Grant demanded. "She's been rubbing her stomach since I got here, she didn't take a single sip of her coffee, and now she's throwing up her guts. And the kicker is, she's not really sick—in fact, I've never seen her more radiant. How long has this been going on?"

"I—I don't know." He thought back, trying to remember.

"Wake up, son. Seems like you've been so busy with your Unseelie problem that you've been blind to what's most important."

Kalen blinked at the man. "You must be mistaken. She wouldn't keep something like that from me." Would she?

"Actually, Dad, I was waiting for the right time to talk to him," Mac said, her voice tight with stress and irritation. "So thanks for bulldozing right over me."

"Shit! I'm sorry, baby girl," he said contritely.

Kalen felt like his head was going to explode. He rubbed his temples, staring at his mate. "You're pregnant."

"Yes." Her blue eyes were clouded with worry. "I was going to tell you. There just hasn't been a good time."

Some thread of knowledge was trying to come to the forefront, but he hadn't grasped it yet. He was still too busy assimilating the facts to think about how excited he was over the news. "How long have you known?"

Her face paled and she licked her lips. "A few days."

A few days. Okay. He processed that and the unwanted information slowly dawned. She wouldn't have—but yeah. She fucking had. A hot flare of anger ignited inside him and built rapidly toward something very, very ugly.

"You knew," he said in a deceptively low voice that quickly ramped up in volume. "You sent me out to battle with the pendant around my neck. The pendant that should have been protecting not only you but our child."

The general frowned. "What pendant?"

"The one she's wearing that protects against evil. I gave it to her, but she took it off when we went into battle against some Sluagh and begged me to wear it."

"Mac," her father began, "what were you thinking?"

"I can explain!" Her eyes filled with tears as she fingered the disk in question. "It seemed safe for me and the baby here, and I didn't want anything to happen to you!"

But Kalen's rage was far from averted. "You chose to protect me over *our baby*? *How the fuck could you?*" he roared. He hadn't even realized he'd taken a giant step toward her until Grant was between them, a palm on his chest, holding him back.

"Okay, let's all calm down."

"I'm sorry!" she cried. The tears broke free and rolled down her cheeks. But Kalen wasn't swayed.

Malik pounced on the situation. *Didn't I warn you, my boy? Do you believe now that I'm the only one you can trust to tell you the truth?*

"You endangered our child, Mackenzie," he said hoarsely, grabbing his head in both hands. The pain of her betrayal was so great, it threatened to send his anger over the edge. "I don't know if that's something I can forgive."

There's something else she knows that you do not, Malik said, his voice sly and pleased. *Ask her.*

"What else are you keeping from me?"

Sobbing openly now, she shook her head in confusion. "What? Nothing!"

She lies. Come to me and I'll forgive your betrayal. I'll reveal the answer to the question you asked me not so long ago. The answer she refuses to give to you.

"You're lying," he hissed at her.

"Wait a damned minute," Grant began, his face reddening in anger. "My girl wouldn't lie to you. Maybe she made a mistake. But she only did that because she cares about you."

A mistake that could have caused you to lose your child.

"I can't—I have to get out of here before I say or do something I'll regret."

Spinning on his heel, he pushed out the door and summoned the rest of his clothing onto his body with a wave of his hand. His mate cried out his name, but he kept going. Faster and faster until he was running, nearly barreling into Ryon as he rounded the corner at the end of the corridor.

"Hey, dude, where's the fire?"

He kept going. But the facts chased him anyway, dogging his steps. His mate had endangered their baby. Sure, the wards over the compound meant that the child was probably safe. *Probably.* But nothing was ever one hundred percent. She'd gambled with a defenseless child's life.

That's right. She refused to protect your child. Just like your mother refused to protect you.

His anger and shock were much too hard to contain. His shift happened almost without conscious thought and his panther was set free. Streaking through the compound toward the rec room, he was hardly aware of the surprised shouts. A teammate calling after him, asking what was wrong. If he could've laughed, he would've.

What was right?

He bolted through the rec room, leaping and easily clearing A.J. and Kira, who were sprawled on the carpet watching television. He ran straight for the outside door—and right through the glass, which shattered on impact. Alarms blared. Somebody would have to fix that. He didn't give a fuck.

There was no pain from any possible injury. Only pain inside that had no outlet.

He ran through the forest for a long while, moving in the direction of Malik's cabin. The place that was nothing more than an illusion, filled with wickedness. So wrong. But he needed to know what the damned Unseelie was talking about. Was his mate really keeping something else from him, or was it a trick? If she was, he might not be able to forgive her.

But didn't everyone deserve another shot? What if nobody had been willing to give him a chance when he arrived in Cody? What if Nick and the Pack had turned him out? They could have at any point in the last few weeks, when it had become obvious Kalen came with a battleship full of trouble. If they had, where would he be now?

Right where he was currently headed. Of that much he was suddenly sure. Malik would have simply lured him in sooner. In an epiphany, it struck him that Malik was, almost without a single doubt, the one responsible for bringing Kalen to the Shoshone in the first place. Until now, he'd always chalked it up to fate that he'd ended up here.

Now he knew better.

The rustic cabin came into view and he slowed, trotting into the yard. The front door opened before he even reached the porch, Malik standing there in his guise as Kerrigan, looking as handsome and urbane as ever.

"You could have teleported," the Unseelie observed with impatience. "I don't appreciate being kept waiting."

Letting his magic flow, he shifted back into human form. "Tough shit. I'm here now, aren't I?"

A flash of anger sparked in his fathomless eyes, but then Malik's lips turned up in amusement. "Come inside, whelp. The last time you were here you asked me a question. I have the answer."

Kalen followed him into the house. Nothing had changed—but something was about to. The air was heavy with the weight of a secret that might soon crush him with the telling. Any secret Malik was excited to impart could only mean bad things for anyone around him.

"What is this answer going to cost me? You want blood?"

"I already have that," he answered cryptically. "And so do you."

Kalen suppressed a shiver. "Are you going to dance around this all night? I don't even remember the question I asked."

Malik walked to the wet bar and removed two tumblers from the glass shelf. Into each he poured two generous fingers of the fine Cognac he'd served before, his stance all too casual. But Kalen had no trouble reading the growing anticipation in the Unseelie's expression. His posture. He turned, a feverish light in his eyes as he brought Kalen the drink, handed it to him.

"You asked me, why you? Why, of all the powerful beings in the world, did I choose *you*?"

"I remember now." Kalen took a fortifying sip of the liquor, let it warm his insides as it went down. "I assumed it had to do with what Grandma told me. That I was born under a black moon, which makes me vulnerable to dark forces."

"That is true, what she told you," he allowed.

"But there's more."

"Of course. Isn't there always?" Malik swirled the amber liquid, took a drink. Then he closed the distance between them, standing casually a mere couple of feet away. Too close. "You are one with the darkness because it's in your blood, Kalen. It's a part of you that causes you intense pain to deny, and yet you fight it so." He seemed genuinely saddened by this.

"I feel it," he admitted. "All the time."

"There is no point in your fighting it any longer." The other male gazed into his eyes. Kalen couldn't look away if he tried. "You were born to be the greatest Sorcerer, the most powerful Fae in the universe. I want you to learn all that you can so that one day, when my time in the universe is done, I may pass the torch. You will rule as I have. You're the only one who can carry on my work."

Kalen shook his head. "That's crazy. I'm nothing like you."

"Remember what I said about blood. You were born under a black moon, which means your sire was a creature of power and darkness. This is what your grandmother kept from you," the Unseelie said earnestly. "Don't you understand?"

His brows furrowed. "Not really. You're saying that my father was, what? A 'creature of darkness,' as you put it? Dave was Unseelie or something?"

"May the gods damn David Ray Black for the spineless human worm he was!" Malik thundered, hurling his glass of Cognac across the room, where it shattered into a zillion shards. The Unseelie's fangs lengthened and his human glamour began to slip. Claws emerged at his fingertips, and his ebony wings erupted from his back as he raged.

"That worthless slug could never sire such a force as you! That is why he hated you so fucking much! That's why he beat you and your mother daily! Why he tossed you out of his home that night, so afraid of you that he almost pissed himself when he realized you were coming into your magic! Don't you get it, boy?"

Kalen swallowed the sickness rising in his throat with the liquor. "He wasn't my father? Then who is?" he rasped.

Oh, God, no. If there's any hope for me at all, please—

"You are mine! *My* son! You have always been mine!"

Kalen's glass hit the carpet. He stared at Malik in sheer horror.

Malik's palms cupped his face, sharp claws digging into his scalp. His dark gaze captured Kalen, refused to let him go. "I am your father, my boy. Your mother was once royalty, a much younger cousin to the Seelie queen who birthed Sariel. I talked my way into your mother's bed in the Seelie court, fucked her right under your grandmother's nose." He chuckled, low and dangerous.

"Then I waited for her to realize I had bestowed a child upon her. She would hand over my son at his birth, and I would take away the evidence of her shame with none the wiser. That was my offer to her."

"Which she refused." Kalen felt numb.

"Yes, which she refused, the stupid bitch," he spat. "She and your grandmother secreted you away to the human realm. There she seduced Black, let him believe the child was his, and he was happy. Until you were born and he overheard the two women whispering that he could never learn you were not his."

"And you left me at his mercy for years," Kalen hissed.

"I did not know where you were! When I finally found you, you were wearing your grandmother's pendant and I couldn't approach you. I waited and bided my time. Allowed you to grow into a man."

"Allowed me to suffer, you mean," he choked, shame and regret clogging his throat. "The pendant didn't save me from doing what I had to do to survive. You should have intervened."

"You grew stronger," Malik countered. "Because of your trials, because of the darkness you encountered at the hands of others, you learned to feed your own."

"So that's the real reason." He hung his head. "You let me suffer to feed this awful rage inside, so you could one day come in and show me how to hone it into a weapon."

"You needn't make it sound like such a harsh decision," the Unseelie said with uncharacteristic gentleness. "Are you not strong? Are you not ready to stand at my side?"

A bitter laugh escaped his chest. "Strong? Not so sure. Stand at your side? I don't fucking think so. I stand alone. You taught me how, remember?"

To his surprise, Malik smiled, looking extremely proud. "Yes, I do. And I taught you well. Had you agreed, that would have been a great disappointment. No one will ever be your equal, boy. Not even me, given time. I have more to teach you yet, but you have all the makings of a fine Unseelie king. My son."

He backed away, panic fluttering. "No, I don't. And I'm not your son. Not in any way that matters."

"You are, and you will prove me correct."

"Yeah? How's that?" He was about two seconds from bolting. Fuck, he needed out of here.

"You will see." Malik paused, studying him. "Have you forgotten why you came here today, to my humble cabin?"

Kalen's mind was a mess. He thought for a few seconds before he recalled his original reason for the visit. "You claimed my mate lied to me. That she knew something and wouldn't tell me."

Malik paused, then detonated his world. "Your Mackenzie knows that you are my son. She knows that the baby she carries is my grandchild."

The room dipped and the Unseelie's clawed hand steadied him on his feet. "You're lying!"

"No. I told her several days ago, a fact that you can easily confirm by speaking with her. Which I assume you will do."

"Does Nick know?" he managed.

"That I cannot say." Malik shrugged. "But he is a Seer, is he not? How many, I wonder, hid the truth from you? Perhaps my other wayward son—your half brother, Sariel? Did he lie as well?"

His conversation with Sariel in the infirmary flashed through his mind in snippets.

As his progeny, I am the only being with the power to destroy him. Or so I believed until recently.

I've known you were Fae since the second you entered the compound.

As humans say, my sire lies like a fucking rug. Don't believe anything that passes his foul lips, Sorcerer. I mean that.

Kalen couldn't speak. There were no words for the agony of betrayal. His mate's, perhaps Nick's and Sariel's, too. So many lies and half-truths, he didn't know who to believe. Who to turn to in his confusion and pain. And Malik understood exactly how to apply salt to the wound.

"Those pathetic humans you've come to trust, they will destroy you," the Unseelie said, placing a hand on his shoulder.

"They won't." But he was no longer sure. Hadn't Nick promised that if Kalen gave in to the darkness he'd be executed as a rogue?

"The commander practically has a hard-on at the possibility of being able to blow your brains out. And Sorcerer or not, there's no coming back from having your gray matter splattered over the forest."

That image reminded him of another, this one very real. "You really did murder my mother and my fa— David Black," he accused, seething.

"Yes. I wiped from the earth the man who had abused you for years and the woman who stood by and allowed it to happen." He regarded Kalen coolly. "And when you saw their bodies, didn't a large part of you wish that *you* had done the deed? Isn't that really why you became ill?"

God help him, he couldn't deny that.

All he could be thankful for was that his grandmother had died months before he was forced from his home. Ida May never knew the horror that befell her daughter.

Wait. "You never harmed my grandmother, did you? Because if you did—"

The Unseelie held up a hand. "On my word, I never touched Ida May. We locked horns many times, but I rather admired the old bat, in my own way. As far as I know, she perished of natural causes, whatever those might have been."

Strangely, he believed that, if anything, was the unvarnished truth.

The two of them stood for long moments, neither speaking. In all of the horrible revelations, the one that hurt the most centered on Mackenzie. She was the sole bright light in his entire miserable existence. If he couldn't count on her, he had nothing.

"You are thinking of your mate," Malik said. "She kept two very important truths from you, but don't take my word. Confront her for yourself and you will see."

"I don't need your advice on how to conduct my personal life."

He shrugged. "Whether you heed my advice or not, it doesn't matter. The reality is what it is."

If only he could grasp what that reality was. He turned to get the hell out, but the Unseelie grasped his arm.

"You're forgetting something."

Kalen glared at him, ready to snap out a retort—and then the Unseelie opened his wrist with a claw and held it out.

"Your blood reward."

"I don't want it." He gritted his teeth against the tantalizing scent of the blood, so intoxicating. Better than liquor. He wanted to resist, but was about as successful as a junkie trying to turn down a hit of heroin.

"Taste. And this time, do so knowing who you are and that you're mine."

The wrist waved in front of his nose and he hesitated a few heartbeats before grabbing it and giving in to temptation. His panther purred, glad to have any blood

that he didn't have to hunt. His other half enjoyed letting the sweetness, so like molasses, slide down his
throat to warm his belly. It infused his body with a shot
of adrenaline, filled his soul with wickedness.

He wanted to hurt those who had lied to and misled
him. Longed to crush them all. Except his mate. Her,
perhaps, he would show mercy. But the others? There
was no limit to his wrath, no stopping his revenge.

Delicious tendrils of excitement snaked around his
balls. This sort of absolute power was pure arousal,
frighteningly addictive. Drugs were never a lure for
him, but this was different.

"My boy," Malik whispered. "My son. Take all you
need. I give you my strength to add to yours."

Kalen drank until he couldn't think straight anymore, while Malik stroked his head and murmured.

"Embrace who you are. Then make them pay."

The wonderful darkness had obliterated all reason.
Hadn't he endured enough agony? What had he ever
done to deserve the abuse he'd suffered his entire life?
All of it was too much. His mind, his will, could no longer stand against this seduction.

"Make them all pay."

Yes. He wanted that. "How?"

"First, you will kill Sariel. He is a threat to me, to
us," Malik said quietly. "I know this will be difficult for
you, but it must be done."

"But . . . he's my half brother."

"Yes, and he must die, or you and I will. If we perish,
so does our mission—to rule the world and put paranormals at the top of the food chain. Remember what I
told you before about the greater good. Sometimes sac-
rifices must be made, my boy."

"I understand."

"Very good." He gave Kalen a sly smile. "Have no fear. You will come to enjoy the killing. Do you feel the wicked rush in your veins from the blood reward?"

"Yeah." He wanted more.

"Killing your prey slowly, draining their life force as you do . . ." He made a sound of satisfaction. "There is nothing like it. Multiply how the blood reward makes you feel and you'll have an idea how pleasurable it is to take your prey."

Against his will, his cock thickened in anticipation. Deep in his brain, some part of the former Kalen recoiled in dread at his own salacious thoughts. The longing to feel what Malik described. But he couldn't deny that he wanted it. He was tired of being the nice guy, of coming in last.

It was time for vengeance.

"I'll kill Sariel," he heard himself say. *What? No!*

"And then you will kill one other Pack member of your choice. Someone you truly like."

"Why?" He frowned.

"Because I order it so, and you must prove your loyalty is to me and none other."

That settled him. He had a purpose. "All right."

Malik looked beyond pleased. "You will be amazed at how easy and satisfying it is to drain the life force of another and take it into yourself. This is your birthright. It is only natural for the strong to consume the weak."

"I'll do it. What else?"

"When I give the order, you will lower the shields on the compound again. And this time they will remain down. I have an army of hundreds of Sluagh ready to storm the base and slaughter every living soul inside. Except your mate, of course. I have big plans for my grandson."

Kalen tried to feel something at that news, any sense of remorse. But it was as though he'd signed away his soul to the devil.

Except . . . his son. The screaming voice was back in his head, protesting. He had to protect his son from Malik. But then the voice was fading away, buried under layers of malice and confusion. Replaced by animal excitement.

Death and destruction. Why did that sound so inviting?

This isn't me. But I can't stop him. Don't know how.

Oh, how he longed to kill.

But can I do it, when the time comes?

"Would you like to practice?"

He blinked at Malik. "What?"

"Trust me. I'll create an avatar for you to practice on." With a wave of his hand, the Unseelie chanted a few words in a language Kalen had never heard before. In moments, a whirl of energy whipped round and round in the living room and slowly formed into a familiar figure.

"Sariel?" he whispered.

In the middle of the room, the prince stood blinking in confusion, uncertain of where he was or what was going on, it seemed. The Fae looked to Malik and then Kalen, fear blooming on his face.

"Why am I here?" the prince asked.

"You were supposed to create an avatar, not bring someone here for real!" Kalen said.

"This *is* an avatar." Malik shook his head. "If it were

that easy to bring my wayward first son here and kill him, I would've done that long ago."

"As if you could ever kill me," Sariel's image sneered. "You're pathetic, both of you."

With that, Kalen let the darkness loose. He shot a bolt of white energy at the blue-haired, blue-winged figure. The bolt hit him square in the chest and he went down.

Kalen pounced, but the prince rolled away, proving to be a more agile target than he'd thought. He went after the fleeing form, tackling the Seelie before he got halfway across the room. A fragile bone in one of the wings snapped and the prince shouted in pain. One tiny drop of blood, and the lust for the kill was ignited.

He let his panther loose and pinned the faery as he would a deer, going for the throat. Just before he struck, the prince turned wide, stricken eyes toward him and whispered, "Brother."

But it was too late to stop the panther. His jaws closed over the vulnerable throat like a steel trap and crushed. Slowly. Flesh, muscle, and bone gave way to his superior strength. *The weak feeds the strong.* The prince's cries were strangled, then silenced, but his body continued to fight.

"That's it, Kalen," his father rasped, his voice thick. "Now feel his life force with your magic and drink it in like fine Cognac. Take it all."

Reaching out with his magic, he did just that. He followed the tendril of life to its source and began to breathe it inside himself. At the same time, he drank. Slurped the blood of his victim and began to feed at his neck, tearing the tender meat. So good. So fucking fantastic. He could *come* from this, feeding and glutting—

And suddenly the body beneath him was gone. It simply vanished into thin air. There was no blood anywhere. Not on himself or the floor. He turned back to human form and scowled. Where had his prey disappeared to?

"I'd say you got the hang of that rather quickly."

"It really was an avatar?"

"Yes. As I said, the real Sariel has been much harder to catch."

Kalen shuddered. He'd known, deep down, the avatar wasn't real and said a silent thanks for it. But he'd still reveled in the act of killing. Could he do it next time, for real?

"You can do it," his father said, as if reading his thoughts. "I would not have chosen you to rule at my side if you did not possess the strength."

"Thank you, . . . Father."

Malik smiled, his expression one of triumph. "You will not let me down."

"No, sir."

"Go, boy. Do what I told you. Kill Sariel and one other, and then wait for my command to lower the wards."

"Nick will execute me as soon as I make a move to harm anyone there."

"If he apprehends you, he'll have you locked up first. That will be his downfall—the hope that he can still save you. Remember, when the time comes, embrace the great Sorcerer you were meant to be. Now go."

The farther he got from Malik's cabin, the more his

returning awareness weighted him down. The end was near. He knew the Pack would never allow him to go rogue. Any more than he could allow himself to follow through with his raw, bestial urge to destroy.

One way or another, very soon, Kalen was going to die.

Thirteen

Mac cried until her dad threatened to fetch Melina or Noah and give her something to make her sleep, pregnancy or not.

His anger over her blatant stupidity had lasted all of three minutes. Just long enough to discern that she hadn't intended to deceive Kalen at all. And she damned sure hadn't meant to endanger her baby—his grandbaby. But that wasn't the only issue.

The general paced while Mac watched him through swollen, bleary eyes. "He acted like you were keeping something else from him. That's what he said. Are you sure you don't know what the hell he was talking about?"

"No, I don't— Oh, no. The nightmare!"

Her dad stopped pacing. "What nightmare?"

"The one I had recently." She wrung her hands on her lap. "I thought—I hoped—it was just a bad dream. In it Malik told me that the baby I carried was his grandson. That Kalen was his son and that he had plans for us. I was so scared. But when I woke up, I couldn't imagine the dream was real."

"Or if it was, that it could possibly be true. Malik is such a goddamned mealymouthed liar," her dad surmised.

"Exactly! I actually planned on telling Kalen, but the creep must've beaten me to it. There just never seemed to be a good time."

"There never is, honey." Sitting next to her on the sofa, he took both her hands in his. "If there's one thing I learned from being married to your mother, it's that there is never a perfect time to deal with the unpleasant stuff. It's always best to get issues out in the open so they can be dealt with and healed."

"And here I am, the therapist with all the fancy college degrees, and my dad had to clue me in." She sniffled, and he handed her another tissue. "Thanks."

"That's what dads are for."

She heaved a shaky breath. "Malik's such an opportunist and a manipulator. I should've known he'd pull something like this. I shouldn't have waited to tell Kalen anything. And I won't from now on, if he gives me another chance."

"I don't think forgiveness is the worst trial either of you are facing right now. It's Malik and how he's going to use this rift to his advantage—and he will. It's just a question of how."

"Daddy, why did Nick bring you here? I know you didn't show up just to surprise me," she said quietly. She was afraid of the answer, but she had to know for sure.

His hesitation, the silence ticking away, was answer enough before he reluctantly shared some of what he knew. "Nick had a vision recently. A couple, actually, involving Kalen and the Pack. He saw that something terrible is going to happen, but he's not certain when or where. Just that it will be soon."

"And what he saw was so bad that he secretly called in the military?" Alarm shot through her at her father's grim nod. "Are your men in the area?"

"I'm afraid so. They're on standby. I had hoped never to have to involve them in the paranormal world, but we don't always get what we want, huh? At least they're good men, trustworthy. They won't breathe a word about their mission or anything they witness."

"Well, it's not like anyone would believe them if they did."

"True." He eyed his daughter. "Are you feeling better?"

"Physically, yes. I wish I knew where Kalen went exactly. And when he's coming back." *If* he was coming back. One thing was for sure: she couldn't sit here anymore feeling miserable and sorry for herself. She needed to get her mind off her troubles with Kalen. "I think I'm going to wash up, then head to the infirmary. What are your plans?"

"I'm going to head out for a while, meet with my units. I don't normally take such a hands-on role these days, but this isn't exactly a typical situation." Kissing her on the cheek, he stood. "You sure you'll be all right?"

"Don't worry." She forced a smile. "Go and take care of business. I'll see you later, maybe at dinner?"

"It's a date."

After seeing her dad out, she took a nice, hot shower, trying to wash away the stress of the morning. All the recent events kept running round in her mind, and it blew her away how fast things had gone from hopeful to hellacious in the span of a few minutes. She liked to think she and Kalen were stronger than the forces trying to drive a wedge between them.

But now she had her doubts.

She hated that, like she hated that he'd run instead of listening to her side of the story. He'd be back, but she wasn't going to make it easy for him. Now that she was over her crying jag, she was getting good and mad. Damned men! They were frequently a huge, collective pain in the ass. It was ironic that she'd taken a job that surrounded her with loads of testosterone on a daily basis.

She dressed quickly, then headed to the kitchen to pour the rest of the coffee down the sink and nibble some crackers. As excited as she was about the baby, the changes to her body made her feel like she'd been dropped into the wrong person. Certain smells made her sick, her breasts were tender, and she was sleepy all the time. She was also weepy, which was problem enough without the rest of the drama.

A few crackers and a cup of juice later, she headed to the infirmary and busied herself examining the latest round of test results on Sariel. He was doing much better and would likely be released, with the stipulation that he take care of himself. Everyone was concerned about the prince, and they would monitor his weight, but there really didn't seem to be a reason to keep him.

She was readying Sariel's release papers when her ink pen hit the desk with a clatter. "Oh my God."

Sariel. If Kalen was Malik's son then that meant . . .

Stunned, she sat back in her office chair and debated

her next course of action. Talk to the prince? Or wait for Kalen? She decided on the latter. Waiting for him was *not* the same as keeping the news from the faery. It just wasn't her place to share what she knew without speaking with her mate first.

"Mac?"

She looked up to see Melina standing in the door-way. "I'm sorry. I didn't see you there."

"You look a million miles away. You okay?"

"I'm fine." She waved the other woman inside. "I was thinking Sariel is about ready to get sprung. What do you say?"

Her friend took the test results from Mac and looked them over. After a few moments, she nodded. "Looks good. Or as good as it can be, considering we don't know what's making him sick. It took him a helluva long time to recover from the witch's attack, much longer than any of the shifters would have taken to heal. He didn't need the injury on top of that."

Mac managed to stifle a smile at her friend's protective tone. Someone was more than a little sweet on a certain Fae prince. Melina would deck her if she mentioned it, though.

"Shall I give him the good news or would you rather do it?" Mac asked innocently.

"I'll do it. I need to give him some instructions or he won't take care of himself," she muttered. Then she glanced up at Mac. "What?"

"Nothing."

All too perceptive even on an "off" day, Melina peered at her face. "Have you been crying? Your eyes are puffy."

"I—maybe."

"What did that dickweed do now?"

"Don't call my mate names," she said in a low voice, bristling. "He's dealing with a lot of shit right now."

"Aren't we all? And if he hurts you, he's a dickweed. End of story."

"We had a misunderstanding, and of course it took place in front of my dad." She grimaced at the memory.

Melina's eyes widened and she sat in a chair across Mac's desk. "No way. How did the general take being in the middle of a spat between his daughter and her new mate?"

"About as well as you'd expect—he got royally pissed at both of us."

"Care to talk about it?"

She hesitated. Actually, it would be nice to have another woman to talk to, and Mac was closer to Melina than to Rowan or Kira, having known the other doctor a lot longer. So she spilled her guts about the nice reunion with her dad that had quickly soured when Kalen learned what she'd been holding back.

Melina listened to the end, her expression softening in sympathy. "Nearly six peaceful years working here at the compound, and then *bam*. When you fuck up, you really give it the old one-two knockout punch."

Mac threw the ballpoint pen at her friend, and it bounced harmlessly off her shoulder. "Bitch. I feel *so* much better now, thanks."

"What are friends for?" Melina studied her for a moment, then grew serious. "Sweetie, what are you going to do if he loses his fight against Malik?"

"I don't know," she admitted, a painful knot in her throat.

"Do you think he'd hurt you or the baby?"

Her gaze dropped to her desk and she studied the wood grain on the surface. "I'd like to think he wouldn't, but honestly? That's my greatest fear. That one day soon he won't be able to distinguish between right and wrong, and he'll do something that will hurt us, even if it's indirectly."

"Is that what you really believe?" Kalen's voice asked breathlessly from the doorway.

Mac froze. Then her eyes lifted and met her mate's. His breathing was coming harshly, as though he'd been running, and his pupils were too large again. She hoped he hadn't been where she suspected. "Have you been with Malik?"

"My question first," he countered. "Is that what you think of me? That I'd hurt you or our child, or that I'd allow anyone else to hurt you?"

"I wish I could say no," she whispered, agonized. "But it's impossible to be sure when you're consorting with the enemy."

Hurt flashed in his expression and his jaw ticced. "I had to ask him whether it was true that I'm his son."

"I think it's sad that you would look to him for the truth about *anything*."

"He *is* telling the truth, at least about this. I have a father and a half brother. I have family."

"Sariel might be your brother, but that *thing* is not and never will be any kind of a father," she said, her voice rising. "A real father wouldn't have left you starving on the streets while he watched and refused to lift a finger to help you."

"Don't you think I know that?" he rasped. "You have a great dad who loves you more than anything and I'll never experience that for myself. Don't you understand how much that hurts? How hard it is to resist any kindness that comes out of his lying mouth?"

"I do—"

"No. You don't. He wants me to—" Swaying, Kalen grabbed his head and hissed in pain. Mac stood and would've gone to him, but he waved her off with a laugh that sounded slightly crazed. "Don't touch me!"

"Kalen—"

"Don't dirty your hands with the likes of me," he snarled, eyes wild. "Oh, wait—too late for that. Too bad you're stuck with Malik's son for a mate."

Fear gripped her heart. He was losing his struggle with his dark half—if he hadn't lost already. "Please, I'm sorry," she whispered. "I didn't mean—"

"Never mind. The truth is, you're right. You *should* be afraid of me. In fact, you need to stay as far from me as you can get."

"I can't do that."

"Don't worry. I'll do it for you." His green eyes were blank marbles as he held her gaze for a long moment, then turned and slammed out.

Melina looked shaken. "My God. His eyes . . . That wasn't Kalen."

I won't cry. It's not over.

"How are we going to help him?" she asked Melina. "Do you think we could try dosing him with the new sedative we've been using on Micah? It's helped him, so why not Kalen?"

"Because we're fighting dark magic here, my friend. I think being sedated will only lower his defenses all the way, leaving him completely vulnerable to the Unseelie's influence." Melina shook her head. "At this point, Kalen is the one who's going to have to save himself."

Mac was terribly afraid her friend was right.

Mac thought he was capable of harming her. Possibly their child.

Nothing could have broken his heart more effectively than hearing that from his mate's lips—except knowing it was entirely possible she was right.

Weary, Kalen paused at the end of the hallway and fought the urge to see Sariel. On the way back to the compound, he'd taken his time. Had fought hard to regain some control over his dark half, and the closer he came to Mackenzie, the more his mind cleared. But not all the way. The need to kill was agonizing. But he had to see the prince, or else he'd be driven out of his mind not knowing if he could resist the compulsion to follow through on Malik's orders.

Outside Sariel's room he knocked and then went on inside. Sariel was sitting on the edge of the bed, dressed in a pair of loose-fitting pants and a shirt that was slit on the back to accommodate his wings.

"Hello, Sorcerer. I'm getting out of here today, or I'm supposed to," the faery told him with a smile.

"Good for you." The flat tone of his voice was unintentional, but it quickly told the prince that something was off.

"What's wrong?" The Fae's brow furrowed.

"I'm supposed to kill you. You get that, right?"

To his surprise, the prince gave a soft laugh. "Am I supposed to be shocked? Afraid? Let me remind you of something, fledgling. I'm more than eleven thousand years old. Can you wrap your brain around that number? Do you actually believe in all that time nobody has ever wanted me dead? I'm a prince of my kind, Kalen. Besides my sire, enemies abound. Been there, done that, got the merit badge in survival, as humans say."

"You're being awfully flip about this."

"Not at all. Simply realistic." Sariel stood, his height equal to Kalen's. He didn't appear to be the least bit alarmed by any threat the Sorcerer might pose. "You could certainly try to harm me and, like the witch, you might succeed if you catch me off guard, not to mention that I'm healing and my system hasn't yet adjusted well to being in this realm. But make no mistake—even with all these disadvantages, I possess power beyond your wildest imagination."

He delivered this statement with such confidence, it gave Kalen pause. "You're saying Malik sent me on a suicide mission, then?"

The prince looked thoughtful. "I don't know. Does he have reason to believe your abilities are equal to mine—other than being Fae yourself?"

Here came the hard part. He took a deep breath. "Because Malik claims to be my father—and he says you're my half brother. Can you wrap *your* brain around *that*?"

Sariel's mouth fell open. "Great gods." He stared at Kalen for a few moments before he nodded. "My brother? That would make perfect sense, that sick old asshole."

"Do you think it's true? Are we brothers?"

"Considering everything you told me before, I'd say it's highly likely. You do realize that I have several other brothers and that would mean you do as well. If it's true, you just gained quite a large family."

"Any way we can ever know for sure?"

"Not if you kill me," Sariel said pointedly. "As if you could."

"If we're related by blood, I'm more than capable."

"And you want to." Sariel observed him with a critical eye. "You're practically vibrating with tension, and your pupils are dilated. Your panther is close to the surface. I can sense that he's dying to rip out my throat and feast on my carcass."

"So badly I can't stand it," he admitted hoarsely. His panther growled in agreement. "And yet the real me doesn't want that at all. I want to get to know the brothers I've always longed for, and fighting the dark half is tearing me apart."

Kill the prince.

Kalen flinched at the order. "He wants me to do it. Help me."

Sariel moved close, laid a hand on his shoulder. "You're strong. And we must be related if you can resist Malik's influence this way for any length of time. Hold on just a while longer. I have a feeling the end of this is near."

"Yeah, but who comes out on top?"

A smile kicked up one corner of the prince's mouth. "Why, the baddest two Fae on earth, of course. And when the day comes to prove it, I'll fight by your side."

Kill him now, boy.

"That's way more than I deserve."

"No. You deserve more . . . brother."

No, you fool! Kill him!

"I won't do it," he whispered to his unseen tormentor. "Go fuck yourself."

Pain stabbed his head again and blood trickled from

his nose. Sariel grabbed a tissue from the nightstand and handed it over. Kalen cleaned up and was about to say something more when the building's intercom intruded into the bonding moment with his brother.

"Alpha Pack to the conference room, stat," Nick ordered.

"That can't be good." Kalen sighed. "We'll finish this later, right?"

"Count on it. And be careful," the faery said, worried.

"I will." Clasping hands briefly with the prince, he turned and hurried toward the conference room. It seemed he could draw the good kind of strength from his friends and loved ones to counter the evil Malik kept pumping into him. That would be what saved him.

Or at least let him live long enough to take out the Unseelie.

In the conference room, Nick was already waiting at the head of the long table, tense and impatient. Next to him stood General Grant, his mood appearing much the same. Kalen took a seat near the back and watched as the rest filed in, some involved in animated conversations, some quiet. But all talking stopped when Nick began, his tone serious yet laced with unmistakable excitement.

"As most of you have heard by now, the general is here to assist us with the problem of Malik and his Sluagh." Aric and Ryon and a couple of others glanced at Kalen. He ignored them. "More specifically, Grant's units are on standby and are fully prepared to accompany us into battle when we eradicate those vermin from the face of the earth."

"We're going to need that many soldiers?" Ryon asked, a tendril of fear in his voice. "How many Sluagh does that fucker have coming for us?"

Nick pinned Kalen with his steely gaze. "Kalen might have that answer. How many?"

It was a test. Nick and the general knew the number, but they wanted him to reveal what Malik had told him. First, he tried to strengthen the mental wall between him and the Unseelie, but it was shaky at best.

"Hundreds," he said. The throbbing started in his temples, but he pushed on. "They're amassing in the Shoshone, far from civilization. He ordered m-me to lower the shields on the c-compound and . . ."

The pain got so bad the rest of the words were strangled in his throat. Hanging his head, he breathed through it as someone clapped his back in reassurance.

"Have you lowered them?"

Kalen shook his head. "No. They won't get in here." He'd die first. They heard that without him saying it out loud.

"All right. We'll face that battle soon enough. But I've brought you here for a different reason. General, you want to tell them?"

"I'd be glad to." The older man stood with his hands behind his back. "Your team has been instrumental in locating and destroying several of the so-called research facilities where Malik, aka Evan Kerrigan, has been funding the creation of his super-shifters. With the destruction of the last couple, as well as with the death of Orson Chappell, NewLife Technology's CEO, you all dealt the operation a serious blow."

There was some agreement around the table on that, and some minor celebrating.

Grant went on. "Be that as it may, the main doctor in charge of the research, Dr. Gene Bowman, has eluded capture time and again." The Pack guys sobered. "But my contacts have found Bowman working in what we believe to be the last research facility in existence belonging to this group of scumbags. Destroy this one, and we've got them all."

"Hot damn!"

"Fuckin' A. When do we start?"

The sentiments were unanimous—the team couldn't wait to get the job done. But Grant wasn't finished.

"Of the enemy, take no prisoners. Of the survivors, bring them home. And there's one more thing—my source indicates that one of the survivors is very special." When he paused, no one so much as breathed. "We believe that Phoenix is among the captives."

There was stunned silence—and then an explosion of questions and exclamations. Nix had gone missing at the same time as Micah and the others. Where had Nix been? How did he get there? Grant held up a hand and shook his head.

"Terry and Jonas truly are dead, according to my source. No one has found any information on Ari, but we're hoping Phoenix can fill in the blanks."

When the guys had calmed somewhat, Jax asked, "So where is this last research facility? I'm sure we'd all like to get on with burning it to the ground."

"It's nestled in a picturesque valley in California. It's a midsized building, situated in the countryside, quiet and unassuming like the old church they used before. Seems to be a favorite MO. But watch for traps, as always."

"Any questions?" Nick called over their excited murmuring.

Rowan piped up. "Just one—when do we leave?"

"Wheels up in twenty," Nick said. "So go put on your party dresses."

That earned a few snickers as chairs scraped and boots clomped. Micah stood back as they filed out, clearly bleak at being left behind again. But the poor bastard was simply in no shape to go along. Rowan, his sister, gave him a fierce hug before hurrying after Aric.

Kalen couldn't pass the man by without saying something. "Soon, big guy. Right?"

"Yeah." Without another word, Micah turned and shuffled off. He looked so alone, even though he was surrounded by friends.

Kalen understood exactly how he felt.

The flight from Wyoming to California was short but turbulent. Very fitting, when Kalen thought about it. By the time they landed the two Hueys a couple of miles from the suspected research facility, he was ready to toss his cookies. A military man he was not. If he could've magically transported the whole bunch of them, he would've.

They scrambled off the copters, and those that pre-ferred to carry checked their weapons. Kalen much pre-ferred to be his own weapon, thank you very much. He didn't care for guns, though he'd use one if he had to.

As they followed Nick through the valley, Kalen tested his mental shield and found it still holding but weak. It seemed the more physical and emotional dis-tance that came between him and Mac, the worse the influence from the Unseelie. Kalen's dark side was slowly overtaking his light, as Sariel called it.

He had to hang on. Just a while longer.

Give it up, my boy. You are mine.

"No." Kalen studied the backs of his teammates, but nobody seemed to have heard.

The lust for blood will rise within you, unstoppable. Give it full rein, feed it. And turn it against the Pack. Be my instrument of revenge.

Concentrating, he tried to shore up the crack in his shield. An almost impossible chore, considering the distractions all around him. He had to watch his Pack brothers, scan for possible traps, hidden enemies. There were sure to be many, if this was in fact the last stronghold for Malik's research.

Did Malik know where they were headed? He couldn't, otherwise the Sluagh guards would be on them already. No, the Unseelie was picking up on his emotions and trying to use them. He didn't really know where Kalen was at the moment.

He'd do his best to keep it that way.

Spread out, they walked through the trees as silently as possible. Using every ounce of their animal stealth, they made their way closer to the building below them. When a grayish blur detached itself from the cover of the forest, it wasn't unexpected, but it shocked the senses all the same.

From their right, a huge Sluagh slammed into Hammer, taking the big man to the ground. His shout was lost in the simultaneous roars from the beast and from the Pack. Rowan was closest, and immediately jumped onto the thing's back, a big Glock in her hand. Without wasting a second, she pressed the muzzle to its temple and blew its brains out. The creature slumped to the side, leaving Hammer staring up at Rowan, wide-eyed.

"Shit! Thanks, Ro," he breathed. "That's one way to take them out."

"And effective, too." Crawling off the beast, she kicked it in disgust. Then she turned just in time to receive a possessive kiss from Aric.

Kalen wondered how the man handled bringing his mate into danger. He wasn't sure he could do the same. Then again, Mac and Rowan were two completely different women. Ro was raised in east Los Angeles and had been an LAPD cop. She was earthy and tough. Kalen's mate was a gentle doctor, and he couldn't fathom her doing what Rowan had just done.

The scent of the creature's blood hit Kalen hard, and the crack in his wall threatened to split at the seam again. Rancid as the odor was, it sparked a fire low in his belly. The need to kill. As he'd done with the avatar of Sariel.

Dammit! He couldn't let the craving get the best of him.

They set off again, the tension high. The Sluagh had obviously been patrolling this section alone, but his brethren might notice his absence anytime. They had to move faster, and picked up the pace.

Once the building was in sight, Nick signaled them to halt and gestured them in close. "A.J., this looks like a good place for you to pick off anyone who gives us trouble."

"I got your backs, boss." The human wasn't a fighter, but he had a high-powered rifle with a scope, and he was deadly accurate with it.

"The rest of us will split into two teams. Kalen, Ryon, Hammer, and Jax take the back. The rest of us will cover the front. Ryon, let us know when you enter the building."

Ryon gave him a thumbs-up and took his group, making a wide circle to the back side of the facility. Kalen couldn't get the stench of the Sluagh's blood out of his head, the itch to shred something—anything— out of his system. The need crawled through him like a disease, insidious. Barely contained.

At the back of the building, they pressed up against the wall on either side of a door that looked to be a service entrance. The lack of guards was disturbing, to say the least. That feeling mounted as Jax picked the lock and they eased inside, still unchallenged.

We're in, Ryon pushed into their minds. *There's a garage area back here, probably where they bring in the prisoners. Three vehicles, two of them vans with blacked-out windows. No guards. I don't like this.*

He paused, presumably getting an answer from Nick. Ryon, as the team's Telepath, could push his thoughts into their heads, but no one could hear a direct mental reply except him. After a few moments, Ryon gestured his group forward, scanning carefully.

With an effort, Kalen kept his mind firmly focused on taking out the enemy when the time came—and *only* the enemy. These were his brothers. His future. Not Malik or his empty promises of acceptance.

He could resist the evil. He *would*.

Across the garage was a door that served as the entrance to the main building. They crept toward it, alert. Something, perhaps some small sound, made Ryon look up, into the beams over their heads.

And he shouted, "Get down!"

The garage erupted into high-pitched squeals as sev-

eral Sluagh swooped down from the rafters at once.
Kalen dropped into a crouch as the others hit the floor.
Facing these numbers, he figured it was better to use
his magic than call his panther.

Ryon and Jax shifted into their wolves and leaped,
tearing into a couple of the creatures. Hammer traced,
confusing the beasts near him. But there were too
many, and they would quickly be overwhelmed in
hand-to-hand combat.

Summoning his staff, Kalen stilled. Focused his
magic on the attacking Sluagh. Then he called the element of water, coaxed it from their bodies. Disseminat-
ing it into the air. The creatures began to shrivel and
scream. One particularly smart one seemed to realize
Kalen was the cause of this development and charged
him, closing the distance between them rapidly.

His heart pounded, but he didn't move. The beast
rushed toward him, roaring his rage, eyes small and
red. And then he too shriveled, dropping right at
Kalen's feet like stone.

"Fuck." Kalen's knees shook at the close call. Uttering a phrase in Latin, he reduced the bodies to ash, and
the particles floated away. His friends morphed back to
human form and picked up their shredded clothes.

"That's a damned nice trick you've got there," Jax
said, pulling on his pants.

"It's saved our bacon more than once," Ryon agreed.
"Thanks."

"Think anyone heard the commotion?" This from
Hammer, who brushed himself off.

Jax smoothed down his goatee. "Only one way to
find out."

They gathered on either side of the door. Ryon

turned the knob and gave it a small push. It swung inward, revealing a long corridor beyond, clean and sterile with white walls and tile. Faint wailing could be heard from a distant room, the soul inside completely without hope.

"Just a few more minutes," Jax whispered. "Help is on the way."

Here is where it can get tricky, Ryon projected as they entered. *We're in the back hallway. It's long and narrow, a tight space for a fight. We'll take it room by room, gather any survivors.*

The first few rooms were being used for storage. Upon inspection, the spaces were surprisingly well organized, with metal shelves storing various useful items. The industrious Dr. Bowman had been busy since they'd nearly caught him last time. One room was full of cleaning supplies, another labeled with medications of all kinds. Jax took an interest in these.

"Before we torch the place, we need to gather this stuff. Maybe it will give our own doctors some helpful research into what these fuckers have been using." He fingered a labeled bottle. "And some free meds, too, if there are some good drugs here."

"Good point," Ryon said.

The next room held shelves of clothing. There were the drab green scrubs that were meant for their doctors and other staff. Some others were plain, consisting of rough tan pants and pullover shirts. Kalen wondered if these were for their unwilling residents, which didn't make sense. Malik's lackeys had never seen fit to clothe their test subjects before. They didn't care about them that much.

"Maybe they got tired of their experiments dying,"

Jax observed, studying the clothing. "Won't matter after today what those assholes wanted, though."

They filed back into the hallway, watchful. At a junction where their corridor was met by another on the left, an armed human guard stood leaning against the wall with his back to them. His stance was relaxed, bored. That would be his last mistake.

Jax quickly sneaked up behind him, grabbed his hair, and jerked him backward. A cry of surprise was silenced as Jax used a sharp claw to slice the man's throat and allowed him to slump to the floor. The guard gurgled, reaching to his neck, but the light in his eyes faded. He was dead in moments.

Kalen's bloodlust rose, hot and shameful. He needed to kill. The next one was his, and he'd enjoy every second.

Good, my son. Feed your need. It matters not what your Pack believes they've accomplished today. What matters is that you use this as your training. Give in to your desires and we'll rebuild together. No one will stop us then.

Dammit, the Unseelie had broken through. The hypnotic words tightened their grip on his soul. He could take out the guards, all the staff here, and that was acceptable. He could channel this need without risking his friends. Right?

A bead of sweat rolled down his face. Control was hard. He wanted to give in to the seductive darkness. Needed to.

As expected, the actual labs and holding areas for the captives were located in the middle of the building. They knew they were upon them when sounds of activity reached their ears. There was a voice here and there. The roll of a cart's wheels along the tiled floor.

Beeping from a monitor. An assistant inquiring as to which subject would be brought to the OR next.

And Dr. Gene Bowman, answering, "Bring the wolf to OR-4. I want to try and splice his DNA with human subject 356 again. I'm on the verge of a breakthrough. I can feel it."

Did you hear that, Nicky? Ryon asked. Then he nodded to Kalen and the others. "His group has taken out the guards in the front and they're approaching from the other side of this central area. We've got them boxed in."

To everyone, Ryon said, *Let's wait and see where they retrieve this captive from and who he is.*

They didn't have to wait for long. Dr. Bowman disappeared, presumably into OR-4, and the assistant buzzed into a cell by punching a silver button on the wall across the hall. It seemed this setup allowed their captives to be conveniently located right next to their torture chamber. The bars slid open and the assistant went inside.

When the lackey came out, he was dragging a tall man with long, filthy golden hair that hung to his waist. He jerked his captive and for a moment his body faced them before both men vanished into the OR.

"Goddamn," Jax hissed, fists clenching. "That was Nix!"

"Those sorry bastards," Ryon said, his voice low and deadly. "Let's go get him and bring him home."

They've got Phoenix! We're on the move.

They closed in fast, and Kalen could see Nick round the corner at the other end of the hallway, the rest of the team behind him. Kalen glanced into the cell the lackey had retrieved Phoenix from and spotted three more figures huddled together in misery. For now they'd be safer where they were.

Ryon led the first strike as they burst into the OR. Bowman looked up, shock blooming on his face. The man grabbed a nearby scalpel and brandished it over Nix's inert body, but the weapon was scant defense against a roomful of enraged Pack brothers out for his blood.

"I'm gonna tear out your fucking heart," Jax snarled. Then he pounced, taking Bowman to the floor. The man's scream as Jax ripped him apart echoed eerily in the enclosed space. The asshole had it coming. He'd hurt and killed so many in the search of world domination, and now it was over.

Kalen turned toward the assistant, who had managed to pull a gun from his lab coat. Throwing out a ball of energy, he zapped the weapon out of the man's hand, and Ryon took him down, ending him in the same manner as the doctor.

Hammer glanced around uneasily. "Is that it? That was too easy, man."

And then the world exploded into chaos. Literally. All around them, the very walls of the research facility detonated, blowing them off their feet. Kalen's back hit a counter hard, and then he was thrown to the floor. Pain radiated through his vertebrae, and he sucked in a sharp breath only to get a lungful of debris.

He coughed as dust and dirt rained down. Chunks fell from the damaged ceiling, which threatened to cave as well. Where the hell was everyone?

Wiping the grit from his eyes, he saw his group struggling to rise. The scent of blood hit his nostrils and this time it wasn't rancid. The aroma was sweet and delicious, and he instantly recoiled. The blood belonged to his Pack brothers. He wouldn't betray them.

Kill. It's what you do best.

"No."

He pushed to his feet, and his heart sank as more Sluagh emerged from the shadows. Malik had sent them here. This was another test. Kalen wouldn't fail. But for which side?

Sounds of battle came from somewhere beyond them. Nick's group. There was no longer a corridor or distinguishable rooms. Just a mess of ruined walls and rubble.

His friends threw themselves into battle with fervor, dispatching Sluagh right and left. More took their place. Using his claws, Kalen slashed, stabbed the beasts' hearts. He used rapid-fire balls of energy to take some down before they could overwhelm his brothers.

But somewhere in the fight, the line began to blur. The craving for the next kill, and the next, mounted with each life he took. It was all too easy and satisfying. Watch the light die; take the next one. Death and more death. So good.

The darkness took him and he was powerless against it. Without a sliver of the light to guide him, the need to deliver death knew no bounds. He turned, searching for his next victim, to find himself staring into wide, light blue eyes, the face surrounded by layered blond hair.

Ryon.

"Kalen! Don't—"

The Sorcerer's hand whipped out almost of its own accord, and he gathered a massive ball of energy. This one would burn right through his opponent's heart, leave nothing but scorched flesh in its wake. And death. Bittersweet and delicious.

But before he could release the fire, a body slammed into him, knocking him to the dirty floor. He roared, trying to dislodge his enemy, to no avail. He fought to gain purchase. Barely understood the words shouted near him.

"Christ, he's gone feral! Hold him!"

Nick?

He struggled harder, but more bodies held him down. He hated being pinned. When men did this, it was for one reason only.

And then he went wild. It was all they could do to subdue him.

"Somebody put him out, goddammit!"

"Sleep, kid," Nick ordered, palm on Kalen's forehead.

And he had no choice but to obey.

Fourteen

Mac picked at her sandwich with disinterest. She'd hardly been able to stomach three bites before nausea played ping-pong with the roasted chicken. The food in the compound's cafeteria was excellent, but nerves and pregnancy were getting in the way of any enjoyment.

The creamy tomato basil soup, one of her favorites, settled much better. She was halfway finished with the bowl when her father came jogging into the dining room. The expression on his face had her on her feet in an instant. She didn't think she'd ever seen the man look nervous before.

"Daddy?" She reached for him instinctively.

"Baby, the Pack is on the way in. They're six minutes out."

"Injuries?" She hurried out, jogging beside him. *Stay calm. Professional.*

"A few lacerations. Hammer had a broken leg, but Zan healed it."

"So why the hurry?"

When he didn't answer right away, she grabbed his arm, stopping him outside the entrance to the infirmary. He gave it to her straight.

"It's Kalen. He's gone feral and Nick had to put him out—"

"Oh my God!" she cried. "He's dead?"

"No! I mean put him to sleep for a while. But it's wearing off and they're having trouble keeping him under control. They've bound him in silver chains and they're bringing him here as soon as they land."

She thought fast. "It won't do them any good to bring him to the infirmary if he's not injured."

"Nick wants him sedated."

"No. That won't help. Sedation will render him incapable of defending himself mentally, and that will only give Malik an easier path into his mind."

"Shit." The general scrubbed a hand through his hair. "Then what do we do?"

God. No. It killed her to say it, but there was only one solution at the moment. "They need to take him to Block R." *My mate, forgive me.* "Call Nick back. I have to ready a cell."

She ran toward Block R, where they kept the creatures that required rehabilitation. The block housed several residents, chief among them Raven and Belial. Raven was the Pack member and former SEAL who'd been stuck in wolf form for more than five years. Belial was a sneaky, seductive basilisk who had yet to earn freedom to roam the compound.

And now it would house Kalen. Her heart ached for her Sorcerer. Quickly she used the keypad to unlock a cell away from the other residents, opened it, and studied the interior. There was nothing in it but a bed bolted to the floor and a mattress on top of the frame. No sheets or pillows. Nothing that he could use to harm himself.

Her father came around the corner and she heard the commotion heading their way from behind him. Kalen was screaming profanities, out of his head, and she braced herself for a horrible confrontation.

Or thought she had until Nick and several others came in to view, barely holding on to the Sorcerer, who was bound in silver chains. Her mate was enraged, twisting his body and slashing with his fangs to try to take a chunk out of his captors. When that didn't work, he tried to utter a spell in Latin, but Nick slapped a hand over his mouth hard, risking a nasty bite to stop the chant.

"Bring him here!" Mac called.

They struggled but managed to maneuver him into the cell, where Nick and Jax tossed him across the space, then let him go and hauled ass out of there. As soon as they cleared the door, Mac and her father slid the heavy bars home. They locked into place with a loud clang that was awfully final.

Hands still bound behind his back with the chains, Kalen hit the bars, causing the whole door to rattle on its track. Mac stood immobile, watching the man she loved slam himself into one wall, then the other, totally out of his head.

"Let me go!" he screamed. "I'll fucking kill you! Every last one of you! And I'll laugh while I'm doing it!"

Tears welled in her eyes, trickled down her cheeks. She couldn't stand seeing him like this. "Daddy," she whispered, grabbing his hand. He held on to her tightly. "What can I do? How do we help him?"

"I don't know, baby girl," he murmured. The entire team gathered around, looking equally stricken.

"Feast on your carcasses," Kalen raved. Laughing, he slid down the far wall next to the bed, uttering curses. Perhaps parts of spells that had no effect in the iron-and-silver-fortified room. His eyes were those of his cat, green, glittering, and elliptical. He smiled, showing off the huge fangs that had almost gotten a piece of his friends. "This is what I am. Blood will tell, won't it?"

Nick stared at Kalen, his eyes suspiciously moist. "We can't let him suffer like this."

"I agree," her father said.

Aric spoke up. "If we can't reach him, he'll eventually bring this place down around our ears. He's too strong to be kept in a cell for long."

Nick withdrew his gun from his waistband. "I'll do it. He's my responsibility."

"What?" Mac shouted. "No! You can't give up on him just like that! I can reach him. I know I can!"

"Honey," her dad began, his face wretched.

"Please. I'm begging you. Give me a chance to get through to him." Her voice broke. She trembled from head to toe, terrified that Nick would deny her plea.

"Mac, he's too far gone," Nick said gently, eyes sad.

"He's a man, not a dog to be put down," she spat angrily, wiping her cheeks. "He promised me he would fight this, and I know he's in there somewhere."

"God," Jax breathed. "Where's the justice in this? We gave him our word that we'd have his back. What's our word worth if we let him drown the first time his head goes under water? Even Raven is still here, though he's been stuck in wolf form for almost six years."

"Raven isn't a Fae Sorcerer with an Unseelie sire and the power to destroy the entire world as we know it."

"Another chance, Nicky. Please."

One by one, the guys voiced their agreement. Against their united front, Nick wavered, then finally relented. "Forty-eight hours. If he's not showing signs of improvement, I won't allow him to suffer any longer. Or to endanger us all."

Even against the backdrop of Kalen's vile rampage, the guys were visibly relieved. Kalen was one of their own, and they didn't want to give up on him.

Nick slumped, looking wiped out. "I need to go check on Phoenix. Melina's taking care of him."

One by one the guys hugged Mac, then headed for the infirmary to await word on their old friend, found and home once more. Mac was torn, but opted to stay with Kalen for a while. Nick wouldn't hear of her remaining behind alone and ordered A.J. to stay with her. Just in case. A.J. nodded, lips pressed into a thin line. He understood the situation very well. And he was trained to handle it.

Mac eyed the rifle with the wicked-looking scope slung over the sniper's shoulder and her gut cramped in dread. She sent a prayer to whatever deity might be listening for her mate to come out of this safely. Alive and whole.

After the others were gone, Mac turned to A.J. "What happened at the research facility?"

The man shook his sandy brown head. "I was on a hillside doing my part to pick off the uglies. I didn't know what was going on inside, but suddenly the central area of the building exploded and fell in. I raced down there, but it was all over by the time I picked my way to where the guys were."

"Surely Nick told you something?"

The handsome man looked away. "Doc, all I know is that the team was ambushed. They were able to get into the research lab and the prisoners way too easily. Then a shitload more Sluagh arrived and they were outnumbered."

"They don't think Kalen had anything to do with that . . ." The idea was horrid. But given the way he was acting now—not unreasonable.

"Nick doesn't think so. But the bloodlust of battle got to your mate. The others said he went into a rage and killed practically the whole damned bunch of those monsters on his own. But they didn't realize he'd stopped distinguishing between 'them' and 'us' until he turned on Ryon and came close to killing him, too."

Mac looked to Kalen, sitting on the floor of his cell. He had his chin tucked to his chest now, dark hair hiding his face, babbling to himself. She couldn't tell what he was saying, but he seemed a bit more calm. But only just. He was still plenty agitated, rocking back and forth, oblivious to her and A.J. watching.

She moved a little closer to the bars. "Kalen? Sweetie, it's me—"

His head came up and he growled, baring his fangs. His elliptical, kohl-rimmed eyes showed not the slightest hint of recognition. He was angry, straining at his bonds. And he was afraid too. Confused.

The emotions slammed into her hard, and she gasped. She felt his fear through their bond, and a ray of hope made a pinprick in the gloom as she recalled that he could feel her emotions as well. She could use that to their advantage. Try to reach him.

Moving slowly to avoid agitating him more, she sat cross-legged on the floor. A.J. leaned on the wall nearby, ready in case of trouble. She blocked out the terrible image of his scoped rifle and concentrated on her bond with her mate. Thought of their baby. Her dreams for the three of them. Sent waves of love to him in an endless stream.

His snarling gradually stopped. His fangs receded and his eyes were humanlike again. But humanity was still absent. He remained confused, but the awful rage had subsided. He studied her for long moments before his lids began to droop. Worn out from the events of the day, he slept.

Slumped against the wall, separated from her mate, so did she. Fitfully.

Kalen was holding her. Stroking her hair. Placing kisses on top of her head. "This is nice," he murmured.

"Yes, it is."

He paused, and she sensed he had more to say.

"This is good, isn't it? Me, holding you?"

He sounded so uncertain, and yet hopeful; her heart swelled. "It definitely is," she said, hugging him. "Why wouldn't it be?"

"This is new to me. Holding someone, being held." His voice resonated a note of wonder.

"Then you've missed out on a lot."

"I'm beginning to see that," he said softly.

A subtle shift was happening between them. Then, gradually . . . comfort became something more. They didn't have to be alone and afraid. They'd begun to bond tonight over a shared terror, and now that connection solidified as he held her against his heart. Tilted her face up to his.

And placed the sweetest of kisses on her lips. He started slowly, one nibble at a time. Paused in between, giving her the chance to put out the flame that had been kindled between them. But she wanted him every bit as much, wasn't about to say no.

Sitting up, he pulled her into his lap. They were both still dressed in their jeans, but situated like this, she had no trouble discerning the erection pressing against her bottom. She wiggled against the hardness, wanting more.

"You're trying to kill me."

"Far from it." Sitting up, she pulled her shirt over her head, baring herself to his gaze. From the sliver of light filtering through the part in the curtains, she could see his green eyes glittering with desire. With need. But also with uncertainty.

"I've never done this before."

"Had sex?" She found that difficult to believe.

"Made love," he whispered. "With someone I care about."

Sweet man. "It's fantastic. Like nothing else you'll ever feel."

"Tell me what you want." Reaching out, he caressed her cheek. "I have to hear it."

"Make love to me. Give me everything."

Capturing her lips again, he lowered her to the bed. Kissed her thoroughly for several long moments. He had the best mouth and he knew how to use it—as he proved by nibbling his way down her throat, teeth scraping. Long ones.

"Are you using your panther teeth?"

"Mmm."

She gasped as one canine grazed a tender nipple. "I'll take that as a yes."

His mouth latched on to the nub, suckling, and she moaned, burying her fingers in his long hair as she'd itched to do for weeks. The black mass was as silky as it looked, thick and just right to get a good grip. She enjoyed the feel of it as much as she loved him lavishing attention on her nipples.

He moved south, kissing her belly. When he moved lower, she had to relinquish her hold on his mane, and whimpered in protest.

"You don't want this?" he teased, settling between her thighs. "You said to give you everything."

"And I meant it. I just love my hands in your hair."

He looked pleased. "Well, you can have it back in a few minutes. Promise."

Unzipping her jeans, he worked them down and off, along with her panties. Pushing her knees apart, he lowered his head. Flicked out his tongue and lapped at her clit. With a sigh of pleasure, she spread for him as wide as possible. It had been much too long, and she wanted Kalen to have her. Like this, or any way he desired.

His mouth was every bit as talented in this area, too. He licked her folds, delved his tongue in between to fuck her channel slowly. Driving her mad. Then he'd withdraw and suckle the little clit, taking her to the edge. And withdraw again. Lick and suckle. Over and over until she was mindless, writhing.

"Oh, God!"

"What do you want, honey?"

"Fuck me," she begged. "I need you."

He didn't require further encouragement and shed his jeans quickly. Crawling over her, he settled between her legs, placed the head of his cock to her opening. Pushed inside.

There, in the darkness, they came together.

Rocking his hips, he began to move inside her. Deep, to the

*hilt, and out again. Slow and easy, stoking the fire once
again, searing her to the depths of her soul. She buried her
fingers in his hair again, watched his face as he made love to
her. The pupils of his eyes had gone elliptical and smoldered
with passion. The muscles of his shoulders bunched and his
fangs protruded as he panted with each thrust, the disk of his
pendant hanging from his neck, resting between her breasts.*

"Harder," she urged. "Faster."

*Increasing the tempo, he did as she asked, moaning. Driv-
ing them higher. She knew he was close when he gathered her
to his chest, hips pumping furiously. She clung to his back,
her own release building until—*

*She shattered with a cry, pulsing around his length. Her
release triggered his and he came with a hoarse shout, sinking himself as deeply as possible. He stayed there, convuls-
ing, holding her close, until at last they were spent. Then a
bit longer as they came down from the high, kissing the curve
of her neck.*

"Thank you," he whispered.

Mac came awake slowly. It took her a moment to realize she was still lying on the floor in the corridor of
Block R—and that someone had placed her on a cot
and put a pillow under her head. She was grateful for
the kindness.

It took her another moment to realize that her sex
was wet and warm, and she squirmed in discomfort.
Lord, she hoped she hadn't been dreaming out loud!
Twisting, she saw A.J. sitting a few feet away, resting
against the wall with his eyes closed, rifle propped beside him. He didn't know she was awake yet, so she
settled again to let herself wake up.

She'd been dreaming of Kalen. Of their first time

making love, in the Wall-Banger Motel, right after the Sluagh had attacked them outside the Cross-eyed Grizzly. That was when they'd made their child together, and no matter what happened, she could never regret it.

Tears pricked her eyes and she finally sat up, searching the inside of Kalen's cell. He was lying on the bare mattress, asleep, his chest rising and falling slowly. He looked alone and forlorn. It was so far from the beautiful memory of their first lovemaking, and all the times they'd been together since then, that it made her ache inside.

A.J.'s low voice broke through her sorrow. "You've both been out for a while."

"What time is it?"

"Two in the morning."

"I'm sorry," she said contritely. "I didn't mean to keep you here this late. I know you're ready to fall into your own bed."

He shrugged. "Got nobody in my bed to make it worthwhile, so I'm just as good staying here, guarding you and Kalen."

She was touched. "Thank you."

"No problem." They sat in companionable silence for a few minutes, watching Kalen. "Melina and Noah brought you the cot and pillow. Said to tell you that Nix is gonna be fine. He's dehydrated and traumatized, but nowhere near as bad as the shape Micah was in when he was found. He was cracking lame jokes in the emergency room, trying to take the edge off the emotional situation."

She smiled in spite of everything. "That sounds like Nix. He reminds me a lot of Aric."

A.J. snorted. "God help us all, then."

"Not with the snark, necessarily. He's got a quick wit that's cutting like Aric's, but he's funny at the same time. He's got the most generous soul of anyone I've ever met, and that's saying a lot considering everyone in the Pack. And he's a notorious womanizer, too. As soon as he's healed, I'm sure he'll round up all the single guys and head to Vegas to party."

"I'll be sure not to miss that trip." He winked at her, and she laughed.

"So, no special lady for you? A.J.'s not going to be the next bachelor to fall?"

"Not on your life," he said with a cocky smile. "I've seen what true luuuv does to you guys, and you're all insane. I'll pass, thanks."

"Hmm. He doth protest too much."

"Say that with a mouthful of crackers."

She giggled. She hadn't really gotten to know A.J. before, and she found she liked him. He was good company, if a bit taciturn sometimes. Though he certainly wasn't being that way right now, with her.

A low growl caught their attention, and she looked through the bars to see Kalen glaring at A.J. Pushing from the bed, he stalked forward, a bit awkwardly with his hands bound behind his back. Wincing, she hoped his shoulders weren't too strained from sleeping like that.

He walked up to the bars, leaning his chest against them. His eyes never left the other male's. "Mine."

Mac's breath caught. If he was aware enough to reassert his claim on her to the other man, then there was hope she could reach him. "Yes, mate," she said softly. "I'm yours."

His green gaze went to hers, and she saw that his

eyes were no longer the slitted ones of his cat. They were no longer feral, but sad. "My mate."

"Yours."

"Need you."

"I'm sorry, but you can't let him out," A.J. told her. "You can't trust him yet."

The knowledge scored her heart. "I need you too," she said, her voice catching. "But you have to stay there for now."

"Need you," he repeated plaintively.

But the battle in his soul still raged. Though there were no outward signs of anger, she could tell by his difficulty forming his thoughts into words that he was struggling. He still wasn't "all there" and she couldn't risk herself, their child, or the others.

"You'll have me soon. I'm here."

"Stay?"

"I will, promise."

"What's happening to me?" he whispered. "Why am I here?"

She bit her lip to keep from bawling. The good side of him had battled to the surface and couldn't understand. When he'd lost it at that research facility, the rush of darkness had been too much. It had damaged something inside him, and she prayed he could recover.

"You're not well, love. We're trying to help you, but you have to try hard, too. Do you understand?"

"No. I want out."

"I'm sorry."

Head hanging, he slid to the floor and rested his head against the bars. He didn't move again for a long time.

Mac sat on her cot and cried, hot, silent tears of misery.

The cold bars of the cell pressed into Kalen's forehead. He sat still and tried to understand what was going on. Struggled to remember.

Why was he locked away like an animal? What had he done?

Flashes of memory assaulted him, but they were from other times, long past. Bad nights when he sold his body for a few dollars or a crummy meal. That was awful, but nobody had been hurt. Well, nobody but himself.

That wasn't why he was here. And where was this?

The compound. Right. Block R, where Nick put the creatures who were almost beyond hope. Almost.

He scoured his brain. Where had he been tonight? Or last night? Something about a mission. A research facility . . .

You did well, my boy. I am very proud of your progress.

"What?" he rasped. "What did I do?"

You defeated my Sluagh, and while that is inconvenient for me, it is important training for you, son. You killed dozens of them and allowed the true predator in you to take over. The bloodlust became one with your soul, and you turned your rage on the one called Hunter.

"Ryon?" Sweet Jesus, no. "I killed him?"

If not for the untimely intervention of those meddling dogs, you would have. The war is near, and when the hour comes, you'll help me destroy them all.

"No. I won't do it."

You will, and you will revel in their blood. Remember the pleasure of bathing in it, boy? Of feasting on your kill? That can be yours, always. You and I will rule, father and son. No one will stand against us.

"The blood *was* sweet." God, no. He was losing his mind. Falling again.

Yes, son. It sustains us, the juices of our prey. Every night we will feast, not on those mangy Sluagh, but on young and succulent meat. Would you like that?

No, no. "Yes, Father."

"Kalen?" a sweet voice called from far away. "Don't listen to him! He's poisoning your mind!" But her pleas faded.

I'll bring the most beautiful specimens for us both, each night. They'll be trembling with desire, eager to sacrifice themselves to the world's most powerful creatures. They will be helpless against our seduction, spread their legs for us so we can feast on their essence before we slide our cocks deep.

Kalen panted, his cock lengthening in his jeans. Fought against the image, but hunger won. His cock throbbed as Malik continued.

You're sinking your cock deep into your willing prey now. The tight clasp of heat writhes against you, and you own this body. You are lord and master and this is your due. More?

"Yes, please. Tell me how it will be." He ground his hard cock underneath himself. Beyond saving.

You own your prey then, for that is what this body is— not woman or man. Simply a sacrifice to satisfy a superior beast. Your rod joins you both as you stroke inside, fanning your flame. Seeking the ultimate high. Just before the peak, you sink your fangs into the delicate throat. Do you taste the sweet, warm blood?

"So good," he moaned.

It fills your mouth as your prey screams out a release of joy at having experienced this joining. Of being your Chosen

One for the evening, your body to enjoy. The prey dances on your cock as you fill it with your seed, until at last the life force begins to leave it. You take the soul into yourself, this precious gift.

His cock erupted, spasming on and on as the decadent scene ended. So wicked.

The sacrifice your prey has given to you is an honor and shall not be wasted. You tear into the throat and feast, and soon move on to the heart, for that is the best meat and will sustain you until the next night. This I promise you.

"You promise," he whispered.

Yes. You are my son. You are the prince of the Unseelie, and this is your destiny.

"Father, I've waited for you for so long. No one else ever wanted me."

I know, my son. We'll be together. In mere hours, it will all be over. You know what to do.

He did, and though the light fought to defeat the darkness, it dimmed to almost nothing. "I'll lower the shields."

Good. And then?

"I'll kill them for you. Kill them all!"

Except the woman. She carries our future.

"Of course." He frowned, but the wisp of light faded away again.

My Sluagh are coming, by the hundreds. You will fight at my side. And when it's all over you'll be rewarded with your first prey. Save your appetite.

He laughed. "Can't wait."

"Oh my fucking God," A.J. croaked, stunned. He stared at Kalen curled on the floor of his cell, consumed by Malik's poison. They'd heard enough of the Sorcerer's side of the conversation to glean what was about to go down. "That's not Kalen anymore. I'm calling Nick."

Sobbing, Mac fled Block R. She didn't know where she was going at first, only that she had to get out of there, now.

Help. She had to get help. She'd get Melina and they'd give him the sedative after all. At least he'd be unable to carry out his father's orders.

"Oh, no. No!"

She'd lost the man she loved to the evil that had stalked him all his life.

And had finally won.

Nick and Jarrod sat in Nick's office at half past two in the morning. Unable to sleep, they'd talked for hours. Something was going to happen, and soon.

The storm was on the way.

As if to punctuate this knowledge, lightning flashed and actual thunder rolled in the distance. Miles away yet but speeding toward them. He should've known the end would come with a real storm to add to the mess, not simply a figurative one.

"I can't get a reading, no inkling at all of a vision beyond what I've told you," Nick said in frustration.

"And that doesn't help much. We know there's a great war and Kalen is there. He's the impetus of the catastrophic event."

"Yeah. And we don't know which side of the fence he comes down on."

The cell phone on Nick's desk buzzed and he glanced at it in surprise. Then the chill of foreboding gripped him even before he saw the name on the screen. "It's A.J.," he told Jarrod. Then he answered. "What's up?"

"Boss, it's Kalen," the younger man said breathlessly. Nick was out of his chair and moving before the guy spoke again. Jarrod ran after him. "That Unseelie creep got into his head again, and—and you shoulda seen it. I think he's gone, boss. Like 'the Kalen we know doesn't live here anymore' *gone*. He's raving about killing all of us!"

"Grant and I are on the way."

"God, it's going to devastate Mac if . . ." The man couldn't finish.

"I know. But I'm not sure I'll have a choice."

But he knew. As soon as they entered the corridor and Nick heard the maniacal laughter, the awful sound of a body crashing into the cell's bars again and again, he understood what he had to do.

And it devastated him every bit as much as it would Kalen's mate.

He was going to have to put down a poor kid who'd never had a chance.

Fifteen

What was with all the attention?

Kalen strained to bring the pieces of his fractured mind back together. To make sense of why he was laughing like a loon, throwing himself at the bars of his prison. Scaring the shit out of A.J. Then the sniper was talking on his cell phone. *Nick*, he heard the man say.

And soon enough, Nick was standing outside, staring in at Kalen with an expression of sorrow Kalen had never seen before. It gave him pause. What did the man have to be sorry about? *He* was the one in here, suffering for something that wasn't his fault.

Was it?

"I'll do it," A.J. said grimly, gripping his rifle. "It's my job."

"No. As I said before, he's Pack. As commander, he's my responsibility, and so is his end."

End. Whose?

Nick took the rifle from A.J., who handed it over

reluctantly. Then the commander faced Kalen again, the weapon in his big hands. "What's your name, son?" he asked, his voice calm.

"Is that a trick question?" he asked snidely. "You can call me Prince of the Unseelie." Yeah, he liked that.

"Who do you answer to?" the commander persisted.

"Malik. My father." But that wasn't right. The man in front of him was his boss. A father figure, too. He was good and kind. But where had those two pipe dreams of goodness and kindness from anyone ever gotten him?

"Jesus Christ," Aric said, walking up to Nick's side. "What the fuck is going on? Kalen?"

"Aric," Nick said quietly. "You might not want to watch this."

"What?" The redhead's mouth dropped open. "No! He goes batty and that's it? You just finish him? I thought we were gonna give him time?"

Aric. A friend, arguing for his life. That sliver of light became a thread in an ocean of black. It grew, slim but there. No! He had no friends. He had only his father. And his father had promised him power; he would never again be at anyone's mercy.

"I can't save him, Aric. He's given himself to the Unseelie, and he won't help himself. He doesn't want us or the good we've brought to his life. He wants blood and death."

Yes, that's what he wanted . . . No, it wasn't! He loved and respected Nick, all of these men. God, his head hurt.

His mate. He needed Mackenzie.

"Where's my mate? Where's Mackenzie?" he asked. God, he was so confused. And now he was getting scared, because Nick had raised the rifle to his shoulder. Kalen was looking down the scope.

Aric stared at his boss in horror. "Nick, you can't. Don't you hear him? If he's asking for his mate, he's still in there somewhere."

From somewhere out of Kalen's line of sight, footsteps sounded, coming fast up the hallway. "No!" Mac screamed. Running up to Nick, she hung on to his arm. "You said forty-eight hours! You can't do this! Melina can give him the sedative!"

And then it happened. Nick whirled and grabbed her arm, and Kalen's vision went crimson.

Mate. The man was touching his mate. Grabbing her and pushing her back as she cried. The cries went straight to his soul, and the light surged. Twined with the dark and exploded outward in a hurricane of power that he gathered and used to snap the silver chains binding his wrists.

Flinging them aside, he gripped the bars and gave a mighty pull, every muscle in his body straining. The entire structure ripped from the stone walls and he tossed it aside just as Nick stumbled backward and opened fire.

The bullet punched his shoulder and he roared in agony. His mate screamed again as Kalen fell back against the ruined wall, clutching the wound. In that moment, their gazes met and he saw her terror, felt it through their bond . . . and the truth nearly sent him to his knees. She was afraid for him. And *of* him. Her pain was all his fault. He had to leave.

"I'm sorry," he rasped. Regret almost felled him.

Summoning his magic, he countered the cell's damaged fortifications and vanished. Transported himself

far into the Shoshone and reappeared in a place he recognized. It was the spot where he and Mackenzie had
made love, so long ago it seemed. He tried to draw
comfort from their place, but there was mostly debili-
tating grief. He'd lost her.

Lost himself, too.

His wound throbbed and he staggered, weakened
by blood loss. Perhaps there was a way to heal. He
shifted into his panther and collapsed under a tree,
panting. He listened to the sounds of the night returning. Crickets and strange bird calls. Somewhere, the
lone howl of a wolf that was a permanent resident of
the forest, not Pack.

Maybe he should've let Nick eliminate him, but the
last shred of humanity in him insisted that he would
never have hurt anyone on his own, especially Mackenzie. There was still good inside him.

Which would be damned near impossible to prove
now that he was a fugitive Sorcerer with a kill order on
his head and rage burning in his almost-black heart.

Mac stood shaking, staring at the spot where Kalen had
been seconds before. There was blood on the wall
where he'd rested his back against it, the shot having
gone through his shoulder.

"You shot my mate," she hissed, rounding on Nick.

The rest of the Pack, along with Sariel, surrounded
them now, kicking through the rubble and taking in the
nasty scene before them.

"You shot my brother?" the Fae asked in disbelief,
appalled. One by one, every man in the Pack turned to
the prince and someone whistled. Apparently not
everyone had gotten that memo.

"He was about to fucking murder us all!" the commander shouted.

"He didn't go nuts and bust out until you grabbed my arm, Nick! Come on. You know it's not smart to touch a man's mate when he's in his right mind, much less when he's struggling like Kalen is!"

"You're so certain he's actually fighting to regain himself? Are you willing to bet all our lives on that?"

"Yes!"

Nick heaved several breaths, making a visible effort to calm down. "We'll find him, or more likely he'll find us. You are not to go looking for him. Is that clear?"

"Nick, that's not—"

"Is that *fucking clear*, Doctor?"

"Yes, sir," she seethed. Turning on her heel, she ignored her dad and everyone else and marched toward her quarters. Once there, she paced and swore until she thought she'd go as crazy as Kalen had. What the hell was she supposed to do now? Just sit here like a good little mate and wait for the big, bad wolves to make it all better?

Well, they'd probably just end up making it worse. Leave a man in charge and it was bound to get worse before it got better.

"Is that clear?" she mocked. "Well, yes, and in fact it sucks. So fuck that."

In her bedroom, she toed off her work shoes; they were flats with cushy soles, but not made for a walk in the woods. Then she stripped out of her black slacks and blouse, which weren't hiking material, either.

From her closet she fetched dark jeans and a T-shirt, as well as her best hiking boots with thick, well-treaded soles, and carried them to the bed. In five minutes she was dressed, had retrieved the flashlight she kept in the nightstand for power outages, and slipped into the corridor.

Luck was on her side as she hurried to the end and through the rec room. That way was the easiest exit without being seen by those inside, who were on the other side of the compound. But she stood outside, gazing at the path leading into the woods, and shivered. Traipsing through the unforgiving Shoshone in the dead of night wasn't the wisest course of action. It wasn't like the compound was situated in a fucking YMCA camp.

But anger and desperation were good motivators. And they had nothing on the best motivator of all—her love for the man who was in so much turmoil. The father of her child. She'd do just about anything to bring him home.

"You and me are going on an adventure," she said, rubbing her flat stomach. "We're going to find your daddy, and we've got his pendant to protect us. We'll be fine."

At that moment she recalled what Kalen had said about the pendant not protecting against stupidity and shoved that aside. If she was going to think like that she'd never leave.

Opening her heart and mind to her mating bond, she switched on the flashlight and followed her instinct. She sent love singing along the golden thread as though it were a telephone line and she had plenty to say. When she felt the love flowing in return, she gasped and followed where the thread was leading her.

She tried to concentrate on putting one foot in front of the other. Not on the rustles in the dense foliage of the nocturnal animals foraging. Not on the call of a wolf that was natural, not a shifter. She reminded herself that there had never been a documented case of a wolf attacking a person, that they shied away from man.

The same couldn't be said of the grizzlies. But surely they were sleeping.

When her flashlight illuminated a tall, dark form ahead, she wasn't afraid. Her heart sped up with happiness. "Kalen! I'm so glad I found you!"

But as she got closer, she saw that the smile in her beam of light wasn't her mate's. Malik stood grinning at her in his true form, huge and frightening. His leathery wings seemed to block out the stars and his fangs gleamed wickedly.

"I'm glad you found me too, sweet. Though I'm not my son."

"He's not any more your son than I am," she told him, anger giving her courage.

The Unseelie chuckled. "He's my flesh and blood, dear. And yet you still want him as your mate. If that's so, then we can't be all bad."

"Don't put yourself in the same category with Kalen. There's no comparison."

"My, you're a feisty thing," he said in amusement. "I used to believe you were a bit of a pushover, but it's nice to see that you have spunk. It will make breaking you all the more fun."

Inside she trembled, but she summoned false bravado. "I have the pendant. It will protect me from all evil, and there's nothing you can do about that."

"Perhaps not. But it only protects the wearer, no one else."

She frowned. "And so it will keep me from harm."

"But not your mate."

"He's strong enough to fight you and win."

"Let's humor you and say he turns from me. All is not lost as far as I can see, because I still have a descendant to take his place." He paused, letting that sink in.

She recoiled, terror rising where confidence had been moments ago. "I won't let you come near our baby! I'll kill you first!"

"You and what army? And the pendant can't protect three people at once." He looked around pointedly. "But come now, there's no need for theatrics. We will all be a family—you, my son, my grandson, and me."

She gave a hysterical laugh. "Yeah, the Addams Family."

"Who?"

"Forget it. I'm not going anywhere with you, so you can just beam yourself back to your cave. And, oh yes, wait to get your ass kicked by the Alpha Pack. Because they're coming for you."

"So you're going to march through the forest all night searching for your wayward lover?"

"Sure. And if you'll kindly move aside, I'll get on with it." She was running on pure adrenaline. No doubt when she recalled this moment sometime in the future, staring up at the most dangerous creature in three realms, she would be amazed that she hadn't fainted.

"No need to go to all that foolishness when you can simply accompany me."

She swallowed hard. "You know where he is?"

"Of course. After the fiasco at your wolves' den, he came to me. Injured, I might add, and I'm not pleased about that."

"Neither am I, so that's one thing we agree on." She studied the Unseelie. "How do I know you're telling the truth that he's there and you're not trying to trick me?"

"The pendant will know," he said, pointing to the silver disk. "I won't be able to touch you if my intent is other than what I say. I will take you to your mate."

After a brief hesitation, she nodded. She had to get to Kalen. That was all that mattered. "Okay."

Reaching out, he placed a hand on her shoulder. In an instant the atmosphere whirled and the forest vanished. The ground disappeared from under her feet. She couldn't scream. But in seconds the trip was over and they were both standing in the living room of a rustic cabin.

"This is your hideout?" she asked, willing down the nausea.

"My nest for the moment. It's really an illusion, but a nice one, don't you think?"

"Where's Kalen?"

"Mackenzie, what are you doing here?"

At Kalen's voice, she looked past the Unseelie to see him standing there, his expression cold. She couldn't lose him to Malik. Not after all they'd been through.

"I came to find you and—and bring you home."

"Home?" he sneered. "Back to my loving boss so he can kill me? Back to my brothers who are going to stand there and let it happen?"

"Nobody wants you dead! But Nick thinks you're past help and he didn't know what to do!"

"The healing bullet wound in my shoulder says differently."

"Think what you want, but the Pack loves you. And I love you most of all." There it was. A spark of humanity that warmed his gaze, filled it with longing. For a few seconds he devoured her hungrily with those green eyes. But then he glanced at Malik, who was observing avidly, and the wall came down again.

"Love has no place in my life now," he said coolly. "The sooner you accept that, the better."

"Wh-what do you mean?" This frightened her, not knowing if he was posturing for Malik's benefit, or if he'd really turned.

"I thought I loved you, but I didn't know what that was. I can't give something I've never had."

"That's not true," she said, holding back a sob. "You have my love. You've felt it. And our baby will love his father."

Another spark. Her Kalen was in there, she was sure of it.

"Our child will follow in my footsteps. In the meantime, you will live here with me. After Nick and his Pack are defeated, we'll move to the Unseelie realm, where we'll stay."

That was so not going to happen. But one look at Malik's sinister expression told her what answer was expected. And she'd give it to buy time until she knew what game Kalen was playing. "As long as I'm with you, it doesn't matter where we live. I'll do as you say, and no one else but you."

Kalen nodded. Malik appeared extremely pleased.

"Make sure the woman stays here. I'm going to gather my Sluagh and then I'll call for you to join in the attack. Oh, and lower the shields on the compound now."

"Yes, Father." Closing his eyes, he chanted softly. The words flowed, faster and stronger, until at last he stopped and opened them again. "It's done."

Mac's heart stuttered in dread. "You didn't."

"I'm going," Malik said. "Be ready."

He vanished and Kalen tugged on her arm, urging her toward the stairs. She opened her mouth, but he silenced her with a finger over her lips.

"We don't have much time."

"For what? You're scaring me."

"Shh."

He led her to a large suite with an opulent bed taking up quite a bit of space. Then he closed the door, turned and took her into his arms. Kissed her with all the pent-up passion they hadn't been able to express for a day or two. When he set her back from him, his face was filled with such love, it took her breath away.

"I love you, baby. Never, ever forget that. No matter what you see or hear before dawn, don't forget I love you so."

"What's going on? I saw you losing your mind in that cell and—"

"I did lose it," he said, his voice aching with regret. "In that cell, the evil consumed me and I longed to kill. But when Nick grabbed you . . . Yeah, I went nuts. You're my mate and seeing his hand on you reminded me I'd do anything for you. For you, not for that son-ofabitch."

"Oh, Kalen."

"I'm still fighting the compulsion, and God, it's the hardest thing I've ever done. But *you* make it go away.

The only time it's really manageable, when I feel like I can win, is when you're in my arms. When he brought you here, I had to make it believable that I'm completely on his side. I do love you. I'm sorry, baby."

She held him tight and they stood together, breathing each other in. Holding on to this moment in time, because it might be all they had. "He's going to attack. What are we going to do?"

He stroked her face tenderly. "*We* aren't doing anything. I'm sending you back to the compound because that's where it's safest. Then I'm joining the fight against that fucking Unseelie bastard who is not my father in any sense of the word."

"But you just lowered the shields there! I don't understand."

"I didn't lower them, sweetheart. I strengthened them."

She sagged against him. "Oh, thank God. I thought . . ."

"I know." He kissed the top of her head. "And I'm sorry all I've done tonight is scare you. This will be over soon. I promise."

"I'll kill you for it later. We need to get going before *he* decides to come back or something."

"He won't. Malik's too focused on his mission. And we have time." He edged her backward, toward the big bed. "Let me make love to you, baby."

"Here? In his house?"

"It's not his house. It's an illusion. But we're not, and neither is how we feel."

"I know, but—"

"Loving you keeps him out of my head and my soul. Help me drive out the darkness for good. I need to show you how much I love you before . . . before I have to fight."

That sounded far too much like goodbye. She wouldn't accept that, but neither would she waste any precious moments with him. And if it would help him, she wouldn't refuse. He undressed her with care, the regular way because he enjoyed it, then himself with magic. He pushed her onto the bed, followed her down.

Covering her, he pushed inside. Made slow, tender love to her, cradling her close. He whispered in her ear, "Never forget this. Never forget me, or how much I love you and our child. How much I want you both."

"I won't," she told him. Tears streamed into her hair. It was a beautiful joining, despite the uncertainty that awaited them.

They reached their orgasm together with mutual cries and floated down. He held her as long as he could, then slipped out of her. Standing by the bed, he clothed himself again, then her, with a wave of his hand.

"I wish I could take you far away from here. Just run from the fight with you."

"But you're not made that way."

His smile was heartbreaking as he took her hand. "No. And you wouldn't love me if I were. Hold on. I'll take you back."

Before she could protest, the room disappeared. The same sense of flying shot a thrill through her, and it wasn't as nauseating as before. In moments, her feet touched solid ground and she found they were standing outside Sariel's room. Kalen knocked, and it took several seconds before the door opened and his brother stood gaping at them.

"Good gods!" The prince ushered them inside and glanced up and down the hallway before shutting and locking the door. He faced Kalen with worry. "Are you mad? If Nick finds you here, all hell is going to break loose. Again."

"He won't. I'm not staying long. I just brought Mackenzie back, and then I'm joining in the fight. On the Pack's side."

"That's not what Nick believes." Sariel eyed his brother.

"He'll believe it when he's faced with the proof. I can't do any more than that to convince him."

"You don't have to do this."

"Yes, I do. I told my mate and I'll tell you—I don't run from a fight."

"You seem in control of yourself. Nothing like what I saw earlier."

"It's a lot harder than it looks," Kalen said, his expression bleak. "Mackenzie grounds me, and it's worse when people or circumstances interfere with our harmony."

"She won't be with you in this fight. How will she ground you then?"

"I'll just have to keep her and the baby in my thoughts. And my real family—you and my Pack brothers. All I can give it is my best shot."

"I'm joining you. I'm not standing by this time and allowing all of you to fight my battles." He held up a hand to forestall Kalen's argument. "I am Malik's son as well, and this conflict started because of me."

"No. It started because of Malik's plot to create

super-shifters. The Pack was already after him. They just didn't know who they were chasing for a long time, and you being related to him and on his hit list was pure coincidence. You're under their protection now and they don't resent that one bit."

"That's true," Mac put in. "Everyone adores you."

Sariel's face colored a bit. "Well, I think the world of everyone here and I'd hate to leave."

Kalen's expression hardened. "You won't have to. We're going to give that asshole a taste of what super-shifters really are—and he's not going to be able to handle the reality check we hand him."

"I think I'm going to enjoy having you for a brother," Sariel told him with a smile.

"Same here." Kalen glanced at Mac. "Give us a minute, baby?"

She nodded and the pair moved across the room, murmuring in hushed voices. Sariel seemed upset but eventually capitulated to whatever Kalen was speaking to him about. Apparently satisfied, Kalen pulled the prince into a brief embrace, then let him go. Kalen returned to Mac and gave her a hug as well, ending hers with another searing kiss.

"When this is over, we're taking a vacation in Fiji. Just so you can start packing."

She gave him a watery smile. "Sounds good to me."

"I love you, baby."

"Love you more," she choked out. Before she could say anything else, he vanished. She gazed at the spot where he'd been. "What did he say to you?"

Sariel just sighed heavily.

"Tell me."

"He asked me to take care of you and the baby if he

doesn't come home. But he will," the prince said fiercely. "We have to believe that."

She was trying. Really, really trying to keep the faith.

But it was getting harder with each passing second.

Nick was perched on the edge of the conference table, slurping as much coffee as he could to keep himself going, like many of his Pack.

They were all tense. Waiting. Jax and Zan were scouting the perimeter, using the cover of darkness to locate Malik and his Sluagh. A crack of lightning split the sky outside the window and thunder rolled again, the time in between shorter. Stronger. The storm was closer and moving in fast.

And out of the blue, the vision held him in its icy grip.

Nick was kneeling in the middle of a field, racked with pain as cold rain lashed down, stinging like needles. Lightning split the sky, took a jagged path to the soaked earth, scorching it in spite of the downpour.

All around him, his Pack battled the Sluagh. His brave men cutting a swath through Malik's batlike Unseelie minions, losing ground with every passing second. There were hundreds of the terrible beasts, swarming, screeching. Far too many for either fierce wolves or men with magical gifts to defeat.

They were all going to die.

High on a pinnacle stood the Sorcerer with his staff, holding it aloft. Screaming at the Unseelie enemy, at the heavens for help that would not come.

And then a bolt of lightning streaked from the boiling black clouds, making the night as day just before it hit the end of the Sorcerer's staff. A massive detonation shook the ground and the world fell away.

Fell and fell. Taking Nick and his men into the abyss.

"Nick!" Was that Ryon? "Nick!"

He blinked to find Ryon crouched over him, patting his cheek. "Shit."

"What did you see, boss?"

He took the hand up Ryon offered and met each of their worried stares. He'd never told his men about the vision before. But maybe it was time he did. They needed to know what they were facing. The dire odds.

So he told them in detail. And when he was finished, the pall in the room was palpable. Never had he seen such doubt and fear on their faces, and he almost regretted it.

"So Kalen's going to save us?" Ryon asked.

"Or destroy us all. I don't know which way it goes, so if any of you want out, now's the time to speak up. Anyone?"

No one moved. Or spoke.

Jax and Zan eased inside, Sariel after them. "What did you find?" Nick asked Jax.

"There's a huge army of Sluagh gathering a couple of miles west of here, in a clearing in the forest. There's way too many, even with Grant's forces meeting us and intercepting them."

Nick and Jarrod shared a look; then Nick repeated his question. "Could be we're all about to meet our deaths. In or out?"

Jax scoffed. "How could you even ask us that? In, dammit."

The rest echoed him, and the Pack took a few

moments to center themselves. To contemplate the monumental task before them. Then they went to face their fate like the men of honor they were. Nick was the last out, but not before he took one more look around the room.

And he wondered, as they all did, whether they'd make it home alive.

Sixteen

Come to me, son. It's time we end the commander and his men.

"The shields are down," he lied. "Come and get them."

To me, boy. We fight together.

Kalen ignored the summons and waited. In the darkness, outside the compound, he knew Malik and his goons would start their way, and he'd gloat when he saw how very outnumbered the Pack was, even with the military black ops groups assisting them.

But he'd soon be in for a very big surprise.

The Pack filed out of the building, tense and battle-ready even though they must be exhausted. They'd already tackled the last research facility, and now they'd battle for their lives. They'd been up almost all night anticipating this, and still they showed. Ready to rumble.

His pride in them, in being a part of them even for a short time, nearly overwhelmed him. If it was the last thing he did, he'd prove to them that he'd been worthy all along. He could resist the lure of evil because of his brothers. Because of Mac and their child. He just had to hold out a little longer.

Kalen cloaked himself from their presence, though some of them sensed something off. He rode right next to Aric in the SUV on the way to the rendezvous point with Grant's men, and the redhead never knew it. That made Kalen smile. Aric would hate that he hadn't known.

Soon the vehicles pulled over near a clearing. The forest edged the open space, and behind that was an outcropping of rock that formed a peak. It wasn't high enough to be called a mountain like some in the distance, but was much more than a hill. Kalen thought that would make a fine vantage point for what he had planned.

Nick and Grant gathered the soldiers and their instructions were simple. Grant took the lead.

"Remember, heart and head. Those are the only two places to kill these bastards, and if you miss, you're dead. What you see here tonight, you didn't see it at all. You were never here. Correct?"

"Yes, sir!" they shouted.

"Excellent. Now, let's beat these fuckers so we can go home!"

More lightning and thunder followed his directive and heralded the beginning of the end. Rain was on the horizon, the scent of fresh earth rich in the air, when a horde of screeching Sluagh broke from the trees, came from every direction. Some men crossed themselves quickly—and then ran bravely toward the enemy.

Dropping his invisibility cloak, Kalen shifted to his

panther form and ran with them into the fray. The attack had happened much more swiftly than he'd expected.

He didn't see Malik. As the opposing forces clashed, both men and Sluagh screaming, he took out the first of the creatures and tried to scan for the Unseelie. It would be so like him to hang back and avoid the real fight.

What are you doing, boy? Over here!

Where? His inattention nearly got him decapitated. He fought on, slashing one creature after another. Lightning and thunder clapped again, and then the rain started. Cold, it stung him like needles in spite of the temperate night. He could hardly see, but he kept fighting. And searching for the one he needed to destroy.

In the flashes of light, he could see the truth. His Pack was losing. They would all die if he didn't do something. They were being overrun, three Sluagh replacing every single one who died. This was hopeless. Victory was up to him.

Or horrible defeat.

Mac couldn't stand it any longer. She had to know what was happening. The site was close, she knew. Just a couple of miles, and there was only one good place close to the compound for a battle to take place.

She borrowed one of the SUVs from the hangar and took off, rubber squealing. Finding the other vehicles didn't take long. But she wasn't expecting the fierce, bloody battle to be taking place so very close to where they'd parked.

There were hundreds. The sight and sound of the conflict was terrible, unlike anything she'd ever witnessed. One Sluagh took notice of her vehicle and she ducked down, her heart in her throat. She waited, and when it didn't approach, she peered out the window. The fight raged on, the Sluagh oblivious to her presence, and she waited.

Please, keep him safe. Keep all of them safe.

She sent love through her bond with Kalen. And prayed.

Kalen spotted Malik beyond the fray, on the peak overlooking the fight, safely out of reach. Without a second thought, he transported himself from the middle of the battle to stand in front of the Unseelie.

"What did you think to accomplish down there?" Malik snarled. "You were supposed to lower the shields and instead you led them here!" Stepping close, he backhanded Kalen hard across the face.

"Fuck you!" Warmth filled his mouth and he spat blood over the edge of the cliff.

"You're mine and you will obey me! You fight *with me.* Is that clear?"

"No, it's not clear, asshole," he called to be heard above the rising storm. Agony speared his brain and Kalen clutched his head, struggling to remain on his feet. Another wave hit, and another. Relentless. He yelled out in pain and anger, swaying.

Through the haze, Kalen swiped at the blood streaming from his nose, glaring at Malik with all the hatred coursing through his body. "Not long ago, you told me that you were intent on creating a breed of super-shifter soldiers. That they would help us usher in a new era where humans were basically cattle and supernatural creatures would rule. Creatures like us."

"Yes! Can't you see that this is our destiny? That it does you no good to resist?"

"There was once a man who believed he could take over the world by annihilating all of those who didn't measure up to his standards," Kalen sneered. "He believed in his sick mind that he would create a pure race, and he murdered millions while millions more bought his twisted lies. His name was Hitler, and his story didn't end so well. Neither will yours."

"You're my son, and we'll rule together! Sariel and those filthy wolves must die! And pendant or not, I'll find a way to slaughter your woman as well, like the cow she is, and take that child for my own before I'll allow you to defy me! You are *mine*!"

At that threat, the blackness within Kalen surged and he welcomed it—but this time to turn it on its creator.

His brothers were losing the fight. He gathered his power and saved it all for the threat to his mate and his family. May the gods give him strength.

"No!" he shouted back, summoning his Sorcerer's staff. "I'll see you in hell first, you motherfucker!"

"I'm your father. You won't kill me." He looked so damned smug.

"Oh, I will. I learned the meaning of *ruthless* from you, after all."

Nick, bloodied and damned near broken, crouched in the mud in the downpour and watched his vision come to pass. High on the pinnacle, the Sorcerer stood with his staff held high. And screamed his rage to the boiling heavens.

"God help us," he whispered.

But there was only the Sorcerer to save them. And that was far from a sure thing.

When the lightning struck the Sorcerer's staff, Nick witnessed a sight he'd never forget—should he live to recall it. Kalen harnessed the fury of the storm, took it into himself, and released it in an explosion that lit the sky as though it were a brilliant summer day.

All around him bodies were blown to bits. Nick scrabbled for purchase and fell.

Fell, thinking he'd never know how the story ended.

And then there was nothing.

Mac heard a powerful scream of rage and peeked out the window again. Kalen stood on the peak facing down Malik. Lightning struck his staff and he channeled the storm into a tool.

The combatants froze in awe—

And then the world was blown away.

Opening his body as a conduit for the storm, Kalen raised the staff high and screamed his rage. "Help me! Fucking help me!"

But he was alone in this. Just him and the elements. He welcomed the lightning and it didn't disappoint him, streaking from the sky as he'd summoned and striking the end of his staff with such force he was nearly blasted from his perch.

But he held firm, harnessing the white light. Because he'd heard somewhere that only light could drive out the darkness. From Sariel? Or someone else?

He used that now, his sole weapon against Malik and the masses of Sluagh below. The Unseelie was the first to realize that his doom was near and made a lunge for Kalen. He didn't make it.

The lightning shot from Kalen's body to Malik's and lit it up so that the Sorcerer could see every bone and organ inside. And then the Unseelie screeched, long and loud—the awful noise ending as he exploded into a million tiny particles to be washed away in the downpour.

A fitting end to the bastard's terrible reign.

No time to celebrate that victory. The Sluagh were next. The Sorcerer channeled the storm at the ugly minions, his own insides burning. His guts, lungs, heart. He could literally feel them starting to boil, the raw, brutal fury of the lightning taking a toll on him as well. But he kept going, long past what any normal human would have been able to withstand. Because he wasn't human.

He was Fae. A Sorcerer. A brother. A mate.

A father.

For the first time in his life, he embraced what and who he'd become. For all of his loved ones, he could do this. They were worth any price. He would die, and it would be okay. The Sluagh froze in confusion, perhaps barely gleaning the loss of their leader when they, too, began to sizzle like bacon. And they exploded, hundreds of them, with such force that his brothers and the remaining soldiers were hurled to the ground. Stunned, many injured, but all right.

It was over.

Kalen Black had finally done something truly good. He'd fought the evil and won, had severed the bond of darkness between himself and Malik. He'd protected his own, and that's all he wanted. His mate and baby were safe. Now he could let go.

His heart stuttered in his chest, the agony tearing him apart. He couldn't breathe. His knees buckled and he collapsed, falling through space, as the darkness took him.

Mac sat up, ears ringing, trying to clear her head. What had happened? The explosion!

She gazed out the SUV's window and spied the Pack guys and some soldiers struggling to sit up. Malik and the Sluagh were dead. She started to smile.

Then she saw Kalen's knees fold. Dropping the Sorcerer's staff, he collapsed, his duster fluttering around him as he tumbled from the summit.

Flinging open the door, she practically fell from it and ran. "Kalen!"

Slipping in the mud, she ran on, screaming his name again and again. She hit a slick spot and couldn't catch herself, went sprawling. Before she could get up, Nick and Sariel were there, helping her to sit up. She tried to pull away, but they held her fast.

"Wait!" Sariel ordered. "I need to check and see if you are all right."

"No! Kalen needs me!"

"The baby needs you too. Hold still."

That got her to cooperate long enough for Sariel to pronounce her and the baby safe. "Okay, help me find him! I saw him fall over there somewhere."

"We'll look together," Nick said. He shared a grim look with the prince.

Mac's pulse jumped, and her lungs seized. She had to find him. They picked their way through the debris-strewn field, the men holding her on each side. Others were up on their feet now, ignoring their own injuries to help in the search. Calling for Kalen.

She spotted him and cried out, jerking from their grasp, and ran. Her mate was lying on his back, unmoving. The rain had trailed off to a soft patter, and steam was rising from his battered and scorched leather duster, from his limbs and black hair. His eyes were closed, his face still and white.

Terrified, she dropped to her knees by his side and searched for a pulse. The beat was erratic, thready. Getting weaker by the second. "Kalen? It's me. Please, hang on," she begged. "It's over and we're all here. We're going to get you back to the compound and it's going to be all right."

But under her palm, his heartbeat slowed. And stopped.

Her world shattered. "No! Kalen!"

Sobbing, she started CPR while Nick tilted his head back, gave him breaths. One minute. Two. Agonizing minutes ticked by with no response. His lips were turning blue. She was losing him. She couldn't lose him!

"Mac, move over."

She found herself shoved aside by Zan. She barely registered that his ears were bleeding and his voice sounded odd. Her entire focus was on her mate lying there not breathing. "Help him, please."

She wasn't sure whether the Healer heard. He didn't answer, but seemed to talk to himself as he placed both palms on Kalen's chest.

"Burned himself out," Zan slurred, his voice odd and garbled. "Don't know if this will be enough."

A green glow began around Zan's palms and spread

to encompass Kalen's whole body. For too long, the Healer's efforts didn't seem to be working. When at last her mate sucked in a breath, there was a collective cheer from the men. But their relief was short-lived.

"Lots of damage," Zan managed, swaying. "Maybe too much."

Then he slumped to the side, unconscious. The Pack jumped into action. Jax and Ryon grabbed Zander while Aric and Nick took Kalen. It wasn't until they started for one of the SUVs with her mate that she remembered her dad. She looked around frantically, calling for him, and he squeezed her hand.

"I'm right here, baby girl. Come on. Let's see to that man of yours."

She rode in the back of one of the SUVs with Kalen, and they had to pry her loose when Melina and Noah rushed out to take over. She tried to follow them into the ER, but Nick blocked her path.

"Let Melina and Noah do their jobs. You need to see to Zan."

"But—"

"That man just saved Kalen's life and now he needs your attention." His voice softened. "Go. Seeing to him will take your mind off your mate for a while."

He was right. All through Zan's examination, she worried for the Healer as well as her mate. By the time she concluded her tests and got him settled in a room, her heart was heavy with the knowledge of the personal mountain Zan now had to climb.

He was going to be all right—but it was going to take a long, long time to get him there.

Once Kalen was settled into a room, no one could pry her from his side. He looked dead, so still and pale, his chest barely rising and falling. He'd given everything to save them all, and there was a possibility he'd never open his eyes.

Taking one of his hands in hers, she stroked his skin as the tears fell. "Listen to me, please. You can't leave us," she whispered. "The baby and I need you. Please stay."

Laying her head next to him, she wept. And began the long wait.

Kalen was at the bottom of a deep, dark ocean.

No matter how he tried, he couldn't swim to the surface. Couldn't breathe. So he let go and floated, rested a while and tried again.

Sometimes he heard quiet conversation. He wasn't sure why or where he was. It scared him a little, not knowing. The longer he floated, the more aware he became that he needed to get to the surface soon, or he never would. Something dear to him waited for him up there, and he had to fight.

So he did, and the voice began to solidify into one that he recognized. *Mackenzie.* His mate, his love. She told him stories all the time, begged him to wake up, and he wanted so badly to respond. To tell her that he loved her and wasn't giving up.

Then one day he broke the surface. He heard a machine beeping nearby. The rustle of someone in a chair, flipping pages, reading something. Stuff made sense and he knew he was back. But how? It didn't matter. He just had to get his lids to cooperate.

Finally he blinked them open to find that everything was fuzzy. But he could make out his mate's figure sitting close to him, bent over something. A magazine?

Yeah. She was reading, and he liked waking up to find her there.

"Baby?" he croaked.

The magazine plopped to the floor and her blue eyes widened. "Oh my God! You're awake!"

Happy kisses peppered his face and he smiled, or thought he did. "I think so. Unless I'm dead and you're an angel."

Sitting back, she stroked his face, touching him everywhere she could reach. When his eyes focused more, he saw that there were tears glistening in hers. He wanted to brush them away but didn't have the strength to raise his arm.

"Hey, none of that. I'm okay, right?"

"You are now." She sniffled.

"You and the baby?" he asked in sudden alarm.

"Relax before you strain something," she said softly. "The baby is fine and so am I. Do you remember what happened?"

He stared at her, thinking. Which was hard since it seemed he was dosed on good drugs. "I forgot."

"The battle. You killed Malik and all his Sluagh," she said gently. "You saved everyone in the Pack."

The storm. The fight. His friends had been losing badly.

Then he'd used the lightning against the enemy.

"I used the light to drive out the darkness." He smiled at his mate. "Sariel told me to."

She smiled back, though it was tired at the edges. "That you did. Do you feel any different? I mean, is there any darkness left?"

Though he was exhausted, he searched deep inside himself. Looked for that awful black thread that Malik had fostered and had wanted to grow into something horrid. "It's gone," he breathed. "For good, I think." He hoped and prayed.

"That's the best news I've had all day. Other than the man I love waking up, that is." Leaning over, she kissed him on the lips.

Something still worried him, though. "I didn't leave here on the best of terms. Last time I saw Nick, he was trying to kill me."

"Well, that changed when you almost killed yourself in the process of saving the world," she told him, love shining in her blue eyes. "The whole Pack has been in and out of here for over two weeks, willing you to get better. Your brother, too. They think you're pretty awesome, and so does my dad. And I happen to think you're fantastic, too."

Damn. His eyes burned.

"You're lucky to have a dad like him."

"He's yours now, too. You'll give him a chance to prove it, won't you?"

That choked him up, and he worked not to show it. "You bet, baby. Say, how are his soldiers?"

She looked sad. "They lost a few, but not as many as they should have, considering how outnumbered they were. There's something else, though." She hesitated.

"What is it?"

"Zan was hurt. Remember how I said he couldn't take another trauma to his head without risk?" Kalen nodded in dread. "He suffered another blow to the skull during the battle, and he was bleeding badly from his ears when we brought him in. When everything was over, he was deaf."

Kalen stared at her. "He can't hear? Is it permanent?"

"We don't know for sure. He's not human, so there's a chance that he'll hear again one day. But for now, nothing."

"Tell me it wasn't my fault," he pleaded. If he'd caused Zan to go deaf with the explosion, he'd never forgive himself.

"I'm not going to lie—we don't know how much the blow to his head factored in, versus the explosion. He's not saying much about it."

"Will he see me?"

"Soon. He needs time to heal and rest, same as you."

There was no arguing that, so his visit with Zan would have to wait. He needed to get well. He had a mate to care for and a baby to buy lots of cute baby things for, too.

"The baby," he rasped. "He's really okay?"

"I wouldn't lie to you, especially about that." She smiled at his use of "he" for their child. Taking his free hand, she scooted forward and let his palm rest on her tummy. "The baby's fine. See?"

Reaching out with a tendril of magic, he searched. And found the tiny life warm and safe in his nest. Tears pricked his eyes. "I don't know how to be a father. It's not like I've had a great example to follow."

"Oh, honey." She stroked his hair. "You're going be a great daddy, because you'll want to give him all the love and support you never had from your folks. If anything, I'll have to worry about you going over-board, doting too much and spoiling him rotten!" Now she'd said "he," too. Kalen's enthusiasm was rubbing off.

Grinning tiredly, he nodded. "I'm gonna buy him all kinds of boy stuff. Footballs, toy trucks, trains—"

"What if it's a girl?" she teased.

"Hmm. Then she'll be a tomboy. All us guys around here will make sure of that."

She laughed. "No doubt."

"I love you, Mac." He yawned.

"That's the second time you've called me that. Or is it the third?"

"Don't know, but it's growing on me. Doesn't make me think of a trucker anymore."

She laughed. "Well, that's flattering. Sleep, Sorcerer."

He drifted off, thinking he was a lucky man. A guy who'd never had a real family except his grandma, whom he'd lost way too soon, now had a compound full of brothers.

And several real brothers, including his and Sariel's half siblings, whom he couldn't wait to get to know better. Though it still wasn't fair that he had to wait a few thousand years to get his wings.

He guessed you couldn't have it all. But you could damned sure try.

Three days after Kalen woke up in the infirmary, the Pack threw him a party in the rec room. Everyone was there, including Sariel and Jarrod Grant. That really got to him. Because in all his life, *nobody* had ever done that. Just celebrated him being alive and loved. It was every missed, lonely birthday rolled into one.

All of them had trooped through his hospital room constantly, jabbering about this and that. But they'd all avoided any conversation that might be deemed mushy in any way. So now, in true guy form, they let him know how sorry they were and how much they cared.

Nick was the first one to speak to him, beer bottle in hand, loud enough that the whole group could hear him. Well, except for Zander. "These damned visions of mine don't always show the whole picture. Wish they did, but they don't. So I'm sorry I gave you such a hard time. And, oh yeah—sorry I shot you."

Kalen smiled. "Forgiven. Though A.J.'s rifle packs a helluva punch. Just sayin', so you'll feel worse."

"Thanks a bunch."

Aric took a turn next. "And I'm sorry I was such an asshole to you in the beginning. Mostly." A few of the guys snickered, and the redhead frowned. "What?"

"So where's *our* apology?" Jax goaded. "You're always an asshole to us."

"Hey, that's my mate, fur face," Rowan said, punching Jax in the arm.

"Ow."

That pretty much set the tone for the party, light-hearted and everyone poking fun at one another. Pointing out their own faults for Kalen's benefit, laughing at themselves. They needn't have bothered, but it was nice. He felt included, and that was a great feeling.

He endured careful hugs, but he didn't mind much. Especially the gesture from Sariel. His brother. He could hardly believe it as they stood regarding each other, the warmth filling his chest. Kalen cleared his throat. "I'm not used to having family that's worth a damn, and it's going to take some getting used to. But I'm glad you're my brother."

"So am I, Kalen." The prince's golden eyes were suspiciously moist. "One day I'll get to introduce you to the rest of our brothers, and you'll love them too."

The idea made him a little nervous, but he smiled

anyway. "I'll look forward to it." They shared an embrace that healed one last hole in Kalen's battered heart. He had a feeling they were going to be close, and he welcomed that joy.

Zan moved from his corner at the fringes of the party and joined Kalen as Sariel released him. They stood awkwardly studying each other until Zan spoke with some difficulty.

"Not your fault," he said with an odd drawl, gesturing to his ears. "Sluagh knocked the shit out of me."

When Kalen replied, he made sure to speak slowly and clearly as Mackenzie had instructed him. "Still, I'm sorry. I wish there was something I could do."

Zan shook his head and tried to smile. "Thank you, but I'm okay." Waving to Aric, he changed the subject. "Presents for you."

"Oh yeah?" He looked to the smirking redhead with interest. "I love presents!"

"Well, you'll love mine, then. We got you something together, but first, this is something just from me." Winking, Aric waved a pink gift sack at him.

More snickers, and a few of them sounded like they knew what was inside. Kalen looked at Mac, who blinked at him innocently.

"Don't ask me. I have no clue what he got you."

Taking the sack, Kalen set it on a table at the front of the room, started pulling out items—and cracked up. He couldn't help it. "Shit! I'm *so* going to get you back for this!"

But he kept laughing, and so did everyone else when they saw what Aric had purchased for him: three colors of sparkly, pastel nail polish and a pack of six different colors of eyeliner. Plus a tube of hot pink lipstick.

"Black is so last week, Goth-boy." Aric winked. "Now you can look all pretty for your next battle."

"You fuckhead!" But it was so damned funny. And typical Aric. He set the sack aside and grabbed the wolf into a big hug. "Thanks, man."

He'd never felt happier or more accepted into a family than he did at that moment. It was just perfect. Couldn't get any better. Or so he thought, until he saw the big box Nick was holding. He let go of Aric and studied it curiously.

"What's that?"

"Well, open it and find out."

He set it on the table next to the makeup and ripped at the paper to reveal a box with the label of a local leather shop in Cody. Glancing at the gang, he saw their excitement and anticipation. He had no clue what it could be.

Lifting the lid, he peered inside. "Is that . . ." Grabbing the leather garment, he lifted it from the box. His heart swelled to clog his throat. "Jesus, guys. You shouldn't have."

More lint in his eyes again, dammit.

The long coat was black, supple, expensive, and gorgeous. He put it on to find that it was fitted, unlike his old one, which had been made for someone else.

Nick cleared his throat. "Your old one got sort of charbroiled. So we got your measurements from Mac when you were on the mend and had it made just for you. If you don't like it, we can't exchange it, so tough shit."

This time his laugh came out a bit choked. "I love it. And I promise I won't wear this one out to fight monsters." He looked around the room. At his mate, Jarrod,

Sariel, the Pack. A child on the way. His family. And he counted his blessings.

"Thank you, all of you. I'm a damned lucky man." He looked at Nick. "Just one more thing would make it perfect."

"What's that?" the commander asked.

"A vacation with my mate," he said, hugging her close to his side. "I've never had a real vacation in my life, and I think we've earned it."

Nick's lips curved upward. "I believe that can be arranged. Put your request on my desk and I'll approve it. In fact," he told the group, "anyone who wants time off, put your name in and I'll stagger weeks so we're not all gone at the same time. We've all earned it."

That idea was met with a ton of approval. Kalen couldn't wait to be completely alone with his baby.

Make that times two.

Kalen lounged on his towel, feet planted off the end so he could dig his toes into the gorgeous sand. "This is the life, huh? God, I never dreamed Fiji would be this beautiful."

His mate eyed his rum concoction with the little umbrella in it, with no little envy. "Some of us get to enjoy more than just the sights."

"Hey, I offered to go virgin! I'm a gentleman that way."

"You are a gentleman, but it's a little late to go *virgin*, I think."

Turning his head, he stared at her for a couple of seconds before he got it and laughed. "Oh, you're so bad. Nope, no virgins around here!"

"You would know."

"That I would." Sucking down the rest of the delicious drink, he removed the tiny umbrella and rolled toward Mackenzie. When she saw him reaching for her stomach, she tried to wiggle away.

"What are you doing?"

"Be still. I need to concentrate." Frowning as though he were creating important art, he placed the tip of the toothpick to rest in her belly button. "Almost . . ." He had it standing upright, but she started giggling and it fell over onto her stomach, where it jerked up and down.

"Kalen, what on earth?"

"I was making a shade for the baby."

"You're an idiot!" But she was still laughing. "We're already in the shade. I think you've had too many of those rum thingies."

He pouted. "Have not." Turning her attention back to her stomach, he studied the smooth skin, then ran his palm over it in fascination. "Do you think he can hear me?"

"I don't know." She buried her fingers in his hair and combed them through the strands, the way he loved. "I've heard that babies in the womb respond well to music and having books read to them. It sure can't hurt."

"Hello, baby," he murmured. "I'm your daddy. I promise I'm going to do my best to be the greatest daddy in the world, because that's what you deserve. I love you, sweetheart, and I can't wait to meet you."

His throat closed up and he couldn't go on. But he'd made the most important promise of all to his child, one that had never been made to him. And he'd follow through.

"Oh, honey. I love you."

"My God, I love you, too."

His mate rolled into his arms, and as they kissed, he vowed he'd never forget what a lucky man he was to have all his dreams come true.

He'd made it out of the darkness and into the light. And that was where he planned to stay. Forever.

Turn the page for an exciting preview
of the next book in the Alpha Pack series,

HUNTER'S HEART

Coming in September 2013 from Signet Eclipse

"The guy bringing up the rear is always the one who gets eaten, you know."

Ryon Hunter made a face at Aric Savage's back as their team of shifters crept stealthily in human form down the garbage-strewn alley. Or half of them, anyway.

The other half were elsewhere in the Big Apple, quickly and quietly searching the night for a gang of rogue vampires who were reportedly on the hunt, draining humans and leaving their corpses to be found by puzzled and alarmed citizens. The Pack's mandate was simple: find the bastards and neutralize every last damned one of them. Otherwise questions would be raised by the general populace, ones that had answers the Pack and the very few authorities in the know didn't want the public getting hold of.

Vampires in New York City. Sounded like an apocalypse movie.

If people only knew of the very real paranormal

world that lurked in the shadows, there would be mass panic. The Alpha Pack's job was to make sure that never happened. They hunted the most dangerous creatures in the world, taking them out before humans had a clue they were there. The less dangerous ones were brought in for possible rehabilitation and integration into the Pack's world.

Peering into the gloom, Ryon forced himself to concentrate. Spirits beckoned to him from every corner, their ghostly forms fading in and out as they entreated him to listen to pleas he couldn't hear. Didn't *want* to hear. As the Pack's Channeler/Telepath, this was his gift—or rather, his curse.

As a Telepath, Ryon was capable of pushing his direct thoughts into other people's heads. He could also catch a reply from one of his teammates if they pushed back hard enough, even though none of the rest of them shared his gift. But his oh-so-wonderful abilities didn't stop there. Being a Channeler meant that Ryon also could communicate with the dead if he really tried. Problem was, he rarely wanted to, but the ghosts just wouldn't leave him alone. Lost souls were drawn to him like metal shavings to a magnet, and New York City held so many of them, it was like wading through pea soup.

Even worse, the ghosts seriously pissed off his wolf, who snapped and snarled inside him every time one got too close. Which was constantly.

Nobody, not even his Pack brothers, knew how very close to the breaking point the ghosts had driven him.

A slight scuffing sound came from behind him, like a shoe on concrete, and Ryon whirled. His enhanced eyesight scanned the darkness, but all was still. Quiet.

So quiet that it took him a couple of seconds to figure out why that bothered him.

The spirits had vanished.

"Shit," he breathed, spinning around to catch up with his group. "Hey, guys—"

The alley exploded in a flurry of dark figures rushing the shifters from all sides. He just had time to see Aric and Hammer engage in battle with four rogue vampires when a fifth tackled him from the side, slamming him into the wall of a building.

Grunting in pain, he shoved at the vamp, grimacing at the stench of fetid breath wafting over his face. The rogue had him pinned and he bared his fangs, going for Ryon's jugular. Twisting, Ryon managed to get enough leverage to put his back to the wall and shove the thing off him. The vamp stumbled backward, and Ryon grabbed for the silver knife strapped to his thigh, cursing himself for not already having it in his hand.

He took the snarling vamp to the ground, and in one swift movement thrust the blade under the breastbone, burying it deep into the monster's black heart. The vamp's squeal joined the others' as Aric and Hammer took out their opponents. But they weren't out of the woods.

Another wave of rogues emerged from the shadows. Before Ryon could stand up, two vamps leaped on him, slamming him to the dirty concrete. He'd fought greater numbers before and won, but this pair had him off-balance. They got him facedown, one sitting on his legs, twisting Ryon's arm behind him and taking his knife, while the other grabbed a fistful of his hair and pulled his head back to expose his throat.

"Get off me, you fucker!" His wolf, enraged, demanded release as Ryon bucked. Tried in vain to throw them off. Knowing he could fight them much better on four legs, with his own set of sharp teeth, he gathered his concentration for the shift.

"Uh-uh," the one sitting on his legs sang. "We can't let the puppy come out to play."

How do they know—

A hard punch landed in his side. Hot, agonizing fire spread through his torso, seized his lungs. His cry came out as a hoarse wheeze as he realized the vamp had stabbed him with his own silver knife. He renewed his struggle to throw them off, but it was no use.

"Hold still, pup," the other crooned in his ear. "This will be over soon."

Then the creature's fangs sank deep into his throat, silencing his shout. The agony was indescribable, drowning out even the burning in his ribs. The sickening slurp of the thing feeding at his neck made him want to vomit, but he couldn't move. Could do nothing as his sight began to dim, his brain spinning with dizziness.

The one who'd been feeding raised his head. "It's true! Shifter blood is like pure cocaine! So good . . ."

"Let me try," the other insisted.

"No! This kill is mine!"

Their argument might have been what saved him. That, and his Pack brothers rushing to his rescue after taking care of the other rogues. Distantly, Ryon heard the sounds of a fierce but brief fight as the vampires turned to meet the new threat. Then sudden silence, broken by harsh breathing. Boots, jogging toward him. Cursing.

"Motherfucking hell," Aric snapped. "Help me turn him over. Careful."

Hands lifted him, and soon he was on his back. He tried to make out their faces, to say he was all right, but warm blood gurgled in his torn throat instead. Fuck, he couldn't breathe!

"Don't try to talk," Hammer instructed him. "You're gonna be all right, my man."

Aric examined Ryon's side, muttering. "Stabbed him with his own goddamned knife. We've got to leave that in there for now, or he'll bleed out."

"But he can't shift unless we remove it. If he can shift, maybe he can heal faster."

Aric's voice floated above him. "Ryon? Can you hear me?"

He nodded once.

"Good. If we take out the knife, can you shift?"

He nodded again, or thought he did. Concentrating, he attempted to call his wolf, but it howled in pain. Retreated deep inside him, his strength drained.

"Ryon? Hang on, man. . . ."

His Pack brothers' curses, their insistent pleas, melted far away. In to nothingness.

Daria Bradford tossed back her single shot of whiskey, relishing the warmth that slid down her throat to her stomach. The nights grew cool in the Shoshone National Forest in the early fall, so the small indulgence was welcome.

Sitting by the fire, she picked up a bottle of water and rinsed her shot glass. Then she dried it before returning the glass and plastic travel flask to her backpack. The nightly ritual comforted her, made her feel more at home when she was so far from civilization. It was a tradition she and her father had shared before he retired from the life's work he'd loved so much. The work that she carried on.

Her father had taught her all he knew about studying wolves. As a young girl, she had accompanied him on many a trip. Unlike most of her high school classmates, Daria had known exactly what she wanted to do with the rest of her life: she would follow in her father's footsteps. And so she did, becoming a wildlife biologist who specialized in the field of studying the most beautiful and elusive creatures on the planet.

Her father had been part of a conservationist group in the 1980s that was instrumental in saving wolves in the Shoshone from the brink of extinction. Watching them thrive once again was one of the two great joys in his life along with doting on his daughter. But eventually his arthritis prevented him from scaling the mountains and valleys he loved so much, so he now lived vicariously through her tales. She made sure to bring him plenty to listen to during their cozy nights by the fire, their whiskeys in hand.

Smiling to herself, she thought of all she had to tell him when she went to visit in a few weeks. The wolf packs she'd checked on so far were doing very well, the pups growing. By the dancing light of the fire, she retrieved her spiral notebook and logged her notes on each of the local pack members for the day. Then she put it away and crawled into her tent, zipping it shut against any nighttime visitors that the flames didn't dissuade.

Exhaustion crept into her bones and muscles, but it was the nice sort earned from an honest day's work. She crawled into the sleeping bag and before long, sleep cocooned her and she drifted off, content.

That's when the nightmare invaded.

She was standing in a dark place. A dirty alley. City noises came from nearby—traffic, people talking. Then came the shouting. She moved closer to the noises, and realized it sounded like fighting. As she crept forward she saw dark shapes. Pale, human-like figures dressed in rags, snarling, yellowed fangs slashing in the gloom.

They were attacking a group of men, and, for a few moments, it appeared the evil ones would win. How she knew the defenders were the good guys, she couldn't say. She only knew she was invisible to them as they battled, as the men gained the upper hand at last.

But one of their number went down under two of the dark ones. There was a flash of silver, his choked cry ending terribly. Suddenly. One of the attackers yanked back his head, and ripped into the man's throat with those awful yellowed fangs.

Stumbling forward, Daria shouted at them to stop, but nobody heard. Her breath froze in her lungs as the man's companions came to his rescue, dispatching the remaining creatures. That's what they were—creatures—but she couldn't put a name to them. Thoughts of the ugly ones vanished as she walked close, looking down to study the man whose friends were trying so hard to save him.

He was, without a doubt, the most beautiful man she'd ever seen. He was lying on his back, arms and legs limp. Moonlight fell into clear, crystal blue eyes and glinted off his shaggy blond hair. His nose was straight, and he had grooves around his mouth and full lips that hinted at his being a man who smiled frequently.

But at the moment he was struggling to breathe. A splash of red marred the torn flesh at his throat, and there was more of the crimson lifeblood flowing from around the hilt of the knife buried in his side. Worry for the man and a deep, sudden sadness overwhelmed her. She tried again to speak but could not make a sound.

Then his gaze found hers, and his eyes widened. Just for a moment, the world narrowed to the two of them. Raising his arm, he reached for her with bloodied fingers. She wanted to hold his hand, bring him what solace she could.

Then she was sucked backward, falling out of the dream as she cried out in protest.

No!

"No!" Daria's shout rang out in the tent as she bolted upright.

Hand on her chest, she sucked in several deep breaths. Gradually her racing heart calmed, but the horror of the nightmare remained. Because she knew better than anyone that it was no dream. The scene had been a vision.

Only her father knew of the "gifts" bestowed on her, presumably by a Native American ancestor. Everyone else would think her crazy, so these were secrets the two of them guarded with great care.

All of her life she'd been plagued with visions of scenes that were either imminent or had just occurred. Most of them were useless, nothing more than innocuous flashes. In the more serious, detailed ones, she typically didn't have a clue where they were taking place or who the people were, and she couldn't assist them. Her other ability—astral projection, the ability to send her physical body into a dreamlike state and visit another place in "spirit" form—was also useless if she didn't know who to help or where they were.

Squirming in her sleeping bag, she worried over the handsome blond man in her vision. Who was he? What were those horrible things that had attacked him and his friends?

Most important, was he going to survive?

She didn't know why he mattered so much. Why the need to find him and make certain he was alive was like ants crawling over her skin. Maybe she could find out with this one. Because unlike all the others, for one brief instant, Daria and the man had connected. Even now, as the rest of the vision seemed distant, a thin tendril remained, trailing from her consciousness to his. She felt it, but would need to project astrally to access it. However, she couldn't do that until she'd recovered some strength. This vision had left her drained.

Settling down again, she tossed until daylight broke, sleep elusive. Rather than being rested, she was tired and rattled. She'd been so afraid she'd fall asleep only to wake up and find that the thread connecting her to the sexy stranger had vanished. It was still there, waiting.

Centering herself, she sat with her legs crossed and closed her eyes, arms loose in her lap. Focusing inward, she let the sounds of the waking forest carry her away. The telltale tingle danced over her skin, signaling that her body was going into its trancelike state. Slowly, her consciousness separated her body, leaving it behind. Looking back, she saw herself sitting peacefully in the tent and, satisfied, set out to follow the thread.

At first the journey was easy. Not confined to flesh, she soared over the trees, basked in the sunlight and the beauty of the day. Onward she traveled, the connection leading her to a curious break in the forest, a place where the trees had been cleared. In the center of the clearing sat a large building. It boasted several wings, and the thread led to one of those wings in particular.

In seconds she stood in what appeared to be a hallway. Before her was a door, and beyond it, she knew she'd find the man she sought. Going forward, she simply walked through it, intent on reaching the still form on the bed—

A loud shriek snapped Daria painfully back into her body. The sound echoed through the mountains, causing her pulse to stutter in her chest. "What the hell?"

As the sound died away, she tried to figure out what in God's name it had been. The creature's angry baritone cry reminded her of something prehistoric out of an old Godzilla movie. As the call died, chills pimpled her skin. Whatever it was, it could be miles away, or a few short yards.

That idea was enough to get her moving. She felt too much like a sitting duck there, and she couldn't try the projection again for a while anyway. She broke camp quickly, packing her tent and supplies and making sure the fire was completely out. Then she headed down the trail, on the way to her next site.

Thoughts of the blond were never far from her mind as she hiked. She much preferred to think of him than of the terrible dream or of the disturbing bellow from some strange animal. Could a grizzly bear make a sound like that if it was in dire pain? She didn't think so. But out here, what could be large enough to make that noise and be heard for miles?

Don't think of it. Think of him.

She put the mystery animal far from her thoughts and lost herself in enjoying the day. She tackled a couple of steep switchbacks and was sweating by noon, when she finally stopped to rest. Dragging off her pack, she rolled her shoulders with relief and bent to reach inside for her water.

A familiar smell hit her nose and she straightened slowly. Blood and rotting flesh. Standing stock still, she turned only her head, scanning the area for signs of the remains that must be nearby. Up ahead, she spotted some broken branches off to the side of the trail. Beyond that, perhaps thirty yards into the foliage, there was something lying on the ground. Studying the lump, she thought she saw denim material, maybe a boot.

"Aw, shit."

She quickly grabbed her handheld radio from the backpack. If it was a body, she'd have to call the ranger's station and report it, then wait for them to arrive. She needed to check in with them anyway, let them know she was all right. Leaving her pack behind, she ventured off the trail and picked her way to the lump on the ground. As she got closer, her fears were realized.

"God in heaven," she whispered.

Once, the body had been a human, but whether it was a man or woman, she couldn't say. The corpse had been torn literally to pieces. She spotted part of a leg, an arm. The torso was mostly gone, eaten. Huge teeth had ripped massive chunks of flesh from its victim, the marks so big she couldn't fathom what creature had made them. There was no head to be seen.

Stumbling a few steps away, Daria fell to her knees and vomited. Her stomach turned inside out, though thankfully there wasn't much to purge as she'd skipped breakfast. As the heaves subsided, one thought screamed into her brain.

What if the killer is still here?

Swiping at her mouth, she pushed up and bolted for her backpack, radio in hand. When she reached it, she dove for the water hooked to the side and rinsed her mouth several times. Then she took a long drink. She had to call this in, but did she dare wait around for the thing to come back for seconds?

Raising the radio to her face, she was about to depress the button when a low growl made every hair stand on end. Turning slightly to the right, she blinked, not sure what she was seeing. As it stalked forward, head lowered, she sucked in a breath.

The creature was a snow-white wolf. It wasn't very large—female if she had to guess. The she-wolf made another threatening rumble and continued to advance. All sorts of useless knowledge came to mind, such as the fact that there had never been a documented case of a wolf attacking a person.

Tell that to this one.

Daria depressed the button on her radio, intending to speak to the rangers, but she was too late. At that moment, the wolf launched itself forward. With a cry, Daria spun around and ran for all she was worth. And knew she'd done exactly the wrong thing. Her dad would rake her over the coals for making such a rookie move.

Legs pumping, she veered off the trail, searching frantically for a good tree to shimmy up. But there were none with branches low enough. Snarling, catching up, the wolf snapped at her boots. She pushed on, faster.

As she topped a rise, the terrain suddenly fell away and she skidded to a stop, right at the edge of a deep ravine. "Fuck!"

She whirled to find the she-wolf right *there*, panting, baring her teeth. Teeth that were nowhere near big enough to have caused the destruction of the dead hiker, but that hardly mattered now. Looking around, she scanned the ground for a rock, anything. She didn't want to throw her radio and risk damaging it, but it might make a good club.

She and the wolf locked gazes, in a standoff. Daria was struck by the intelligence in the wolf's eyes, the lack of madness. What the hell was going on? Then a crash sounded from the forest. And another. The sound of heavy steps. More hikers? Maybe help was there.

The moment of distraction cost her. The wolf gathered itself, leaped, and knocked her backward. Daria staggered, trying to regain her balance.

And stepped into thin air. She fell, screaming; then her back connected with the rocky ground, knocking the breath from her lungs. She tumbled, ass over elbows, rocks gouging and scraping her skin, tearing her clothes. The slide went on forever, it seemed.

Until she came to an extremely abrupt stop that made her bite her tongue. Warm blood flooded her mouth. She tried to move but couldn't. She was lying mostly on her back, her body wedged in a crevice formed by some boulders. Her left arm stuck out at a weird angle, bloody bone protruding through the skin. Trying to move, to get some sort of leverage, only caused waves of agony to pound her battered body.

Her radio? She moved her neck, attempted to see if she could spot it. There was nothing but rock all around, her broken body firmly trapped. The radio was gone . . . and nobody knew Daria's exact location. In the Shoshone, it could take days for her to be found. Months.

Or her bones might still rest here decades from now.

She thought of her father, and of his devastation when he learned his only child was dead. Lost to the very forest they had both loved so much. It would kill him.

Though it was too soon to attempt another projection without draining the last of her strength, she had no choice. Ignoring the horrendous pain of her injuries, she closed her eyes. It took much longer than usual but she found her center.

Eventually, she felt the familiar tingle, the buzzing sensation that meant she was leaving her earthly form and traveling over time and distance. Determined, she once again followed the thread to the one she knew in her gut who would understand her message. There was no time to lose.

She flew over the trees, soaring. Eventually she found the place she'd sensed him before, the big building in the forest. A curious place that appeared to be some sort of compound with another big building next to it—a hangar, going by the jet parked nearby—and a third building under construction not far from the main one.

Within moments she found herself in the hallway. This time, a woman with wavy shoulder-length brunette hair emerged from a room, carrying a clipboard. She wore a lab coat, and Daria realized she must be a doctor. The woman was taking care of the sexy stranger. The doctor passed by, not having seen Daria at all.

Daria drifted into the room, her attention immediately focusing on the tall figure in the bed. Knowing time was short, she moved forward to his side.

She reached out tentatively and gently touched the

face of the handsome blond man. Watched as he opened his gorgeous, crystal blue eyes—eyes that widened as he saw her astral form hovering by his bed. He might not hear her or understand her. But she had to try.

"Please, help me."

Also available from

J.D. Tyler

Primal Law
An Alpha Pack Novel

Meet the Alpha Pack, a top-secret military team of wolf-shifters fighting the most dangerous predators in the world, human and nonhuman. After a massacre leaves Jaxon Law crippled, he must relearn how to fight—and battle the anger and guilt threatening to overwhelm him.

But when Jax rescues a beautiful woman who awakens his primal instincts, he is unprepared for the dangers that lie ahead. Soon he must decide if the deep connection he feels with Kira is worth defying the ultimate shifter law...

Available wherever books are sold or at
penguin.com

facebook.com/ProjectParanormalBooks